I0664395

KEEP CALM AND STEAMPUNK ON

The whole of Victorian London knows there is something not quite right about the Lady Verity Hart. She may be the daughter of an MP and the sister of famed inventor Lord David Hart, but she is a spinster whose own father threatens to send her to the madhouse every fortnight. Because Society is correct—Verity Hart is no lady. If they suspected how quick with a quip she is, let alone the majority of her brother's ingenious machines were her design, the sale of fainting couches would double.

Verity requires one herself when her beloved brother is kidnapped by vampyres in the dead of night. With the aid of an aggravating, rude American bounty hunter with a secret of his own, Verity takes to land, sea, and even air to rescue the only person who could ever love and truly accept her. Or is he?

VERITY HART

VS

THE VAMPYRES

OMNIBUS

A HART/MCQUEEN

STEAMPUNK ADVENTURE

BY JENNIFER HARLOW

DEVIL ON THE LEFT BOOKS

COPYRIGHT

Devil on the Left Books
Copyright © 2014 by Jennifer Dowis
All Rights Reserved
First Edition

ISBN-10:098939445X
ISBN-13:978-0-9893944-5-1
Library of Congress: 2014943233
Devil on the Left Books, Peachtree City GA

The characters and events in this book are fictitious. Any similarity to real persons, living or dead, is purely coincidental and not intended by the author. No part of this book may be reproduced or stored in a retrieval system or transmitted in any form or by any means electronic, mechanical, photocopying, recording or otherwise without the express written permission of the author.

ALSO BY JENNIFER HARLOW

THE GALILEE FALLS TRILOGY

In The Beginning...A Galilee Falls Short
Justice
Galilee Rising

THE F.R.E.A.K.S. SQUAD SERIES

Mind Over Monsters
To Catch a Vampire
Death Takes A Holiday
High Moon (Out 9/14)

THE MIDNIGHT MAGIC MYSTERY SERIES

What's A Witch To Do?
Werewolf Sings The Blues

For All the Women Who Paved the Way And Those Who Continue To

CHAPTER ONE

THE NOTORIOUS COUNT DARLOCK HAS A BALL

Oh, heavens, did I leave my blowtorch on?

As I sit in our carriage, waiting behind one of those new motorcars I have been dying to tear apart, fear grips me like a vice. Burning the house down would certainly be the final straw with Father. He would surely lock me away as he has threatened countless instances these past eleven years. Did I leave it on? I was in such a rush to get ready for the ball, it is certainly possible. I swiftly run through my movements. I was welding the hinge on my latest invention, the Artemis, when David poked his head into my workshop to inform me Father was home. I set down the torch, removed my goggles, then quickly changed out of my leather work clothes into my lavender tea dress. Then I made sure the gunpowder and petrol were stowed properly, checked the hinge, then…I did shut it off. Oh, thank the Lord.

"Verity, did you hear a word I said?" Father asks harshly, bringing me out of my head.

I gaze across the carriage at my father. He's dapper tonight in his tuxedo with white handkerchief, bowtie, and white rose in the lapel like David. At four-and-fifty my father is still handsome, even though at forty his hair turned pure silver in the blink of an eye. Strangely his eyebrows remained dark brown and are only now beginning to match. He's known for his patience and grace under pressure, though one would not know this judging from his expression now. As always when his attention is directed at me his face is filled with an undercurrent of contempt with each passing moment. I believe I am the only person in all of Christendom who can crack the façade.

"Yes, I mean no, Father. I was daydreaming. I apologize."

His lips purse. "I was saying, try to refrain from garishly flirting with *that man* tonight. You are to be on your best behavior. Several other Parliament members shall be in attendance, along with the head of the India bureau. Avoid that man as much as possible."

"You mean our host?" I ask.

"I heard Isobel Derbyshire was seen departing his villa most late at night un-chaperoned not a month past," Mama says, ever the gossip.

"My point precisely. Even a hint of impropriety, and people will talk."

"Father, people do little else," I counter. If possible his lips tighten further. I gaze down to the floor. "Sorry, Father."

"If you will not behave for me, then do it for Margot. She has only three years until she is presented into society. Do not make your sister pay for your ill behavior."

As always, my father cuts right to the quick. Worst, he is not wrong. "I shall be the paragon of ladylike virtue all evening, Father."

"See that you are."

Two weeks. Only two more weeks until my obligation is fulfilled for the year, and I may return to Somerset. Then, unless summoned, I do not have to see him until Christmas. May the good Lord give me strength to hold my tongue, keep my head high, and behave as the lady the whole of London believes me to be. Our coach pulls to a stop at the entrance of the hotel. *You are Lady Verity Hart, daughter of the Eighth Earl of Carlisle tonight, nothing more. Bloody well act like it.*

The automaton footman dressed in livery with powdered wigs opens the carriage door and holds out its metal hand to help us debark. I have never liked these machines. Created to resemble humans in both form and height with their smooth, blank brass faces, jerky movements, and the strength of three men. Unnatural.

More human than human in some respects. I do appreciate their mechanical intricacies, the innovation as dozens of gears, pistons, cogs all firing and moving together as if God himself designed them. I do not spy a bulky engine with exhaust pipes shooting out hot steam on its back, so it must be a newer model powered either by battery or electrical oscillator. What a difference five years makes in terms of progress.

I am surprised that so many of the upper crust would deign to travel to Chelsea from Mayfair and Belgravia but here they are, the men in pressed suits and the majority of women in white, though I would wager there is not a black glove left in the whole of London. The Count always throws *the* party of the Season, which is the only reason Father deigns to be in the same room as him. And we, I mean I, had the added honor of being personally invited by the Count. It would be a slap in the face should we not attend, even with the theme of "Black and White" with mourning clothes encouraged. As always, tongues wagged about the request, with those not invited most vocal.

As white washes me out, I selected a black lace gown trimmed with white, and both my slippers and elbow length gloves are white as well, with a spare pair in my black reticule. I never leave the house without two pair in case of emergency. My hands resemble those of a laborer with calluses, scars, and burns difficult to explain away. I learnt from experience.

My brother David holds out his arm for me to take. With a smile, I lock my arm with his, and we trek toward the hotel door. We usually all but read each other's minds, but my scowl says it all.

"Father is in rare form tonight," David says. "Attempting to guilt you with destroying Margot's reputation? Low swipe, even for him."

"I know. One would think I was constantly throwing myself at the Count every chance I had."

"He does flirt with you a considerable amount."

"He flirts with everyone, I am nowhere near special in that regard. When I do seek him out, it is simply because I find him agreeable. And honest, which is most refreshing." With a sigh, I shake my head. "I am eight-and-twenty years old, and our parents treat me as if I am a three-year-old who throws temper tantrums whenever there is company about. I just want to…scream. I should be able to speak and dance with my friend if I so choose."

"You should. Without question. But tonight, please Very, be cautious."

"Am I not always?" I ask with a rueful smile.

An actual human takes our invitations and informs us the location of the cloakroom. I have never been to this particular hall no one has as the Count just completed its construction for this ball, but it's cheery with pale yellow walls. Most refreshing from the usual dark wallpaper or red walls found everywhere else. I especially adore the roses in the vases, most white but some literally painted black. David and I stop to admire them until Father and Mama reach us. "Shameless," Father huffs.

The men break off to the hat room and Mama and I to the cloakroom. "You look quite pretty tonight, darling," Mama says as we stroll past more shameless displays.

Despite my swift preparation for the night's event, I do agree with her for once. My naturally thick, honey blonde hair is in a chignon held by diamond encrusted silver geared barrettes that match my interlaced silver clock gear necklace. My grass green eyes, the only indication I am my father's daughter, are as always offset by my milky skin, as are my pink lips with Cupid's bow. Even my figure is impressive with the torturous corset doing its job, giving the impression my small breasts are fuller and my waist a near perfect seventeen and a half inches on my 5"4' frame. Still, I cannot wait until I am back in my real clothes: leather trousers, billowy white shirt, all of me covered in oil or grease. I may not be worthy of note then, but at least I can breathe. Bloody corset.

"Thank you, as do you, Mama."

I hand the maid my cloak and receive my programme and dance card as Martha Templeton and her eight-and-ten-year-old daughter Emiline begin commenting on the odd décor and apprize all who can hear of the latest gossip. I maintain a smile as I pretend to find it all fascinating until we return to the hallway where Father and David wait. The moment Emiline catches sight of my dapper brother she smooths her pink hair, which is the newest colour in the D.V. Hart Hair Dye line. I've heard that many ladies use the product simply so they have a conversation starter around my brother. He never notices a one of them. Poor dears.

I understand his appeal. Beyond the fact my brother is rich as Crocus, a future Earl to a grand manor, and one of the greatest inventors of our time, but is also quite handsome. He has a lean body, rich brown eyes, thick brown hair that at thirty shows no signs of grey. If he weren't my brother, I would probably be in love with him as well.

David and I trail behind our parents, who nod at the few people loitering in the hallway. Once again we have to wait in line at the arching entrance of the ballroom to be announced. A lady always enters a room with a smile, so I affix mine. *You are Lady Verity Hart. Lady Hart...*

"Lord Edmund Hart, Earl of Carlisle, accompanied by Countess Edith Hart with Lord David Hart, Viscount of Lovell, and the Lady Verity Hart."

The majority of the guests gaze our way. David and I spend ten months a year at our manor house in Somerset, coming to town only for the end of the Season to avoid gossip, so when the magnificent, brilliant D.V. Hart deigns to venture into society, there is always a reaction. Quite a few ladies brighten up. I heard two hundred fifty invitations were sent out, and by the size of the crowd, I would say most are here. The doors and windows are already open to aid with the heat. Balls in mid-June are always rather uncomfortable, not to mention stench filled. Hand fans are already being put to use, mine included. A lady never sweats. *Never.*

I spot Aunt Esme gliding toward us with her daughter Cricket and Cricket's husband Arthur following behind. The sisters kiss cheeks as I smile at my cousin. Though she's two years younger than I, we used to be good friends at least until her marriage. Gone was the bright, exuberant girl who loved watching me weld. Four children, two who didn't survive infancy, have taken their toll on her. Her blonde hair remains limp even though it is wrapped around various gear ornaments, and figure fragile underneath the ivory taffeta gown. Arthur's a good man but dull as dishwater. He towers over his wife and is as gaunt as she. As Mama and Esme repeat all the conversations they've had since arriving, the men begin with politics. Even Cricket's eyes glaze over. "Cricket, could you show me where the refreshment room is? I'm parched."

"Of course," she says.

Taking her arm, I lead her from the group. "I am sorry my dear, I have not been available to keep you company this week," I begin. "I—"

A tall woman with flaming red hair and skin the colour of snow bumps into my frail Cricket. Instead of apologizing, and her equally pale escort scoff and continue on their way. Our mouths plop open. "How rude," Cricket says. My jaw drops further as I watch them approach David, but Oliver Blaylock reaches him first. The rough couple exchanges an angry look but change course away from him. What odd people.

As we make our way to the refreshment room, I nod and smile at those I recognise as Cricket updates me on her children. We get our lemonade, even if I asked they would not serve me whiskey, and sink gracefully into chairs near an open window to people watch. A few ladies rebelled against the theme by wearing bright colours and dying their hair the same colour with greens, purples, blues all the colours of the rainbow both garishly adorned with clockwork gears similar to mine. David commissioned the clockwork gear necklace I wear tonight for my twenty-first birthday as an inside joke. I wore on a few occasions, blinked, and the whole of society were adorned in rivets and gears. The style was then translated into home décor, ours included. Brass gears and rivets now adorn most light fixtures, lampshades, even wall moldings like those in this very hall. Took some of the fun out of it.

It is easy to glean why the dye is David's highest seller. Where the women try to distinguish themselves with said colours, the men could be interchangeable with the same tuxedo, clipped mustaches, and short hair parted down the middle. I spot the always delightful Lord Dickie Hopper, the last of my three potential husbands, holding court amid a dozen people, only one whom I do not recognise. The stranger's black hair peppered with grey is longer than is fashionable as it reaches his shoulders, and his skin is dark from hours spent in the sun. Not from London then. He's also most handsome in a rugged way not often appreciated in society. It must be tonight as everyone seems fascinated by him, and judging from the near scowl on his face, he does not enjoy said attention. Dickie collects people to show off, so the stranger could be an exiled crown prince or circus performer. His new friend just sips his tumbler of liquor between deep scowls.

"American," a familiar voice purrs behind me, "among other interesting characteristics."

With a smile I pivot around and find our host looming over me with his usual catlike grin. Another man of mystery. He simply arrived in town five years past, purchasing a large parcel of Chelsea and throwing the most elaborate parties I've ever attended. Fire eaters, swamis, tigers, even ballet dancers have been showcased at his events. Tonight men in black and white jester costumes with kabuki masks juggle or perform mime around the ballroom. I've heard he hails from Russia, but others insist it's Romania or Hungary. It is difficult to gage as when he speaks, there is only a trace of Eastern Europe in his voice. I do know one or two people who affirm they met his father in Austria at balls decades ago. His name wasn't Orrlock, but they swear based on the uncanny resemblance, the men have to be father and son. The mystery rages on, and my unconventional friend revels in every wagging tongue.

He looks to be in his mid-thirties with olive skin, dark brown hair the same colour as his eyes, athletic physique, and straight nose. I have only ever seen one man as beautiful as he, though Jolyon's was restrained whereas Orrlock's is wild like a gypsy, though a dandy gypsy. Though we flirt, there is no real romantic attachment towards one another, at least on my part. Ever since I rapped his hand with my fan and told him I would break his nose if he was ever forward enough to attempt to touch my neck again, we have been good friends.

"That fact alone makes him more interesting than the whole of the room put together," I say.

The Count glides around, fixing his jewel encrusted gear cufflinks as Cricket rises. "I had best be getting back to Arthur," she says, curtsying. "Pardon me."

Orrlock furrows his brow as she scurries away. "Am I that repellant?" he asks as he sits.

"The family does not approve of you. I am sure she received the same speech I did about keeping away from you."

"Well, thank you for not obeying. And for wearing black. It was most bold of you."

"Bold nothing, it was purely for cosmetic reasons. White washes me out. People would think I was a member of the undead, haunting the hall otherwise."

A large yet private smile crosses his face. "Now there is a thought, Lady Hart."

I smirk back. "So, I have not seen Isobel Derbyshire here tonight. Will she be attending?"

"I very much doubt it, I am afraid. I am not her favourite person at present."

"And you wonder why proper ladies flee in your presence."

"Yet you never do. Are you not a proper lady?"

"Depends on whom you ask, Count Orrlock." We both grin and grow silent before the sound of laughter draws our attention. Dickie imitates gunfire with his fingers as all but the American laugh at his antics. "Poor American," I say. "He looks about ready to scream. Shall we attempt a rescue before the gunfire begins in earnest?"

Orrlock rises, holding out a hand for me. "I would be remiss in my duties as host if I did not."

I take his perpetually chilly hand and accompany him to the jubilant group. Halfway to our destination, the American notices us approaching. Staring straight at Orrlock, his back straightens and shoulders fall back as if he's threatened. Orrlock smirks. Are we that frightening? Dickie notices us a second later and lights up further, smiling enough to show teeth. Even that's boyish. "Our host and my favourite heartbreaker. I am honored." The men bow except the American who just nods.

"Heartbreaker indeed," I say as I curtsey. "You proposed to Hester not two weeks after you did me." To avoid going to debtor's prison. I suppose I should be flattered he thought of my fortune first. "And speaking of, where is your lovely wife this evening?"

"Home with one of her headaches per usual," Dickie says. He smacks the American's back. "Thankfully, I met Jamie here two nights ago, and he agreed to keep me company tonight." Everyone in the group exchanges a look as Dickie should have introduced us right away and failed to do so. He realizes it far too late to avoid impropriety. "Oh, forgive me! Your beauty made me forget my manners. Lady Verity Hart, Count Ivan Orrlock, may I present Mr. Jamie McQueen of the Oklahoma territory of America."

"Pleasure to meet you, sir," I say, but the man doesn't remove his eyes from Orrlock, who still smirks.

"Yeah," the American says.

"Jamie McQueen, an Irish name if ever I heard one," Orrlock says. "You look remarkably like an Irish acquaintance I once had. James Roarke? Are you by chance related?"

"He's my grandfather, but I never met the man," the American says icily.

"A shame. He was a colourful man."

"He's dead?" the American asks.

"I heard of his death almost ten years past, though I do believe the rest of your clan is still on that island of theirs." Orrlock's smile grows. "You know it has been years since I ran into one of your kind." He glances at the confused group of which I am a part. "An American that is."

"And it is always a pleasure to meet one of yours," he says with a sneer.

What an utterly rude man, and judging from the ladies pulling their escorts away, I am not alone in thinking this. Orrlock does not seem to mind. "Cats and dogs, ha ha," Orrlock says gaily. He glances behind Dickie. "Oh my, it seems as if I must attempt another rescue. Mr. Stoker has been cornered by an aspiring actress hoping to join the Lyceum."

"I heard you two were working on a book together," I say. "Whatever is it about?"

"He's simply interviewing me for research. It's hush hush at the moment, I am afraid. Excuse me." Orrlock steps away but instantly thinks better of it. "I almost forgot. Lady Hart, I demand the first dance and you cannot refuse me. I am the host after all."

Blast. I shall never hear the end of this from Father, but I do have no choice. "I would never dream of refusing. 'Til then."

He bows and nods at the men. "Gentlemen, enjoy yourselves." He walks away to help poor Bram from acquiring another mistress.

Dickie pouts. "Oh, foo. I was hoping for that honor, Lady Hart. You can make it up to me by giving me every dance after."

I start penciling names on my dance card. "You may have the second, no more." I glance at the American, who if he had one ounce of breeding would ask as well.

I take this opportunity to size him up. I would place him in his third decade. Up close he is far more handsome than I first thought with almost black eyes with wrinkles around, whiffs of grey in his black hair, and thick physique that even in ill-fitting evening wear looks rough. I suppose it could be the fact he's sporting black cowboy boots. He's quite imposing, easily over six feet tall. He feels our stares and lowers the tumbler. "I don't dance. Ever. Sorry."

"Perfectly alright, Mr. McQueen," I say, ever the lady. "So, I am sure you have been asked this question many a time already, but how did you and Lord Hopper come to be acquaintances?"

Dickie throws his arm around Mr. McQueen's shoulder. As I suspected he is already halfway toward inebriation. "Why, he saved my life, Lady Hart. I would be shot dead if not for him."

I press my fan to my heart in mock shock that always appears genuine. Practice makes perfect. "Oh, my. How dreadful."

"I was in this club, which one doesn't matter," he adds quickly, meaning it was an East End den of iniquity, "merely playing cards, when this brute accused me of cheating and drew a pistol. I pleaded, but the blackguard would not listen to reason. That's when my savior rose from the chair next to my assailant, and with one deft punch, knocked him into oblivion. It was nothing short of amazing."

"I gather."

"After that I insisted I show him the best of London."

"And is this your first time in England, Mr. McQueen? Are you here on business?"

The American opens his mouth to answer, but Dickie interjects. "Oh, guess his occupation, Lady Hart. It's too extraordinary."

"Judging from your boots, I'd say cattle baron?"

"Bounty hunter!" Dickie exclaims.

"Oh. I thought they only existed in stories."

"We're real," the American says dourly.

"He was a Pinkerton as well. Chased the Jesse James gang."

"Impressive," I say, meaning it.

He nods. "That you, ma'am."

Dickie sips his gin. "He's the one who brought Algernon Bishop back."

"Algernon Bishop…" I prompt.

Dickie downs the rest of his drink. "He stole Countess Lacey's jewels and fled to America a few months past. She put up a five hundred pound reward for his capture." Dickie smacks McQueen's back again. "McQueen here tracked him down and brought him back here to face justice."

"Once again, most impressive," I say.

Dickie takes the American's glass. "We require refills. I shall return."

I gaze around and realize I am now alone with the American as the rest of the group, who knew the story already, left. I have a million questions, but most shouldn't even cross my mind let alone my lips. The standards will have to suffice. "So, how long are you staying in London, Mr. McQueen?"

"My ship leaves tomorrow afternoon."

"And your crossing. Was it enjoyable?"

"I was stuck in a closet with a no account criminal for five days. It wasn't great."

I am a tad shocked by his response, but only my eyes show it. "I'm sorry, but hopefully your time here has been more agreeable. How do you find our fair London?"

"It's crowded, smells worse than a slaughterhouse in August, and y'all keep looking at me like I was a damn zoo animal. I'm counting the minutes until I leave. No offense."

Before I can retort, Dickie returns with a huge smile. "Ha ha, old chap, you are the topic *du jour* tonight. People are talking," he says in sing-song.

McQueen takes his tumbler. "Yeah, well, people don't do much else, do they?"

In spite of myself I quickly smile, which judging from his narrowed eyes, the American sees. I clear my throat. "Well Lord Hopper, Mr. McQueen, I have monopolized enough of your evening. Please excuse me." With a curtsey, I take my leave.

I spot David across the room speaking to the couple who bumped into Cricket, but am waylaid by Agnes Townsend, her brother Robert, and two other gentlemen who help fill my dance card. By the time we are done discussing the ball and gushing over how attractive we all are tonight, a new group of men surrounds my brother, one of whom sports two canes and the Hart mechanical braces. I always swell with pride when I see them. The man's thin legs are encased in metal struts acting as an outer skeleton with hydraulic joints and tubing spiraling around the struts, leading to a small steam engine attached to the back vertical brace like a knapsack. My, or rather D.V. Hart's greatest triumph. Men, women, even children who could not walk now can because of me. All creating them cost me was the man I loved, and my Father's infinite wrath. Still worth it.

"...and nobody has seen him since," Lord Stone says as I approach the group. "It has been close to three months now and no trace."

"He simply vanished?" Lord Hepburn asks.

As I step beside David, the men bow and I curtsey. David turns to me. "Dr. Rathbone is still missing. Scotland Yard has run out of leads."

"How dreadful."

Dr. Charles Rathbone is the closest thing D.V. Hart has to a rival. A year after the braces became available, Rathbone unveiled his first automaton. A year later, he had usurped David's title of "Inventor of the Age." We've had him over to dinner a few times. A lovely man. His disappearance was most shocking.

"We really needed those plans for his defensive automaton," Lord Stone says. "He was on his way to deliver them when he vanished from his train. Lord Hart, I don't suppose you would reconsider—"

David holds up his hand. "Lord Stone I have stated my position on automatons for years now. I design to improve lives, not create machines that will takes jobs from flesh and blood people in dire need of them," he says, giving my reason.

"So, what have you been working on lately?" Hepburn asks.

David glances at me, and I smile. As always, my dear brother reads my mind. "Gentlemen, please observe my ring." David holds up his pinky with a brass clockwork adorned ring on it. When he rotates the small gear, a tiny needle springs forth, startling the men. "I call it The Stinger. There is a powerful sedative I developed inside injected on contact. It is one of the many covert weapons I have created for covert self-defense purposes. Flamethrowers that resemble bracelet cuffs, a fob watch and cigarette case both with syringes much like this, just to name a few. I plan to test some tomorrow in Hyde Park."

"A bracelet? You intend to make these available to ladies?" Hepburn asks, eyeing me. "Is that wise?"

"Lord Hepburn, I told him exactly the same thing. They are quite impractical, but he was so enjoying his lethal phase he would not listen. I cannot see my peers desiring to set anything ablaze. Besides their husbands, that is," I say with a titter. The men do not smile back. I drop mine. "The Ministry might have use though."

"Perhaps," Hepburn says. "What about the project I proposed last month? To improve air quality around the factories?"

"I'm afraid my mind has been elsewhere," David says.

"Lord Stone," I say before anyone else can make demands, "how is Constance enjoying India? Have she and her husband settled in?"

I know this is a sore spot for him as Constance eloped with a soldier and fled to India. "She's fine. Excuse me." Using his canes he walks away, hydraulics whirring, with his toady Hepburn in toe.

"Thank you," David says with a sigh as he turns the gear to hide the syringe.

"You're almost as popular as Dickie's bounty hunter friend over there. Who was that infernally rude couple you were speaking to before?"

"Which one?"

I glance around the room and find them in a heated discussion with Orrlock. "The ones arguing with our host." The woman all but hisses at Orrlock before her companion takes her arm and drags her toward the exit. Our host glares at them until they are out of sight, then shakes his head to regain his composure. I have never seen Orrlock angered before. They must really be wretched people.

"Frank and Megan Smith. Irish. They have a commission for D.V. Hart. Something about custom braces for their child who is paralyzed from the neck down."

"Heavens."

"I told them I would meet them tomorrow night at nine." And I will be eavesdropping in the next room as always. "And, as you heard, the crown desperately wants those air filters, and Sir Lucas wants to commission a self-flushing privy, and—"

"Please stop. No more demands tonight. I am trying to enjoy myself."

"And are you succeeding, sister dear? Is your dance card at maximum capacity yet?" He glances at it. "Not even half full," he tuts. "This will not stand, not one whit. Come. This must be remedied at once."

We spend the preceding ten minutes moving from small group to small group, making polite conversation with members of his club who, being the proper gentlemen they are, request dances. Bless them. If I'm truthful, I never care who I'm dancing with as long as I can perform the act. It's the one activity I look forward to during the Season. It grows harder to find partners year after year as most of my male peers have married, and the younger men use these functions to find potential wives, and an eight-and-twenty-year-old spinster is not considered a good prospect. After I flirt an offer from Hugh Wilmore, we notice Antony Graves, one of David's old Oxford friends and my second former potential husband, waving at us. Lovely fellow. He took a post in Australia five years ago after his marriage, so we rarely see him. I know David still misses their relationship to this day. We excuse ourselves and walk over to his group. Halfway on our short journey, the tall gentleman Antony speaks to pivots around, and my stomach drops.

Oh, Lord no. Not him. Anyone but *him.*

Even after ten years, he is still the most beautiful man I have ever laid eyes on. Over six feet tall, soft dark brown hair, hazel eyes, pale skin even women covet, clipped moustache that gives him a roguish air, and that cleft chin I adored kissing every chance I received. Now whenever I set eyes upon him, which are mercifully few and far between as he resides in Paris, I just want to strike that spot. At least he has the decency to appear frightened, mouth dropping open, when he notices me. David stops mid-stride but I continue on, pulling my brother along with me. I will not give Jolyon the satisfaction of seeing me weak. A Hart never backs down. *Never.* It is quite a good thing I chose not wear The Artemis as intended or former prospective husband number one might have found himself riddled with tiny spikes. Death by a thousand tiny pinpricks. Why should his fate be different from the one he prescribed for me?

Despite my deliciously murderous thoughts, I smile at the men and curtsey as they bow. Jolyon peers away toward the dance floor, but Antony takes my hand, kissing the top. "Lady Hart, you are tonight as always a vision."

"Thank you, Lord Graves. It appears Australia agrees with you as well."

"Hot and wild always has," he says, eyeing a blushing David.

Jolyon's jaw tightens as he sips his brandy. "And does your wife enjoy it?" he asks.

David and I momentarily scowl, but Antony smiles. "You may ask her, Mr. de Luce. She's around here somewhere," he says, searching for her. "We came to visit Father. His health is failing."

"We heard. I am so sorry," David says.

Antony merely shrugs. No love lost there since his father vowed to disown his own son if he failed to marry. I was his first query since he knew of my situation and I his. I actually gave the proposal serious consideration. It was mutually beneficial to us both after all. I would not be under my father's thumb or reliant on David for protection. And there would have been no nocturnal wifely duties to worry about. But in the end I could not bring myself to say yes. It would have meant leaving David, who had fallen out with Antony months before. They have since made up. Every chance they receive. Lucky for Antony, Margaret Huxtable was in the same predicament and with the same proclivities as her future husband. It is wild in Australia indeed."Father wants us to move back and take over his seat in the House, but we so love it there."

"You two will have to come for dinner before you depart," I say.

This would be the time when I ask Jolyon and his wretched wife over as well, but I'd rather shove needles in my eyes than break bread with them. Unless it was poisoned. Jolyon takes another sip of his drink as we fall into uncomfortable silence. My breeding will not allow this for too long. "And how is Ariadne, Mr. de Luce?" Hopefully she's grown fat and warty so her outside matches the ugly inside.

"Well. She's eagerly anticipating our third child," he says apologetically.

Another boulder plummets in my stomach, though I refuse to show my response. "Really? Congratulations." And that is enough of that. Social contract terms officially met. I spot Cricket and Arthur across the room. "Oh, excuse me, I believe my cousin requires me." I do a quick curtsey and flee. I managed an entire minute that time. Certainly progress.

"Is that who I think it is?" Cricket asks when I reach her.

"Oh, yes."

"Who is it?" Arthur asks.

"Is he watching?" I ask Cricket.

"He's glanced twice."

Arthur stares over my shoulder at Jolyon. "Who is he?"

"Arthur, stop staring," Cricket whispers. "That's Jolyon de Luce. He and Verity were attached."

"He's the one who broke your engagement?" Arthur asks me.

"Yes, and then not even a month later, he became attached to Ariadne Lester. He's looking again," Cricket tells me.

"I need some air. Pardon me, please."

Head still high, I walk toward the nearest veranda but find it full of people. Fine. I move to the double doors which open onto a brick patio amid a large English garden where men smoke. It will have to do. I locate a quiet spot near the far back corner near the seven foot hedge blooms with white roses, but the cigar smell is still overpowering. I can already hear Mama's complaints on the ride home. No matter. I—oh, blast. No sooner that I sit and take a long, controlled breath, Jolyon steps out. Peace. One moment's peace tonight. Is that too much to ask? He examines the area, spots me, and strides over with purpose. I used to admire that quality in him, his self-assurance. No more. Every centimeter of me wants to flee, but instead I straighten my back and stare him square in the eyes. "Leave. Now."

"I must speak with you," he says.

"We have absolutely nothing to say to one another," I whisper, which is a useless gesture.

My gaze juts to the men on the patio who watch and even whisper about the scene before them. We are breaking a golden rule, no private conversations in public. He shouldn't even be approaching me like this. My father will blow a gasket when he hears about this. Of course Jolyon cares not a farthing for my reputation. He proved that ten years ago and continues the pattern tonight, sitting beside me on the bench. I make a show of moving as far as I can from him, not that this act will make it into the gossip tomorrow.

"We need to rectify this animosity between us." His jaw sets. "Especially since Ariadne and I are returning to London in a month."

As if my night could not get worse. "You are returning to England?" Which means I shall be seeing the joyous couple every time I am required in London. Oh, joyous day.

"Yes. I'll be overseeing our London office, and Ariadne misses her family."

"Of course she does, they're as wretched as she is."

His face contorts into the exact expression I never wanted to see from him. Pity. Once more I resist the urge to strike his face. It does prove far more difficult this time. "I never thought you could grow so bitter. It was over ten years ago, Verity. I want us to be civil, friends even. We all were once."

I literally balk at his gall. "*Friends*? Your wife made my formative years a nightmare, spreading vile rumors regarding me and my brother and our…relationship. She turned multiple friends of mine against me with lies when I did absolutely nothing to her save for existing. And what you did to me was far more reprehensible. You all but ruined my life. My reputation remains tarnished to this day. We shall *never* be friends. I will be civil to you both in public because I am a lady, and that is what is expected of me, but I will not seek you out, and I would greatly appreciate if you hear I shall be attending a party, that you both refrain from attending as well. That is the very least you can do for me. The very least."

His handsome face falls even further, gripped by sadness this time. "You shall never forgive me, will you?"

"For which offence? Making me fall in love with you, and believing you felt the same? Breaking our engagement when you found out I was not the perfect lady you imagined me to be? That I failed to live up to your ridiculous expectations? Or perhaps for making me the laughingstock of society when a month later you became engaged to my rival? My father almost disowned me. He still constantly threatens to lock me away and all but has. If David hadn't threatened to cut his money off, Lord knows what would have happened to me. So, which sin shall I forgive first?"

By the time I met Jolyon just before my coming out, D.V. Hart was a sensation. Not only were David's roll-on odorizer and hair cream just released, but so were my home alarm and crank washing machine. I had been tinkering with machines ever since David gave me his discarded erector set when I was two-and-ten. By three-and-ten I developed my first invention, a walking wind-up doll. My parents had tried to sway me from my hobby early on, downright forbidding me on several occasions from working, but it was of no use. Around age ten-and-five they finally gave up when my patents paid off the mortgage on Foxfire manor. The only condition was that no one could discover my secret. It would not only ruin my reputation but the family's as well. Thus D.V. Hart was born. All the money, all the acclaim, it all belongs to David. Not a soul doubted us. I could continue my projects, and my reputation would remain intact. It was rarely a problem until Jolyon.

I considered revealing my secret before the engagement but something stopped me every time, though I convinced myself the man I loved could not help but be proud and amazed at my accomplishments. Deep down I knew the truth. The fact men do not want an ambitious, intelligent wife had been drilled into me for years, only hope and denial made me believe Jolyon was different. He wasn't. When I finally showed him my workshop, he was shocked which quickly became anger at my betrayal. Admonishments that I was not the woman he thought I was, that I'd lied to him sprang forth like bullets, killing my soul with each word. I was so in love I swore I would stop, and for over a month as I planned my wedding, I kept my promise. Until tragedy struck.

When Brutus, our two-year-old bulldog was hit by an Omnibus, paralyzing his hind legs. At first I built him a whicker buggy he could wheel around in, but he would whine when we left him on the ground floor. One such time, as he stared up at me with pitiful brown eyes, I received an epiphany straight from God. Then it came to me. My wind-up doll. The same principals could be applied. I drew up the plans in two days and began building. Jolyon's reaction barely crossed my mind. Soon, during the process, I realized the braces could be fitted for humans as well and worked twice as hard. When Jolyon found out, from my own mother no less, he was livid. Utterly livid. During his tirade, the truth of the matter finally walloped me out of denial. It would never work. *We* would never work. He had fallen in love with the mask, Lady Hart—beautiful, sweet, demure, all I pretended to be. Verity Hart was none of that and never could be. She could never be content sitting by, simply running a household while her husband was out conquering the world. Thinking only of him, of his accomplishments and ambitions. Turning into nothing but a pretty doll, an accessory like my mother. I could not think of a worse fate.

When I told him that I wouldn't, no I *couldn't* stop, even for him, he ended the engagement. I was so devastated so mortified I fled to Foxfire, burying myself in work around the clock until the braces were complete. I had to read in the paper about his engagement. Just like that, I was replaced. Forgotten. Work and David helped me through the melancholia, and a year later when people walked up to David on the street with tears of gratitude in their eyes and tales of their first ever steps due to my braces, I knew I had made the right choice. I still know it. My heart was never the same though. No woman should have to reconcile herself to spinsterhood at ten-and-seven. At any age I suppose.

"I never told anyone your secret, not even Ariadne," Jolyon says.

"And I am supposed to thank you for that? For not further besmirching my name?"

He lets out an angry, frustrated sigh. "There is no talking to you. Never was."

"Well I am, what did you call me, abnormal? Manish? Stubborn? Not a proper lady, and I never would be? I would hate to disappoint you again."

Shaking his head, my old rises. "I had hoped the years had changed you, softened you. I am disappointed it is not so. Have a pleasant evening, *Lady* Hart." He bows and finally leaves me in peace.

My hands ache from ringing my fan with all my might, so I stretch my fingers to help ease the pain. Better it than his neck. Just when I think I've accepted the past and moved on... It's not so much him—I knew it wasn't his fault he was raised to believe a certain thing—but the whole of my situation. They are all the same. Why is it so threatening for a woman to be educated? To want something more than only supporting her husband and children? It's so bloody unfair some days I want to sc—

The sound of gravel crackling behind the hedge startles me out of my mental tirade. I cannot see who's there behind the tall hedge. "Who is there?" I ask as I leap up. "Show yourself!"

"Just me," a familiar American voice says as he steps into view.

"How long have you been standing there?" I ask, horrified. Dear Lord, please don't say, "Since before you sat down."

I attempt to gulp down the large lump in my throat. "How much did you—"

He cocks an eyebrow. "Really want to know?"

Oh, please let the world end right now. "You should have let your presence be known, sir," I hiss. "And how dare you eavesdrop on a private conversation!"

"Sugar, I was here first. I wanted to finish my cigar in peace then you showed up. This close it was pretty damn hard not to hear you row that man up Salt River this close. Sounded like he deserved it, though."

"Thank you?" I ask. I do not understand half of what this man says.

"Welcome." We stand staring for quite a few moments, neither of us sure what to make of the other. He does not appear apologetic, in fact he seems amused, mouth curled into a faint smirk. I look away first. "So, exactly how many of the men here have you been engaged to?"

I raise an eyebrow. "I beg your pardon?"

"Hopper told me you two were engaged, then the guy out here. I—"

"I was never engaged to Lord Hopper. He asked, and I declined."

"It have something to do with your secret? Or why you smell like metal and grease?"

"I do?" I sniff my arm but find only my perfume, honeysuckle and vanilla. When I glance up, his smirk has grown. "First you listen to a private conversation, then you lie about my odor. I know Americans are meant to be rude, but you trump them all, sir. Excuse me."

I advance to depart but the American sidesteps me, turning his back to the door. "Hey, look shug, I'm sorry, alright? I am sorry. I don't mean to pile on the agony. I'm just not good at this social malarkey. It's been a tough night. I didn't mean to take it out on you."

I meet his eyes, finding them sincere if not a tad weary. They are quite nice eyes, dark like a gypsy's, with tiny lines around that only add to their untamed charm. I pull mine away before I give away my thoughts. "We are a trying group, that is certain. Especially to outsiders."

"I do feel like I should be performing circus tricks or wrestling a bear while they throw pennies at me."

"I know exactly what you mean, sir," I say with a half smile.

His eyes narrow as he studies me for a moment. "I get the feeling you just might, shug." My new acquatience's grin grows as if he knows what I look like without my chemise. I should be outraged, perhaps give him a good telling to, but instead I'm...exhilarated. Flattered. Beautiful even. I had forgotten how marvelous a male's attention can be. These stirrings must show on my face because his eyes brim with merriment. Something passes between us for a long, glorious moment, a heat that awakens the butterflies in my stomach that have been dormant these eleven years. Oh, how I have missed their playful fluttering. They—

Suddenly, the mood breaks as the American's grin drops, and his head cocks to the side as if he hears something. "Oh, hell," the American says before disappearing behind the hedge again. "I'm not here."

What... Not a second later, Dickie steps onto the patio, surveying the area. How on earth did he know—?

"Lady Hart," Dickie says as he approaches, "have you seen Mr. McQueen? The American? I seem to have misplaced him."

I receive sweet revenge for his eavesdropping, but instead find myself saying, "I am afraid not. Apologies."

"Oh, I do hope he has not left yet. I wished to introduce him to Antony. He refuses to believe I am acquainted with a real cowboy bounty hunter."

"Dickie, Mr. McQueen is a human being, not a show pony. He most likely has no desire to be put on display like one all night."

"He doesn't mind," Dickie says, waving his hand.

"Well, if I locate him, I shall tell your American you are searching for him."

"Thank you," Dickie says before venturing off once more.

"He's gone," I say a second later.

The America emerges from his hiding spot. "Thanks. That guy is working my last nerve."

"Then why associate with him?"

"Nothing better to do until my ship sails, and your friend pays for everything." He pulls out a cigar case. "Not to mention he's got great taste in cigars."

"My friend does not have a farthing to his name. He gambled through his own trust and now has debts all about town that the modest allowance his father-in-law provides does not cover, I recommend you maintain a close eye on your billfold, Mr. McQueen."

He lights the cigar, giving me a cheeky grin in the process. "Always do, shug."

The way he says that last word sends the butterflies into a frenzy. A few more minutes with this man and I shall be in peril of forgetting myself. "*Lady* Hart," I correct. "Terms of endearment are meant only for those one is…intimate with."

All the mirth drains from his face. Blast. "Excuse me, *lady*." He shakes his head. "Lord, y'all have so many rules I can't keep half of them straight. No wonder y'all are such sticks in the mud."

I open my mouth to take umbrage, but seeing as I agree with him on both points, the words will flow. "Rules create order. Without them there would be chaos."

He cocks an eyebrow, adding to his roguishness. "Damn, we wouldn't want that, would we? We might actually end up having some fun. You ever have real, pure, exhilarating fun before, Lady Hart? The kind where you can't catch your breath? Where every second is more…delicious than the last? Where your skin tingles like someone's blowing on every inch of it?"

Without a doubt this man could hold a salon about that topic. Oh, how I would love to attend. "I…I…"

"Don't know what you're missing, shug," he says, licking his chops at me.

Oh, merciful heavens, thank you. The trumpet sounds in the ballroom, signaling the first dance. He smirks. "And we're off to the races."

"I-I had best get in there. Count Orrlock will be looking for me."

"Don't want to break anymore hearts, right?" he says with a glint in his eye.

"I do have a reputation to protect. Enjoy the rest of your tenure in England, Mr. McQueen." I curtsey with flourish and begin walking away. "Try not to eavesdrop on anymore conversations."

"No promises, shug."

Oh, I do enjoy how that word rolls off his tongue. The Count meets me at the patio door, glancing back at the American. "Making friends with the wildlife I see. Be careful Lady Hart, he looks like he bites."

"Whatever do you mean, sir?" I ask with a smirk to rival Mr. McQueen's.

The master of ceremonies saves me from yet another inappropriate conversation. "It is time for the first dance," the M.C. says inside. "Please join me on the dance floor with your partner."

Orrlock crooks his arm for me to take. "Shall we make the tongues wag?"

I glance back at the American as he takes another puff of his cigar. He winks at me, and I turn back around, blushing. I take my friend's arm and stroll inside, past Jolyon and my glaring father. I give them both the patented Lady Hart smile. Sweet, gracious, and pliable. Just as they want me. Well, not tonight. Tonight may chaos reign. "Nothing would give me greater pleasure."

Time to burn this house down.

CHAPTER TWO

When Worlds Collide

We don't arrive home until three, and I am thoroughly exhausted having danced all but two of the twenty. I can barely remove my gown before passing out in my chemise. Next thing I know Croft, my ladies maid, is bringing me brunch at eleven, drawing me out of a dreamless sleep. After a much needed bath, Croft dresses me in my pink and white muslin dress with matching hat. She's a young thing, barely six-and-ten from a small village up North, but quite sweet. When I told her I was taking her to London with me from Somerset, she burst into joyous tears. Ah to be young and full of stardust once more.

Ready for the public, I stroll up to my workshop to collect the weapons for the day's demonstration. The smell of burnt metal and oil. Gears, pistons, cylinders, tubing, gages, rods, extenders, girders, vices, oscillators, wires, bolts, drills, my blowtorch all scattered around the room or on the drafting table with the skylight, bay window, and gas lamp chandelier above providing illumination. Not as grand as the one at Foxfire, but without measure it is the only place in the whole of London I feel at home.

The Artemis remains right where I left her last evening. At first glance she seems to be nothing more than a large iron cuff with tiny cylindrical chambers around the bracelet, a clockwork gear on top for decoration, and a chain leading to a ring. As usual appearances can be deceiving. After I add the gunpowder to the cylinders, I latch her on, and turn the gear until the click. Raising my arm at the level of the dartboard, I lower my ring finger, putting pressure on the chain. There's a loud pop as three two inch spikes fly into the dartboard in less time than it takes to blink. I pull the chain again, rotating the chambers and gear before a thick spike fires. A proud smile crosses my face. Death by a thousand tiny pinpricks indeed. I toss the Incinerator and Artemis into my carpetbag and return downstairs. Time to have some fun.

Or not.

When I meander into the drawing room, I am pleased to find Cricket, Arthur, Aunt Esme, David, and Margot waiting amid our wicker chairs in the cluttered room. Like most of the other houses in London brass rivets forming flowery patterns adorn the curtains with gears embedded into the end tables and desk. Mama's lips purse when I enter, and the others shift uncomfortably in their chairs, refusing to gaze my way. The already dark room dims further. I believe I am in trouble. Again. Only Brutus, our bulldog, appears happy to see me. The hydraulics and tiny steam engine whirr as his braces clack on the floor as he walks over to me, tongue lolling out of the side of his mouth.

"Hello love," I say as I pet him. With a false grin now plastered on, I turn to the others. "Beautiful day is it not?"

Silence, then Cricket mutters, "Yes," followed by more uncomfortable silence.

I drop the smile. "What?"

"Cricket, Arthur, Margot, will you please go wait for us in the carriage?" David asks. "We shall be with you shortly."

My four-and-ten-year-old sister pouts but follows the others out. When the doors slide shut, with the expression of a martyr facing the stockade, Mama rises, plots to the sideboard, retrieves two newspapers, and hands them to me before sitting again. Each is turned to an article on the ball, both of which I review. My name is mentioned a few times but nothing too lascivious, just speculation that the Count is in love with me since we danced together three times. I knew the third would cause a ruckus, but I love a good Volta and no one else offered. The gossip page is far more disconcerting. My three private conversations, two with married men, are chronicled. Blast.

"Your father was beside himself when he read these," Mama says. "As was I. We ask so little from you. What were you thinking? Not of us. Not of your poor sister. You promised to behave. I swear you mean to put us in an early grave."

I set the papers down. This is ridiculous. "Mama, this will be forgotten in days. I'm not worried, and neither should you be."

"She's right, Mama," David says, standing up from the red velvet chair. "They were minor infractions which she shall not make again."

"Does your selfishness know no bounds, Verity," Mama says, ignoring him. "Sometimes I believe you do not care a whit about the rest of us. Not a one."

"I am selfish? When beckoned, who drops everything so we can pretend to be the perfect family? Who pays for this house? That dress you have on? All the money you give to charity to appear as the bastion of moral rectitude? I—"

"Verity, stop," David snaps. "Apologize to Mama for raising your voice at her."

My anger swells enough to flush my cheeks, but when I look into my brother's pleading eyes, it wavers. He can only protect me so much and getting into a shouting match with Mama might just nudge Father over the edge, if he has not already reached the precipice this morning. I have lost count of how many times he has threatened to send me to a sanitarium. He has every legal right to. So I take a deep breath, push this day's rage down with all my might, and smile. "David is right as always. I am sorry I spoke so cruelly to you, Mama. I shall do my utmost not to be so selfish in the future."

"See that you don't." Mama's pretty face softens a little. "Oh, Verity. You must know I have no desire to quarrel with you. Nor does your father. Truly. We love you."

"As I do you." I pick up my bag. "David? Our party is waiting."

My dear brother kisses our mother's cheek and follows me out of the room. "Good show, old girl," he whispers.

"Get me out of this house. Now."

Our carriage is one of the few left in London to use real horses. Outside the street is busy with our neighbours strolling and other carriages and cabs with their steam-powered automaton horses, for lack of a better word, running hither and yon. Really the automatons are merely the size of horses with four brass pillars ending at wheels, a cylindrical body, and a steam engine controlled by leavers from the carriage. I think I shall always remain a Luddite in certain ways. David hypothesizes my animosity towards automatons stems from jealousy, that I wish I had conceived them. In actuality I merely like horses and have no desire to increase the poverty rate already on the rise as more jobs are swallowed by machines. Just because one can create something does not mean one always should.

David helps me in where the others wait, and when we are seated our driver Larkin pulls away."Are you alright?" Cricket asks.

"Fine," I say, staring out the window.

We ride in silence for a several seconds, but my sister cannot stop fidgeting or glancing at me with curiosity. She's a pretty thing just now growing into her looks. Like David she takes after Father with brown hair, thin frame, but Mama's brown eyes. I was her age when she was born. Oh, how I adored her. I carried her around with me everywhere, doting on her as if she were my own. That ended with Jolyon. The bad seed would not corrupt his new growing flower. Father does his utmost to keep her away from my influence, but every chance I get I spend time with her or write. She is the closest thing to a child I am ever likely to have. It is my duty to encourage her curiosity because no one else shall. "Yes, Margot?"

"Did you really dance with the Count thrice?" Margot asks.

"I did. He's a wonderful dancer."

"It was rather imprudent, Verity," Cricket chides. "As were those conversations."

My anger threatens to boil over again, the heat rising from my gut. "*They* approached *me*. *They* are the married ones. Why am I the guilty party?"

"You knew better," David says.

Something snaps inside me, and I grow so angry I am afraid I might implode, goose pimples rising all over my skin. I am so sick of being talked down as if I were twenty years younger. "What did I do that was so wrong? I danced with my good friend, and I had brief, innocuous conversations with three gentlemen. It is not as if I dragged them into the coat cupboard to have my way with them!"

There is a collective gasp. "Verity!" Cricket admonishes.

"And even if I did, whose bloody business is it?"

"Verity, please refrain from using that type of language. There are children present," Arthur hisses, eyeing Margot.

"I don't mind," she says. She's heard our father say far worse.

"I do," Arthur says. "It is improper, and my wife should not be exposed to it."

I shake my head and throw up my hands. "Excuse me Arthur, but your wife has a voice of her own. If she has a problem with me or my language, *she* can tell me. Or are you afraid of what else she may have to say once the precedent is set, Arthur?"

"Enough," David shouts, jolting all in the carriage. My mouth snaps shut. "Verity, we understand your frustration, but I must ask you do not vent it at us. No one in this carriage has wronged you, so please do not treat us as if we have. We are trying to enjoy the day, and so should you be."

I look around the carriage at Arthur's angry face, David's stern one, Cricket's pleading eyes, and Margot's excited ones. Oh blast. I've done it again. I've forgotten myself. I take a deep breath, accepting defeat. "I am sorry. I apologize, especially to you

Cricket and Arthur. I fear I have grown feral out in Somerset. I am so sorry all."

"We accept your apology," Arthur says.

Cricket does not utter a word. I did not expect her to.

We ride the rest of the way in silence, uncomfortable though it may be. The whole of London have found themselves in Hyde Park taking advantage of the beautiful summer weather. Every avenue for three blocks is filled with carriages and people ambling around the lush green in their fine suits and parasols with street performers plying their trade all around them. Larkin maneuvers our carriage into the waiting area, and we climb out to join the polished horde. "You three, please go reserve us a spot. We'll be right behind," David instructs. The trio exchange a weary glance but obey. Larkin hands the picnic basket, satchel with my toys, and Margot's photographic equipment to David and I. "Thank you, Larkin. We should only be an hour and a half."

"Yes, milord," Larkin says.

We start walking to the field, past the promenading peacocks who either refuse to gaze upon me or smile then whisper to their companion as we pass. One would think I would be used to their silent slights. Not one whit. "Did you have to chastise me in front of them like that?"

"Yes, I did. You embarrassed Cricket and put her in an untenable position with her husband. She did not deserve that."

"She deserves her own voice and opinions."

"Not everyone is up to the task of revolution, Verity."

"But you agree with me, nonetheless? Were I a man, the fact I spoke to three ladies in private wouldn't even be noticed, let alone printed for the whole of London to read."

"Very, of course I agree with you, you know that. But you are a lady, and therefore put under more scrutiny."

I shake my head. "It's not fair."

"No, it is not, just as it is not fair that I am a member of the Queen's Privy Council and you are not. Or that we have a wall of awards with the wrong name on them, or a million other much larger injustices on this earth. But that is not the world we live in, and I am sorry to say there is precious little you can do about it without harm coming to all those you love, yourself included."

"I know!" I hiss in a low voice. "I am reminded of it twenty bloody times a day! It is just…for whatever reason, it grows harder and harder to bear. I am afraid I am going to burst. Or worse go mad as Father wishes I would."

"We live a privileged life, Verity. We have wealth, status, respect, we want for nothing when so many others can barely feed themselves. But there is a price to pay. You bear the brunt of it, and I do know the pain it causes you."

"How could you? You're not at the mercy of Father. You're not sniggered about behind your back. Stared at with naught but pity. You're D.V. bloody Hart, everyone adores and respects you. I'm simply your spinster sister who is barely allowed to leave her house." Amanda Potter, with her blue hair and matching frock, and her fiancé Kyle Fairfax pass by, and an automatic smile crosses my face. We all nod and continue walking in silence for a few seconds. "I'm sorry. I don't mean to be cross with you."

"I know, as I know you did not mean to act out last night. It must have been a shock seeing him."

Sometimes my brother knows me better than I know myself. "They're moving back to London."

"I know, he told me. He even tried to get me to speak to you on his behalf. I told him I'd rather eat glass, and if he upset you again, I'd sock him in the jaw."

I smirk as only he can make me do. "Thank you."

As we continue strolling, my smile fades with each step as dark thoughts I try to keep at bay invade. My brother reads my face as one would a book. "Do you ever regret it? Your choice?"

"On occasion," I say, staring down at the gravel path. "It was the right decision, I know that. It's just…hard. I love what I do, you know I love what I do. And I love you. But sometimes I wonder…why not me? What is so wrong with me?"

"There is nothing wrong with you, Very," he says adamantly. "You recognise who you are and remain true to that. You see the world how it is and how it could be, and the lack of overlap breaks your heart. It is the same for me. And if we are branded freaks because of that, then so be it. I would not have you any other way than as you are. My beautiful, intelligent, brilliantly marvelous baby sister. My best friend."

I lock my arm in his and rest my head on his shoulder. "At least we have one another, right?"

He kisses my hat. "And always will."

I can live with that. I hope.

*

"D.V. Hart Invades Hyde Park," reads the evening's headline. They even included a picture of David surrounded by a crowd at the archery range, arm outstretched, testing the Incinerator. A plume of fire streams like a bullet from the reservoir. My shenanigans from last night are all but forgotten as once again my brother's genius overshadows anything I contribute to society. People were already approaching him, asking where they can purchase the cuffs. London is either about to become a great deal safer or far more dangerous in the months to come.

Both devices required adjustments as the petrol reservoir on the Incinerator was leaking, which can result in a burnt hand, and there was not enough gunpowder in the cylinder to launch the spikes more than a few feet. As always work takes my mind off my troubles. I get lost in the puzzle where nothing matters save for solving it. The outside world with its petty concerns fade away. Mrs. Cooper, the housekeeper, comes up with my tea tray and informs me I am not needed tonight for dinner with the Pertwees. I would not be surprised if later tonight Father informs me I must return to Somerset on the first train tomorrow. I have no intention of putting up a fight.

I finish the corrections with time to spare so I begin the preliminary sketches of a full body mechanical brace for the rude Irish couple David is set to meet tonight. A thing like a child forever paralyzed from the neck down most assuredly puts my insignificant problems well into perspective. Obviously I'll take the job. It should only take two to three months to assemble once I receive the measurements.

David returns home around nine with mere minutes to spare before the appointment. Antony always did make him forget himself. My brother joins me in the drawing room where I enjoy the latest H.G. Wells novel curled up on the dark red velvet loveseat. A pleasant breeze blows in from the open veranda door and bay windows so the flames in the gas lamps dance. Father really needs to convert the house to electricity. "How was Antony?"

"Good," David answers, kissing the top of my head. "Very good."

"Will we be seeing more of him?" I ask with a raised eyebrow.

"Tomorrow actually. We're going to an exhibition at Burberry's gallery. You can come if you wish."

"Yes, I'm sure that's what you both want. Your spinster sister tagging along on your...outing." I close the book and stand as David adjusts one of the silver framed photographs along the wall. "No, thank you. Besides, if this meeting goes well, I shall be far too busy."

"You definitely think you'll take the commission?"

"I have already begun the blueprints. Here's a list of questions to ask," I say, pulling them out of the book and handing them to him. "Barring the usual reasons, I don't foresee a problem." We hear the doorbell ring in the foyer. They are right on time.

Watson, the butler, steps into the drawing room a minute later. "Mr. and Mrs. Francis Smith, milord."

The Irish couple steps in. I only glanced upon them last night but their strangeness is amplified upon examination. Her blazing red hair is pulled into a frizzy bun, and his matching shade is longer than is fashionable, reaching his shoulders. Their clothes are of good quality, though store bought and not tailored. What's really striking is the total lack of colour to their skin. I can spy webs of criss-crossing blue veins in their necks and faces. If I did not know better I would say they had not been in the sun in decades. Perhaps they haven't because when the duo step in, both shield their eyes against the gaslights above.

"I'm sorry, is it too bright in here?" David asks.

"A tad," the man says with an Irish lilt. David turns the clockwork gear on the wall to lower the flames on all the lamps. "Thank you."

"Um, may I present my sister, Lady Verity Hart."

"Pleased to meet you both." I nod, and the couple barely acknowledges my presence with the quickest glance. Their rudeness has not waned in the passing day. "Well then, best let you get on with it. Excuse me." I walk past, and Mrs. Smith all but glares at me. I can only hope they treat the child kinder than they do strangers.

As I tip toe to the dining room, I hear David offer refreshments, but he is quickly rebuffed. When I get inside I can hear every word inside the drawing room. David and I used to sneak in here to eavesdrop on our parents when we were children. Still do on occasion. I sit in the chair next to the adjoining door to listen.

"…actually looking forward to it," David says. "I just finished my last project yesterday so you are in luck."

"Fantastic," Mr. Smith says.

"Now, first things first, what is the name of your child?"

"Child?" Mr. Smith asks. "What ch—"

"Michael," the woman cuts in, also with an Irish accent. "Our son's name is Michael."

David must think it as odd as I do that a father forgot his son's name because he clears his throat. "And how old is Michael?"

"Um, five," Mrs. Smith answers, as if guessing, "about."

"And what vertebra is he paralyzed down from?"

More silence, then, "What?"

These Irish are a few cards short of a deck. "I need to know. Um, top of the neck? Closer to the shoulders?" David asks.

"Shoulders I guess," the woman says. "So, you're going to do it?"

"Perhaps. I need to know more about your son and his situation to better determine that."

"But you *can* do it?" the woman asks urgently. "You can build a full body automaton?"

"Um, what I'm proposing wouldn't be an automaton, simply a mechanical brace."

"Can you build an automaton?" the man asks.

"I have a strict policy against it, but actually the brace is more common for your son's situation."

"But the design and concept are the same, correct?" the woman asks. "That's what we were told. You could build one if you wished to?"

What are they on about? "I—I suppose," David says, "but an automaton would not be suitable for your son. And if your hearts are set on one, then I cannot help you."

"You *can* do it, but you won't?" the man asks.

"As I said I need more information," David says. And for you both to stop making it so bloody hard for us to help your son. "Now, is you son allergic to any metals? Copper? Iron?"

"Silver," the woman says.

"And what are his proportions? How tall is he?"

"I—I don't know. Why?" Mrs. Smith asks.

"Because I'd like to get started before you bring Michael back to our house in Somerset. He—"

"Wait, you want him to come here?" the man asks. "To England?"

"Well, yes, of course. I'm willing to pay for your hotel and crossing if money is a concern."

"No, no that's not possible," the woman says. "We thought you would come with us."

"To Ireland?" David chuckles. "I am afraid that is impossible."

"But we thought—"

"My workshop is in Somerset, all my materials, not to mention I do have other duties. I cannot leave England at this time. If your son is immobile, perhaps we can—"

"No, you have to come with us," the man says urgently. "It can't be brought here, and-and-and you are the only one who can finish it."

I am taken aback, as is David. He remains silent for several seconds. "*It*? I'm sorry are we still discussing your son?"

"You ponce," the woman snaps. "I told you to let me do the bloody talking."

"He's not going to do it! What are we supposed to do now?" the man asks with terror in his voice. "Michael will stake us if we return empty handed. Think of something! This was your bloody plan!"

Steak? They are out of their minds.

I hear the chair creak as if someone rises. "You will have to forgive me," David says, "I am sorry. I do not think—"

"Sit down and be quiet," the woman orders.

David's chair creaks again as I believe he obeys. What—

"You said this would work," the man whispers, "that he'd agree."

"I know, shut your gob," she snaps. Her skirt rustles as she hurries somewhere across the room. "You. Don't struggle, don't make a sound until I tell you to. Now sleep." She pauses. "Grab him."

"What about—"

"*Grab him!*"

This has gone on long enough. I leap to my feet and rush through the door without another moment's thought, a horrified gasp escaping when I enter the parlor. Oh, my word. The man has my unconscious brother slung over his shoulder like a sack of potatoes. The gravity of the situation wallops me like a mallet. This is an abduction. They are attempting to steal my brother. My body begins trembling from shock. "What..." I choke out.

Like a wild animal, the woman hisses, even exposing her white teeth. I blink to clear my vision because I cannot be seeing what I am seeing. Terror has driven me into the mouth of madness, it is the only explanation. The woman's eyes are two balls of onyx with no white visible. But it's those fangs...sharp as needles. Fangs. Oh God. I know what she is. I've seen a picture in a book of a creature such as this, but it was fiction. Folklore. Faeiry stories. I believe I just fell into one.

With a grin, the vampyre lunges at me. I gasp and smack into the wall, framed photos falling around me. I catch one in my trembling hands. My fear widens her smile until it is stretched all the way across her pale face. *Fangs.* God protect me. "You know, I have never tasted a real Lady before. You look scrumptious," she says, licking her teeth. The monster takes a step toward me, and I do the only thing I can. Shrieking, I throw the silver frame at her face. It singes her flesh like a hot poker. She screams in pain, turning her back to me, but I am too petrified to move. To blink even. She quickly pivots back to, clutching onto her face, eyes wide in shock. The stench of burnt skin alone makes me want to vomit, let alone the sight of her bubbling, seared flesh visible when she removes her hand. Shock transforms into white hot fury on her grotesque face. "You...*bitch!*"

A glimmer of intelligence fights through the fog of fear. I grab another picture, holding it up to strike once more. "Get out! Get out of my house!"

"Megan! People coming! Let's go! Now!" the man with David says urgently.

She curls her lip up, boring her hate filled eyes at me. "See you later, girlie."

The vampyres turn their backs to me before dashing toward the open veranda door. I'm trembling, afraid to even close my eyes, but only for a moment. One glance at my helpless brother, and I charge forward, but I am too late. I step out into the warm night just in time to watch as they lift off into the air like birds, the woman holding the man by the hand. David's limp arms flap as if waving good-bye to me as they disappear into the starlit sky.

For the first time in my life, I faint. Gone. He's gone.

*

The foul stink of noxious chemicals draws me out of the abyss. I jerk awake, flailing my arms to stop the assault. The pain in my head is instantaneous as if someone has knocked a chisel in its base. The various people weeping or gasping around me do not help matters. I blink to clear the miasma, and find Dr. Cumberton sitting to my left with Mama, Father, Watson, Mrs. Cooper, and a crying Croft encircling my four-poster bed, all gravely concerned. "What? Why—" I say, attempting to rise. The chisel is hammered in even harder, and the doctor pushes me back down onto my pink bedspread.

"Do not sit up, Lady Hart," the doctor orders. "You have a mild concussion."

I touch the source of the pain, finding matted hair and a bump. "I do? What happened?"

"Mrs. Cooper discovered you unconscious on the veranda," Father says. "You hit your head on the stone. She immediately sent for us and the doctor."

"We were so worried, darling," Mama says, taking my hand.

The doctor shines a light in my eyes, and I wince. "Yes, simply a mild concussion. There should not be permanent damage. What precipitated the fall? Did you swoon?"

Everything is still a bit fuzzy, so I have to think for a moment. "Yes, after...*David!*" All the night's events stream though my head like a nightmare. "Oh, my God, David's been kidnapped!"

Everyone's face contorts with shock and dismay. "He what?" Mama gasps.

"What are you talking about?" Father asks.

"They—They took him! They must have drugged him or performed some sort of spell, but they took him and flew off. We have to save him!"

"Calm yourself, darling," Mama says.

"No!" I try to get up again but am forced down by the doctor. "No! Let me go!"

"Milord, should I go fetch Scotland Yard, or—" Watson starts.

"Hold off a moment," Father says. He turns toward me and sits on the bed beside Mama. "Who kidnapped David?"

"The Irish! The vampyres!" The second after I let those idiotic words escape my mouth, I know I've said the wrong thing. Father's face falls, Mama drops my hand, and the others exchange a distressed glance amongst themselves. Damn my scrambled brain.

"The vampyres?" Father asks slowly.

Mama gasps, holding her hand to her mouth. "No! Edmund, what is the matter with her? She's gone mad."

"I am not making it up, and I am not mad," I say, voice quaking. "They have him right now. Lord knows what tortures they are inflicting upon him. You have to believe me!" I stare at our butler in the corner of the room. "Watson, you showed them in. Tell them I'm not mad."

All eyes move to him. "Master David had an appointment with an Irish couple, milord. The Smith's. I have not seen them or him since."

"I told you!"

"You didn't see or hear them leave?" Father asks.

"No, milord, but I was on the other side of the house in the kitchen until I heard Mrs. Cooper scream that Lady Verity needed assistance."

"So he could have left with them?" Father prompts.

"He didn't! They abducted him!"

"The vampyres?" Father asks. I don't answer. He glances at the frightened Mama, then at Dr. Cumberton. "Doctor, may I speak with you in the hall?" Father, Mama, and the doctor rise and make their way out if the room with Watson and Mrs. Cooper in tow. The adults are off to decide my fate. Only the quivering Croft remains.

The moment the door closes, Croft rushes beside me. "Did they bite you, milady?" she asks urgently. "Did they force their blood upon you?"

My eyes narrow. "You believe me?"

"Of course, milady. One came to our village years ago. He killed three children, my cousin included. My grandfather helped stake him. So, did they bite you?"

"No, they didn't get the chance. What do you know about them?"

"They only come out at night. The sun burns them. Silver too." Which explains the frame. "They have magic in them too, like witches and faeries. If you look into their eyes, they take control of your body and mind."

That must be what they did to David. Thank God I was too afraid to meet her eyes. "What else?"

"Some can fly, others can raise and control the dead or animals. As they get older their magic grows, and they're stronger than ten men. Fast too. And they need blood. Human blood. They kill people to get it, milady. You don't think they will—" she says, on the verge of hysteria.

"No, they require him for something," I say, more to calm myself than her. "How do you kill them?"

"You have to destroy their heart and burn them. They hate holy items too, crosses and such hurt them, but they heal quickly too, in *seconds,* milady. They're almost as scary as the devil himself. They're not coming back, are they?"

"I don't know. I—" The door opens again and the adults step in, faces expressionless. "So, is the carriage from the sanitarium out front yet? Finally going to put me away, Father?"

"Lady Hart," Cumberton says in a soothing voice, "you have suffered a traumatic brain injury. Delusions like the one you are experiencing now are not uncommon. When the swelling ceases, they should abate."

"I saw them fly away before I hit my head."

Father's jaw tightens. "Verity—"

"I did!"

Cumberton clears his throat. "As I said, they should fade in the next few days. As for tonight, I have given your mother medicine to administer for the pain. You should not leave your bed for at least twelve hours, and when you sleep, someone should watch over you."

"Thank you very much, doctor," Father says. "Watson shall see you out." The doctor nods and leaves with our butler.

And then there were four. "What about David?" I ask. "I know you think I'm insane, but—"

"You are not insane, darling," Mama says, "you have a brain injury."

"Father, please. Even if I imagined the vampyres, the fact is that David is not here, and no one knows where he is. That is not like him, and you know it. He is in danger," I plead, voice cracking. "Please. You have to do something."

"If he has not come home or sent word by morning, I will contact Scotland Yard, will that suffice?"

"No! They could have him in Ireland by then. He—"

"That is my decision, Verity, do not question it," he says, voice hard as steel. I meet his cold blue eyes, and my heart sinks. There's fear in them, but I know it is not for David. He doesn't believe me. He's worried of what Scotland Yard will uncover about David, about all of us, if there is an investigation. Public perception trumps the life of his only son and heir. At this moment, I hate this man, my own flesh and blood, more than I have ever hated anyone before. "You need to rest. You are not to leave that bed for the required time. Mrs. Cooper will watch over you." Like a prison matron. I always knew he would imprison me at some point. "Rest. You will feel better in the morning. Good night." With that, he departs. After blowing me a kiss, Mama trails behind him. My loving parents. I would be better off with wolves.

Mrs. Cooper steps forward. "Croft, I shall take over from here. You're dismissed." My only ally frowns but obeys, and I'm left with my jailer. She begins mixing the medicine Cumberton left. "You will feel better in the morning, Lady Verity. You just need to sleep. You'll wake and the bad dream will all be over."

"It's only just begun, Mrs. Cooper." And I am the only one apparently willing to end it. I turn on my side away from her, shutting my tear filled eyes. Hold on, David. I'm coming.

CHAPTER THREE

VERITY HART SPRINGS INTO ACTION

Mrs. Cooper must have doubled my dose of pain powder on Father's orders because I drink it and a few minutes later become too woozy to put my escape plan into action. I shut my eyes, and when I open them once more the sun has come out to play. At least the pain has abated. I glance at the clock and realize I've been asleep for twelve hours. Precious time stolen. Wherever their destination is they are well on their way. He's gone.

I need a plan. My best option is still Scotland Yard. If Father will not alert them then I shall go myself. I will just tell them the truth, save for the vampyre part. I witnessed an abduction. I can give a description and names of the culprits, assuming those were not aliases. Yes, Scotland Yard it is. They *have* to believe me.

A silent Croft assists me into my most serious outfit, the one Father insists I wear to press functions: white shirt, dark blue jacket and skirt with rivets forming roses, and tight bun underneath a structured mini top hat with white netted veil. As I walk past the servants to breakfast, most glance at me as if I were about to strike them. Word about my ravings has spread. I keep my head up and spine stiff. The rest of the family, minus David, is already at the large mahogany table with Father reading the paper. Part of me hoped David would be here, but I knew the moment I opened my eyes this morning, and he wasn't by my side, that he was really gone. Part of me did think it had been a delusion or nightmare. I do not have that luxury now.

"Glad to see the vampyres didn't get you, Verity," Margot says as I step in.

"Margot!" Mama scolds.

I handle frightened servants and mouthy sisters the same way, by ignoring them. I silently serve myself from the sideboard before sitting across from Mama. "Have you contacted the Yard yet?" I ask Father.

"No need," he says. "We received a note from him. He took that commission in Ireland and had to leave right away."

"Was it a telegram or hand written note?"

He pulls out a paper from his pocket, handing it to me.

"*Dear Family,*

I must apologize for my abrupt and unannounced departure, but an opportunity has arisen that I must act quickly upon. I am leaving for Ireland tonight. Please do not worry. I will send telegrams as often as I can, but do not know when I shall return. I love you all.

D.V. Hart"

"They forced him to write this," I say, crumpling up this falsehood. "David never signs anything D.V. Hart, and it is far too impersonal. It sounds as if an automaton transcribed it."

"Verity you must stop this. He is fine, he's working," Father says.

"Without me? When has he ever gone off on a lark, let alone on a project without me?"

"He is thirty years old. He does not need his younger sister by his side at all times."

"And he decided to go off for who knows how long without any clothes? Or his chemistry books and tools?" I am assuming.

"They probably had a train or boat to catch, and there was not time to pack," Mama offers. "He will send for them later."

My mouth drops open big enough to catch flies. "This is madness. I saw what I saw. They kidnapped David."

"You will stop this now," Father says, anger simmering in his voice.

"I will not! Whether you choose to believe it or not, David is in mortal danger and you are standing by doing nothing."

"There is nothing to do. Stop being hysterical," Father orders.

"I am not hysterical, I am perfectly calm." And I am, at least on the outside. "David needs help. If you will not acquire it for him, I shall. I will go to Scotland Yard myself."

That was the exact wrong thing to declare. Intense fury crosses Father's face as I have seen only once before. He stands, and at the same time thrusts his fist down on the table, making the silverware and plates clatter. Mama gasps and Margot flinches. "Stop this!" he roars. "Stop these fantasies at once! Your brother is fine, and I swear to God above if you set foot in Scotland Yard, if you persist in feeding these delusions, I will call the sanitarium myself, and you shall never leave. I should have done it bloody years ago. All the money in the world is not worth putting up with *you*. I am at my wit's end with you, do not push me over the edge!" He storms out of the dining room before he can strike me. He never has before, but the last time I saw him this infuriated was the one time he came close.

Mama, near tears, tosses her napkin down. "Now look what you have done! You're breaking our hearts, Verity. Our hearts!" She follows Father out, off to comfort him. If I ever needed proof she valued him over her own children I now have it.

I am brimming with so much rage my hands tremble. Margot has lost her smile as well. I wish she did not have to witness all this strum and drang. "You best listen to him," she says. "He will do it."

I know he will, and it breaks my heart. "You don't believe me either, do you?"

"No. Sorry. The bobbies probably won't either."

My baby sister is correct once more. With only my word against Father's, and a letter in David's own handwriting, I would be laughed out of the station or placed in a straightjacket. "Excuse me."

I flee to the only place I can fall apart, my workshop. When I reach the third floor, I am on the verge of hysteria and cannot breathe. I slam the door shut, crumbing to the hardwood floor. It takes several breaths and a lot of willpower to fight the hysteria back enough to think. Form a plan. Every problem has a solution. Yet the answer to this one…have I the strength to carry it out? I have no choice, do I? But if Father discovers I'm considering chasing after David, he shall imprison me for life without hesitation. This realization gives me further pause. Oh Lord, do I actually intend to do what I am contemplating? Forget the fact I am dealing with vampyres, if I do survive another encounter with them and retrieve David I shall be returning home to the very great possibility that I will spend the rest of my life exiled halfway across the world or imprisoned with the barking mad. Am I really going to do this? *Really?*

Yes. Absolutely. David would move heaven and earth if the shoe were on the other foot. I can do this. I *can.*

Very well then. Where do I begin? What do I know about the enemy? They're Irish, vampyres, and they seemed to need him to build an automaton if last night's conversation could be believed. Oh dear Lord, what will they do when they find out David can't even use a hammer, let alone assemble a complex machine? Do not think about that. Focus on the task at hand. What else do I know of them? Their names, though those are probably false. I wrack my brain for every word said, every gesture, and every person they came into contact with. *Orrlock.* They were his guests, he has to know them, especially considering he had harsh words with them the other night. He'll help me. He has to.

Making sure that no one sees me, I sneak out of the house through the library window, my heart racing the entire time. Even on the street, when people smile and nod, I glance behind to see if they're racing toward the house to tattle on me. I hail a hansom cab, one of the newer models pulled by automaton horses, and only then relax. I have only just begun this journey, and I am frightened enough to give up.

As usual the London streets and sidewalks are clogged with carriages, cabs, and sellers peddling their wares. The ride to Chelsea takes donkey's years, time I haven't to spare. The Count rarely has parties at his home, only the odd concert or theatrical presentation, so I have only been once or twice. It is a smallish white two-story villa wedged between two others. There are no signs of life inside with all the curtains drawn. The moment I exit the cab, I feel as if the spotlight is on me again. If anyone saw me alone on this block, let alone walking up to his house unescorted, my already shaky reputation would be ruined. Of course it will be shredded to tatters after I leave for Ireland.

I ring the bell, glancing behind myself every few moments. It takes a few nerve-wracking seconds, but the door opens. His valet stands at the threshold. "May I help you?" he asks with an Eastern European accent.

"Lady Hart to see Count Orrlock on a most urgent matter."

"I am afraid the Count is not in."

"I can wait. It is imperative I speak with him right away. It regards a matter of life and death."

"The Count is out and will not be available until this evening, I am sorry."

"Then tell me where he is. I will go there. A person's life is at stake, do you hear me? Tell me where he is!"

The valet is taken aback by my vehemence. "Lady Hart if I could help you I would, but the Count is out of reach until nightfall, seven at the earliest. I shall give him your most urgent message when he arises."

"Arises?"

"Good-bye, Lady Hart." The valet shuts the door in my face.

No, no, no this cannot be happening. Is he simply asleep in there? I pound on the door but receive no answer this time. If he's simply asleep in there I will murder…a horrific realization ceases my knocking and sweeps my breath away once more. Our entire relationship, all our interactions, flashes through my mind. He has never come to events during the day or taken us up on our invitations to Foxfire, not once, and I have invited him numerous occasions. He rarely attends dinner parties, and on more than one occasion, I caught him hiding food in his napkin. He would wink at me, and I'd smile back. And he always walks around with a drink, but upon second examination it is always been full. Dear Lord, I simply thought he tended to business during the day and hated English cuisine. I back away from the house cautiously. One of my best friends is a soulless vampyre. I have been flirting with an undead monster. Father is going to have my guts for garters.

I hail a hansom cab to return home, climbing in. When it moves, I sigh again. Nothing has changed with this revelation. Orrlock is still my best lead. He probably knows the Irish intimately. I mean, how many vampyres are there in the world? If they were legion they wouldn't be just myth. Obsess about your choice of dancing partner later, Verity. Onto the next phase of the operation. Prepping for when I locate him.

After I sneak back into the house, I make sure Mama sees me so she believes nothing is amiss before returning to my workshop. All this subterfuge is exhausting. I sit at my work table cluttered with pistons and cogs, closing my eyes to focus. I need weapons. Lots of weapons. Holy items, silver, guns, knives, perhaps even explosives. Thankfully, through the course of our business, I know just where to acquire them all. Materials first. I pilfer all the silver jewelry, candlesticks, and picture frames in my room, before moving onto David's. Getting my parent's trinkets and the silverware from the closet is a bit trickier with the servants wandering the house. I only take what will not be missed for a day or so. After I begin my journey to Ireland, a few stolen forks will be the least of my crimes.

Mama checks on me in the workshop before leaving for her afternoon social rounds. The moment the door shuts downstairs, I sneak out again, huge carpetbag in hand. On my way to the silversmith I stop in a few shops, buying as much silver as I can find. If David lives he will have a heart attack when he receives the bill, especially from the silversmith. A rush job for forty silver spikes, arrow heads, and daggers do not come cheap. For the silver bullets a gunsmith is required. I find one three shops down.

The shop is empty, even of the shopkeeper, but there is plenty to capture my interest. There are dozens of guns along the walls, mostly rifles for hunting but a few pistols as well. I have only fired a pistol once or twice, and a rifle a few times more than that, but my years of archery have made me a good shot if I can compensate for the blowback. I do hope I have no use for them in this endeavor. Still. Better to have one and not need it…

The shopkeeper, a haggard old man in a leather apron, finally emerges from the back of the shop, sweat covering his face. "May I help you?"

"Yes, I have an urgent commission for you from the inventor D.V. Hart."

"I've heard of him. What's he need?"

"It is an odd request and discretion is required." I place the frames and candelabras still remaining from my previous stops on the counter. "We'll pay you handsomely, of course, but the order must be complete by tomorrow."

"I don't take trade," he says, eyeing the items.

"These are for materials. I require silver bullets, as many as you can make by tomorrow."

I expect him to balk, but instead he says, "Vampyre or werewolf?"

My first instinct is to lie, that he is attempting to trick me, but he is so serious staring at me I decide to tell the truth. "Vampyre. They kidnapped my brother."

"Are you going after him alone? Because they will eat you alive. Literally."

"I have no choice. No one believes me. Have you ever fought—"

"No, but I've known a few people who have through the years."

"Can you give me their names? Maybe they would—"

"They're dead. Vampyres are nasty bastards. Your brother's dead, ma'am." He pushes the candles back to me. "He wouldn't want you going out the same way."

I thrust them back toward him, mouth set level straight. "He is not dead. I *know* it. Now, if you will not assist me, then my money and I shall go to someone who will. Are you able to make me the bullets in time or not?"

The gunsmith stares me square in the eye, finding them as hard as his. "I'll put crosses on the tips. It won't affect velocity or precision. You have guns to go with the bullets?"

I square my shoulders and toss my head back. "No, but luckily I find myself in a gun shop. What do you recommend, sir?"

I leave the shop with two sleek six shooters and the promise the bullets will be ready tomorrow. Next stop is church. As we're Church of England, I have never been inside a Catholic church but I know they have holy water. The few people praying in the pews barely notice as I place two flasks into the water, filling them to capacity. Stealing from God's holy house. I barely recognise myself. When I sneak back into the house with my bag full of contraband I feel faint. I must remember to eat during this adventure.

I stop in the kitchen for a snack and cup of tea before retiring to my workshop to retrofit my latest line for field readiness. I'll be up all night building another Incinerator, which instead of firing petrol spews holy water. A miniature air fan may be required. I'll also need to remove the arrowheads from the archery sets to replace them with silver the ones. And I know

David has silver nitrate in his lab, which I might find use for. I just wish I knew where I was going so I can begin my travel plans. I need the quickest route, which has to be by train no matter the destination. I'll examine the train schedule later. Work now.

Time does not fly as it usually does when I am on a project. I cannot stop glancing out the window, willing the sun to set or distressing myself with thoughts of the torture they are putting my poor David through. When it's time for prayers and supper, I've barely begun on the new cuff. At this pace, it will never get done.

Dinner is a somber affair with my parents almost making it a point of not to acknowledging my presence. I only open my mouth to ask for a servant for water. We pretend nothing is amiss as Father recounts his meeting at 10 Dowling St and Mama about visiting a flower show with Aunt Esme. Just as we are about to leave the table, the doorbell rings. Oh, he has the most despicable timing.

"Who the devil can that be?" Father asks.

Trying to remain calm, I rise. "I believe it is Count Orrlock come for his appointment with David. I shall just inform him of the cancellation. Excuse me." Before they can protest, I rush into the hallway. Sure enough Watson steps aside to allow my undead friend entrance. "Count Orrlock, always a pleasure."

His usual *joie de vive* is missing this evening, replaced with a gravity that does not become him. "I received your—"

"I am afraid David is unable to make your appointment," I cut in. "He has been unexpectedly detained."

"I beg your pardon? You—" I theatrically eye Watson as I step next to our butler. Orrlock gives a little nod. "I understand, Lady Hart."

"I have no idea when David will be available again. I do apologize for any inconvenience. I shall walk you back to your carriage." I take his arm, leading him outside with Watson close behind us. "Meet me at the end of the block," I whisper. "I am so sorry, Count, but these things do happen," I say louder. "You know geniuses. So eccentric."

"All is forgiven, Lady Hart," he says before kissing my hand. "Until we meet again." He nods at Watson and Father, who stands at the door with a glower on his face, and disappears into his carriage.

Father's glower grows in time to my proximity as I walk up the path. "I do not like him coming here, let alone kissing your hand like that."

"Sorry, Father. I will not allow it to happen again." I pass through the foyer to the staircase. "I have a headache. I am going to lie down." Slowly, I walk upstairs, but when I reach the second floor hallway away from all eyes, I dash to my room and shut the door before ringing for Croft. I throw on my black cloak with the large hood as she enters. "I must go out again. I need you to scout ahead for me, then return here should anyone come to check on me. If they do, tell them I have taken medicine and am about to drift asleep."

"Yes, milady."

Croft pokes her head out of my door and waves for me to move. She does this again on the stairs, but I have to hasten into the hall closet when a servant passes downstairs. My heart about to pound out of my chest as I stand in the dark enclosure. I am more nervous about leaving the house than meeting a suspected vampyre alone in his carriage. When Croft knocks on the door, I sprint to the library to make my escape through the window I have been using all day like a common burglar.

Checking over my shoulder to make sure I am not followed, I rush down our busy street holding the hood to hide my face. His carriage waits at the end. When I climb in, I draw the shades. "Tell your man to drive around," I order. "I don't care where."

"Canterbury, around the park please." The steam engines on the automaton horses wheeze, and we jolt to a start. "I was most concerned when I received your message. I am sorry I could not respond sooner. You appear to have all your appendages. What—"

"David's been kidnapped."

My friend's face falls, disquieted by my news. "I had not heard. I'm sorry."

"You haven't heard because no one believes me. The culprits were vampyres."

His eyes narrow with disbelief. "Vampyres? Lady Hart—"

"My brother does not have time for playacting, Count Orrlock," I snap. "Please spare me sentiments that I have gone around the bend when we both know I have not. You are proof of their existence, are you not? Or shall we continue this discussion in a church? Or during daylight hours?"

His pretty mouth opens to protest, but my steely gaze makes him think better of it. I have him. "How long have you suspected?"

"I pieced it together today. Until last night I believed your kind were merely faeiry stories, until two of your kinsman attempted to eat me before flying off like a pigeon with my brother."

"Who were they?"

"An Irish couple who attended your ball. I saw you speaking to them, so I thought you might know who they really are and where I can find them. Do you recall them?"

"Oh, yes," he says with a scoff. "They came uninvited, so I asked them to leave."

"Who are they?"

"Underlings of an old *friend*," he says with disdain, "or so they claimed."

"They said they needed David to travel with them to Ireland to help build something, I believe a new form of automaton. Do you know where in Ireland your friend is, or why they would go to such great lengths to abduct my brother?"

"Since he moved his in a year or two ago I have heard Michael's been involved in a dispute with another local cabal who control the bay."

"Bay? Which bay?"

"Why?" Orrlock stares at me with confusion until the obvious conclusion is reached. "You mean to go after them."

"Of course."

"Lady Hart, what you are proposing is tantamount to suicide. However dangerous you believe my kind is, multiply by ten. We can rip you apart with our bare hands as if you were made of paper. We can make you leap off a bridge with a glance of our eyes. You do not stand a chance alone."

I anticipated his reluctance to assist me. There is only one thing to do, no matter how distasteful it is. In for a penny, Verity. "You could come with me. I would do…" I slide my hand toward his, caressing it, "whatever you asked of me."

He glances down at my trembling hand, eyes narrowing. He pulls away from my touch. "Lady Hart, that is beneath you. I could have had you many times over if I wanted with a mere look, but there is no sport in that, nor is there any now. And I have managed to remain alive for centuries by not aligning myself for or against any one faction. I will not do it now, not even for a friend. I am sorry. It's a fool's errand. Michael has a cabal of over twenty vampyres under his rule. The best thing to do is wait and pray they free your brother when he completes this automaton."

"And… if he cannot complete it?"

"Why would he not?"

If a vampyre cannot keep a secret, who can? "Because David never designed a machine in his life. It was me. They were all me. He only develops the chemicals should I need them, but nothing more. What will they do to him when they find out of our deception?"

My friend is hesitant for a few moments, no doubt wanting to spare me pain. And they say vampyres have no souls. "Either kill him or keep him to control the real D.V. Hart, who they *will* come after."

"Then kill us both to silence us when I have given them what they desire," I finish for him. I knew all of this, but hearing it spoken aloud makes the situation that much more real. "And you suggest I wait around for that to happen? That is your council? Bide my time until I am abducted as well? Should that happen, there will be no one looking for us, no one to rescue us if they trap me as well. The only real chance I have is to free him before they realize he is a fraud then go to the papers with his kidnapping. They wouldn't dare attempt the same crime twice if we named them as kidnappers, would they?"

"It is possible," he says with reluctance.

"Then I have no choice, do I? So if our friendship means *anything* to you, you will tell me where they have taken my brother. Give me a fighting chance. *Please.*"

He remains silent for a few seconds, studying my stony face. One cannot argue against hard logic. "Last I heard, Michael had taken a manor just outside of Galway in Barna."

A weight lifts from me. I have my location. "Thank you."

"But you *cannot* go alone. You will not make it out of London."

Of course logic can backfire on one as well. He is correct on this point. "I am open to suggestions, Count."

He ponders this for a second. True heroes are few and far between in our group of acquaintances. "What about the bounty hunter? The American you flirted with?"

"I did not…never mind. He's gone. He returned to America yesterday."

"You did not hear? He was arrested after the ball for grievous bodily harm."

My mouth pops open again. "Whom did he assault?"

"Whom do you think? Lord Hopper of course. The American claimed he stole his money then hit him. Dickie denied the entire thing and pressed charges. The American's at Newgate as he could not make bail."

"Because Dickie has his money," I say with a scoff. Dickie. "Do you think he would help me?"

"If the price were right I do not see why not. He will be desperate for passage home."

For a fleeting moment I am almost hopeful, a little of the weight of the situation lifts, but reality steals it from me. "I would have to tell him what we were up against. He would never believe me."

"Well, there you are in luck, Lady Hart. He is in a unique position to believe."

"How do you know?"

Orrlock smiles. "Because, if I am not mistaken, your American friend is a shifter, more specifically a *loup-garou.*" I shake my head. I have never heard the term before. "A werewolf, Lady Hart."

Dear Lord. "They exist as well?"

"As do witches, warlocks, trolls, faeries, the entire rogue's gallery. Your American friend comes from one of the longest known shifter bloodlines in the world. They actually live on an island not far from Galway."

That might prove useful. "But he, I mean, his condition doesn't make him dangerous, does it?"

"I would not want to be around him in wolf form but no. His condition makes him ideal for this task. Werewolves have superior senses, not to mention exceptional strength and healing capabilities that rival those of my species."

The American is becoming more and more attractive a prospect with each passing second. "Very well, I shall get him released."

"It is still a fool's errand, especially for a woman."

"Well, we are known for our foolishness and lack of intelligence," I say with a false smile. "Take me to Dickie's. I must speak to him at once. It isn't far from here."

"As you wish."

Ten minutes later, the carriage pulls up to Dickie's three-story villa. "Come in with me?" I ask Orrlock. "I may need your powers of persuasion."

"I am your humble servant, milady."

The Count and I walk up to the door, and I ring the bell. The butler answers. "Yes?"

"Count Ivan Orrlock and the Lady Verity Hart to see Lord Hopper," Orrlock says.

"Is he expecting you?"

"No, but I'm sure he will see us," I say. "Please. It is most urgent."

He nods. "You may wait in the parlor," the butler says, stepping aside.

Dickie's parlor is quite like ours, dark and cluttered from wall to wall with furniture. I do find it odd there is not a single frame or painting anywhere. He probably sold them all for poker debts. I hear Dickie tromps down the stairs then enter the room a moment later. He's dressed in a tuxedo to go out and spread joy to all the men who will beat him at cards tonight, but his black-eye really draws my attention. Much deserved, I'm sure. Good for the American. "This is a surprise, though a pleasant one of course."

"We have come to speak to you about the American. I need you to drop the charges you leveled against him right away," I importune.

Dickie chuckles. "Why on earth would I do that? You see what he did to me."

"And the whole city knows what you did to him," I parry.

The blackguard's smile drops like a stone. "I didn't touch a penny," Dickie spits out. "And why do you care? Did that

Neanderthal finally melt the ice maiden's heart? Or is it something lower that's drawn to him?"

"Watch yourself, Hopper," Orrlock warns.

He turns to Orrlock, scoffing then smiling cruelly. "You after sloppy seconds there, old chap? I'll take her after you."

Neither of us sees him move. One blink and Orrlock has traveled ten feet, his lean fingers wrapped around Dickie's throat. "That is no way to speak to a lady. Look at me!" He shakes Dickie, who winces in pain. Orrlock stares into the frightened man's eyes. "You will never do it again, will you?"

"Never again," Dickie says as if in a daze.

"Good. Now at nine tomorrow morning, you shall meet Lady Hart outside Newgate Prison. You will enter and do whatever you have to to get Mr. McQueen released. *Anything.* Then you will return home and forget we were ever here or what was asked of you. Do you understand me?"

"I understand," he says.

Orrlock releases him, shoving him against the piano so hard it shakes, expelling sour notes. He clears his throat. "Lady Hart, time to depart." The vampyre strolls out as if nothing happened. I hesitate for a moment, still in shock by the strange scene I witnessed but rush out when my senses return. *That* is what I am up against? I'm doomed.

When we get back inside the carriage Orrlock smiles. "I never tire of doing that. Now, let's get you home." He hits the top of the carriage with his cane. "Canterbury, Mayfair."

Thank the good Lord he's on my side.

We ride in silence until we reach the edge of Hyde Park near the house. "Thank you for all your help. I appreciate it more than words can proclaim. You are a true friend, I mean that. Good-bye."

I am about to climb out when he grabs my arm. "Lady Hart." I turn around and before I can stop him, his lips are upon mine. They're far colder than I imagined, which might be why no passion rises from me. He pulls away a moment later. "Be careful. I would hate to lose my favourite dancing partner."

I kiss his cool cheek. "Thank you." I leap out and the carriage pulls away, leaving me alone in the dark night. So. Galway. I've heard it's lovely. Hills, sea, vampyres. I cannot wait.

Now I just have to get there intact.

CHAPTER FOUR

THE AMERICAN WEREWOLF IN LONDON

Around four in the morning, I pass out on the fainting couch in my workshop still dressed in my leather trousers only to be finally awoken three hours later by Brutus attempting to leap on the couch beside me. My brain is in a daze from the lack of sleep and pouring rain outside. This is the kind of day I would spend reading in the library or tinkering in my workshop. I haven't that luxury today. Literally miles and miles to go before I sleep again.

First stop after changing into my grey muslin suit with ruffled white shirt and grey hat with iron gears along the rim is sneaking out to Victoria Station to purchase train tickets. After studying both the train and steamship schedules, I deduced that by train and ferry we would arrive half a day sooner than by ship. The vendor eyes me suspiciously as I purchase two first-class Pullman tickets for Holyhead, Wales. An unmarried man and woman traveling alone together is all but illegal, so I casually mention I'm traveling with my brother, which only makes it a tad more seemly. The train doesn't leave until four thirty-five so I have plenty of time to finish my other projects. We should get into Barna late tomorrow night if we stay on track. Now to retrieve my American.

I have driven past Newgate Prison countless times but have never had cause to go inside. It's a gloomy, cold foreboding place with few windows that takes up the whole block. It almost resembles a cross between a rectangular grey brick three-story castle and manor house but far more imposing. There are thousands inside that behemoth, the worst of the worst. I'm told they used to execute people almost right where I sit now. I shudder at the thought.

As ordered, Dickie waits outside the iron gates of the prison when my cab pulls alongside. The moment he spies me through the window with the visage of an automaton and about as much free will he treks through the gates. I haven't a clue how long it takes to release a man, but my cabbie gets antsy, as do I as the minutes pass. Half an hour after my arrival, just as I am about to charge through that gate myself, Dickie emerges, walking over to the cab. "I dropped the charges."

"Good. Thank you. You may go home now." He obeys. I'm forced to wait another two hours as miserable people filter in and out of those gates. Precious time I do not have wasted. I barely recognise the American when he tromps out with his fuzzy face and stringy black hair. "Mr. McQueen!" I call, but he doesn't hear. "Mr. McQueen, wait!"

I toss money at the cabbie before leaping out of the cab in pursuit, not even bothering to open my umbrella. "Mr. McQueen!" When I reach the American just past the dome of the Old Bailey, he spins around and stops dead. Not prepared for this, I gasp as our bodies smash against each other. I stumble back, holding my unsteady hat. Eyes narrowed and glare affixed, this man is not pleased to see me. In fact he looks downright frightening with three days worth of beard, disheveled greasy hair, and soot on his tuxedo. He reeks of stale sweat and body odor as well. Prison did not agree with him. "What?"

"Do you remember me?" I ask, out of breath. "Lady Verity Hart? We met at the ball, in the garden? I'm the one who convinced Dickie to release you."

"Thanks. Bye. Whatever you want, the answer is hell no." He spins on his cowboy boot and continues down the street.

"Mr. McQueen, please wait! Please!" I shout as I take off after him again. "I have a job for you! Wait!"

When I reach him again as we round the corner, I tug on his jacket sleeve and he rotates around, the sides of his mouth twitching in anger. "Lady, you can take your job and..." He sees my horrified expression and instantly softens a little, the corners of his mouth dropping. He takes a few seconds to calm himself, taking several deep breaths. "Look, I'm sorry, okay?" he says, running his large hand through his now soggy hair. "It was a swell thing you did getting me out of there. I'm grateful. Really. But I am leaving this disgusting, rainy cesspool of a country on the first steamship I can get before I kill someone, okay? Whatever you want done, find someone else."

"There is no one else. No one believes me. My brother will die, probably me as well, if you do not help us. I'll pay you handsomely. Five hundred pounds, a thousand, I don't care." I grab his forearms, clutching tight. His lip twitches, I believe in disgust. *"Please.* I am *begging* you. I shall fall to my knees if necessary, Mr. McQueen. Help me."

He glances down at my hands digging into his arms then back at my face. Relief washes through me when his brown eyes meet mine. Pity brims from his. For once, I welcome the emotion. "Let's go and talk about this, alright? No promises though."

I release his arms, grinning. "Thank you, sir. Thank you so much."

My hero nods and steps away from the crazy lady. We find the nearest café four stores down, taking a table in the back. "I'm fuc—" He glances at me. "I'm starving."

"Order however much you wish. I'm paying."

"Good because your friend Hopper stole all my money. I don't have two nickels to rub together right now. Don't even know how I'm paying for my hotel room."

"I warned you to watch your billfold."

"That you did, sugar," he says, sitting back in his chair. "But I think he took it before the ball so too little too late, huh?" The server gets our large order, every type of meat available for him, though I only get tea. The server walks away, eyeing us like all the other patrons. "So, someone's trying to kill you and your brother, and nobody believes you. I got that all right?"

"Two nights ago my brother was kidnapped in front of me. I believe they have taken him to Galway."

"Sounds like a police matter to me."

The waiter brings our drinks. When he's gone, I whisper, "Except the culprits were vampyres."

He cocks an eyebrow. "Vampyres?"

"Yes. And before you try to convince me you do not believe they exist, which we both know is a lie, I should tell you I know of your…condition that flares up during the full moon."

His eyes double in size as his face falls. "I don't know wh—"

I hold up my hand. "Please, just don't. Count Orrlock informed me, about himself as well, so there is no point denying it. The simple fact is you know that world, the…supernatural, and I do not. Therefore I need your unique set of experience and skills if I have even half a chance of succeeding in this endeavor."

"So what exactly do you want from me?"

"I need you to accompany me to Galway to help me free my brother."

"Galway as in Ireland?"

"Yes. I believe they are keeping him in a manor house just outside there."

He sips his black coffee. "Why'd they take him?"

"They need him to build a machine, but he will be unable to. When they discover this, they will probably come after me because I…can."

It takes a moment before he comprehends my meaning. He scoffs. "I wondered why you smelled like metal and grease." He takes another sip of coffee and chuckles. "So they got the wrong Hart, huh?" He sets the cup down. "They'll kill him, you know, if he ain't dead already."

"He isn't. I would…sense it if he was. I would. I felt it when he broke his arm, when he had pneumonia, I would *know*." I sip my tea. "Besides, he's leverage. They already have him, they might as well put him to use. Keep him to control me."

"Shug, I'd still put it at fifty-fifty. You don't know what these bastards are like. I've only run into their kind a handful of times, and it was never pleasant. And you're suggesting you and I travel alone across two countries to storm a castle filled with the buggers, trying to save your brother who is probably already dead?"

"Three countries. We would take the ferry in Holyhead, Wales."

He stares, studying me to see if I am serious. When he realizes I am, he chuckles. "Lady, you are a piece of work. You really are."

"I have weapons. Guns, knives, even a few I designed myself all equipt with silver. We get there, sneak in during daylight, retrieve David, and go to the authorities about the kidnapping."

"Got it all planned, huh?"

"Absolutely. The train leaves today at four thirty-five from Victoria Station, I have already acquired our tickets," I say, removing his.

He glances at it, shaking his head. "Mighty presumptuous of you."

"I am desperate, Mr. McQueen. I'm not staying here waiting around for them to abduct me as well. I'm venturing to Galway regardless."

"Do that and your parents will be burying two kids, not just one."

"Then do the honorable thing. Help me."

As he studies me, I study him. He's exhausted, dirty, and almost feral in a way, angry at the world. Dangerous. The exact type of man I need on my side. What he sees in me I do not know, but while the rest of his face is stony his eyes tell the real story.

They soften for a moment, and I know I have him. I am so relieved I could kiss him.

"A thousand, up front."

"Five hundred when you step on the train, the rest when we reach Barna. Should something happen to me before then, you forfeit the rest. I pay all expenses within reason, and if you are injured, I will pay all medical bills, and you will get a bonus to be determined."

He mulls the proposition over. "Sounds fair." Then he leans in, affixing a scowl to his face. "But I have a few conditions of my own. No talking down to me, no acting like the biggest toad in the puddle. Just because you got money don't make you better than me. You may be fronting the bill, but I don't work for you. You're buying the expertise, not the man. I'm not gonna be your pack mule or whipping boy. I am here for one reason, to see you to your destination and get your brother. And should shit go down, you listen to me and obey without question."

"Sounds fair. So, we have a deal?" I ask, extending my hand.

He shakes it. "Deal."

I stand from the table, tossing enough money on it for the food and his hotel. "I shall see you this afternoon then. Enjoy your breakfast." As I walk out, I sense his eyes following me as I sashay away. When I step out into the rain, I feel infinitely better. Things are coming along quite nicely. This may actually work. I'll worry about the fact I'm traveling alone with a handsome werewolf later. I have an arsenal to complete.

*

Both the silversmith and gunsmith appear haggard most likely from lack of sleep, but I am most pleased with the quality and amount of ammunition I leave with. They have earned every shilling. When I return home I am drenched, covered in mud, and exhausted, but there is no time for a bath. I change into my leather work clothes, affix my goggles, and attempt to finish the Fountain.

The jet of holy water is propelled from the reservoir by a puff of air heated by a miniature steam attached to the top of the cuff. It only spews three feet and it quite clunky and nowhere near as fashionable as the others but will have to do. There is no time to tinker. I pack my trunk with the weapons first only to cover them with my clothes and other essentials like books, hats, gloves, and so forth. By the time this is all done, and I change into my peach tea dress with matching top hat with white veil, I have only twenty minutes to get to the station. On my way out, I hear music from the library. Only one person in this house plays that beautifully. I take one last glimpse at my baby sister from the threshold of the room.

Watching Margot, so beautiful and impassioned by Handel, intense panic grips me to the point I cease to breathe. Despite what I've told everyone, myself included, I'm aware the odds are against me. What I'm intending is insane, absolutely insane. I am outmatched, outgunned, and haven't a clue what I am doing. Vampyres? Werewolves? Maybe I have gone mad.

It makes no difference, though. I know without a doubt David would do this for me. He would walk through the gates of hell for me. He's not only my brother, he's my best friend. The only person in this world who loves me unconditionally. He has protected me all my life. From Father, from my so called friends, even from myself. I have to go.

One obstacle left. Watson stands at the door, staring as the footman carries my trunk to the hansom cab. "Lady Verity, where are you going?"

I need a head start before Father calls the men with butterfly nets, so I say, "You did not hear the bell earlier? We received a telegram from David asking us to send his things. Croft and I packed for him. I'm taking the trunk to the steamship then meeting Cricket for tea. I shall be home in time for dinner. Have to dash, don't want to miss the ship!" Before he can query me further, I dash out the door to the cab. I climb in and sigh. It begins. "Victoria Station, and please hurry." Croft is near tears as she stands in the door, waving as I pull away. I feel like weeping myself.

Traffic is wretched with the ill weather, and my tension increases threefold with each delayed passing minute. When we finally pull up to the station, my body trembles like a leaf on the wind. The trip itself may very well do me in before we even reach the vampyres. A porter unloads my trunk and follows me swiftly through the busy station, with its arched ceiling held by girders and noisy train whistles, to the platform and finally onto the train. I maneuver through second class where businessmen and their companions already sit on upholstered benches or stow their suitcases on the railing above. When I get to the Pullman smoking car, men are already enjoying their cigars while chatting in high back, plush chairs with gas lamp chandeliers above. Automatons dressed as porters stand by to light their cigars or roll up with trays of drinks. Oh, dear. I recognise a man in the corner, one of Father's M.P. colleagues, and quickly glance away before he can see my face. The problem of notoriety arises again in the dining car with Penelope Pace and her husband Benedict. I pretend to adjust my veil to shield myself. Pitfalls everywhere.

When we finally reach my sleeper suite, I am about to swoon from fear. There are only two suites on the Pullman that are actual rooms with a door while the rest of the passengers have to sleep in literal holes in the wall, though beautiful holes in the wall with chandeliers above and geared ornaments in all the moldings. My suite is roughly the size of a small closet with a plush bench and folding upper berth where I'm to sleep. Close quarters. As the porter stows my trunk under the bench, I step out into the lounge to search for my "brother." No sign, only men and women taking their seats along the windows. Outside someone shouts, "All aboard!"

My stomach clenches. No. This cannot be happening. He has to be here. He promised. Didn't he? The past few days are something of a blur. I can barely recall what I was doing ten minutes ago. He must have promised. The train lurches forward. No. *No.* Tears rise again. Of course he isn't coming. He hasn't a death wish as I apparently do. I am completely alone. I—

"There you are."

I pivot around to find the American sauntering toward me. He is dressed in black trousers with matching cowboy boots, white cotton shirt, black calfskin vest with brass buttons, and light linen coat, competed by a black broad brimmed Stetson with circular buckles and belt with a row of bullets along it. Despite his conspicuous appearance, once again I have the strongest urge to kiss him. I really must stop having those. He must have them as well because when he reaches me, he pecks my cheek. My entire body alights with the mere brushing of his lips. I am too shocked to move. "This one's ours, right, shug?" he asks, nodding toward the suite. "Come on."

Oh, dear. The other passengers eye us with suspicion as he takes my hand, leading me into our suite. When the door closes, he releases my hand and throws his suitcase on the seat. I hug the door in case he decides to pounce. "Mr. McQueen, I believe I should clarify what exactly I do and do not expect from you."

He glances at me then chuckles. "You look like a cornered rabbit there, shug. Calm down, I ain't gonna attack ya. You aren't even close to my type. That there was just for show," he says, nodding at the door. "The only way tongues won't wag is if they think we're married, so congratulations. You are now Mrs. Jamie McQueen. To avoid any problems, we'll just keep ourselves to ourselves."

"Well, you're not *sleeping* in here," I say, aghast at the prospect.

The large werewolf steps toward me, amusement fading as he does. "Oh yes, I am. You're paying me to be your bodyguard. I need to be near your body to guard it."

"You will not need to do a thing until we reach Barna. I am perfectly safe. No one knows where I am, not even my family."

"Maybe, but better safe than sorry. And before you forget, I believe you owe me some money."

As yes. That. Scowling, I maneuver around him to reach my trunk. The banque note is between my clothes and weapons. "I do not like this arrangement, not one bit."

He whistles when he catches sight of my arsenal. "Damn, shug, we invading all of Ireland or what?" Once again he steps beside me, far too close for comfort. As least he's bathed in the interim, shaved as well so he only has a moustache and light beard around his chin. A vast improvement. He picks up the Artemis. "What on God's green is this?"

"I designed it. It fires silver spikes." Next, he picks up the Incinerator. "It emits a stream of petrol ignited by the flame at the tip." Then the Fountain. "Projects holy water." I show him my ring. "Syringe inside with a sedative. The cigarette case injects silver nitrate via syringe, as does the card case. Then, of course, pistols and miniature rifle with silver bullets, daggers, and crossbow, though I didn't have enough time to replace the old arrowheads with the silver ones I acquired today. Will it be enough?"

"Um, yeah," he chuckles and shakes his head. "Shoot, I don't know if I should run screaming from this room or marry ya. Damn."

"Thank you?"

"Welcome." He shrugs off his jacket, where I am shocked to find two six shooters in a black shoulder holster lined with more bullets. He removes the straps and belt with the bullets. "Glad one of us came prepared. Any of those silver bullets for a .44 Peacemaker?" I dig around for the box of .44s. "You best load them for me."

I rise from the bench. "Why? Oh…" I keep forgetting about his condition. "Wait, your condition shall not be a problem on this trip, will it?"

"'My condition,' I like that," he says, shaking out the regular bullets into his hand. "No, the full moon ain't for awhile." We exchange his pistols for my banque note. "Thank you kindly, ma'am."

I sit on the bench and start loading the silver bullets. "There is one more matter we need to discuss. There are several people on this train of my acquatience. Hopefully they will debark soon, but still, if you see someone speaking to me, it would be best to pretend we are strangers. If people even *suspected* I was traveling unaccompanied with a man, my reputation would be ruined. That *cannot* happen."

"Let's agree on one thing right away: life first, reputation second, okay?"

For me they are one in the same, but I still say, "Of course."

"Good." He picks up his jacket. "Now, I'm gonna check out the layout of the train," he says putting it on again. "You stay put, Mrs. McQueen. Don't miss me too much."

"Perish the thought."

With another grin my way, he walks out. When the door shuts, I breathe a literal sigh of relief. Being around him makes me feel as if I have to be on constant guard, against what I do not know. It must be the werewolf factor, primitive warnings against a predator and all. The train jostles and his worn suitcase bumps against my leg. An impish notion crosses my mind. Before I can stop myself I open his case. I should know *something* about the man I'm sharing close quarters with. It is the prudent course of action. It's mostly dark wool trousers, animal skin vests, cotton shirts, and another light linen duster, brown this time. There are a few books too, one Dickens novel and two on farming. There are also hygiene items like razor, soap, D.V. Hart roll-on odorizor, and toothpaste.

What really captures my interest is the sole photograph in his possession. A grinning McQueen stands in front of a tiny ramshackle house though hut would be more appropriate made of wood with a field, if it can be called that, behind it. Really it's a plot of dirt with wild grass as tall as my waist around. Must be his home. No wife in the picture, though she could be the one taking it. He doesn't wear a ring. Not that I care if he's married or not. It has no bearing on the job. I place everything back inside, close the case, and resume my task. I fill not only his pistols but his belt with my silver bullets. He returns twenty minutes later reeking of cigar smoke.

"Train looks clear for now," McQueen says, opening the top fold-out bed. He takes one of the guns from beside me and climbs up. "I'm bushed. Gonna take a nap while I can." He lifts off his hat, placing it over his eyes. "Don't leave the room, but try to keep quiet."

"Do you always sleep with your boots and guns on?"

"I do everything with them on, shug."

Thank goodness his eyes are covered because I turn as red as an apple with the image that pops into my head. I return to my bench and start replacing the arrowheads, which does not take long as I only brought ten. Too bulky a weapon in most cases, but I'm a regular William Tell with a bow and arrow. It is important to be prepared for every contingency. When I'm done, I pull out my H.G. Wells novel, *The Island of Dr. Moreau,* but cannot concentrate. It is too on point with half man/half animal creatures as protagonists. I should have brought *Journey to the Centre of the Earth* instead. Soon I simply stare out the window at the passing countryside of green fields with sheep on the rolling hills. My eyes grow heavy within minutes, and I feel myself nodding off as well to the sound of his light snores.

I jerk awake sometime later as the train lurches, and find it's now twilight. I groan and take off the jacket smelling of cigars covering me to stretch. That was quite nice of him. Maybe underneath that coarse exterior he *is* actually a gentleman.

A missing gentleman. I rise, and notice his bunk is empty. Probably off to smoke again. I stretch to work the kinks from my back—sleeping in a corset is never advised—as I watch two big men, one bald and the other with blonde hair, race to catch our now moving train. The sign reads Northampton, so I've only been asleep only an hour or so. I need the privy and something to eat. Really what I want is to stretch my legs and get out of this stuffy closet. I fasten my hat with the netted veil, snap the Artemis on over my white glove, and step out. A few passengers sit in the parlor chatting or reading the paper. They pay me no mind as I move to the washroom. When I catch sight of myself in the mirror, I cringe. I am a fright. Wan, pasty, my hair wild. I fix myself up as best as I can, even pinching my cheeks to get some colour in them. Only a few hours of traveling and I'm wilting. Food will help.

There are only a few empty seats in the dining car with automaton waiters rolling back and forth with trays of food and drink. No one I recognise is here, so I take a seat beside a window and write down my order of salmon with lemonade. Just as the automaton rolls away, Penelope and her husband walk in. She is hard to miss with bright green hair, purple hat with peacock feathers and green netting, and matching purple silk dress with brass rivets in a swirl pattern. It takes her all of a second to notice me. "Verity!" Oh, blast. She leads Benedict over, an interesting looking man with small nose but large lips, and we kiss cheeks. "We thought that was you. What a surprise."

"It certainly is. Where are you off to?" I ask.

"Benedict's father summoned us to Birmingham, something about one of the factories." They sit in the chairs across from me uninvited. "What about you?"

"Holyhead. David has a commission in Ireland. I decided to travel with him."

"Where is he?" Benedict asks, wiping his monocle with his handkerchief.

"Poor lamb has a wretched headache. He took some powders. He will be out until we get there, I'm sure." The automaton rolls over with my food.

"Poor thing," Pen says. "Please give him our best." The Paces write down their orders and give the paper to the automaton. "Such good service since they switched to machines. They—" Pen gasps. "Oh, my! Look who it is!" I spin around and find McQueen filling at the door, glaring at me. "That American who struck Dickie. I heard he was in jail. You don't think he's dangerous, do you?"

I turn back to them. "Only to those who steal his billfold. We all know Dickie has sticky fingers."

"Should we invite him to dine with us?" Pen asks in a low voice. She's a notorious gossip who I am sure is chomping at the bit to get the scoop on the real story. "It *is* the polite thing to do. Ben, go over there. Go!" Her husband obeys. Seconds later the men return with McQueen lowering himself into the chair beside me. I can't look at him for fear of turning bright red. "Lady Hart, did you have a chance to meet Mr. McQueen the other night?"

"I did." I have no choice but to turn to him. "It is lovely to see you again," I say with a gracious smile.

I do not get one in return. "Same here, Lady Hart. It's surprising to see you *out here*."

"My brother is asleep in our suite, and I was hungry."

The waiter returns with our meals and McQueen places his, red meat of course. There will not be a cow safe in this country until he departs it. "So, Mr. McQueen," Benedict says, "we are pleased to see you are no longer a guest of Newgate." The table rattles as Pen kicks her husband under it. "Ow!" Be winces.

"Yes, we heard about your unfortunate incarceration Mr. McQueen," I interject. "It must have been dreadful."

"Yes," Pen says, "and I hate to speak ill of anyone, especially Dickie, I adore him to death, but he can be a handful. He has asked Benedict for money on several occasions. I can safely say everyone at this table believes in your innocence."

"You have no idea what that means to me," he says with a fake grin.

"You are most welcome," Pen says with a proud smile. McQueen's food arrives, and we all begin eating. "So, where are you traveling to, Mr. McQueen? Chasing another fugitive?"

"I'm visiting relatives in Ireland."

"Have you ever been before?" I ask.

"Uh, no ma'am. My parents moved to America before I was born. My grandfather didn't approve of my father, so they left."

"They eloped? How wonderfully romantic," Pen says.

"Why didn't he approve?" I ask.

"My mother was the only daughter of a powerful...*family* with a long, proud bloodline. She was promised to a similar family in Scotland, but fell in love with my father instead."

"An arranged marriage, how positively medieval," says Pen, who when she became Mrs. Pace her family's estate was saved from foreclosure. At least she liked her husband. "Are you married, Mr. McQueen?"

"No, she died of consumption many years ago," he says, cutting his meat as if this news was nothing.

We stop eating, glancing down at our plates. "I'm so sorry, Mr. McQueen," I say.

"It was a lot of years ago, it's fine."

Silence, then Benedict says, "My aunt died of consumption. Ghastly way to go." The table rattles again. He deserved that one.

"You never thought of remarrying, Mr. McQueen?" Pen asks as if nothing happened.

"No, work kept me busy and moving around."

"You were a Pinkerton, correct?" Ben asks. "You chased the Jesse James gang?"

"Once or twice. The Reno clan was tougher, though. John Reno actually clipped me in the side when we arrested him."

"Clipped?" I ask.

"Shot."

My mouth drops open. "You were shot?" As I turn to see his reaction, I notice he is barely paying attention to me. I glance in the direction he's staring. The two men, the bald and the blonde, at a nearby table glance at us too. "Mr. McQueen?"

He leaves his head and looks at me, blinking more than normal. "Oh, uh, sorry. Um, I was shot a few times, but I've shot more than have shot me."

"You've actually killed?" Ben asks, almost awed by the prospect.

"Only when I had to."

I know the next question will be, "What does it feel like?" and no one should have to reflect on that, so I say, "Is that why you left the Pinkertons? Because of the danger?"

"No, I didn't agree with my last assignment, spying and breaking up this union in Pennsylvania. When they opened fire on all those people, I couldn't work for them anymore. It'd been over thirty years anyway. Needed a change."

"My goodness, you must have been a baby when you joined," Pen says.

"I'm older than I look, ma'am," he says with a smile that makes her blush.

Not quite sure I like that. "And now you are an international bounty hunter. What do you do when you're not chasing fugitives?" His attention has returned to the men, whose heads are huddled close together. "Mr. McQueen?"

"Oh, sorry shug." Pen raises an eyebrow at this faux paus. "I, um, have a farm in Oklahoma I'm trying to start up. Afraid it's harder and more expensive than I thought, so I take a few bounties here and there."

"A farm?" Ben asks.

"Yeah, it's a beautiful plot of land. Got a creek twisting through these rolling hills that seem to go on forever. When the breeze blows, the tall grass ripples like waves. I miss it like a limb."

"It sounds divine," I say, meaning it. "Whenever I'm in the city, I miss our country home in Somerset like mad. There's no room to breathe in London."

"Didn't peg you for a country girl, shug."

The Paces both scrunch up their faces at this second impropriety. "That's *Lady* Hart, Mr. McQueen," I correct.

The side of his mouth twitches either from embarrassment or anger. "I apologize, Lady Hart."

"Perfectly understandable," I say with a gracious smile. "So, Penelope, how is Lionel enjoying his time in Jersey?"

We finish our dinner as Pen lists her son's accomplishments, and their planned trip to Brighton when the Season is over in a few weeks. McQueen devours his meal but barely takes his eyes off the men, why I know not. They cannot be vampyres because they're eating, and it's barely grown dark. His staring is making me quite nervous, though. It must have a similar effect on the men because after a few more glances our way, they don't finish their meals before retreating to the smoking car. Soon after the men depart, the automaton returns for our empty plates, and we all stand.

"Mr. McQueen, join me for an after dinner cigar?" Ben asks.

"Love to." He turns to me. "Nice seeing you both again, ladies."

"And you, Mr. McQueen," I say. "Have a safe journey." I nod, and begin walking back to the parlor car with Pen beside me.

When we're out of earshot, Pen whispers, "He is quite delicious, is he not?"

"Penny, you are a married woman," I admonish.

"I do have eyes, Verity. He's so…rugged and exotic," she says, almost growling.

"And rude," I point out as we sit across from one another in the parlor.

"He's American, they're all like that." She leans back in her chair with a private smile. "He strikes me as the type of man who'd just grab you and kiss you until you swoon. Oh," she sighs dramatically. "I believe I am going to suggest Benedict purchase a hat and cowboy boots."

"What on earth for?"

She tuts. "Oh, Verity. You're not married, you know nothing of it's peaks and troughs. Things become quite stale quite quickly. One looks for spice where one can." It takes me a moment to comprehend what she is speaking of, and my mouth drops. She grins mischievously. "He seemed to like you. He was frightfully familiar, *shug*. I heard he was one of the gentlemen you spoke to unaccompanied, you naughty girl. Is it mere coincidence you are both on the same train at the same time, or is something more nefarious going on?"

"He and I spoke for exactly five minutes before tonight, only two of those alone. And during that time he simply asked me if I was alright after I conversed with Jolyon. The entire event was blown wildly out of proportion. I have not run off with a coarse American who shoots people, I assure you."

"Such a shame," she says, smiling.

I return the gesture before standing. "I had best check on David and finish my letters before I forget. Good luck with the cowboy boots."

"Enjoy Ireland, if possible," she says as I step into my suite.

The moment the door closes I lean against it, take a deep breath, and let it out. That could have gone worse. Much worse. I think they believed us, but that was far too close. He really must be reminded not to be so…familiar with me. One word, no one *look* and our little charade could be exposed. I sit on the bench, staring out the window again. He is going to be cross with me later if he can ever get back into the room. His problem, not mine.

I settle in and begin my book again, but my mind wanders from Dr. Moreau's island. Outlaws or no, I have hired a man who has taken lives. Strange but this does not bother me as much as it should. Or as much as the fact he was married before does. I wonder how long ago she died. I wonder if he has children. Probably not as he has no pictures of them. Perhaps they died too. How horrid, poor man. She must have been—

Oh!

The sudden stopping of the train, which throws me forward onto the floor, knocks out the rest of my thoughts. I fall with a thud, sharp pain darting up my arms when I land. The screeching brakes are so loud I wince. What on earth? There's a commotion in the parlor, and I debate remaining in the suite, but have to know what has transpired. Truly I simply do not wish to be alone. I pick myself up to join everyone.

Gentlemen and the human porters aid the women and children off the floor while others upend fallen automatons whose wheels still spin. Penny adjusts her hat as I dash over to her. Fashion first. "What happened?" I ask as I help her find her feet.

"Penny!" Benedict shouts as he rushes into the car with McQueen close behind.

"Are you okay? Are you hurt?" McQueen asks, visually examining me.

"I'm fine. Why did we stop?"

"I don't know," he says gravely, which brings a chill down my spine.

"Is David alright?" Ben asks.

"David?" Why is he…oh. "He's fine. He went right back to sleep."

"He did?" Ben asks with skepticism.

A lie is not forthcoming. "He just, um…"

"Lady Hart," McQueen cuts in, "you look like you could use a stiff drink."

"I shouldn't," I say, glancing at the Paces.

"No, I insist ma'am. Come on. Let's go see if the hooch was destroyed, okay?" He places his hand on the small of my back, leading me toward the bar. He smiles at the bartender, who is sweeping up the broken glass tumblers. "Give us anything you have left."

When we collect our glasses of brandy, we step into a private corner. "Is it them? Did they tamper with the train?"

"I don't know, and my guns are in your room, which I can't get into with your friends watching." He sips his drink. "I told you not to leave that room for exactly this reason."

"I had to use the powder room, I'm sorry. Do you believe they know we are traveling together?"

He scowls at me. "Get your damn priorities straight, girl. We could be under attack here." He downs the brandy with one gulp. "I didn't like the look of those two guys in the dining car."

"Why not?"

"Forty-five years of law enforcement experience, that's why. They kept looking at us. At *you.*"

"Oh." A realization hits me. "Exactly how old are you?"

"Sixty-two. I age slower than normal." Dear Lord he's old enough to be my grandfather. "Here's what you need to do, shug. Go back into the room and don't leave for *anything*. There are only two ways in, the door and window. They could come through the window, and if they do, scream your lungs out. I'll position myself right outside the door. The second I can, I'll slip in. We—"

"Attention, everyone!" a porter says as he walks in. "I apologize for the abrupt stop. A tree has fallen across the line and must be removed. We expect a delay of an hour or two." There is a collective groan. "We shall be underway as soon as we can. Once again, we are sorry for the inconvenience."

I sip my brandy, the warmth tricking through me. "Do you think they did it?" I ask.

"Don't know. Just go to the suite, okay?"

After downing my brandy to help my nerves, I obey, shutting the suite door behind me. Immediately, I move to the window but cannot see anything except the outline of a field below the midnight blue sky. I shut the blinds, and curl up on the bench far away from the window. With the Artemis cocked and ready, a few minutes pass as I stare at the blinds and nothing. This is intolerable. I am shaking like a leaf. I couldn't hit an elephant in this state. Another few minutes pass and still nothing. I calm down enough to relax my body and stretch out on the bench. A few more and I uncock Artemis. I suppose sometimes a fallen tree is just a fallen tree.

Now I feel ridiculous, like I am jumping at shadows. If I keep this up my heart will give out before I even face the vampyres. I take off my shoes, jacket, and the Artemis, setting them on the floor beside me. I need to relax. I grab my book, blanket, and pillow, settling in. I take a long, deep breath and let it out. There is nothing to worry about. McQueen is right outside, he will not let anyone touch a hair on my head. For some unknown reason, I trust him. Stay strong, David, little sister is on her way.

Or at least she will be when this bloody train starts again.

CHAPTER FIVE

MURDER ON THE LONDON EXPRESS

What a beautiful world we live in. I meander through our field, long grass and wheat tickling my palm and fingertips as I run them over the tops. A gentle breeze blows through, shifting not only the grass but my billowy white dress and loose hair, the tendrils caressing my bare skin. I pause to breathe in the sweet smell of nature's bounty as the sun above kisses my skin with its warmth. Marvelous. Simply marvelous. When I open my eyes again a smiling David strides over the crest of the emerald green hill, waves, and blows me a kiss. I do the same back before his smiling face turns, returning the way he came. I have never seen him so tranquil. Then, just as I lower my arm, someone gently wraps his arm around my waist, pulling me back against his fiery body. I do not glance back. I simply close my eyes and guide his other arm around my upper chest while resting my head against his steady heart. There is no misery, no rancor, no dismay in the world as long as he holds me and never lets me go.

"Sugar…" he whispers. I hug his arms with mine, pressing them closer. The entire world jerks. "*Lady.*"

My eyes fly open, but instead of a field I'm greeted by an intense werewolf's face inches from mine. Not the worst wake-up I've ever had. But… "What—"

"Get up," he commands, standing up straight.

I toss off the blanket, and pick up my shoes, but then McQueen's gaze whips like quicksilver toward the door. As the door handle turns, in one fluid movement he grabs my wrist, jerks me up, spins me around, places one arm around my waist and other hand over my mouth, and ducks us into the corner. The door slowly opens, and McQueen holds me against his body tighter. In the dream this was far more pleasant.

The gun enters before the man holding it. A gun. My stomach drops, and it is a good thing McQueen has covered my mouth because I gasp. *A gun.* The bald man McQueen was concerned about at dinner takes a step into the suite. I stop breathing and even blinking for fear of discovery. McQueen's heart is throbbing so loudly I pray our intruder cannot hear it. If the man moves his head an inch or two to the left, we will be spotted. But God smiles upon us. The intruder quickly scans the room, mutters "Shit," and then departs.

The moment the door clicks shut McQueen lowers his hand, and I can breathe again. I rest the back of my head on his chest as we both let out literal sighs of relief. "That was close," I whisper.

"Yeah. They approached me, asked how I knew you," he says. "Wanted to know where you were going."

"Who are they?"

"Hired thugs if I had to guess. I've been watching and listening to them all night. I think they have people waiting for you at the next stop. We have to get off this train."

I stare up to meet his eyes and he gazes down. "Oh."

It's then we realize he is still holding me. As if a snake were slithering up toward him, his arm jerks away. I step forward, blushing. "Um, they'll be back," he says, glancing everywhere but at me. "We have to pull foot. We'll hide on the caboose landing until the train slows then walk to the last station. Get dressed." As I put on my shoes and jacket, he fastens his gun belt and slips on his shoulder holster. Before he closes the trunk, I retrieve a gun and dagger which go in my purse and snap on the Artemis, praying I will not have to use any of them. Fleeing in the night from men with guns, how extraordinary. I knew this was possible, but now the danger is here I am not as frightened as I thought I would be. My heart is racing but my head remains crystal clear. "I'll check to see if the coast's clear," McQueen says, putting on his coat. "Hold on." He opens the door a crack. "I don't see 'em. Walk quickly to the back. Go."

I brush past him out the door. Only a few people remain reading in the parlor. As if nothing were amiss, I stroll toward the back, nodding as I pass. So far so good. I—oh, blast. Just as I reach the end of the car, the bald man steps inside the train from my intended destination. He looks as surprised to see me as I am him, both our mouths popping open in unison. We stand staring at each other for a moment, neither sure what to do next.

Fleeing is always the best option.

Pivoting on my toe, I bolt the way I came toward the dining car with the villain only a few paces behind. I glance back to see if he's pulled the gun again, but he hasn't. He is trying to remain inconspicuous as I am. I pick up my speed through the dining and smoking cars. I have no idea where I am going, I have no plan. Should I enlist someone's help? He may shoot them. Confront him? No. Where is McQueen? Has he abandoned me? Of course not. Just keep walking, Verity.

I realize I am running out of train as I pass through second, then third class where the passengers are packed on wooden benches like livestock. A young man in a bowler hat stands after I pass and my pursuer is momentarily blocked, but he shoves the boy back in his seat. At least I gain a second. I'm through the door and across to the next car, the cargo hold, without him at my feet. I slide open the cargo door, stepping in among the wooden boxes and crates with clucking chickens. There's no lock on the inside of the door, so I do the only thing I can, try to hold it closed myself with brute strength. My assailant jerks it open a tad, but with strength I did not know I possessed I slam it shut before he can step through. The noise from the engine is close to deafening, but I hear him shout, "Gus!"

Blast! The blonde man, his partner, steps from behind one of the huge stacks of wooden boxes with a pistol in hand. Oh no.

No. How could I have been so bloody stupid? I walked right into their trap.

"Hello, pretty," Gus says.

There is nowhere for me to go, nothing else to do but raise my hands in surrender. The second man throws the door open to step in. "She's a wily little thing. Tie her up, and stick her in the crate. Tom's waiting at the station, we'll sneak her out."

They each take a step toward me. "Whatever they are paying you to capture me, I will double it if you let me go."

Both men leer at me as if I were nude as the bald one circles me like a shark. "Tempting, but we have a reputation to protect," he says.

"Triple."

This time they exchange a glimpse. I may have them. Before they can agree, the door flies open, startling us all. The men's guns swing toward the door. They're matched by McQueen's two six-shooters pointed right at us. "Duck!"

Without hesitation, I drop to the ground as the shots ring out, so loud I cover my ears. McQueen dashes behind a box of chickens to the left as the men sprint behind the tall wooden crates. All the bullets miss their intended targets, lodging in trunks and the walls. They all fire again with the same result. "Shug, move!" McQueen stands and shoots again twice to give me cover. I leap up and dash beside him, one bullet literally whizzing past my cheek. "Give me the gun in your purse." One of the men fire, splintering the wood of the crate inches from my head, as I remove the pistol. He sticks it in the front of his trousers. "I'm gonna lay more cover fire, and you're gonna run to the door."

"But I don't want to lea—"

He stands again, gun at the ready. "Go!"

As he fires, I rise and barrel toward the exit. Just as I am through the door, with the wind whipping around me like a cyclone I notice the blonde man, Gus, stealthily walking toward McQueen in a crouch. After I close the door and catch my breath I realize what that means. My body's working on its own, so I take a few steps toward the next car before I stop myself. I want to run away, I absolutely do. Every part of me urges me forward to safety. But I cannot move. I cannot leave him in there alone outmanned. They will not kill me. They need me alive. They need him dead. *No.* Before I can talk myself out of this lunacy, I arm the Artemis and sprint back into the fray.

When I slide the door open and step in, McQueen's attention diverts to me, his face toppling. Gus uses this to his advantage. He rises from his hiding spot ten feet behind McQueen, gun moving right toward the back of his head. My stomach drops as my arm rises. The squeal of the steam engine almost bursts my eardrums as McQueen turns to see what I am aiming at. I'm faster. Just as the blonde man levels to fire his pistol, I pull my trigger. The three inch spike strikes his left eye, a burst of blood spewing as his head jerks back. He crumples to the floor. Dead. Oh, God forgive me. Please forgive me.

"Gus!" the bald man shouts. "You—"

Two things happen simultaneously. The bald man rises across the car with his gun pointed at me. Before I process this, McQueen yanks me to the floor, aims, and the men fire at the same time. Bald's bullet hits exactly where I was standing, but McQueen's hits its target. The back of the man's head explodes in blood and bone all over the crate behind him. I scream in horror. The body slumps against the crate, sliding down it, dead eyes staring at me. I turn over on my hands and knees to toss up dinner.

"Are you okay?" McQueen asks, rubbing my back. It feels lovely. "Just…sit down. Breathe. I have to get rid of the bodies."

He has other concerns so I obey, resting my back against the bullet riddled wall. Quickly McQueen maneuvers around the crates, to the sliding train door and throws it open before hustling to the blonde man. My victim. McQueen rifles through his pockets, finding only a piece of paper, before hiking the corpse over his shoulder. McQueen tosses the man out the door onto the countryside before doing the same to the other villain as if it were nothing.

Then he cleans up the blood with his handkerchief and a cloth before moving another box to fully cover the stain. He is so calm. I imagine he's done this before. I am so glad he has. I am in no state for complex thoughts needed when covering up a double murder.

Wiping the extra blood from his hands on his black trousers, he walks over to me. "We have to go. Can you walk? Come on." He helps me stand, but my legs are shaky. They only support me until I attempt to move. Before I fall, McQueen wraps his arm around my waist, pulling me to his side. "It's okay, lean on me. I gotcha, shug." It's difficult but I put one foot in front of the other as he leads me out.

The third class passengers downright stare as we pass. We must look like lovers with him holding me and my head on his shoulder. As long as they do not suspect the truth. I don't care one whit. The gazes continue all through the train, though I keep my eyes straight ahead. A porter comes the opposite way saying, "Woverhampton next. Woverhampton." McQueen quickens our pace.

When we reach the first class parlor, he releases me. I am shocked to find I can stand on my own. "Keep walking," he whispers as he enters the suite. "Be there in a second."

I manage the rest of the way to the caboose alone. The wind rushes into the car as I open the door and step out onto the landing outside, which is only few feet across and wide with a guardrail. In the darkness all I can see are the outlines of hilly fields and fast moving train track. I have a problem with heights, even a few feet up I suffer vertigo, so I look away. There is enough terror in my life without adding to it. I take in massive lungfulls of fresh air in an attempt to stop the screams that desire to fly out. I just killed a man. *Killed* him.

As the train begins decelerating, McQueen steps out with my trunk and his suitcase. "Take my case," he says.

"We're not really going to jump, are we?" I ask, grabbing the case from the top of my trunk.

"Don't worry. I've done this a few times before. Just bend your knees when you land and roll. Easy as pie. You can do it." The brakes squeal as the train slows further. McQueen slides my trunk over the side, and I hear it hit the ground with a thud. He takes his suitcase, sliding it off too. "Ready?"

I glance at the still moving ground below. "Absolutely not. No," I say, shaking my head. This is insanity. I am not jumping off a bloody train. I back into the wall as far as possible.

He grabs me by the shoulders, meeting my eyes. "You can do this, shug. You *have* to do this. We're only going about five miles an hour. You *will* be okay. Trust me."

Gazing into his earnest eyes, some of the fear dissipates. I believe him. I trust him. I *can* do this. "Okay." He releases me and steps aside so I can do what I must. Only three feet off the ground, five miles per hour. I can do this. I will do this.

"Go, shug."

One small step and I'm airborne for a moment until I hit the ground. Hard. My ankles give way as slivers of pain shoot up to my hips. I tumble down a small hill onto my stomach, knocking the air out of me along with my brain for a few moments. I lie on the ground staring up at the stars, mind reeling like a whirligig. *Did I just jump off a bloody train?*

After a few seconds the shock wears off. As much as I would like to remain prostrate gazing at the tranquil night sky, I need to keep moving. I push myself up, gloves becoming as soaked with mud like the rest of me. My ankles are tender but if I move slowly, I can walk. McQueen is quicker to recover, running over to help me. Unlike me, he looks pristine. Even his hat is straight. "You okay?" he asks, giving me the once over.

"I believe so."

His gaze stops at my face. "You have mud…" Without hesitation, he wipes my cheek with his jacket sleeve.

Oh Lord I must resemble a bog monster. "Thank you."

I smile, and for a moment his eyes soften. Who knew a bounty hunter could be so tender? Then for whatever reason, a change washes over him, a darkness. McQueen backs away as if I really were a monster. "We, um, have to go. Come on."

After an awkward glance my way, he takes off in a quick clip. If I didn't know better I would think he was purposely trying to flee from me. Within a few silent minutes of me hobbling behind him, we come upon our luggage. Thank goodness. I open the trunk retrieve new gloves. "What the hell are you doing? We don't have time for a costume change," McQueen says, almost snapping the lid shut on my fingers.

"I am wet and covered in mud. What—"

"Lady, we have to walk about ten miles through open countryside. Move your ass." He starts walking again with his suitcase in hand.

"Wait, what about my trunk?"

"Told you, I ain't a pack mule," he says, not turning around. "It's yours. Your responsibility."

He is having a laugh. I can't carry this ten miles, it weighs almost as much as I do. McQueen simply continues walking. Brilliant. Having no other choice, I grab one of the handles to drag the trunk behind me. In short order my hand, arm, back and still tender ankle are in agony as McQueen moves farther away. If he glances back I cannot say because within minutes, he is out of sight. We make it perhaps half a mile before I need a rest. I sit on the trunk and flex my sore, creaking hands. My ankles are not much better. This is ridiculous. This whole thing is madness. What on earth was I thinking? Chasing vampyres, jumping off trains, shootings? Those men tried to…and I…

"Lady, why the hell are you stopping already?" McQueen calls in the darkness.

"I need to rest."

My so called bodyguard quickly comes into view, stalking toward me. "We haven't even gone a mile. Get off your bony ass and let's get moving!"

"Do not speak to me in that manner. And stop using foul language. My ears are not bogs, which is the only place words like that should go!"

"What, 'ass?' I will fucking say whatever I fucking want to!" He stops a foot away, looming over me with a scowl that would frighten the Devil himself. "Now, get up! We agreed I'm in charge here, so I say when we stop. If that trunk is too much for you, then leave it behind."

"It has my clothes, money, and oh yes, the weapons that just saved our lives. I am sorry if I do not have supernatural strength or endurance like some, but us mortals need to rest when dragging an object half their bloody body weight!"

We just stare at one another with matching scowls for a few seconds anger darting back and forth like bullets. He looks away first. "Fine." He thrusts the suitcase into my lap. "Get up."

I rise. He lifts the trunk onto his shoulder much like the dead men before, turns his back to me, and begins trekking away again. Verity Hart one, McQueen zero. He remains ahead of me, but only by a few paces as we continue on along the train tracks. This close I can practically sense the anger radiating from him. It must be a werewolf idiosyncrasy, this rapid mood change. Or an American one. Whichever, this cannot continue. We must be united, no matter what imaginary crime I have committed to offend him. We have enough problems as is without us quarreling. As a lady it is my job to incite harmony. And I cannot bear the silence a moment longer.

"Are you as strong as a vampyre?"

"What?" he asks, glancing back.

"The Count said they have the strength of ten men. Do you?"

"Why? You worried I can't handle them?" he snaps, sounding even angrier than before.

"No, I am simply making conversation to pass the time. Good lord. Please let that bee in your bonnet fly away, it is making you insufferable. Forget I spoke." *That* was a dismal failure.

We continue in silence for a few seconds with only crickets carrying on with their symphony, then he says, "I'm about as strong as a vampyre, yeah. We heal at about the same rate too."

With his back to me, I do not quell my smile. Lady Hart scores another point. "I think I read someplace you need a spell to transform. Is that true?"

"No. I can do it just with concentration, but on the full moon I can't stop it. Something about the position of the planet or something."

"Have you always been able to transform? Is it something you were born with?"

"Yeah. Started when I was thirteen. I was in this fight with two guys, sons of some of the other ranch hands, and it just rose up. Scared the hell out of all of us. Spent a week in wolf form running around the arroyo until the morning after the full moon. Pa about lost his mind."

"Did you know about your condition before that?"

"Yeah, Pa told me it could happen. He went through it with my mother, so he knew it would probably happen to me too. Still a shock, though."

I am certain it was. "Is the transformation painful?" I ask.

"More than you can ever imagine, shug. Every time."

"I'm sorry." We continue in silence for a few more seconds. "So, your mother was a werewolf. Have you encountered any others on your travels?"

"Hell, I never met *her*. She died having me. Lost too much blood, even for our kind. I didn't happen upon another werewolf until I was sixteen. There was this tribe, the Cheyenne, when I was in Wyoming working another ranch. They took me in, showed me how to control it. I lived with them for about a year."

"There must not be many of your kind then. How lonely that must be."

He scoffs. "What the hell would you know about lonely?"

I scoff back. "I know what it is to be an aberration, Mr. McQueen. I know what it's like to be shunned for being different, even by your own parents. Being told everything you love, everything that makes you you is unsuitable. Being forced to hide your true self because when you do reveal it, no matter how much you believe a person cares for you, they just treat you as some miscreant when they discover there is more to you than a fine figure and ability to adhere to asinine rules of conduct. So do not dare say I know nothing of loneliness. I could write a bloody book on the subject."

"I stand corrected," he says, actually sounding apologetic. Good. More silence, then, "That why you got so mad at the man in the garden? He wouldn't marry you because of your gadgets?"

"That was a large part of it, yes." His shoulders loosen as he relaxes again before chuckling and shaking his head. What he finds comical about my misery I know not. "What?"

"Well, then he's a grade A moron, shug. That's the stupidest reason for not marrying someone you love I've ever heard. I thought you liked other ladies or something."

"I beg your pardon? You thought I...enjoyed the poems of Sappho?"

"If that means you sleep with women instead of men, yeah. He called you mannish and abnormal, what else was I supposed to think? Now *that's* a reason not to marry someone, not because she knows her way around a blowtorch. He *should* have been proud of you. I would be. You've done a lot, especially for a woman. I know a lot of guys who can walk because of those braces of yours. And I use a lot of your toiletry products."

"David develops the toiletries. He adores working with chemicals. He's almost blown us up half a dozen times, but he always says, 'Faith, Very. Patience and faith. It will all come together in the end. And if I die, at least I die doing what I love.'" I chuckle sadly.

"We'll get him back, shug," he says after a pause.

I do not like where this conversation has veered. A few more words and I'll begin on a much needed sob, for which there is no time. I clear my throat. "So, after we do rescue my brother, will you go visit your long, lost relations? Meet your cousins?"

"Hell no."

"You should. They might be lovely people, you never know."

"I *know*. My Pa worked in their stables, and his father before him. You know what James Roarke did when he found out Pa went walking, just walking with my mother? Whipped him in front of the other servants. Pa had scars for the rest of his life. They hurt until the day he died."

"But your grandfather's dead. They can't all be like that. Is your grandmother still alive?"

"Don't know, don't care. If my father wouldn't be welcome there, then I won't go. End of discussion."

There goes the possibility of werewolf allies. "You must have been close to your father to still have such a strong devotion."

"He was all I had. We moved around a lot from ranch to ranch, wherever he could get work. He had this way with horses and cattle like he could talk to them. It was uncanny. He was just so gentle and patient with them." He looks back at me. "In case you hadn't noticed, I did not inherit either of those traits," he says with a smile.

I smile back. "David and I used to joke we were changelings. You know, faeiry children replacing ordinary ones? We look like our parents, nothing more."

"I take it y'all don't get along?"

"That is an understatement, Mr. McQueen. I am a disgrace to the Hart name. After the Jolyon debacle, Father threatened to lock me away for the rest of my life if I ever picked up a piece of metal again. If David hadn't been there, defending me at every turn, I would probably be babbling in a straightjacket right this moment."

"What did your brother do?"

"Threatened to out us all, all our dirty secrets, his included. He and Father struck a bargain. I would remain in our manor at Somerset with limited visitors, coming to London only when Father needed us to play happy family. In exchange, our money would continue to keep him in the style of which he was accustomed to. Yet should I embarrass or disobey him, then to the sanitarium I shall go."

"Jesus Christ, shug," McQueen says with a sneer.

I see the pity returning, and glance away. "And I am sure Father has already contacted Shadyville Sanitarium to chase me down and lock me away. Do you think those men could have been sent by him?"

"Carrying weapons? He hate you that much?"

Sadly, I have no idea. "I hope not."

"What I'm trying to figure out is how they knew where you were so quick," he says. "Who knew which train you were taking?"

"Just my maid, but she wouldn't say a word, especially to strangers."

"When I was going through their pockets, I found a telegram with your description and the train number. How could they have known? What name did you buy the tickets under?"

"Mine and David's."

He stops walking to spin around. "Why the Sam Hill did you do that?"

"It's my name. Why?"

Shaking his head, he turns back around and starts walking again. "You know for someone so damn smart, you can be downright dumb, Lady. That was probably it. You practically left them a treasure map. *Never* use your real name when on the run."

"Well, I'm sorry," I snap. "This is all just a tad new to me. I have never had need to travel incognito or find myself in a gun battle before."

"They are going to be on our asses the rest of the way now. They know where you intended to go, and probably how you were going to get there too. Great."

Marvelous, I've enraged him again. At least this time I know why he's angry at me. Neither of us utters a word for a mile or two. I could remind him I saved his life tonight, that should count for something, but that would mean talking about the event, and I am not ready to face it yet. Or ever. Silence is good. This way I can hear the crickets chirping and breeze blowing through the trees. I can pretend I am home in Somerset. If only.

We tromp another mile before he stops dead, even setting down the trunk. "Stay back there," he says before advancing forward again.

Not likely. I hurry to reach him. "What is—oh." The bald man lies in a heap beside the tracks, his arm at an odd angle and back of his head a mush of pulp and splinters of bone. Revulsion makes me shudder.

"I have to move him so no one ties him to our train," McQueen explains. He lifts the man and carries him to some nearby bushes. Food for wild animals. That image brings the contents of my empty stomach up again. I gulp it down. The fact I vomited once in front of him was dreadful enough. McQueen covers the body with brush before returning to me. "They probably won't find him for weeks." Another image I do not need. He takes one look at me, and his face falls. "Are you okay, shug? You look a little—"

"I am fine. Let's carry on, unless you require a break."

With my chin miraculously up, I continue walking as fast as I can away from the dead man. Though he is out of sight, he will not vacate my mind. Both men probably had families, a wife and children who are expecting them home. I hug McQueen's suitcase to my chest as if it were a teddy bear. What's going to happen to them? Are they going to end up in work houses or forced into prostitution because of me? Am I going to hell? As if it is occurring all over again, I see the blonde man as my spike penetrates his brain. I killed a man. Gus. His name was Gus. I took a life. I could go to prison. I could face the gallows. Oh, God in heaven. What have I done? I cannot breathe. I double over, dropping the suitcase and gasping for air that will not enter.

"Shug?" McQueen asks as he dashes over to me. "Hey, hey." The trunk falls before he wraps his large arms around me again, hugging me tight. "Just breathe, shug. Let it all out, it's okay."

I clutch onto him as my gasps bring wracking sobs. I cry for Jolyon, for David, for Father, for the man I killed, for letting McQueen down, all of it. How can this be happening? How? In all probability, David is dead or worse lost his immortal soul forever. We won't even be reunited in heaven, if I even get to ascend there now. Murderers don't.

"I killed him," I sob into his shoulder. "He—I…"

He gently strokes my muddy hair. "Don't you dare feel guilty, not for one second, shug. You saved my life. And yours. You did what you had to; there ain't nothing wrong with that. Look at me." He releases me so I can look up at his hard face. "That man doesn't deserve one of your tears. Not a one. Neither of them does. Listen to me, okay? That man was gonna shoot me. Dead. Lord knows what they would have done to you when they had ya. It wasn't your fault. You didn't ask for any of this, and the fact you could pull that trigger when you had to shows how strong you are. You saved me. You saved us both. You did good, shug.

Real good. You're a hell of a woman, Verity Hart. I'm damn proud of you."

I have no clue why, but his declarations lift my spirits a hundred fold. He's proud of me. So few people have ever told me that. His words comfort me almost as much his embrace. "I'm sorry I used my real name and almost got you killed."

"Well, you won't make the same mistake twice, will you? That's all I can ask," he says, wiping a tear off my cheek with his thumb.

Despite my damp state the breeze, that small touch sparks a heat that travels like lightening through my entire body. It is...marvelous. Kindness turns to confusion to concern in his eyes. He backs away, as if I were a rabid dog about to strike. Thank heavens he does because a few more seconds and I would forget myself and possibly do something I would later regret. Now I am mortified on top of all else. I only pray werewolves cannot read minds as well. Mine becomes a cesspit around him.

I turn away to hide the uneasiness written all over my face. "I have recovered now, thank you very much," I say. "I apologize for that display of emotion. I will do my utmost to make sure it does not occur again." I wipe my face, lift his suitcase, and square my shoulders. "Shall we go?" Without checking to see that he follows, I continue on as if nothing had happened with my head held high all the way to our destination.

It is the English way.

CHAPTER SIX

MR. AND MRS. MCQUEEN
TERRORIZE THE COUNTRYSIDE

By the time we reach Bridgnorth the blisters on my feet have blisters, my back aches with every step, and neither I nor my companion has uttered more than ten words to each other in three hours. If he is half as exhausted as I he welcomes the silence as well.

The Bridgnorth train station is deserted when we finally come across it. Like most rural stations it is nothing more than a brick platform amid the rolling hills with a one-story stone building acting as the station. Bridgnorth sets itself apart with adjoining stairs up to a steep iron foot-bridge leading to the town. On a high hill chimes three times as we approach. Three in the morning. It's later than I thought. No wonder I am beyond fatigued. As I rest my weary body on one of the benches, McQueen enters the station. Without forward motion my eyes grow heavy, and just as I'm about to drop off, he says, "Hey!"

I jerk awake. "What?"

"I got some pamphlets to plan the next leg. Let's go find a hotel."

That is the most marvelous idea I have heard all night. It takes effort but I manage to stand again and trudge up to the town proper, no easy feat as I am certain the footbridge is as steep as two mountains. Despite this instrument of torture, Bridgnorth is a cozy little hamlet with buildings of all heights side-by-side like books on a shelf, most red brick but some in the Tudor style, black and white and partially timbered with cupolas. Luckily we don't have to walk far on the empty cobblestone avenues before we chance upon an inn, though the door is locked, and there are no signs of life inside. The owners are going to be most displeased at us for waking them at this unseemly hour, but I don't care. They can spit on me as long as they give me a bed.

McQueen pounds on the door. A few seconds later a light turns on inside, and the door is opened by a man in night clothes and robe. "Do you know what time it is?"

"I do, and we apologize," McQueen says. "We need a room."

"Gerald?" a woman calls inside.

Gerald examines us in the candlelight. We look how we feel: exhausted, dirty, and desperate. He takes pity on us. "Come in." Bless him. We walk into a small sitting room with a wooden reception desk and large wicker chairs providing the only accoutrements. A woman about Mama's age stands on the stairs with a candle, clutching her robe. She seems shocked when she lays eyes on us, even gasping a tad. We are a sight with him in cowboy attire and I covered in mud. I am shocked they allow us entrance. As McQueen and Gerald move to the desk, the wife descends the stairs to join her husband, most likely for protection. "How many rooms?"

I am about to open my mouth when McQueen proclaims, "Just one."

Both stare, eyes narrowing in suspicion. We are an odd pair in the best of circumstances. "My husband and I are on our way to Scotland. We were in a carriage when one of the automaton horses broke down. We had to walk all the way from Broseley which is why we're so unkempt. It has been a dreadful night."

Their expressions soften at our tale of woe. "Poor things," the wife says.

"I know, and on our honeymoon no less," I add. "We were married just last night."

"Were you?" the woman asks, brightening up.

I wrap my arm around McQueen's, beaming up at him. He remains impassive. "We eloped. My father refused the match, so we just ran off."

"How romantic. Isn't that romantic, Gerald?"

He nods. "Fifteen shillings a night, with breakfast at eight."

I open my reticule and hand him the money. "It was *so* romantic, but now Father's gone mad. He's actually hired men to take me back to London, as if I were a child."

"Shug, she doesn't need to know all of our business," McQueen admonishes. "Sorry. My wife tends to run her mouth when she's tired. Can we see the room?"

"Right this way, Mr. and Mrs. McQueen," Gerald says. McQueen's eyes narrow at me in warning before we follow them up to our small room. It is barely the size of a servant's quarters, with only a dresser, nightstand, and single bed inside. "Outhouse is in the back. No plumbing yet, I'm afraid."

"I'll bring you both some water to freshen up," the wife says before walking off.

"Thank you," McQueen says. Gerald goes the way of his wife, and McQueen shuts the door. "Went a little overboard back there, don't ya think? Made us sound like we were in some trashy dime novel."

"Trust me. There is method to my madness." I flop down on the soft bed. It is such a wonderful bed, the best I have ever lain on. "Oh, I could sleep for years."

"Not yet. We need to figure out our next move." He sits on the bed to remove his boots and jacket. "We should avoid trains if we can, and Holyhead is out."

"The ferry only departs from Holyhead. It's the only way across the Irish sea besides…" I snap my mouth shut. The only other option is *not* an option.

"Besides?" McQueen queries. "We don't have many choices now, shug. Out with it."

Blast. "Dirigible. But I absolutely positively will not set foot on one of those deathtraps," I say adamantly. "*Never*."

"Why? They ain't that bad. Slow but safe. What, you afraid of heights?"

There's a knock on the door, saving me from further embarrassment. The wife enters with a jug of water, basin, rags, and soap. "Here you are."

"Thank you kindly, ma'am," McQueen says, ushering her out. "Good night." After closing the door, he picks up the pamphlets he placed on the dresser and removes his hat. "Here's the one for a dirigible line." He reads it quickly before smiling. "Says non-stop to Dublin from Treuddur, Wales. Bet they have one to Galway too. Sorry, shug, you're just gonna have to suck it up." He reviews the next pamphlet. "And look, the 9:10 train tomorrow morning goes right to Treuddur." He sets the pamphlets down again. "I love it when a plan comes together. Shug, seems our luck might finally be changing."

"If you say so," I say under my breath. I close my eyes. I shall panic tomorrow. I haven't the energy tonight. The sound of his suitcase opening and rustling of cloth a few seconds later causes me to open my eyes again.

Oh. My.

With his back to me McQueen peels off his shirt, revealing a broad, tan back with hard muscles rippling as he moves. My mouth gapes open at this marvelous sight. The only man I have ever seen with his shirt off was David, and his gaunt frame was nothing like this, just pale skin and bones. I watch, captivated, as McQueen washes his torso with a soapy rag, wet body glistening in the soft light. His neck, his arms, I assume even his legs are as sculpted, as his back. Michelangelo's David made flesh. I never knew a man could appear so…powerful yet beautiful all at once. My stomach flutters as if it is about to take flight.

"Enjoying the show there, shug?"

Horror and mortification snap me out of my lustful state as he glances over his shoulder with a mischievous grin. I turn beet red from tip to toes. "You are being immodest, sir," I admonish.

McQueen spins around, revealing a strongly muscled chest covered in dark hair. I make a point of looking away this time. "I'm not the one doing the ogling, lady," he says, pulling out a fresh shirt.

I harrumph. "I was not ogling. Do not flatter yourself." I stare down at my destroyed skirt and fidget with the fabric. "And while we are on the subject of impropriety, I know we are alone in a small room with one bed masquerading as husband and wife, but if you so much as *touch* me, I shall scream this inn down and have you arrested. Do you understand me?"

All amusement drains from his face, being replaced by disbelief. He scoffs and chuckles cruelly. "Lady, I have no desire to touch you. I like my women a hell of a lot less uppity and prudish."

This stings more than I care to admit. "Meaning you like loose, stupid women."

"The looser and stupider the better, shug."

I look up at him, scoffing. "I wouldn't expect anything less from an American."

I believe I hit a nerve. Glowering, he stalks over to me. I stare back as he looms over me, daring him to do something, what I do not know. My heart is about to leap from my chest as we just gaze at one another, locked in a ballet of wills for a second. When his hand moves toward my head, I tense. Is he going to hit me? Grab me and kiss me? My stomach flutters considering that last option. Neither. He snatches the pillow from under me, my head plopping onto the bare mattress. "You get the bed, *I* get the pillow." Still glaring, he tosses it to the floor, grabs his hat and jacket, and turns off the gas lamp so it's close to pitch black before settling on the floor. "Night, Lady Hart."

I remain perfectly still for a few seconds, afraid to move. He…I…that man is insufferable! I've never encountered someone so exasperating. I flip on my side with my back to him, grabbing the perfectly good pillow from the other side of the bed. Well, I don't have to like him, I just have to tolerate him until Galway, then I shall never see him again. I hit the pillow to soften it before resting my head again. I just hope we make it there without killing one another. The image of his chest pops into my mind, followed by that mischievous grin. Or worse.

*

A shutting door wakes me out of dreamless sleep far too soon. I force my eyes open and sigh. I am still dressed in my muddy clothes as all I could muster was removing my shoes before passing out, and I feel disgusting, skin flaking or slimy. I need a bath. Or three. I blink to allow my eyes to adjust to the light from the window and notice my companion is missing. His suitcase is still on my trunk so he hasn't abandoned me, which relieves my momentary panic. I know he would not do that, not unless I made him. I shall make a resolution. Today is brand new, all that transpired last night is in the past. I *will* make an effort to be more polite today like the lady I am. And certainly no more ogling.

There is not an inch of me that does not ache like mad as I get up. I can barely hobble over to the basin due to the blisters on my feet. I somehow remove my now ruined clothes and stand naked for a minute, doing my best to wipe off the dried mud and grime before putting on a fresh chemise. Getting dressed without help is new to me as my ladies maid always assists, so I am at a loss as to what to do about my corset. I should have planned better. None of my dresses will fit without it. As I position the corset, I catch sight of myself in the mirror and cringe. My skin is almost grey, with dark circles under my eyes, my hair is limp, and my body hunched like a crone. At least no one will recognise me.

As I try to lace my corset, an exercise in futility if there ever was one, someone knocks on the door. I grab the quilt off the bed, wrapping it around myself. "You may enter."

McQueen steps in with a tray of food. Unlike me, last night's events took no evident toll on him, at least not physically. He is dressed in light brown pants, white shirt, completed with hat and boots. He even shaved. I still prefer him shirtless. "You missed breakfast. Mrs. Mullen insisted I bring you a tray."

"Oh, thank you. Just set it on the bed."

"Did you sleep okay?" he asks as he does.

"Fine." I nervously touch my damp hair. "Um, how long until the train departs?"

"Half hour or so. You should get dressed. I'll…" he points to the door before stepping toward it.

Having no choice, I say, "Um, actually, I need some assistance. My corset. I can't…"

He looks disquieted by this request, blinking more than normal. "Oh. Okay." He walks over to me, obviously as uncomfortable as I, and I move the quilt to my front, clutching it to my chest the best I can. No, this is not awkward at all. "Tell me if it's too tight. I haven't done this in awhile." With more gentility than I thought him capable of, he pulls on the stays to lace me up. I try to think of anything but him close by and seeing me in nothing but my under garments. Croquet. Aunt Esme talking about her boils. The dirigible a thousand feet up. Oh, he smells so lovely today, like lavender shaving cream. Right, stop. Vampyres. David. "That okay?"

"Yes, thank you," I say, stepping away.

Neither of us can look at the other. His eyes settle on the door. "I, uh, got our train tickets. Second class."

"That's fine."

He nods repeatedly head bobbing up and down as if it were on a spring. "Well, I'll uh, let you finish up there. Excuse me," he says, hustling out of the room. I release the breath I was holding when the door shuts. I think I prefer us at each other's throats than whatever just passed between us. He—

The door swings opens again and a dead serious McQueen rushes in. The look on his face, the intensity freezing the wrinkles around his eyes, stops my breath again. We're in trouble. "We got company."

Blast. As he opens the trunk to retrieve his gun belt, I dash to the door, opening it a smidge to peek out into the hall. It is empty.

"…a lady," a man says downstairs. "Her family is worried."

"What did she do?" Mrs. Mullen asks.

"Ran away from an asylum," another man says.

McQueen, gun up and at the ready, steps mere inches behind me to listen as well.

"Poor thing," the wife says.

"So, have you seen her?"

McQueen cocks the gun, that click retching up the tension, and I hold onto the edge of the door for dear life. *Oh, please…*

"No, sorry. We haven't had a new lodger since yesterday afternoon. But should she arrive, I'll call the constable and have him hold her for you."

"Thank you," the first man says. A few seconds later the door shuts downstairs.

McQueen uncocks his gun, but I still clutch the door so I do not topple. "That was too damn close," he says, breath hot against my neck. I still get goosebumps.

There are hurried footfalls up the stairs, and Mrs. Mullen hurries into the hall. "Two men were just looking for you."

"We heard. Thank you for lying," I say. "I am sorry you were placed in that position."

"They said you escaped from an asylum."

"I guess better insane than married to a penniless American, right shug?" McQueen says with an undercurrent of anger. "We'll leave as quick as we can. We don't want to cause trouble."

"Well, best be careful. They said they'll be around town checking at the other inns and train station."

"Thank you *so* much," I say. "You have been so kind."

"Anything for love, right Mrs. McQueen?" she says with a smile before leaving.

"I could kiss that old lady," McQueen says as I shut the door. "I can't believe she lied."

"She's a fellow woman. We never stand in the way of true love, even involving strangers." I toss on a white ruffled shirt and royal blue skirt with silver rivets in swirls with matching bolero. "So, what do we do now?"

"Well, it sounds like they don't know about me yet, so that's in our favor. They're looking for a woman traveling alone, not a couple. Still. We won't go to the station until the last possible minute. Less chance of you getting spotted."

I pull out the aid kit I packed and sit on the bed. "Good. I have to care for my feet. It shall be a miracle if I can get my shoes on."

"They're that bad? Let me see." McQueen lowers himself beside me, and before I can protest, he grabs my bare foot. I have no choice in this corset but to lie down. "Yeah, they're big. I have to pop them." He rises to retrieve a rag, and I scoot up on the bed to get more comfortable, leaning against the headboard. My nurse lifts both my feet into his lap. "Don't worry. I've done this a million times."

"Okay," I say. As I feel the pin enters the blister on my heel, I wince.

"Stop being such a baby," McQueen scolds as he drains the fluid. "Just don't look. It'll hurt less."

I grimace and avert my eyes to the ceiling. "The human body is so disgusting."

"Not all of it. Some parts are mighty beautiful, not to mention damn enjoyable."

"I am sure I have no idea of what you speak," I say, knowing full well his insinuation.

"Oh, I'm *more* than sure you have no idea, shug. There is no doubt of that."

I wince again, and not only from the pain this time. And to think I was going to apologize for my rude remarks made last night. He's so coarse he probably thought they were compliments. McQueen finishes his nursing duties within minutes, and my feet are now more plaster than flesh. As he rummages around in my trunk, I pull up my skirt to roll on my stockings, exposing my legs. He doesn't glance back.

The clock tower chimes nine o'clock as I try not to scream in agony as I put on my shoes. McQueen shuts his suitcase and my trunk before turning around. "We have to go. Can you see my guns?" I shake my head no. "Here." He tosses me the Artemis. "Just in case."

"Thank you," I say, snapping her on. I place the toast and apple from breakfast into my purse for later, gulp down the milk, and find my feet. Time to depart Bridgnorth.

After we get the descriptions of the men, we say our farewells to the Mullens. McQueen checks to see if there are any villains outside before we brave the streets. I do not say a word when he slips his free arm around my waist before we step out. The town square is busy as people walk to shops while buggies haul cargo on the streets. The train station is just as bustling as men load or unload crates from a train, though how they can see through the steam I do not know. There are a few passengers waiting for a train as well. I can tell the urbanites from the country folk by the ladies multi-coloured hair and fine clothes adorned with bejeweled gears. Though I know who to avoid, I purposely keep my head and large white hat down to obscure my face from all eyes. "I have to use the powder room," I say.

"Hurry."

I use the facilities and take a moment to enjoy the solitude. No baddies in here. Oh, how I wish this would all end. I haven't had a moment's peace in days. Even around McQueen it's as if I must remain on guard. His presence is meant to put me at ease, not add to my confusion and agitation. One glimpse from him and I'm all at sixes and sevens. He—

The train whistle screeches outside announcing its arrival. Blast! I rearrange my skirts and dash out of the stall. If I miss the train I'll...I step out onto the platform and five feet away I spot McQueen talking to two men whose backs are to me. "...Hart. Seen her?" One holds up a photograph, I presume of me.

Oh God. Too shocked to even blink, I stand stone still, willing myself invisible, until I get my wits back. I leap back inside, hugging the wall and panting. Thank God there is no one else in here to see me acting like a lunatic. What do I do? Make a dash for it? I cannot miss the train. I—

The door swings open, and I spring a foot off the ground while outstretching my shaking arm with the Artemis. McQueen steps in, and I almost double over from relief. Without a word, he grabs my hand, yanking me out of the bathroom. As we sprint across the platform to the waiting train, I notice the two men rushing the opposite way into the station. McQueen all but shoves me into the train and shuts the compartment door. Since it's an older train there are no sleepers, only tiny private compartments with two benches looking out onto huge windows. I lean back so the people outside will only view McQueen.

"Was that them?"

"Yeah. They were showing around a picture of you, giving the asylum speech. I told them I recognised you from the train yesterday, said I thought I saw you get out at Coventry."

"Do you think they believed you?"

"Seemed so. Time will tell."

"All aboard!" a porter shouts.

Thank the Lord. A few seconds later, when the train begins to move and we leave Bridgnorth in our steam, I realize I am still holding McQueen's hand. I loosen my grip. "Sorry," I say, swallowing my embarrassment. "Do you think we're safe now?"

"They're probably desperate for leads, so they'll have to follow this one up. Hopefully it'll give us enough time to get on that dirigible."

"And if they discover us on that?"

He smiles. "Then you may earn that fear of heights after all."

Gulp.

*

The sun shines down from that vivid blue sky onto me, those rays washing over me like a lover's kiss. Just as sweet. Fluffy clouds in the shape of animals pass by as a gentle breeze rustles not only on them but the soft blanket of grass we lie on. The scent of lavender and fresh cut grass embraces me as *he* does. With a feather light touch he brushes a loose strand of my hair off my face, tucking it behind my ear. With a serene smile, I settle into the crook of his arm, which tightens around me even more. His heartbeat is as strong and steady as the rest of him. Such a good heart. The best. I close my eyes so there is nothing but that beat, his body, and peace.

The tranquility does not last. Even with my eyes closed, I sense when someone obstructs the sun. Gone is the scent of lavender, overshadowed by the putrid stench of decomposition assailing my nostrils. I open my eyes, finding a dark figure standing over us. "Verity," David moans. Moving fast as lightening, my brother contorts to all fours beside me, snarling like a beast. Blood pours out of his ears, his eyes, his nose, and his mouth onto my face as he pleads, *"Save me!"*

I wrench awake with a gasp, the image of David still fresh in my mind as if he were still bleeding on me. It takes me a moment to realize I stare at an empty bench. That I am on the train, with a jacket draped over me, resting my head on McQueen's shoulder. His arm is wrapped around me just as it was in…never mind.

"Bad dream?" he asks, looking away from the window.

I push myself away from him. "Yes."

"Seemed good there for awhile."

"What?" I ask, rubbing my eyes.

"You were making these baby noises and grinning. You looked real cute."

"I—I don't remember what I was dreaming," I lie. "Here," I say, handing him the jacket back. "Thank you."

"Think nothing of it, shug."

I adjust my hat to regain some dignity and scoot to the other bench to face him. "How long was I asleep? Where are we?"

"You were out for about four hours or so. I just woke up myself, but I think we're in Wales. The last stop was Tre-wal-ch-mai," he says, butchering the name.

"Sounds like Wales." I grimace as the wet Welsh countryside, exactly like the English kind, with hills and thatched cottages rolls by. "It's raining again?"

"You're surprised? I've been in this country a week, and there was only one day it hasn't. And I was in prison at the time, so I didn't exactly get to enjoy the sunshine."

"It doesn't rain in Oklahoma?"

"Not like this. Last year it didn't rain for three damn months. The creek dried up, the crops that weren't already dead died, thought I'd lose some animals too. Then one day I woke up and it was pouring. Huge, *huge* storm blew through. Couldn't see two feet in front of me. Had two twisters in as many days. One took out my barn, killed the horses. Still haven't rebuilt it."

"Why not?"

"Can't afford to. Besides, don't see much point. I put all my savings into that land. Almost died to get it during the land rush. Guy tried to trample me with his wagon while I was putting in the flag to claim it. Four broken ribs and a head wound. And what the hell do I have to show for it? Small herd of cattle, few chickens and goats, one bedroom shack with a leaky roof, and not one successful crop in three years. Don't know what the hell I was thinking."

"You were thinking that you wanted a home. A place to call your own. From what you've told me, it seems like you never really had one. Or people. You wanted roots."

He gazes out the window away from me. I believe I struck a nerve. My companion remains quiet for a few seconds, and then says, "No, I had a person for awhile. Roots even. It was a short while, but still."

I hesitate, but curiosity wins over propriety. "What was she like? Your wife?"

His gaze whips back to me. "What makes you think I was talking about my wife?"

"Logic."

His face softens. "I forgot I'm traveling with a bonafide genius. Thought you was a mind reader there for a second."

I avert my eyes to my lap. "You don't have to tell me. Forgive me for overstepping my bounds."

"No, hey, it's fine. I don't mind talking about her. Just haven't thought about her in awhile. I mean, Josie'd been dead for over forty years, and we were only married for one. She was a sweet thing, a school teacher in Kansas City when I was working there as a Marshall. Taught me to read and all. I fell in love with her over those lessons. She was this...fragile little doll you couldn't help but love." He smiles at this memory, and something twists inside my stomach. I suppress a wince. "I took one look at and knew I had to protect her. She kept a good house too. Great cook. I loved her something powerful."

My stomach twists again with I believe jealousy. Envious of a woman dead forty years. I really have come so low. "Did you have children?"

"Came close twice, but she…you know. Her body couldn't take it I guess."

"I'm sorry."

"Probably for the best. At least that's what I tell myself."

"And you never re-married?"

"No."

"Loose, stupid women are more your style now?"

"Something like that," he says with a smirk. "No, I just think I'm a lone wolf, shug. I've gotten so used to being on my own, it'd take one hell of a woman to make me want to change that. And there ain't many of those who'd marry a penniless, failed farmer with no connections, and who has my curse to boot."

He says this nonchalantly, but staring at him I recognise what I sometimes see when I gaze at myself in the mirror. Deep, fathomless loneliness only those who stray from the crowd experience. Waking every day knowing you are disparate from all those around you. That they will never understand or fully accept you. *Never.* At least I have David. McQueen has none of his own kind. He's been alone in the wilderness almost all his life. Lord, do I want to throw myself into his arms and give him a huge—

"What about you?"

I snap to. Wait, is he asking if I would marry... "What about me what?"

"Think you'll ever tie the knot?" Oh. I should be relieved that is what he is asking, correct? "Been asked three times, right? I know about one. What happened with the others?"

"One wanted me solely for my money, and the other to mask his unnatural proclivities."

"Still. It could happen, right?"

I scoff. "I am eight-and-twenty, a clandestine suffragette, too intelligent for my own welfare according to most, and cannot help myself from engaging in masculine activities. One of those traits might be overlooked but not all together. And I will not change. I had ample opportunities, but I am no man's accessory.

He takes me as I am, as I would take him. As an equal. No, some of the best women are spinsters: Queen Elizabeth, Jane Austen, my Aunt May. They all led full lives without the aid or need of a husband. I am in good company."

"You know, not all men are like that no-account bummer from the ball. There are some who like brains and fire in a woman."

Says a man who admits to valuing the exact opposite. "Well, I have yet to meet one. And if I ever do meet this unicorn, I shall marry him on the spot should he be worthy of me."

McQueen raises an eyebrow. "Worthy of you?"

"Yes. With a strong character, a romantic and brave soul, and keen intellect."

"And rich. Don't forget that one." He shakes his head. "You're right. You have a better shot at the unicorn, shug," he chuckles.

I scowl. "Do not mock me."

"I'm not, I swear I'm not," he says as the chuckles subside. He calms himself. "You're just so…I can't get a handle on you. I'm usually better at sizing people up. You just keep surprising me. Thought you were smarter than to buy into all that soul mate, true love bunkum. There is no such thing as a perfect match, shug, because people ain't perfect. They're shallow, stupid, and afraid of their own damn shadows. They care way too damn much about what others think about them, especially you English. Face it, if a factory worker or one of your servants, who had all you ever dreamt of in a man, asked you to marry him, you'd say no because deep down you're just like all the rest of them."

I scoff. "You really think I am some snobbish, poor little rich girl don't you? You know *nothing* of who I am. I was born with money, yes, but I was also born with a brain and the ability to form conclusions on my own. I know what is fair, what is logical, and what is not. And I can also recognise its antithesis, which is magnified by the shallow, stupid, frightened upper class in which I unfortunately find myself in. My life is governed by their rules. I am imprisoned by them. My brother's name will go down in history affixed to my visions, *my* hard work, and I will not even be a footnote. Is that fair? Do I not wish to scream my house down in frustration and anger? Of course I do. But I am part of a family, and part of what keeps me silent is them, especially my little sister. She should not pay for my alleged crimes, which is exactly what would happen. I have seen it time and time again. She would be shunned before she even had a chance to find happiness. I would never do that to her. *Never.* So I keep quiet and play the role of the sweet, complacent Lady Hart. So don't you dare presume to know me or my heart. There is precious little I would not do, would not sacrifice, for someone I love. Which, if you had an ounce of emotional intelligence, should be apparent as I am not only risking my reputation, my freedom, and my life by traveling with you to Ireland to save the one person on this bloody planet who truly loves *me*. So keep your closed minded, obtuse, and downright idiotic observations to yourself. Excuse me."

With what dignity I can muster, I rise and try for the door before the oncoming tears burst forth. He is too quick for me. McQueen blocks the door with his hands up to stop me. "Wait. Wait."

"Let me pass, sir!" I try to move around him, but he steps the same way so I cannot flee. "Please!"

"I'm sorry, okay? I'm sorry. Shug, I'm sorry. I didn't mean to…"

"Insult me? Again?"

"Yeah. I'm sorry. It wasn't my intention, I swear. You're right, I don't know jack squat about your life, or what you've been through. I just…I don't know if I'm coming or going with you, and that bothers the hell out of me. You keep knocking me off centre. I ain't used to it. Sit down, come on. Sit." He gestures to the bench before sitting himself. Wiping my face of the two stray tears, I toss my head back before lowering myself on the bench directly across from him. "We have to stop doing this. We're gonna end up saying or doing something we can't take back, and that'd be bad all around. Things are too tense. We have to fix this."

"I agree," I say.

"We should just…" He shrugs.

"What—"

McQueen lunges across the narrow gap, and his mouth is on mine before I can finish. At first I am too shocked to do anything but remain still, but that lasts barely a heartbeat before my body ignites like an exploding steam engine. I find myself clutching as desperately onto him as he is me. I've never experienced anything remotely like this, not even with Jolyon. And he certainly never parted my lips with his tongue to massage mine, exploring me like a conquistador. Oh Lord he tastes glorious, everything about him is divine. I am swept away in the current of this…raw, primal pleasure. It's bloody transcendent. But too soon he pulls away, leaving desolation in his wake.

That's it?

As the steam engine whistles to signal our stopping, he straightens his hair, which has gone wild underneath my fingers, and returns to his side of the compartment. "Whew," he whistles as I stare at him slack jawed. "There. Done. Got that out of our systems. I feel a hell of a lot better, don't you?" I am not capable of speech yet. My tongue has found its true use now. Speech seems ridiculous. The train slows to a stop. "I'm gonna hit the latrine and grab something to eat. I'm starving. Want anything?" No words will come. "Get ya something anyway. Be right back." He puts on his hat and leaps out of the compartment before the train comes to a complete stop as if nothing happened.

I just sit staring at his empty seat with my mouth open wide enough to park a monopede. Did that actually happen? I would think I was imagining it except I can still taste him, still feel him on my lips. I touch them with my gloved finger to make sure *they're* real. He kissed me. Actually that word seems as insignificant in describing what he just did to me. I should be appalled. I *am* appalled. Oh Lord, what if he never does it again?

"Hello," says a woman with a Welsh accent. My gaze whips over to the door as an elderly man and woman climb into the compartment. "Room for two more?"

"What?" I ask breathlessly.

The woman glances at me, face falling with concern. "Oh, dear you're flushed. Are you feeling alright?"

I touch my cheeks and sure enough I'm as hot as a furnace. "I'm…" Jamie strolls past the window, and it is as if the world slows. As the white steam swirls around him, he notices me and smiles like the Cheshire cat. With a tip of his hat and wink, he disappears into the white cloud. The man literally takes my breath away.

"I'm…*marvelous*."

CHAPTER SEVEN

A Wales of a Time

Bloody Charles Dickens. Why did he ever put pen to paper? If he never did perhaps McQueen pay attention to me instead of Little stupid Dorrit. Oh, I forgot he likes his women insipid and dull. No wonder the book holds such fascination to him. And the Ifans are lovely people, but how can he speak to me if they will not cease asking questions and fretting over me? The only time he acknowledges my presence is to smirk and give me sideways glimpses when Mrs. Ifans carried on about what a nice, young couple we are. It's intolerable.

The train pulls into Trearddur Bay as Mrs. Ifans finishes the story of the birth of her first great-grandchild two days before. It's a beautiful village right on the shore with sandy beaches beside rocky headlands and green fields with the odd cottage or lighthouse along the expanse. The rain has let up so only a mist remains, giving the bay an ethereal quality as if we have landed in Avalon. Boats ranging from large cargo ships with billowing steam stacks to cruising sailboats swan in and around the tranquil blue bay. In the sky, amid the multitude of flapping seagulls, a brown dirigible with a dangling gondola slowly lifts into the grey sky like a leaf on the wind. I see they use older models judging from the multi-coloured patches along the brown canvass. Brilliant.

Mrs. Ifans notices me staring up at the floating deathtrap. "Beautiful, isn't it? What an exciting time we live in, getting to touch the clouds."

"I prefer the ground," I say, looking away.

"She's afraid of heights," McQueen says, speaking more than a syllable for the first time in over an hour.

"Oh, our dirigibles are the safest in all of Wales," Mrs. Ifans proclaims. "One hasn't gone down in over two years."

"Marvelous," I say under my breath.

The train pulls up to the wooden platform with red brick station about as big as my bedroom. If I recall correctly this is mainly a cargo port, so immediately workmen begin unloading boxes from the train to take to awaiting ships of both air and sea. As I step down to the platform, McQueen holds his hand out with a gracious smile. Though our skin does not touch through my gloves, I still get tingles under his touch as if a Tesla coil were nearby. Delicious. "Thank you."

The moment my other foot hits the ground, he yanks his hand from mine as if it were cursed, and starts walking toward the cargo area where they unload luggage. He retrieves my trunk and strides out of the station without a glimpse back my way. I follow behind with his suitcase. A few silent minutes later, a wooden cart with a real horse arrives outside the station with familiar faces on it. The Ifans offered to take us to the dirigible station, and we of course accepted. A young man, probably in his late teens, and a pretty girl a few years older sit in the back. The boy holds out his hand to aid me, but McQueen grabs hold of my hips to push me in. Those tingles return. When we're all loaded, we leave the station on a gravel road.

"These are our grandchildren, Gwenda and Clyde," Mr. Ifans says as he leads the horse.

"Very nice to meet you both," I say.

The girl's doe eyes do not move from McQueen, but Clyde nods. "How long will you be in town for?" Gwenda asks McQueen.

"Depends on the dirigibles," McQueen says. "Hopefully there's one tonight."

"Well if you can, we'd love to have you over to dinner," Mrs. Ifans says. "Seven o'clock, shepherd's pie."

"We shall try to stop by if we can," I say with a gracious smile.

Through the bumpy ride the girl keeps stealing glances at McQueen then down to her hands as if shamed. She bloody well should be. He catches her once, giving her a smoldering smile. The girl turns red all over. I have the strongest urge to shove her off the cart. Lucky for her the dirigible station is only a few minutes away because my patience is waning.

The East/West Dirigible Line station or "airport" is barely more than a wooden box in the middle of a field with a blue uniformed man inside. There are two brass tanks filled with hydrogen the size of a buildings with hoses attached. Two smaller airships are tied to the ground beside the tanks being topped off with fuel for their voyage. They are still enormous, easily the size of a large schooners. The brown gasbags on each bobs up and down in the wind as the open gondolas, held by naught but metal cables, continue smashing against the ground. Some workmen clean the gondolas while others climb the cables to check the gasbag or simply stand around smoking. Near the highly volatile flammable gas. Lovely.

"We need to get to Galway," McQueen says to the man in the ticket booth.

The clerk checks in the book. "Galway…two options. We have one to Dublin tonight, but then you'll have to wait until noon for the next one heading west. Or you can take the ship leaving here tomorrow at two-thirty. It's our express, only stops in Dublin and two others."

"Which will get us there faster?" I ask.

"The express by a few hours. It's a nicer ship too. Sleeper cabin, salon, deck."

"Two for the express then. A sleeper," McQueen says. I set down his suitcase to retrieve the banque notes from my purse. "Thank you, shug."

2:30 tomorrow. I hope that is enough time for me to grow a backbone. After we get the tickets, McQueen lifts my trunk and I his suitcase before starting down the road to town. "We could take the Dublin flight then the train the remainder of the journey," I point out. "We've already lost so much time."

"No, they'll be expecting you to use the train. If they took the bait, they'll be searching around Coventry and Holyhead. And if they're this organized in England we'll have to be triple careful on their home turf. Probably have men at every station, especially in a hub like Dublin. No, fewer stops means fewer chances of them boarding."

"What about David?"

"Well, they seem to want you mighty bad, so that means they know you're D.V. Hart. Either they already killed him or they'll keep him alive to use against you. Either way, *when* we get there doesn't matter anymore. Safety before swiftness from here on out."

I cannot argue with the logic. Really I just do not want to get on that bloody balloon.

Though my still tender blisters sting like mad, I keep up his pace into the village. It is smaller even than Bridgnorth with only a general store, butcher shop, pub/inn, tea shop, and a few separate houses all along the two lane gravel road. For mid-afternoon it is quiet with open carts rolling into town from the fields. Our destination is the pub. I've only ever been inside an actual pub once as a child when our train to Edinburgh had to stop in Haworth, and we had no place else to stay overnight. We walked through their small, smoky pub to the rooms upstairs, not acknowledging anyone as we passed. Father forbid us to venture downstairs in case ruffians attempted to steal or violate us. This pub reminds me a lot like that one dark with small tables in the centre, wooden booths along the perimeter, and a bar with stools with a man behind it. A girl walks to the patrons seated in the wooden booth in the far corner with a tray of food. Two men playing darts in the corner size us up as we walk in. I keep my eyes on the worn hardwood floor.

"We need a room for the night," McQueen says the man behind the bar.

"An American, eh?" the bartender asks with a Welsh accent. He removes the register from under the bar. "Don't get many of you in here. Which part are you from? New York? Chicago?"

"Oklahoma," he says, filling our information into the register.

"Don't think I've heard of that one."

McQueen hands the ledger back. "It's new."

"Nineteen shillings a night, Mr. and Mrs. McQueen." I involuntarily smile when he calls us that. It has a lovely ring to it. "Give you the honeymoon suite."

I wrap my arm around McQueen's and rest my head on his shoulder. "Perfect, because we are on our honeymoon."

"New love, I can smell it a mile away," the man says with a grin. He nods for us to follow him, and when his back's turned McQueen wrenches away to retrieve the trunk. As we move upstairs to the room, I retell the story about our elopement and my father's objections just in case. He seems to believe it, calling us brave even. No one can resist a love story.

The honeymoon suite is not much bigger than last night's room, but at least has an indoor bathroom with an actual bathtub down the hall. I practically salivate upon hearing that. The owner, Mickey, leaves us in what should be peace, but is far from it. We are alone in a small room with one bed and a million mixed emotions. Perhaps only on my part because McQueen gingerly shrugs off his hat, coat, and guns as if I was not a few feet from him in turmoil. I cannot let him know his effect on my though. I take off my bonnet and sit on the bed while he rummages around in his suitcase.

After thirty seconds, I cannot bear the silence a moment longer. "I think I should send a telegram to my family to let them know I'm alive. What is your opinion?"

He starts examining his guns. "I wouldn't. They're probably watching your family. They can intercept it and track it back here."

"I could send it to my cousin Cricket or Count Orrlock. I doubt they would be watching them as well. I'm just worried my father will do something rash like alert the authorities if they fail to hear from me. We have enough troubles without police or men from the sanitarium after me, if they are not after us already."

McQueen lays the gun on the nightstand and shuts his suitcase. "I guess as long as you don't say where we are, and you send it to your cousin, it'll be okay."

"Or I can send one to my parents but inform them I'm in Dublin already," I offer. "The vampyres do not know I am aware they are chasing me. By the time they realize the wire didn't originate from Dublin, we'll be in the air."

A grin forms on his handsome face. "You're getting better at this, shug."

"I've had a great tutor," I say with a matching smile.

We stay staring and smiling for a few seconds before he breaks the spell, turning away. "You write the address and what you want to say down, and I'll go send it when you're in the bath."

"I suppose I should freshen up before dinner with the Ifans," I say.

He turns his back to me to fill the basin. "You want to go?" He starts wiping his face with the rag.

"It would be rude if we did not. Besides a home cooked meal might do us good, and we don't have much to do for twenty-four hours. Unless you wish to spend them alone in here with me." The moment those words escape my mouth I want to gobble them back in. "No—Not that you do, or even that I do for that matter. I was not suggesting *that*. And—"

"You're right," he finally says, turning around, "we'll go to dinner. It's been months since I had a home cooked meal."

"Right. Yes. Good." I'm flushed again, I know it. As I write out the two notes and addresses to the house and Cricket, telling them both I am safely in Dublin, McQueen puts on his holster and jacket. "Here," I say, giving him the note and money to pay.

"I'll get these off right away. I'll be back to tie your corset later." He retrieves his hat, putting it on as well. "Lock the door and carry a weapon at all times. If I'm not in here, I'll be down in the pub. Have a nice bath, shug."

As he takes a step toward the door, before I can stop myself, I ask, "Why did you kiss me?" And instantly want to die from embarrassment.

He spins around, face neutral. "The usual reasons."

I wrack my mind. "Which…are?"

A look of disbelief crosses his face before he chuckles. "Damn, shug. It has been awhile for you, huh?"

I scowl. "Do not make jokes at my expense, please."

His face softens. "Sorry, shug. You're right." He sighs, taking a moment to search for the right words. "I kissed you…because I wanted to. I've wanted to since the first time you smiled at me at that ball, and a blind man could tell you felt the same way. And you needed kissing. Bad. But that's it. It was just a kiss to get it out of our systems, like letting out some steam so the boiler doesn't blow. It won't happen again."

"Why not?"

He chuckles. "Because you're emotional and excited right now, and I don't take advantage of emotional virgins. You wouldn't even consider what you're considering if we weren't in this situation. You're not in your right mind. I'm not the kind of man a gal like you takes home to Daddy, especially yours. So it's over. It's done. It was a great pleasure to kiss you, a great pleasure, but I won't do it again. End of story." He sighs. "I'm gonna go send that telegram now. You enjoy your bath, shug." He gives a quick nod before walking out of our room.

The moment the door shuts, I cover my face with my hands and curl onto the bed with embarrassment. I feel like a total imbecile. I *am* a total imbecile. He is correct, of course. He's acting like a gentleman, and I want to chastise him for it. What on earth was I thinking? We have no future. I know he has no intention of proposing, and I would not let things go farther without one. At least I hope I wouldn't as I have committed enough sins in this life without adding a mortal one like making love out of wedlock to St. Peter's list. And he's not the first man since Jolyon to steal a kiss. He's just the first where I really, really, with every fiber of my being wished for him to do it again. Lust. Just pure lust. The man emits it from his pores. Perhaps it's a werewolf trait. I will just have to be on my guard because if it does happen again…God help me.

*

I feel human after my bath, and after applying more plaster to my still tender feet, I lounge in bed reading for some time. McQueen has vanished, and I have no desire to search for him. The more time apart the better. I do find tea and biscuits when I get out of the bath, but that was probably the chambermaid, the same one who knocks on my door around six to help me dress. Wonderful service. Since I doubt it's a formal dinner, I choose my red and white roses tea dress with my hair plaited across my head, adorned with my ruby encrusted gears made to resemble roses and lips painted red. If not for the dark circles under my eyes, I would look ravishing.

Having no choice as it's time to leave, I vacate the room to locate my wayward bodyguard. I haven't far to go. McQueen sits at a table playing cards with four other men. The one with muttonchops utters something, and my bodyguard laughs. McQueen shakes his head and throws back his whiskey before laying his cards down. There's a collective groan from the men, who toss their cards down with grimaces. Guess he won. Watching him in his element, so gay and relaxed, releases the butterflies again. Not even the harsh reality of our situation can stop their transformation. I wish they would remain in their cocoons. As he collects his winnings, he notices me staring with a sly smile on my face, and his drops. All the butterflies are stabbed to death with tiny daggers.

"The old ball and chain's here," McQueen says to the men as I walk over.

The men's eyes grow wide when they see me. "Holy shite," muttonchops says.

"Hello, gentlemen," I say, basking in their adoration. Like gentlemen, all but McQueen stands. "Oh, please sit down. I do not mean to interrupt."

"*This* is your wife?" the young man in spectacles asks.

"Nice work, son," says muttonchops. "How'd you manage it? Blackmail?"

McQueen grabs his coat from the back of the chair. "Are you kidding? *She* paid *me*." The men laugh, as I flash him an "I am not pleased" smile. He stands. "See you later. Don't lose all your money. I'll be back to take it later." He pats spectacles on the shoulder before walking toward me. "Come on, Mrs. McQueen. Don't wanna be late."

The village is busier than before with carts pulled by real horses and people hustling up and down the road. People smile and nod as we pass. "Nice night," I say for lack of something better. It is. The rain has stopped allowing the smell of the sea to waft through the air. It's that rare mix of cool and warm, so my white shawl suffices.

"House apparently isn't that far. You okay to walk it? I think this town has only one cab."

"I shall be fine, thank you." And not another word is spoken between us until we reach the Ifans' one-story, brown stone cottage with thatched roof tucked against the calm blue bay with its slow, lapping waves. Cozy and serene. They are lucky people.

"You came!" Mrs. Ifans shouts from the front door.

"Of course," I say as we stroll up the gravel walkway to the door.

"Oh, what a beautiful dress," she gushes. "So fancy. Come in!"

The house is smaller than it appears from the outside and darker. The sitting and dining rooms are one in the same with the kitchen attached so the house is smoky enough my eyes water. It's sparsely furnished with only a worn green canvas couch with a wooden chair beside and table in the front of the fire. I've visited houses like these when I do my charity work in the village while at Foxfire. Poor but brimming with love.

"You have a lovely home," McQueen says.

"Thank you," Mrs. Ifans replies. That girl, Gwenda, ambles into the kitchen from the outside carrying wood. "Gwenda, our guests are here." She glances up, and if I did not know better I would assume she had just been caught in her underclothes. Her mortified wide eyes immediately divert to McQueen as she opens her mouth to speak. She does look a fright in her dirty apron and cap. She sets her load down, half smiles, and retreats to the back of the house. Poor thing. I almost feel sorry for her. Kindred spirit in McQueen misery and all. "She's shy," Mrs. Ifans says. "Supper will be ready in a few minutes."

"Anything we can do to help?" McQueen asks.

"No, just sit down. John and Clyde will be back in a minute. May I get you both something to drink?"

"Water's fine, thank you." McQueen says.

"Same for me, thank you," I say.

We sit on opposite sides of the couch, and after she brings us water, she returns to the oven. Gwenda comes out a minute later with her long brown hair brushed and I'd bet her best dress, a green muslin with white lace, on. She is rather striking with big brown eyes and thick brown hair. Judging from McQueen's glances he believes so as well. Even from this distance I can view her blushing when she catches him. The empathy from before burns up, and I have the strongest urge to press the Artemis to his leg and fire.

He is saved by the male Ifans walking in. We rise to greet them. After the usual felicitations the men begin chatting about poker, and I am forgotten. Time to join the women in the kitchen just as Mrs. Ifans pulls out both a shepherd's and mincemeat pie. Delicious. Gwenda eyes me with the full force of her misery from her post of slicing bread. Even though it has been years since I have seen that look I recognise it right away. It was often present on women while I spoke to a man they fancied. Since this one obviously has designs on my supposed husband, I lack sympathy.

"It smells delicious, Mrs. Ifans. Please allow me to set the table."

"Thank you, dear. Gwenda, get Mrs. McQueen the silverware."

The sullen girl moves to the drawer and practically shoves the pile at me. "Thank you," I say with a gracious smile, a lady's finest weapon. When I complete my task, I call the men to dinner as Mrs. Ifans places the pie on the table. I sit across from Clyde and McQueen from Gwenda, who sweetly smiles before coyly looking away. Flirting at the supper table. How uncouth. After grace we all serve ourselves. "This must be so different from your dinners in London," Mrs. Ifans says.

"London? You're from London?" Gwenda asks with longing.

"Just during the Season. My brother and I spend the majority of our time at our manor in Somerset."

"The Season? Were you presented to the Queen?" Gwenda asks.

"Oh, yes. Some time ago."

"What does your father do?" Mr. Ifans asks.

I open my mouth, but McQueen says, "He owns shoe factories."

I wasn't going to tell the truth, I'm not *that* stupid. "Best shoes in England."

"So how did you two meet?" Gwenda asks.

"At a ball," I say, making a show of taking his hand in mine. "We married a few short weeks later. He couldn't take his eyes off me then, and still can't." So back off, girlie.

"And is it true you were a Pinkerton?" Clyde asks.

"Yes son, I was."

"You must be so brave," Gwenda says almost breathless.

"On occasion," he says with a flirtatious smile as he removes his hand from mine. "With men shooting at you, you have to be or you end up dead."

"You were shot at?" she asks.

"A few times. Worst was when I was trying for the Reno clan." We all listen with rapt attention as he describes tracking them down to a saloon, before chasing them on horseback into the woods, bullets flying the entire time. He was hit twice, once in the arm and hip. But he had to give up when they hit his horse, bringing it down. These tales would have more impact with me if he did not spend the entire tale glancing and smirking at the beautiful girl across from him, whose glows with each exchange. This affront continues for the whole of dinner as he's grilled by Clyde and Mr. Ifans about his various death defying adventures in the Wild West. I fight being quite impressed by his prowess in the face of certain death with the growing anger ratcheted up with every smile he gives her. When he has the audacity to wink at her, I reach my breaking point.

Without preamble, I leap up, startling the table. "Will you all please excuse me? I need to use the w.c."

"It's out back," says Mrs. Ifans. "Are you alright, dear?"

"Yes. Excuse me."

Head bowed, I quickly dash through the kitchen and out the back door into the lovely night air. The lapping waves and slight breeze quell my rage to a manageable level. A minute. I just need a minute to regain my composure so I can return all smiles and sunshine. I must stop letting that man burrow under my skin. I am usually better at containing my emotions in mixed company than this, with one understandable exception in the form of Jolyon de Luce. That had to do with love, which is *absolutely* not the case in this situation. I am simply exhausted, and my nerves are a jangle. Nothing more.

"Are you okay?"

I twirl around and find McQueen shutting the cottage door. "I'm fine," I say with an angry edge. "Needed some air. Alone."

"The stories getting to you because of what happened last night?" he asks as he slowly approaches. "Sometimes folks get flashes of it happening again. Is that—"

"No. I'm fine. Please go back inside, they shall think something is amiss."

"Nawh, they think you're with child. Figured, let them."

My mouth drops open. "That just makes what you did far worse!"

"What?"

Let it be Verity. Don't—

"You flirting with that slattern in there! Are you going to maul her like you did me? Do you just go around dallying with everything in a skirt until one of us is foolish enough to…you know." I ball my hands into fists to stop them trembling with rage.

His face contorts with indignant anger. "Are you kidding me with this? She's a damn baby. I do have some morals. I'm just trying to give her a little thrill, and even if I did have designs on her, it isn't your business. We ain't together."

"Yes, you have made that quite clear, Mr. McQueen," I say, back straightening. "However, while you are under my employ, and we are pretending to be husband and wife, I would appreciate it if you would act accordingly. Which means no insulting me, no flirting with other women in my presence, and—"

"No kissing you? That a condition?" He bridges the short gap between us, and bends down with a mischievous, almost cruel grin. "Or maybe the exact opposite is." His body is inches from mine, and he gazes down at me, daring me to do something, I don't know what. "Huh? Want to take a walk on the wild side, Lady Hart? Expect me to be your tour guide? Or maybe that's what you had in mind the whole time. Lord knows you could do with a good rutting. I think you're paying me enough."

I slap his face as hard as I can, hand stinging as if I touched a jellyfish. McQueen doesn't even flinch yet the moment I pull my hand away, mortification strikes me harder than I did him. I've never hit anyone in my life. Though he remains impassive, I cannot stand to be near him a millisecond longer. Still shuddering from wave after wave of countless emotions, especially the urge to murder him, I begin walking back to the house. I take a second to compose myself, at the door put on a smile, and step back into the house.

"Are you feeling better dear?" Mrs. Ifans asks.

"Actually, no, I'm not feeling the thing at the moment. I need to return to the inn."

"Of course," Mrs. Ifans says. "Clyde, go hitch the horse. He'll take you both back to town."

"Thank you." As Clyde steps out McQueen comes in cool as ice. I square my shoulders to regain some dignity but keep my eyes to the ground. "I'm returning to the hotel. You may stay if you wish. You haven't had *dessert*."

"Tempting," he says, "but where you go, I go. You know that."

"Do you have to go? Really?" Gwenda asks.

McQueen places a hand on my shoulder, and it takes all of me not to bat it off. "Yeah, sorry. It was nice to meet y'all though. Dinner was great."

"Yes, thank you. I apologize for our abrupt departure," I say, retrieving my shawl.

"I remember what it's like," Mrs. Ifans says. "I just hope you feel better."

With a smile and nod, I walk out with McQueen behind me. A few silent minutes later with only angry glimpses are exchanged, Clyde pulls the cart around. Nobody utters a word on the ride, for which I am grateful. If he never speaks to me again, it will be far too soon. I can feel all the patrons' eyes on me as I storm up to my room, slamming the door shut when I reach its safety. Finally blissfully alone, I take several deep breaths to calm myself as it seems to be the only thing that works. This cannot continue. What—

Angry thumping footsteps in the hall cuts my breath short and fear grips me. I fling myself in the bed with my back to the door just as it opens. He slams it shut. "I am not doing this with you. I am not putting up with this shit, lady!" he shouts.

"Watch your filthy, disgusting language around me, please. My ears are not a w.c."

"See? This. This right here. I told you when you hired me I would not put up with this hoity toity, holier than thou bullshit."

I jump off the bed to face him. "I said watch you filthy tongue around me."

"Oh, now my tongue's filthy huh? You didn't seem to mind my filthy tongue earlier when you were sucking on it."

I pick up the teacup on the nightstand, flinging it at him. "You pig!"

He dodges it with a grin. "Attacking me won't get you a second kiss, Lady Hart."

"Really?" I grab the saucer, launching it too. "I wouldn't kiss you again if my life depended on it. You disgust me. You…coarse, rude, ignorant, prejudiced wolf man!

He puts his hands on his hips. "Well, you're a prudish, uptight, spoiled little rich girl who takes everything so damn seriously she turns a simple, fun thing like a kiss into a damn war for supremacy."

"Oh, I'm uptight, am I? You know nothing, Jamie McQueen. *Nothing*," I hiss.

I'll bloody well show him. I stalk out of the room and down the hall to the stairs. As I descend I shout, "Next round of drinks are on me!"

The fifteen or so people all cheer. Mr. Reynolds, the innkeeper/bartender, watches in confusion as I saunter down to the bar. "Right nice of you, Mrs. McQueen," Reynolds says.

"Whiskey and water, please. And call me Verity."

A few patrons, men mostly, come over to get their drinks and thank me. I am one of only two females in here not counting Kate, the chambermaid/waitress. The other woman looks to be a fellow traveler, judging from her purple hair with matching iron riveted dress, enjoying supper with her husband. Speaking of husbands, mine finds me knocking back the entire glass of whiskey with one chug. It takes concentration but I suppress the shudder and hacking cough that want to accompany this feat. "May I have another, please?" Reynolds glances at McQueen who moves beside me. "Do not look to him, he is not my mother nor my keeper. And he's only with me for my money. Pour." A reluctant Reynolds fills my glass. "Thank you."

McQueen grabs my arm, yanking me off the stool. At least my drink doesn't spill. "What the hell are you doing?" he asks as he drags me to a corner table.

"Having a drink and taking in the ambiance."

"You're making a spectacle of yourself." He tightens his grip. "Low profile, remember?"

I snatch my arm away. "I am enjoying a drink not dancing the can-can on the billiard table." I swig the whiskey but fail to hide the aftershock this round.

"One more of those and you will be."

"I can hold my liquor, thank you very much. I have drunk my brother under the table more than once."

"Right," he says with disdain.

With a scowl, I meet him square in the blue eyes. "You think you know me, but you don't. You don't know me at all." I break away, stalking over to the poker table where the same four men from before sit. They all smile, as do I. "Room for one more?"

"You play?" asks muttonchops.

"Only once or twice. Jamie loves it so much I thought I should learn the basics. So may I play? Pretty please?" I ask with my patented Lady Hart smile.

"Guess I'll join too," McQueen says, all but glaring at me. I bat my eyelashes and grin.

We all move to a bigger table with muttonchops, or Barry, pulling out a chair for me. "Thank you, Barry, you are such a gentleman. I do so appreciate that in a man." McQueen rolls his eyes. "Okay darling, it goes one pair, two pair, three of a kind, five cards in sequence, five of a same suit, full house, four of a kind, five in order of the same suit, and royal flush, correct? And aces completely confuse me. Are they highest or lowest?"

"Both," McQueen says sullenly, passing out the cards. He knows I am up to something. He's right.

"Right. Ugh, there are so many rules I hope I can keep them straight. You'll be gentle with me, right gentlemen?"

"Of course, Mrs. McQueen," spectacles, or Jack, says with a smile.

This is far too easy. Men. Of course I know how to play, I have since I was ten-and-three when my cousin Francis taught David and I. I have spent many a night sitting at a table with some of David's more tightlipped and liberal friends using this very act against them. Math, reading people, then acting accordingly? This game was made for Verity Hart. Tonight I lose seven hands, utilizing the time to study my opponents for their tells and working the odds. Even McQueen begins buying my grift enough to let his guard down until his tell becomes salient. It's subtle. While bluffing, his eyes veer a tad to the left, and when he's telling the truth they move right. I file that away for future use.

When I actually win a round, the men applaud. Fifteen rounds and a hundred pounds later, I do not even receive a smile. Except from the werewolf dealer across from me. I am the only one who has gone toe-to-toe with him and won more than once. Fairly soon it's as if it were just the two of us. Parrying and thrusting in a dance of wills. He smirks, and I sweetly smile back, batting my eyelashes. But all good things must come to an end. I knew that fourth whisky was a mistake. The world lags a second behind my thoughts, and I cannot sit still. Time for bed. I bet the lot on a pair of fives against Jack.

"Oh, no," I groan. "So stupid of me. Deal me out, please." I stand on uneasy legs as the world tilts. I need some air. "Gentlemen, it was a pleasure. Enjoy the-the evening."

The smoke is making me nauseous, as is the fact the floor will not stop wobbling as if we were on a sea voyage. Oh boats. I do like boats. Should have taken a boat. Boats remain on earth. People weren't meant to fly. Okay, I am tipsier than I thought. Still beat them all. Ha ha. I need air.

It is chilly, chilly, chilly out here with the breeze blowing from the bay. There are no people on the streets and all the shops are closed, so it's quite dark with the only light emanating from inside the pub and train station in the distance. I sigh as I plod toward the street. He was impressed, I could tell. Not that I care what he thinks. No, not at all. Nope. Oh, I should not shake my head like that, it's making me seasick. He is an excellent kisser, though. Far more tender than I imagined. I close my eyes to relive those seconds. He even tasted divine. No it was me, I was a bad kisser, but he caught me off guard. I wasn't ready, and it has been years. I'm out of practice. We really should do it again. Multiple times until we get it right. I...am thoroughly pissed. Without a doubt, I shall regret that fourth whisky tomorrow. McQueen—

"No, don't! Stop!"

My eyes fly open. I hear the same girl yelling and groaning in pain. Before I realize what I am doing, I sprint in the direction of the noises around the side of the pub, cocking the Artemis along the way. With the dim light of the pub's upper window, I can make out the silhouettes of two people writing against the wall, a taller man looming over a girl as she emits small whimpers. Oh God. As I run closer, I can make out more of their features. I recognise the man from the pub. I noticed him as he sat in the back staring at Kate. He was so pale and his clothes were too nice for this crowd, with golden gears on his lapel and fob watch dangling in his vest. There was something off about him, but I was too busy awing McQueen to give him a second thought. Now here he is bending over a whimpering girl with his mouth on her neck.

"You bastard!" I shriek as I shove him away from the girl.

"What—"

Apparently even when undead a swift kick in the bollocks hurts like mad. The man groans and doubles over in agony, clutching the family jewels as he falls.

"Mrs. McQueen!" Kate pleads behind me.

Her assailant writhes around on the pavement as I level the Artemis at him. "Wanted a snack before you attacked me too, huh? Who sent you? Michael? Where is my brother? Talk—"

"Verity!" McQueen booms as he rushes down the alley. Artemis still leveled, I glance behind me. "What the hell is going on?"

"He's one of them. He was attacking Kate!"

"No, he wasn't," the girl cries, "we were just kissing. I swear it. Don't tell my Da."

I look back at her, actually taking the time to look carefully. There is no blood on her neck or clothes. Oh no. "What?" I ask.

"Kate, go back inside. *Now,*" McQueen orders. The girl winces, then flees back to the safety of the pub. McQueen steps behind me, touching my arms to get me to relax. "He's not one of them, shug. Stand down, hon, stand down. It's okay."

Trembling, I lower the Artemis. "I'm sorry. I'm so sorry."

"It's okay," he whispers before moving toward the still agonized man, bending down beside my victim. "You'll be fine. Ice them when you get back to your room."

"Your wife...crazy..." the man says through the gasps.

"Mister, that girl is fourteen. You're lucky she's the one who found you and not me. I'd a broken your damn jaw, among other things, so shut your mouth, get your ass back to your room, and forget this ever happened." McQueen turns back to me. "You okay?"

I take a step. "I—" The world tilts and me with it. The only reason I fail to fall is that McQueen catches me. "I don't feel well."

"Yeah, that'll be the fourth whiskey, shug. Come on," he says, lifting me into his arms like a princess in a faeiry story. I wrap my arms around his neck and rest my swimming head on his shoulder. It's such a lovely shoulder. Broad and strong. Perfect for my head. I close my eyes to savor this. I never wish to leave this spot. Not for all the spices in India. "Bedtime."

My prince carries me through the pub and up the stairs to our bedroom, setting me gently on the bed as if I were made of China. I gaze up at him and want to die. "I'm sorry, I'm so sorry," I mutter. "I really thought he was a vampyre. Kate was whimpering, and he was pale..."

"It's okay, shug," he says, pouring me a glass of water. He sits on the bed with the water and waste bin. "Sit up and drink this." I manage to push my heavy body up to sip the water. "Finish the whole thing." He sits there with a sympathetic smile as I do. "Good girl."

"I'm sorry," I whisper as my eyes coat with tears. "I am so sorry. I was cruel. I don't really think you are disgusting. Quite the opposite in fact. I think you are bloody marvelous."

"Thank you. And I'm sorry too. For everything."

The tears threaten to spring out. "Even kissing me?" I ask miserably.

"Maybe not everything," he says with a sly smile.

A warm blush cascades across my face. "I hate fighting with you. I want you to like me ever so much. I want it more than almost anything."

His face falls under the weight of his regret. "I do like you. A great deal."

"I really am a good kisser. I swear it. You simply caught me by surprise."

"Shug, you are an excellent kisser. And damn fine poker player."

"Did not see that coming, did you?" I giggle.

"Lady, you are one of the most surprising people I have ever met, and that's the biggest damn compliment I have ever given in my life."

My heart swells with pride. "Really?"

His smile stretches across his entire face and beyond. "Really. Now, lie down. Time to sleep."

A most brilliant excellent idea. My eyes close on their own before I even scoot down and adjust the pillow. The bed moves as he rises, but shifts again as he moves farther down to remove my slippers. "I like you a lot too." And I drift to sleep with the blissful sensation of his hands on my bare feet. Skin to skin. Bloody marvelous. Being bad sure does feel good…

However, the day after…

Oh, blast. My eyes fly open only to be scalded by the sunlight from the window. More pressing problems at present. I barely have time to pick up and aim into the waste basket beside the bed before expelling the whole of my stomach and several other organs as well. Dear Lord in heaven, take me now.

"Oh, shug," McQueen says as he stands from the floor where he was sleeping. I take a moment to catch my breath before the urge to purge swells again. McQueen perches on the edge of the bed, rubbing my back as I lose the rest. My governess used to do that when I was ill. Feels lovely. "Good girl, get it all out."

I rest my head on the rim of the bin before retrieving the water from the nightstand, rinsing my mouth out and spitting it in with the rest. "The vampyres can kill me now. I would not mind one whit."

"Feel better?" he chuckles.

"No." I set the bin on the floor and lie down with water in hand. "I used to be able to hold my liquor better. I hate getting older. I am beyond mortified." Yes, nothing makes a man want to fall in love with you like watching you attack someone, then vomit up not only your emotions but last night's supper as well. We should announce the wedding at once.

"Don't be. Last time I drank too much I woke up in my own juices, more than one kind."

"How vivid." I settle into the bed a little more, my stomach still churning with every minute movement.

"Drink lots of water and take a bath, you'll be right as rain in a couple hours. Drink." I sit up to get some water down as he watches like a mother hen. I can now add nurturer to his growing list of attributes. Anymore and I shall be in *real* trouble. "Get about five more of these under your belt. I'm gonna shave then run you a bath, okay? Keep chugging." He stands and walks to the jug, bringing it over to the nightstand. My nurse smiles before pulling on his boots and getting his shaving kit from the suitcase. I pretend to focus on my glass, but really never take my eyes off him. "Be back in a few. I want that water gone when I get back."

As he's about to step out, I say, "Mr. McQueen?"

He spins around. "Yeah?"

"Thank you." I pause. "For taking care of me. It means more than you know."

For a moment I swear something akin to terror fills his dark eyes, but he blinks it away. He nods. "It's what you're paying me for, shug." He quickly smiles and walks out.

I do not know why but those words hurt more than twenty hangovers combined. Blast.

CHAPTER EIGHT

FREUDIAN SLIPS

He's right. I hate those words, but they are accurate. After an entire pitcher of water, soak in the tub and headache powder, I am finally able to face the day, at least physically. Sadly last night and this morning's event plague me so I cannot simply enjoy my change of health. I acted like a drunken, jealous madwoman with low morals. I haven't a clue how I'll be able to meet his eyes from now on. No more. No more idiotic flights of fancy about romancing Americans. I have shown restraint all my life, I can do so now as well.

When I return to the room from the bath, I find a tray of food on the bed but no McQueen. It's only ten and our flight isn't until 2:30, so I climb back into bed and start picking at my food. My stomach is still too tender to imbibe more than a few bites. My employee returns a short time later. I'm only in my chemise, so I pull the covers up more.

"Feeling better?" he asks.

"Yes, thank you," I say, clutching the covers. "And thank you for breakfast."

"Well, you gotta eat," he says, leaning over me to grab a piece of toast. Lord he smells marvelous, like tobacco and lavender. He sits in the chair across from me, chomping on my toast. "So, you up for a little excursion? Apparently we can't leave town without checking out Porth Daforch. The beach. It's a good day for it too. The sun is actually out, should take advantage of it. Unless you want to stay in the room."

"No, I'd love to go. I haven't been to the shore in ages."

"Great. I'll find Kate to help you get dressed." He brushes the crumbs off his pants before leaving again.

A lovely day by the shore. Perfect to keep my mind off everything. I chose my outfit carefully, my light pink silk dress with white Brussels lace embellishment. Light enough for the summer heat. There's a knock on the door, and a sheepish Kate steps in. Neither of us can meet the other's eyes. As we stand in front of the mirror, I spy her uncomfortable glances as she laces my corset. What happened last night was my fault, it is up to me to fix it.

"Kate, I need to apologize for my actions last night. It was not my intention to scare you."

"It's okay, ma'am," she says in a low tone. "Thank you for not telling Da. He…" She goes into her head for a moment. "I don't know why I did it. He just seemed so…elegant. He told me I was pretty."

"You are pretty."

"No, I'm not," she says, blushing. "I've got unruly hair and nothing up top. Nobody's gonna love me like Mr. McQueen loves you."

My mouth sets in a straight line. I could lie, stick with our story, but fear the words will choke me. "He doesn't love me. Our marriage is simply a business arrangement, nothing more."

"Really?"

"Yes. If not for my money, he would not be here with me. I think he likes me on occasion, perhaps even a great deal, but love? No. I do not think that will ever be possible." She glances at me with pity, so I smile to reassure us both. "Don't be sad for me. It simply is what it is. Sadness and pity will not change that universal truth. My fate is sealed. But yours is not. Many men will tell you you are pretty to get what they want. Do not throw your entire life away for a few sweet words and one night of passion. Wait until you're in love, and he is willing to give you as much as you do him."

"You didn't," she points out.

"Yes…I did."

There isn't any more to say. She helps me with the dress and petticoat then at my request leaves me to finish the rest. Her sympathetic looks are driving me mad. I take time with my make-up and hair, a simple chignon held by my tri-geared hair pin, and select a white cameo necklace with pink ribbon, before latching on the Artemis. Don't want McQueen to think I am ill prepared for danger. With my white parasol and bonnet, I am a vision. When I descend the stairs to the pub, people do stop and stare, well save for the one person I desire to. His comely appearance today rivals mine with black pants, white shirt, black leather vest, and black jacket with boots and hat. What a fine pair we are. He continues reading his book in the corner even when I stand a few feet away.

After clearing my throat, he finally glances up, emotionless. "About time. Ready to go?"

I am taken aback by his bruskness. "Um, yes."

He places the book behind the bar, and I follow him out. He is correct, it is a wonderful day. The street is busy with carts and people walking on the street to and fro. In the clear blue sky a brown dirigible floats up, shining gondola dangling below, as another lands. I nibble on the inside of my mouth. One good thing about my new obsession, it has helped me forget I have to ride one of those death traps in a few short hours. Maybe McQueen can knock me out and revive me when we arrive in Galway. He must notice me staring because he says, "You'll be okay." Those are his only words the entire walk to the shore.

We are not the only ones taking advantage of the fine weather. The coast is filled with families resting on blankets, enjoying picnics, flying kites, building sandcastles, or promenading in their finest clothes. Small children frolic in the water, squealing as their siblings or parents chase them into the water as waves lap against their bare legs. As I watch a father spin his young daughter by the arms in the surf as she giggles, melancholia grips me.

One of my fondest memories of my father was when I was seven and we let a house Cornwall right on the shore. He spent hours building sandcastles with us when he wasn't teaching us how to swim. I felt so safe in his arms, my big brave father. I trusted him without reservation even the one time he dunked me under the waves. Panicking, I got lost under the water, not knowing which way was up. Father pulled me up and hugged me until my tears ceased. That was before he gained notoriety in Parliament and people expected so much of him. Before he stopped loving me.

"We should take our shoes off," McQueen suggests, drawing me out of the darkness. "Feel the sand between our toes."

"I have stockings on."

"Then take them off."

"I couldn't! There are people everywhere."

He raises an eyebrow. "Thought you didn't care what people thought, wild woman of the Bay Pub & Inn."

I know a dare when I hear one. "You're right. I do have a reputation to uphold," I say, smiling sweetly. I spy a large rock up the shore near the headlands where I can sit. I turn my back to both him and the others as I lower myself onto the boulder and remove my shoes and stockings. As I do, I glance behind a few times to see if McQueen is sneaking peeks at my bare legs, but he just stands there with his back to me. Blast. I fix my skirts and rejoin him. "You're right, that does feel lovely. Shall we?"

We walk side-by-side along the shore, passing and nodding at people as they do us. I do adore the sensation of the warm sand between my toes. It's so decadent. One couple has a liveried automaton following behind to hold the ladies' parasol. Its gears will clog with sand if they are not careful.

"I never liked those things," McQueen says. "Especially when they're dressed up like us. It ain't right." He glances at me, the side of his mouth twitching. "Oh, sorry. Forgot you made them."

"I have many sins to atone for, Mr. McQueen, but introducing those monstrosities to the world was not one of them. No, I agree. Ever since Rathbone introduced them, good people have lost their jobs and homes England's already high poverty rate exploded. I have seen the consequences firsthand, especially in the East End. The whole neighbourhood is like hell on earth. Children starving, women having to sell themselves to support their families because their husband cannot find factory work anymore. Tragic does not begin to describe it. People are always going to David to build a newer, better automaton, but I always refuse. I want what I create to improve lives, not destroy them. Just because something can be created does not mean it should." He's been staring at me with interest during my tirade, making me even more uncomfortable. "What?"

He looks away, embarrassed at being caught. "Nothing. Not a damn thing."

Again we walk in silence except for the crashing waves and sounds of laughter. I tolerate it for sixty seconds, not a moment longer. "So, how do our shores compare to those in America?"

"A lot calmer. Some places in California the waves get up to ten feet high. Florida too. Pretty warm in both all year round. Sunny too."

"Have you traveled all over America?"

"Most of it. Work took me around a lot. Been coast-to-coast, Canada and Mexico too. Didn't like to stick in one place too long."

"Beholden to nothing and no one," I add. "A lone wolf, pun intended."

"I reckon."

"It must be lonely though. What little I know of wolves, I do recall they travel in packs. It is most unnatural for them to be alone. Your condition must have affected you a bit in that regard."

His eyes have narrowed. "Not so much. And I had companionship here and there along the way."

"*That* is not the same, and you know it. There is no substitute for love. And family. People who understand, support, and love you come what may. If God provides you the chance of having that, it would be a crime an affront to Him to toss it away out of fear or pride."

Once again, I sense him peering intensely at me. My eyes remain straight ahead. "If you have something to say, you should just come out and say it, shug."

Not until you say it first. "I have no clue what you are talking about. I was just sharing my opinion."

He shakes his head. "You're barking at a knot, shug. I'm not doing it. It's a bad idea."

"Why?"

"Because I have no desire to meet them, not now or ever."

"What?" I'm lost.

"I know you think getting the pack to help us is a good idea, and under other circumstances it might be, but they don't know me from Adam. And you don't know werewolves. Just me setting foot on their property could be seen as a threat. I may be blood, but I ain't pack. We can save your brother without them."

"Right, whatever you think is best." Blast. Double blast.

More silence as we walk, before he says, "Which reminds me. We haven't talked strategy much. I've done simple extractions before, not many but some. Blending in is always key. Don't know how, but we'll have to get our hands on some servant's uniforms. We can walk right in and out if we play our cards right. Of course I'll know more once we get there. Are you nervous?"

"I haven't really given it much thought. At present I am more worried about the trip there."

"Flying really is a piece of pie. You can stay in the cabin, and you won't even know you're fifteen hundred feet up."

"That high?" I ask, my voice going up an octave. He chuckles. "What?"

"Nothing. You were just a hell of a lot less fearful the other night when people were shooting at us then you are now."

"I am aware it is not rational, and I am not proud of the fact, but it just is. I can't even climb a ladder without panicking. It is not funny."

"No," he chuckles, "it's just nice to know you have flaws. That you're as irrational and human as the rest of us, present company excluded."

He thought I was perfect? I quickly smile. "So you don't think I am prudish, uptight, and spoiled?"

"Only if you don't think I'm coarse, rude, ignorant, and prejudiced."

I wince. "I said those things in anger, I apologize."

"Nothing to apologize for. You're right," he says. "I ain't refined, I tell it like I see it, I don't got book smarts, and hoity toity people who look down on me piss me the hell off. Money don't make people better, in my experience the opposite is true. The most evil sons of bitches I ever met were the wealthiest. Not a one was happy either." He scoffs. "You're rich, and you're one of the most miserable people I've ever met."

I have no retort for that. "Still if I made you feel inferior, or that I do not have anything but the utmost respect for you, I am so sorry. Quite the opposite is true, in fact."

"Don't worry, shug, you haven't. You're one of the good ones, any fool can see that. Even this fool."

Inside I swell with delight, but try to conceal it. We promenade on, the edges of our arms occasionally brushing. To be so close yet so far away, it's growing intolerable. I am about to leap out of my skin or worse have words blurt out that I cannot take back. Thank goodness a ball rolls in front of us a few feet away. A smiling McQueen trots toward it, tossing it back to the little boy and girl it belongs to. They both grin and wave before returning to their game of catch. I stare at the boy for a moment.

He looks like David did at that age, all gangly limbs and floppy brown hair.

David.

Guilt overshadows all other emotions. Here I am strolling along the beach on a beautiful day, my thoughts on romance rather than saving my brother. They could be torturing him while I'm making eyes at an American wholly unsuitable for me. McQueen glances back with a smile. I stare down at the sand. I must stop this. I absolutely will not allow myself to fall in love with him. Every rational bone inside me is screaming at this horrible notion. He will be gone tomorrow, and I shall never lay eyes on him again. David is all that matters. Getting him back in one piece. Everything else is a distracting folly.

When I reach my employee, I toss my head back and jut my chin out as Father always does when speaking to the help. "I wish to return to the inn."

"Already? You feeling alright, shug?"

"I feel like lying down. I do not require you to follow me. I shall be fine alone."

His eyes narrow again. "We both know that ain't happening. If you want to go back, we'll go back. No big deal."

We change course back the way we came. As always, I am aware of the distance between us, but instead of bridging the gap, I widen it. If he notices my chilliness he does not let on. He must know something has shifted between us because he does not attempt to speak. Mores the better. Whenever he opens his mouth I either want to slap or kiss him. Seeing as I have done both in the past day I think I have reached my limit.

A wonderful hypothesis forms inside my mind. Perhaps what I am feeling is simply an illusion, a distraction to ease my worry about David. I believe I am falling in love with an inappropriate man so I can obsess on that and not on my brother's likely demise. That must be the cause. Before this journey began, when I met him at the ball, I thought he was interesting and moderately handsome in a rugged way I have never been partial to, but there was only the tiniest spark of attraction, nothing to account for this. Yes, I am simply displacing my emotions to a safe area. It makes perfect sense. I must write Dr. Freud about this should I survive. And Father called his theories poppycock.

Feeling much better now I've sorted myself out, and knowing my madness is only temporary, I enjoy the rest of the walk. I think I shall bring David here on our way home to rest. I am sure he'll need it, as will I. Delay Father's wrath as long as possible. He—oh.

An old gentleman up the beach sits on a blanket as his wife attempts to help him stand. What really captures my attention is the fact he sports Hart braces. I've witnessed this scene before. The braces have broken down, locking the joints in place. With proper maintenance and upkeep this rarely happens, but when it does it is a pain.

I am surprised when McQueen beats me to their rescue, walking over to them before even I do. "Everything okay here?"

"There's something wrong with his left leg," the wife says.

If the other leg is functional that means the miniature steam engine in the back is functioning, which is the most common problem. "When was the last time you changed the hydraulic fluid?" I ask as I bend down.

"We're supposed to change it?" the wife asks.

Why is it so hard for people to follow simple instructions? "Is there one spot that is malfunctioning or the entire side?"

"Joint at the knee. It's been stiff," the man says.

"Then it is probably a clog in one of the hydraulic lines. It clots if the whole system is not flushed every so often."

"Flushed?" the man asks.

"Drain the old and replace it with new," I instruct. "If you don't, the heat from the engine congeals the fluid until it clots, and the braces malfunction. We simply have to remove the clog. Turn the engine off please."

The wife switches off the small steam engine soldered on the metal back plate which pumps the fluid to the gears. The easiest thing to do is pull the mass out. I remove my tri-gear hat pin before unhooking the tiny copper tube at his locked knee. Brown fluid spills onto my hands before I lift up the tube to stop it. Another pair of gloves ruined.

"You shouldn't do that!" the wife says. "Do you have any idea what you're doing?"

"Ma'am let me assure you there in no one better equip to handle your problem then that lady right there," McQueen says. "I guarantee it."

I smile in spite of myself. Mind on the work, Verity. Mind on the work. Since I haven't a clue exactly where the clog is, I gradually press the hat pin up the tube until about three inches in I hit resistance. There it is. With the gentlest of care, I pierce the gooey clot and slowly draw it out of the tube. No wonder it malfunctioned. It's the size of a ball bearing. It is a miracle the bugger didn't wreck the entire apparatus. As I remove it from the pin, I accidently prick my finger. I wince but nothing can be done at this moment. Once the tube is reconnected I say, "Restart the engine, please." The wife obeys, but I wait thirty seconds when I see the wisps of steam out of the small exhaust pipes, before saying, "Attempt to move it."

Sure enough his leg bends back and forth, hydraulics whirring. "Oh my goodness, she did it," the man says.

McQueen holds out his hand to help me stand, then assists the elderly couple as well. The old woman gives her husband his canes. "Chances are there are more clots in the system, so at your earliest convenience you must replace the fluid. They might have some at the General Store."

"Thank you, thank you so much," the man says.

"You're welcome. Enjoy the rest of your day," I say before walking toward the water. As I do, I unlatch the Artemis and remove my gloves. The fluid has soaked through, and my index finger bleeds. Disgusting. I wash my hands in the sea, the cut stinging a bit.

"You're bleeding," McQueen says as he steps behind me. There is no way he can tell that from where he's standing. I turn with a confused expression on my face. "I can smell it." He pulls out a handkerchief. "Here, let me see."

He makes a move to take my hand, but I hide it behind my back. "I'm fine."

"Stop being a baby," he says. "Give me your hand."

No, this is good. When he sees my hand I'll view his revulsion, and that will push me one step closer to breaking the illusion. Before I can change my mind, I thrust my scarred hand at him. Cuts, burns, calluses, chipped fingernails, and now blood, hardly an enticing sight. I watch his face closely, but find no revulsion or any reaction whatsoever. He simply examines the prick and wraps his handkerchief around my finger. "You'll live."

"Will it scar? Not that it matters, as you can plainly see."

"Yeah, you got quite a collection here, but this won't scar." He smiles. "At least one mystery is solved."

"What?"

"I was wondering why you never took your gloves off."

Why didn't I bring a spare set? I know better. "Yes, they're disgusting, aren't they?" I ask as I yank my hand away, balling them both into fists.

"Wouldn't go that far, though I know why you keep them hidden. You can tell a lot about a person by their hands."

I am more than a little afraid at the answer, but find myself asking, "And what do mine tell you?"

"That you're a hard worker. You're not afraid to get your hands dirty. That you work through the pain when you think something is worthwhile, but I already knew all that. The hands just confirmed what I already suspected."

"What?"

He meets my eyes, my stomach twisting for fear of his next words. "That deep down, you ain't no lady." He smiles as brightly as the sun. "And thank God for that." He winks and strolls away, leaving me slack jawed and reeling. When he is far enough away, I gasp.

Because with those words the illusion *is* shattered, but not the one I wanted. Damn it all to hell. Not him. Anyone but him. But no it's too late. I feel it down to my very soul. I love him. I am officially in love with a penniless, vulgar, American werewolf. I am.

And I have never felt so sad and hopeless in my entire life.

CHAPTER NINE

FEAR OF FALLING

Years of practice have made it possible for me to mask my true feelings. It is one of the first lessons taught to all us ladies, so in spite of my revelation, I am able to act as if nothing were amiss. The man I love and I return to the inn with few words spoken, and he resumes reading in the chair by the window of our room. I attempt to do the same on the bed, faking it well. H.G. Wells words have no meaning, but I flip the pages anyway. I breathe a literal sigh of relief when he announces he's going to the General Store to replenish supplies before our flight.

How did this happen? How had I allowed this to happen? I must be mad. That's it. It is the only explanation. I have officially gone around the bend. Sure he is the strongest, bravest, most fascinating man I have ever met, and he kisses like a god, but he also infuriates me on an hourly basis. And he's made it clear he has no intention of staying in England, let alone marrying me. Unrequited love is the most torturous kind on the planet because no one is at fault. I cannot blame him for not reciprocating my feelings any more than I can blame myself for having them. This is why I prefer machines to people. No messy emotions involved. Logic is better, a problem and solution. The only solution to this problem is to magnify his faults until he sails out of my life for good. I'll remember him fondly, then as the years pass, not at all. I survived love once relatively intact, I can survive it again.

When he returns with toothpaste, magazines, and two new books, it is time to check out. At the very least my emotional upheaval has blocked the intense panic I would be feeling regarding the flight. I suppose I should get something good from this mess. We pay our enormous bill, liquor for an entire pub is expensive, and say our good-byes to Reynolds and Kate, who smiles sadly at me. I appreciate the sentiment more now than ever. A hansom cab takes us to the dirigible station but the jostling makes me keep bumping against McQueen. Every time our bodies touch I receive a jolt, as if my dirty little secret could be discerned through touch.

"You okay?" he asks as we near the station.

"Yes, why wouldn't I be?" I ask shrilly.

By the time the cab stops, the inside of my mouth is so raw from my nibbling on my cheeks I am close to drawing blood. McQueen gets out first then extends his hand to help me out. I yank my hand from his the moment I can.

Unlike yesterday the station, or according to the sign "airport," is a flurry of activity. There are two dirigibles tethered to spikes in the ground by a dozen ropes, one only a barge with metal railings being loaded with crates, and the larger, our destination, with a porter assisting people up a ramp to the cigar shaped gondola, or passenger compartment. It hangs from metal cables attached to the balloon or gasbag, which means we will literally be dangling by strings the entire trip. There are also wings, or flaps, and a metal rudder on the brown gasbag, all used to steer the airship. Braver men than I crawl like monkeys on the gasbag from the cables, checking all the lines. Normally such a beautiful piece of mechanical ingenuity would excite me, this one makes me want to gag. Sheer terror immobilizes me.

No, not doing this. No way.

A porter walks up with a handcart and bends to pick up my trunk. "Don't touch that!" I shriek. "Get away from here!"

"I'm sorry, I thought—"

"It's fine, put it on the cart," McQueen instructs. "We're in sleeper seven." His gaze whips to me. "You, come here." He grabs my arm and leads me out of earshot. "Talk to me."

I love you. I adore you. I am on the verge of a nervous breakdown and will have one if I have to set foot on that death trap. "I've re-examined our strategy. If they intercepted the wire, they already believe we're in Ireland. There is no reason we cannot take the ferry and train now. It will be faster."

"But this is safer."

I yank my arm away. "Are you mad? *Safe?* That monstrosity is nowhere near safe! It is powered by an internal combustion engine and hydrogen. My brother is a chemist, I have seen firsthand how volatile hydrogen is. One spark, one tiny spark, and we explode with nowhere to go but a thousand feet down! I prefer our odds with the vampyres, thank you very much. I am *not* getting on that deathtrap, and that is final. End of discussion."

McQueen's silent for a few seconds as his narrowed eyes bore into mine. "Shug…man the hell up."

"Pardon me?"

"You are acting like a frightened five-year-old, and that is beneath you. There is nothing to be afraid of, and deep down you know it. You've got more grit than any woman I have ever met. This thing ain't gonna beat you. So stop your bellyaching, and get your ass on that ship!"

I consider all he's said for a second, I swear I do, then say, "No." I make a break for the cab, but he's too fast for me. I barely make it three steps when he grabs my wrist, swings me around, and slings me over his shoulder. "Put me down!"

"Ornery as a damn mule." I kick his stomach and whack his back with my fists as he walks us toward the ship, but he will not release me. "Stop that, or I'll take you over my knee and spank you."

I gasp. "You wouldn't!"

"The hell I wouldn't. You act like a child, I'll treat you like one. Lord knows you could use a good hiding. Don't tempt me, shug."

And this is the man I love. I have abysmal taste in men.

All wide eyes are on us as he saunters over to the porter, handing our tickets to the stunned man. "Fear of flying," McQueen says, I am sure with a grin. Wretched man.

"Welcome aboard," the porter says. As I pass, he nods. "Ma'am."

Oh Lord. I am mortified beyond words as we move into the gondola, which oddly helps with the panic. Not a great deal but enough. The inside of the ship is grander than I imagined, much like a Pullman car, with the same dark red carpeting and gas lamps flickering above. We pass through lounge area with tables for dining and rows of smaller tables or lounge chairs against the huge bay windows where people are already enjoying drinks served by rolling automatons. Instead of taking in this beautiful day, the stare at me, mouths dropping as we pass. If it were possible to die of embarrassment I would at this very moment. We move from the lounge to a tight corridor with doors, the sleeper compartments I assume. McQueen carries me to the last one on the left. The compartment is smaller than the one on the train, about the size of my water closet at Foxfire Manor, barely enough room for two people. We have to wait for the porter to stow my trunk under the plush burgundy bench, and walk out before we can enter. McQueen shuts the door, then practically flings me on the bench as if I were a sack of cloth.

"There. That wasn't so hard, was it?" he asks.

I leap up, shaking with rage. "You...brute! How dare you manhandle me like that?"

"And here I thought you'd like it."

"I...am sure I have no clue what you mean, sir. All I do know is I am not staying on this thing, I don't care what you do." I attempt to sidestep him but he moves in front of me, I try the other direction with the same result. "Stop it! Let me pass!"

"Not happening, shug."

Rage possesses me like a demon, and I point the Artemis at him. "Let me pass."

Instead of fear I find amusement. "You're gonna shoot me?"

"Technically you are kidnapping me, so I am well within my rights. I do not want to but—"

Before I can finish, he lunges at me, grabbing my outstretched wrist first, then the other. With one swift move, he raises my arms above my head while at the same time using his body to push me onto the bench with him on top of me. One moment I am standing, and the next I realize we are lying on the couch with him straddling me at the waist with my arms pinned above, his face inches from mine. "Stop acting crazy and calm the hell down."

I wriggle and writhe under him, trying to break free. "Let me go! This is grievous bodily harm! Release me at once!"

"Not until you—"

We both notice his reaction to our closeness at the same time. Oh, my. He… The only reason I know what is pressed against my thigh is that Jolyon sometimes had the same affliction while we kissed on the duvet. One time he even attempted to guide my hand into his britches, but I balked. There was plenty of time for that after the wedding. At this moment, with this man, I have no idea what to do except stay still so as not to make matters worse. Or better depending on how one views it. We both glance down at the bulge then back into each other's eyes. My breath catches as I see the lust and turmoil gazing back at me. He stops breathing as well, afraid as I am by what is passing between us, a deep, primal hunger I never knew myself capable of. A sweltering, tingling fire that radiates from my most intimate centre to my very core, melting away any reserve, and reservations I have about loving this man. And he wants me just as violently as I do him. *He wants me.*

He can bloody well have me.

I bridge the gap between our lips, but the moment I move the spell breaks. He springs up, shock and disgust written in every tense line and muscle on his rugged, beguiling, befuddled face. "Um, sorry."

Sorry?

The knock on the door jolts us both. "Excuse me, please open the door," a man orders.

McQueen turns his back to me, taking a few deep breaths as I quickly sit up and adjust my skirts. He opens the door. "Yes?" McQueen asks the porter in the corridor.

"We had reports of shouting," the porter says, glancing at me. I smile to reassure him.

"My, um, wife has a fear of heights. I was trying to convince her to stay on the ship."

"Are you okay, ma'am?"

"Yes, thank you. I apologize for my loud outburst. It shall not happen again."

Judging from his narrowed eyes, he isn't quite convinced, but still says, "Very well. We'll be lifting off shortly."

"Thank you," McQueen says as he shuts the door. Alone again. He takes a moment to compose himself, shoulders raising and slumping as he huffs and puffs, before turning to face me. Any trace of lust, or any emotion, has vanished. He has the same expression plastered on he did whilst we played poker last night. He presses his back to the door to get as far from me as possible in this closet. "I am not moving from this spot until we are in the air," he says, refusing to look at me. "You can shoot me if you want, I ain't moving."

"I wasn't really going to shoot you," I say meekly.

"I know," he says after a pause.

Obviously we are not going to speak about what occurred, which is fine by me. Part of me is elated that I could inspire such lust while the other part, now unclouded by my baser instincts, is disgusted by my behavior. To think I…ugh. I forgot myself. That is all. Neither of us utters a word as I watch through the window as the last of the passengers arrive, including the dandy from last night's debacle. As if this flight could not be any worse. Workmen scurry about, untying the tethers and pulling the gas hoses away to safety. Terror rears its ugly head again as I watch the lines tying us to earth unfurl. My hands begin trembling.

"Close the curtain," McQueen says. I glance at his impassive face. "You'll barely be able to tell when we lift off."

I do as he instructs, but keep my eyes on that maroon covering. The room jostles a little, like a flicked piano wire, and I grip the edge of the bench for dear life as a whimper escapes me. I shut my eyes tight to lock my oncoming tears inside. I'm close to sobbing my eyes out for everything. For David, for the man I killed, for fear, for my broken heart. I begin rocking back and forth like the bloody madwoman I have become. I cannot do this. I can't. It's too much. I want to give up. It's time to give up. I'm sorry David. I'm not strong enough. I—

McQueen lowers himself beside me, but I am afraid to open my eyes. His hand slides over my clawed one. He extracts it from the seat and entwines his fingers with mine. It helps a little, enough to stop the rocking. "Tell me your happiest memory of your brother."

The ship shifts again. "What?" I ask breathlessly.

"Think back. What's the best memory you have of him?"

"I, there are so many." I wrack my brain, and one moves to the forefront. "It's not a happy memory, but…it's the time I loved him the most. When he saved my sanity."

"What happened?"

"It was just after Jolyon broke off our engagement. He spoke to Father on his way out. He told him every detail of our conversation. How it was my fault and mine alone. David had been out for the day, and when he returned home he found us in the parlor. Father was…unhinged as if a demon had taken possession of his very soul. He had been shouting at me for twenty minutes straight. How I had shamed the family, how I had let him down, how he'd lock me away in a sanitarium, disown me if I continued my inventions. How…he wished I had never been born. His face was as red as a tomato. His voice had grown hoarse ten minutes prior yet he continued on and on. Years of disappointment and hatred had finally come to a head. He had never lost control like that, then or since. Mama sat in the corner weeping as if I were dead. At that point I was so numb he could have struck me, more than once I believed he would, and I would not have felt the sting. I hadn't even cried yet. It was as if I was outside my body looking down at this pathetic, ashen creature who wouldn't utter a word in her own defense because a large part of her believed every cruel word.

"Then David returned home. He heard the yelling, and of course came to see what was happening. Father told him, and a rage I didn't know he had rose in David. It is the first and only time I ever heard him raise his voice, let alone to Father. He was shouting, 'How can you treat her this way?' and 'What kind of parents are you?' Father was aghast, especially when David told him to go to hell. After he said those words, David took my hand and dragged me out of that room to my workshop, locked the door, and pulled me into his arms. The moment he did, I finally broke down. He did not let go for two hours as I cried until I feared my eyes would bleed.

"We did not leave that room for almost a full day. At first we just talked. About Jolyon, about our parents, about being aberrations of nature. That was when he finally admitted he was attracted to men, though I had suspected as much for some time. Of course I didn't care, nothing let alone that could make me love him any less. He cried then, I think it was the first time he ever said it aloud, and I did for him as he had done for me. When there was nothing left inside us, and I remember this moment as clear as if it were occurring now, my brother, my best friend stared into my eyes and said, 'Listen to me, Very. We are who we are. We cannot change, and we shouldn't have to, because there is nothing, *nothing* wrong with either of us. It's *them* with their small minds and closed hearts. We have accomplished more now than most do in three lifetimes. We make this world better. And *no one* should try to take that away from us. He didn't deserve you. Very few men will. That is the price of genius, my darling. But no matter what, I swear, I *swear* we will always have each other. Come hell or high water, I am on your side just as I know you are on mine. 'Til death and beyond.'" I open my eyes and look at my saddened companion. "So, that's the memory. My happiest," I say with a wry chuckle as I wipe the stray tears.

"I'm so sorry, Verity," he says in a low voice.

I don't want his pity. I want to live in a perfect world where two aberrations live happily ever after with those who love them for them. Where I can foster a shred of hope that the man holding my hand and I have a future, in spite of the odds against it. Where I get my brother back untouched and alive. But it does one no good to dwell in fantasy to the detriment of reality, no matter how bleak it may be.

I pull my hand away from his to open the curtain. The ground grows farther away as we float into the blue sky among the puffy white clouds. "We're up in the air."

"So we are."

I take a moment to compose myself, to push my emotions down, and even manage to give him a small smile when I turn back around. "Thank you."

"Even the strongest of us lose our way from time to time. Then we just need a little help to find our way back. No shame in that, Lady Hart."

"Well, I'm back. Thank you."

I return to my window, gazing down as the bright green grass leagues below us fades into the blue water. There was nothing to fear after all. It was all for nothing. I almost threw away all my hard work, David's life, for naught. If McQueen had not been here…but he was. He *is*. This wonderful, aggravating, marvelous man knew the exact right thing to say, the very thing I needed to continue on. He saved me. And I am now resigned that no matter what happens between us, no matter that without a doubt he will break my heart intentionally or not, no matter what I shall love Jamie McQueen with the whole of my soul until my dying day.

And beyond.

CHAPTER TEN

DO NOT LOOK DOWN

He was right, the journey across the Irish Sea via airship is smoother than a train ride. After some time, I even forget we are moving so high in the sky birds would swoon should they look down. I even venture a glance out the window once or twice with little to no anxiety. I can understand why more and more people are choosing this mode of transport. It is a modern miracle. Had we lived a century ago flying through the clouds could only occur in the wildest of dreams. I still don't like it but I can appreciate that fact.

Jamie excused himself soon after lift-off to learn the layout of the ship. Really I suspect it was to get away from me. I did not fault him that or chase after him. At least not right away. I finally work up the nerve two hours later to leave the relative safety of my cell. I do not find him in the lounge where automatons in brown service suits roll over with their libations to passengers. The dandy from last night notices me, and when my eyes narrow at him, he leaps up, knocking tea into his lap. The nervous Nelly does not bother to clean up before fleeing. I smile to myself. I could get used to striking fear into the hearts of men. It's rather delightful. And now I can enjoy teatime. I'm ravenous after all the strum and drang.

When I return of my room, belly full of scones and clotted crème, I am surprised to find Jamie's suitcase ajar with his book and packet of cards missing. Fine. When we land in Dublin, that same uneasy mania returns, but Jamie does not. I hear that familiar American baritone out in the corridor speaking to a porter, until we lift off again and then the footsteps fade away. Either he has great faith in me or he cannot even stand to be in the same room as me for even a few seconds. Perhaps both.

I do not see him again until around eight when I grow hungry again. I find him in the lounge sitting right by the door with three other men playing cards. We glance at each other, but he returns to the game with nary a word. I might as well be a stranger. Fine. It barely stings. Okay, it bloody well hurts like a swarm of wasps upon me, but I refuse to let this snub show. I dine alone with my back to him and *20,000 Leagues Under the Sea*, my favourite book, to keep me company. Other patrons keep glancing at me, either because they recognise me from my memorable boarding or from the fact I am alone. I ignore them, eat quickly, and retreat back into my cabin. So far my fake marriage is quite like a real one. Dinner with friends, arguing, making up, arguing again, and a lot of time alone hating one another. At least according to my observations regarding my parents' marriage. No wonder they are both so miserable.

I am sick to death of reading, and should try to sleep since in a few scant hours we will land and have to siege a house filled with vampyres, but I am not sleepy. Instead I check through my arsenal to make sure all is in pristine condition. For whatever reason cleaning guns and sharpening dangerous implements is rather soothing. Soon I will be in battle, and for some reason am calmer than I should be. I'm close to tranquil with this six shooter in my hands. We won't be entering the manor until daylight, so I have a little less than twelve hours. I should be frightened, and I suppose I am deep down, but nowhere near the terror that gripped me before. Jamie doesn't return to check on me when we land in Athlone, which brings the wasps back. I take my ire out on the arrowheads. They can cut through metal now.

The unnatural chemical stench from the gun cleaning fluid is so overpowering in the small room, and I feel a headache coming on, so when the porter arrives to let down the second bed, I scoot out to take the night air. It is a little past ten, so I'll spend a few minutes on deck to clear my head before attempting sleep. Busy day tomorrow and all. It would be bad form to fall asleep in the middle of a fight.

I have avoided coming up to the observation deck for obvious reasons, but fresh air is more important than my imagined fears at this moment in time. And my fears are unwarranted. The edge is barricaded by a metal and rope railing with cables every few feet leading up to the gasbag twenty feet above with empty deck chairs like those on an ocean liner line the perimeter. I do wish I'd brought my shawl. The frigid, gusty wind creates a thumping above. The wide, fin-like flaps adjusting to the wind.. A couple I recognise from earlier in the lounge nods as they pass me toward the exit, which leaves only one person on the deck. He must have finally grown bored with cards. I would abandon my plan except he turned and spotted me the moment I stepped outside. It is dark with only a few lanterns around to provide light, but I would recognise that hat and that smell anywhere. He does love those cigars. Having little choice, I stroll over to him, though stop a few feet from the edge.

"Thought you'd be asleep by now," he says, coming toward me, bridging the gap between us.

"No, I was prepping for tomorrow, making sure everything was ready should we need it."

"Smart," he says, stubbing out his cigar. "Here. You look cold." He removes his jacket, handing it to me. It's so warm and smells of him, of lavender and tobacco.

"Thank you," I say as I button it up.

"Apparently we're gonna land in Galway in about two hours. Figure we'll get a room, sleep, find this house, and scout it out at first light."

"Fine." I avert my eyes down to the creaking wooden deck, and we stand in uncomfortable silence.

He breaks it first this time. "It's, uh, really a nice night, don't ya think? You can see all the stars." I glance up but only see the gasbag. "No, you have to…the railing. You have to go to the railing. It's really a sight. You wanna…" He gestures to the edge.

"No. Absolutely not. No."

"Shug, you'll never be this close to them again. Really, it's worth it. Come on, I won't let you fall. I promise." I swallow my ridiculous fear and follow him to the railing, my heart all but leaping out of my chest. "Just don't look down."

As if I would. Ever. I gaze up at the night sky with Jamie right beside me. He was right, it is remarkable. A million lights twinkling in the darkness with the half moon filling the sky, all close enough to touch. "It's beautiful."

He leans on the railing. "Yeah."

I study the sky. "There's Orion."

"What?"

"The constellation. See?" I point to the grouping of stars that comprise him, tracing them with my finger. "There's his belt, body, and outstretched arm and bow."

He shakes his head. "I don't…"

"Here." I move closer and grab his hand, holding it up to the belt. Oh, he smells heavenly. "Um, start at the belt. Those three bright stars close together?" I guide his arm that direction. "Then there's the rest of him. His bow's out, ready for battle. See it?"

"Yeah," he says with a smile.

"And if we move up a bit we find Perseus. The legend is he defeated Medusa and the ocean monster Cetus to save the princess Andromeda. She's next to him, right there." I move his hand her way. "Side-by-side until the end of eternity." I smile. "We should all be so lucky."

I glance over to make sure I am not boring him. Another unfounded fear. He's staring at me, his expression catching my own breath a heartbeat. It is the same look he had before when he was on top of me, lust and turmoil revolving like gears. It disappears the moment my eyes catch his, and he yanks his hand away. Guess our lesson is over. "I, uh, only know the north star and Big Dipper, to uh navigate at night. I mostly used my nose and hearing to track, though. And, uh, knowing which moon is in the sky was important for obvious reasons."

"The full moon's soon, correct?"

"Yeah, in about eight days. Don't know what the hell I'm gonna do then, though."

"What do you normally do?"

"Scout out the most isolated spot I can. Sometimes I lock myself in a root cellar."

"Are you dangerous when you change?"

"Sometimes. I mean, I'm aware of what I'm doing and all, but I don't know how to explain it. I'm me, but I'm not. There's something…animal that takes over. Primal. I'm reduced to the bare essentials. It's like all societal niceties vanish, and all I want to do is run and eat and hunt. It's freeing. There are no rules. Whatever I want to do, I do, and damn the consequences."

"Have you ever hurt anyone?"

He shrugs. "If someone runs, I chase. If they hurt me, I hurt them right on back."

I take a few seconds to let this sink in. I have tried not to think about that side of him, the beast inside. This marvelous man before me becomes a wild predator without conscience. It's not his fault, but it is a part of him. The man I love is not human, not fully. He shall never be normal. Yet this does nothing to dim my love for him. Quite the opposite in fact. What he has to endure month after month, all alone until the end of his days, and the fact he's as well adjusted as he is is a testament to his strength. I couldn't bare it.

"When our mission is complete, there is no need for you to rush back to America. If you require a safe haven to change, Foxfire Manor has multiple rooms that might suit. The countryside is quite beautiful. We have a forest, a river, and it's isolated. It would be the smart thing to do, staying. I—we'd love to have you. I know I haven't been the best of traveling companions at times, so it's the least I can do after all you have done for me."

"I haven't been much better," he admits. "I know I've been changeable, and it-it really ain't your fault. It's all on me, try not to take it personally. I'm just…" He chuckles. "I have no idea what I am. You…confound me at times, and I don't know. I try to gage which way is up, and flail around in the process. I'll try to handle things better from here on out."

My eyes narrow. "I confound you? I don't know what that means."

"I—you—you just," he stammers, trying to find the correct words. He grunts in frustration. "There's a saying back home, 'You can't hitch a coyote to a horse.' It always ends in misery, at least for the horse. Get it?"

"No."

He sighs, turning away from me to the railing and dark empty abyss of the night. "Everyone has a way they view life, and a way they try to live that life. A guiding principal, I guess. The thing that keep 'em going, lights the way when they're lost. My light is honor. Doing the right thing, no matter the personal cost." He spins back around, mouth straight. "And for the most part I've stuck to my guns. I've tried to live an honorable life. I make a mess, I damn well clean it up. And no matter how tempting, how much you might want something, if it hurts another person, you have to step back. It's been tough at times, no question, but I've always managed to stay on the path. But with you…I messed up, shug. I shouldn't have kissed you. Deep down I knew it was wrong. That you weren't the kind to just brush something off like that. That it'd mean something to you. But I did it anyway. I forgot myself, just like what happened this afternoon. That's why you confound me. You mess with my compass, but I've got my bearings now. I won't lose sight again."

"Lose sight of what? You have done nothing wrong, Jamie. I wanted you to kiss me. I want…I—I—" I cannot say the words. Not yet. "You are the most marvelous man I have ever met.

Around you, I feel…I can be myself without repercussions. Without judgment. I trust you. I feel safe."

"You're paying me to—"

"Stop it! That is not what I am speaking of, and you know it. I kill a man, and you comfort me. I tell you of my inventions, and you're impressed. I drink too much and kick a man in the bollocks, and you tell me job well done. I threaten to shoot you, and you hold my hand. I know I am considered…a discredit to my sex. I am an aberration, Jamie. I accept that. But save for one person, no one ever has, let alone been proud of my alleged faults. How can I not—" I stop myself from saying that word again. I swallow it down then take a moment to compose myself. "How can I not hold you in such high esteem?"

He stares at me with a mix of sadness and pity, remaining silent for a few seconds before taking a step my way, but only the one. "You're a hell of a gal, you know that, right? You are one of the bravest, smartest, most aggravating woman I have ever encountered, and I've lived a hell of a long time. Longer than you, so trust me like you say you do. As of right now, I have five hundred and two dollars and a shack on dead land to my name. My few friends are card sharks and killers. I've been alone for almost forty years. I live thousands of miles away, not to mention my damn condition. You and I might as well be from different planets. Use your head, shug. Esteem? *It ain't enough.* We're too different. I got nothing to offer you. *Nothing.* I'm sorry."

Before I can respond, he walks toward the exit without looking back, leaving me alone to the cold night. I clutch his jacket tighter around me, hugging myself but not only to ward against the chill. I should feel dejected. Morose. The man I love just told me he could not see a future for us. But I don't. Not in the least. The opposite in fact. He just…he cares for me. He wants me. A great deal. So much he's attempting to protect me to the detriment of himself. Oh, I did not think I could possibly fall deeper in love with him. He's an idiot, but a chivalrous, honorable, marvelous bloody idiot. There's hope. I just need to convince him—

Though there's minimal light I notice a flash of movement on the other side of the railing in that dark abyss with a fluttering sound too large and loud to be a bird. By the time I glance in that direction, it's gone. Goosebumps rise all over my skin and not from the cold. I do believe it is time to go inside. Now.

I spin toward the door and gasp from fright. Crouched on top of the railing, arms dangling like a monkey's, is a familiar, grotesque face. The last time I laid eyes on her, the monster was flying off with my brother. Guess the Dublin telegram ruse failed. Bugger.

"D.V. Hart, I presume," the vampyre says with a sickening grin. Tonight all pretense of gentility is gone as she's dressed in black leather trousers, jacket fastened closed with brass buckles, knee high black boots, all offsetting her almost glowing pale skin. The round goggles she sports fails to hide the burn from the silver frame that left a scar on her cheek. As if she was not frightening before. I am frozen in place from shock and fear as she leaps off the railing. "You have been a pain in my backside, girlie, let me tell you." She lifts her goggles to her forehead. "I should kill you where you stand for that alone. Let alone this," she says, caressing her scar.

She moves toward me as somehow I step back. "Is—is—is my brother still alive?"

"Come with me and find out," she says with another step.

"I-I asked you a question." I back against the railing, hiding my hands behind my back to cock the Artemis. "Is he alive, you bitch?" I shout.

She's taken aback. "Language, milady, language," the vampyre chides. "He is alive, for the moment. But give me any problems, and that will change."

"How can I believe a word you say?"

She grins maliciously, exposing those sharp fangs, and I suppress a shudder. "You can't, but you are coming with me regardless, so whatever you chose to believe is not my concern. I do hope you haven't a fear of heights otherwise this will not be as much fun—"

Instinct takes over. As she bridges the short gap between us, I raise my arm at the elbow. The moment she lays a frigid gloved hand on me, I fire the Artemis through Jamie's jacket sleeve. The she-demon's body jerks five times, one for each shot directly into her chest. Blood spurts from her mouth onto my face as she stares at me, shock radiating from her eyes. She seemed to think I would make this easy for her. What fools these immortals be.

Trembling as if I were in the midst of a fit, I step aside as the vampyre stares down at her bleeding, smoking chest. She collapses against the railing like a sack of rancid potatoes. I sprint toward the door, shouting, "Jamie!" I make it halfway down the spiral iron steps before in my haste I miss a step, and if I was not holding the railing I would topple over head first instead of just on my bum. Jamie appears at the bottom to witness my blunder, but I care not. "I killed her!"

He grips my arm to help me to my shaky feet, not that I let that stop me. I am first up the stairs with him close behind. But the sight on the deck is not what I anticipated. She's vanished. Gone. Jamie moves behind me, gun at the ready. "Wh—"

"She was here! I swear it! I shot her five times in the chest. She—"

I feel a body slamming against me without seeing it, shoving me to the ground. Before my mind catches on, I fall on my stomach. At the same time a gunshot rings out nearby, then something goes skidding in front of me. A gun. *His* gun. Everything has happened so fast I take a second to get my bearings and catch my breath. What is...? I look to the source of the guttural grunting. With one deft kick, Jamie sends my assailant stumbling backwards like a drunk. Judging from his white skin and leather outfit complete with goggles, I gather he's another vampyre. The vampyre soon recovers from the assault, cocking his head to the side. "Strong. Faerie?"

"Werewolf," Jamie says with a cruel grin.

"Mongrels."

The vampyre rushes toward Jamie like a bull and Jamie him. Instead of horns, they lock fists. Jamie draws first blood with a hit to the jaw that sends the vampyre stumbling back, but he recovers too fast, pelting Jamie in the stomach. He doubles over, and the vampyre scores another strike to the jaw. Jamie smacks against the railing, his hat plummeting to earth as the man I love is about to do with one more hit. I have to do something. I push myself up and crawl toward the discarded gun. It weighs heavy in my hand yet I still rise while pointing it at the men.

Jamie half hangs over the railing, the only thing stopping him taking a dive is his grasp on the cable. I level the gun as a calm washes over me like before. At least this one is technically dead already. Without hesitation I fire twice, both men jerking as the bullets hit the vampyre's back. The vampyre spins around, baring his fangs. I shoot again, the bullet penetrating through the glass of his goggle. He collapses to the deck, incapacitated but not dead judging from the groans of pain. I run to the vampyre, aiming right for his heart. Looming over him, I empty the chamber point blank into his heart. The groans cease. "Is he dead now?" I ask. Jamie slumps against the rail, grimacing in pain as he holds his chest. He takes a few ragged breaths before he finds the energy to fully stand. He pulls out his other gun from the shoulder holster and fires twice into the vampyre's head and four times into his heart. Never can be too careful.

"Help me throw him over," Jamie says through gritted teeth, holstering the gun.

I hand him the gun I'm holding onto for dear life to holster before we pick up the vampyre. He is literally dead weight in our overtaxed arms, but we manage to push him over the rail. The bastard plunges down into the darkness below. Oh, please let him be dead. Her as wel—

Like a sea serpent rising from the depths of hell, her pale goggled face and hands break the surface of the darkness, grabbing me and taking me back down with her. My stomach brushes the railing then there is nothing but open air. Even with it in abundance, none enters my lungs. Water, water everywhere. God help me. God please help me.

I'm falling. I have actually fallen off the dirigible. I'm going to die.

My stomach feels as if it has escaped out the back of my ribcage as the wind whips all around me. I am too shocked and petrified to even scream. What feels like eternity is I believe only a second or two before something hooks me under my arms. I jolt upwards and glide like a bird for a moment before there's another jerk. The hands release me into free fall again. This time the screams flow freely. A second later the same something grabs me again by the collar, choking the shrieks from me. This time I have the wherewithal to glance up for a second. The vampyre holds me with one hand as the other reaches around clawing at Jamie, who clutches onto her with the use of a chokehold. Down and down we go plummeting to the earth.

Everything changes again as we reach the tree tops another second later. Once again I am discarded, tossed against a tree branch as the other two fly away. Instinct takes over. The moment my chest hits wood, knocking the wind out of me, I wrap my arms around the top of the branch. With more strength I knew I possessed, I pull myself onto it, holding on for dear life. Thank you, thank you, thank you God.

I take a moment to savor being alive, the sensation of the rough bark against my cheek, the gentle song of the birds, my stomach remaining in one place before I open my eyes to assess the situation. I'm not as high as I thought, about forty feet from terra firma, though high enough to break my neck or both legs should I jump. But I cannot remain up here no matter how much I desire to. That she beast shall return for me, plucking me from here as a bird snares a worm. I'll have to move down from branch to branch like the monkeys at the zoo. Charles Darwin's theory is about to be put to the test.

The next branch large enough to support me is eight feet down. If I jump to it, I risk not catching it in time. *Think.* I just require a foot or two more to be safe. I run through the possibilities, my mind not moving nearly as fast as my blood, but come up with the jacket. After unbuttoning Jamie's leather coat, I fling it across my branch and use the sleeves to lower myself down, arms quaking from the effort. My feet touch the branch below, and I fall onto the narrow wood. So far so good. This may—

As I try to retrieve the coat I lose my footing, landing miraculously on my stomach. Half an inch either way and game bloody well over. It takes a few seconds for breathing to be possible again. Hell. This is sheer hell. "Okay, okay," I whisper.

A man's scream in the distance burns away the fog of fear. Jamie. I was wrong, now I'm in hell. A second before I realize I am doing it, I apparently lower myself to the next branch. Then the one after that. The next branch is easier, straight across to take me down to the next. Then the one below that, and the next. The last branch is about ten feet above the ground. The man I love howls in agony again. No choice. Get on with it. After slipping the jacket back on I leap, landing on my feet. Slivers of white hot sharp pain fires up my entire right leg, and I drop onto my tender stomach again, but I don't care. I literally kiss the ground. I am never leaving terra firma again.

But there is no time for further celebration. Faintly I hear painful grunting. Jamie. *Get up.* I push myself up, though my legs almost give out as if I were on a pitching ship. *One foot in front of the other as fast as possible, Verity.* My legs and ankles scream in pain from the fall, but my walking soon becomes a good trot as the grunting, groans, and laughter grow closer with each agonizing. The rows of trees I follow soon end at a large clearing. It is too dark to see far ahead, but what I can is simply rocky ground. I stop to catch my breath. This is—

Cutting through the tranquility a woman cackles as Jamie howls in pain reserved only for those consigned to the pits of hell. What do I do? I have no weapons save the Artemis, and she's proven less than effective. I need something else. Something…? The only possibility is a large fallen branch on the ground. Maybe I can club her with it. Better than nothing. *Keep moving.* I do, following the shrieks of agony through the dark. About a hundred feet away, I can make out two blobs of black moving near a trickling river. I must be quiet, so I slow my pace and breath. There is nothing I can do about my throbbing heart.

The vampyre has Jamie on the ground, straddling him and chortling as she slaps him. "Tough, tough, tough little werewolf," she taunts with the smacks. "Pathetic, pathetic, pathetic." She gazes down at him, and sighs. "Well, at least you're tasty." Quick as lightening, she lowers her head to his neck as he whimpers in pain. She sits up and caresses his neck before licking her fingers as she chuckles. "Yummy." I am within striking distance right behind her, raising the branch. *Please, oh please…* Just as I swing her arm moves, catching the club. It disintegrates into splinters around her fingers. He blood soaked face whips toward me. "Fair attempt, I heard you ages ago."

Oh, dear God save us. I take off running the way I came, only making it a few steps before she appears in front of me, smiling with bloody fangs bared. Blast. The moment I stop moving she grabs the back of my hair, yanks me around, and hurls me onto the grass. My head hits with a thud, and I see stars. The vampyre straddles me, pinning my arms to the ground, not that I am in a fit state to fight. The world will not stop tilting. She lowers her face close enough to kiss. "You are a right pain in the arse, you know that? Burn me, shoot me, sic your wolf on me?" She slaps my face. Hard. Stinging barbs bloom up and down my cheek as if a jellyfish struck me. "Made me look bad to Michael?" She slaps me again, bringing tears. "Oh, is the lady scared? She should be. We just need your brain." She leans down to whisper in my ear, Jamie's blood dripping from her goggles onto my face. I close my eyes. "Your body is forfeit."

As her tongue rolls along my neck, I sob even harder, bringing more cackles. Suddenly, her violently body jerks as she screams bloody murder into the night. My eyes fly open. A ravaged, beaten, bleeding Jamie stands above us both, hands still wrapped around the stake inside the vampyre's back. I didn't hear him coming either. Years of practice stalking prey. Shaking, Jamie yanks the wood out. The vampyre continues shrieking as she rolls next to me. Without missing a heartbeat, Jamie plunges the stake into her heart. In out, in out, drops of blood splattering from the stake onto my face. I watch in horror as she wails in pain as he does it again, and again, and again. I lose count of the blows, but eventually her cries end. He raises the stake above his head again when all of a sudden Jamie cries out in pain. The stake drops as he clutches his chest, his eyes roll back, and he collapses next to the vampyre.

"Jamie!" All the carnage I just witnessed is nothing but a memory when I watch him topple. He's dead. Oh God, he's dead. I sit up and crawl over the dead vampyre to the man I love. "Jamie? Jamie?" I do not believe there is an inch of him not caked in blood. He is a mess with cuts, swollen cheekbones, and even chunks of hair are missing from his bleeding scalp. The neck wound oozes the worst, so I put pressure on it. Rivets of blood still pour between my fingers. "Jamie, please wake up. Jamie?" I cry. I quickly kiss his split lip twice as I shake his shoulder. No. "Jamie!" I slap his face as hard as possible, and his eyes fly open, looking around wildly. "Oh, Jamie," I gasp. I cannot help myself. I shower his face with kisses. "I thought you were—"

"I'm okay," he says, an obvious lie.

"Oh, Jamie," I say as I lower my head onto his shoulder. He groans as I touch his chest. "Oh, God I'm sorry."

"It's fine," he says through gritted teeth. "I just, take off my shirt. I need to see how bad it is."

My quaking hands can barely undo the buttons on his vest and shirt. I gasp again when I see his chest. I was expecting bruises and cuts, not two streaming bullet holes. Two. That means... "Oh, God. I—I—I shot you?"

"They went through him. It's fine."

"But I shot you! Oh, my God," I cry as I cover my mouth. This is not happening. It is not happening. Too much. All too much. "I'm sorry. I'm so sorry. I didn't mean to. Forgive me. I—"

His hand squeezing my wrist to the point of pain keeps the hysteria from taking over. "*Stop it.* Fall apart later, I need you, shug okay? Breathe." I nod and whimper, but force the air in as I rock back and forth. "That's my girl," he whispers. "Good girl. It wasn't your fault. Look at me!" I meet his pained eyes as he breathes as heavily as I do. "You saved my life. Again. You did what you had to. They ain't deep. I'll be okay, I swear it. I'm damn lucky, okay?"

"Lucky? Are you mad? I shot you! We just fell off a bloody dirigible!"

"Well I jumped," he chuckles, then winces in pain. "And we made it, didn't we?"

"For how long? They might not be dead. There could even be others. You could still die due to me. You need a doctor, and I have no clue where we are, let alone how to find one."

"Listen, I can take care of me. And her," he says, glancing at the vampyre. "You just gotta go, okay? Follow the river downstream a piece. I think I smell smoke that way, there have to be people. You run full chisel, okay? Like the devil was chasing ya."

"I am not leaving you!" I say, voice hard.

"Shug, I will be alright. Just do this for me, okay? Here, take my guns and the belt. You may need them."

"Why do I need a gun? Wh—"

"Just do it!" he snaps. With a nod, I unhook the belt laced with silver bullets and his holster. He bites his lip in pain as I move him. "Load them." I shake out the shells to slide in fresh bullets. "I can give you a ten minute head start. I'll try to keep away, but if I come near you, don't hesitate. Aim for the heart, use 'em all if you have to."

"What?" It finally dawns on me. "You're going to—"

"It won't be me in there. You find people, and you keep 'em inside until morning. I'll change back when I can, but don't come looking for me until first light no matter what."

"I understand," I say, slipping the holster and gun belt onto my shoulder.

"Then go. Now. Don't look back."

I nod as I manage to get to my feet. I turn, taking two steps before spinning back around. I kneel beside him and smash my lips against his. This time there is no hesitation. He kisses me back with equal fervor. He tastes of blood, but I could kiss him for days, and judging from the way his mouth moves with mine, he feels the same. I break the seal first. "That is for jumping off a dirigible for me." I give him another quick peck. "See you in the morning." I leap up and begin running.

Ten minutes.

After one minute it grows difficult to breathe, after two I must stop for a few seconds to catch my breath, and at four the stitch in my side might as well be a dagger. Running in a corset is never advisable. I lose a minute to massage it out, and now can run only at a quarter chisel which I consider a victory as I have not run in over two decades. I know I've passed the ten minute mark when I hear a faint howl. I stop dead in my tracks to scan the countryside behind me. Nothing but the night. *Move.* I reach half chisel now with terror fueling my legs.

My heartbeat is so loud in my ears whenever I try to hear footfalls, it blocks all sound save for the rush of the river beside me. Then, just as I am about to collapse, I see it up the hill outlined by the moonlight. A crumbling ruin of a castle half decimated with only two walls forming overrun covered with vegetation remaining. There is no roof, only jagged stone half walls with a few large windows sans glass where the floors used to be. A closer howl scares not only me but the birds perched at various locations around the ruin. This will have to do.

I need to get to higher ground. One of those windows must suffice. I run up to the ruin, which is covered in more ivy than mortar yet the wall slopes like a hill. Despite being elbow deep in foliage, it's as easy as a staircase with abundant foot and handholds. My luck runs out when I reach the top. The third story window is six feet away with only flat stone from here to there. I take a minute to compose myself, allowing the gears in my mind to churn out a solution. My body and mind are well beyond exhausted so none readily presents itself. Perhaps this is good enough. I am sheltered in this small nook where part of the wall remains vertical. I sit, resting in the corner. Yes, this will do. It will have to.

I pull his jacket around tighter, lean my head against the wall, and sit with my knees cuddled to my chest. I fight my closing eyes. I am nowhere near comfortable with rough stones and pebbles underneath not to mention the cold wall for a pillow, but could sleep on a bed of spikes after all that's happened. Eyes open, Verity. Be vigilant.

I manage that for five minutes before my eyes win the war. I must fall asleep because I jerk awake sometime later to the sound of falling rocks. Oh, bugger. Climbing up on all fours is a large, snarling animal with pointed ears and a growl vibrating from his pointed snout. With a gasp, I leap to my feet which enrages him further. I've never seen a wolf, were or otherwise, before but I doubt they are this enormous. He is roughly the same size as in his human form, about six feet long and the same weight. His blackish fur stands up on end along the spine. What really captures my attention is the clack of sharp claws on rock as he stalks closer.

Time to move.

I reach to my left along the flat vertical wall for a raised stone or hole in the mortar. I find one, moving as fast as I can while doing my best to ignore the charging werewolf. For a moment only my fingers keep me from crashing to earth until my foot taps against a centimeters big foothold. My quivering arms and fingers are in agony as I hold on for dear life. Ignore it all and focus. *Focus.* I locate another hole and stone hold, propelling myself forward as the werewolf reaches my nook. About two feet to go. He growls, reaching for me claws first. I shriek as I search madly for another hold. "Go away!"

The monster swipes again, missing my arm by an inch. Bugger. Bugger! I find the last hold and move into the stone enclosure. There is no time to celebrate. The moment I am inside, the werewolf springs toward me, front and back legs stretched out almost the entire length. For a moment I think he might make it, and my heart leaps into my throat. On instinct, I reach for the gun, but only his paw brushes the landing, claws scraping the mortar, as he plunges three stories down. He lands with a painful yelp on the broken stone and grass below. "Jamie!"

When I gaze down, the wolf writhes around on its side attempting to stand. He whimpers as he finds his four legs, though he holds up his front paw like it's injured. "Jamie?" The wolf throws his head back to howl in agony. He throws himself at the wall as if attempting to climb it, leaping from his hind legs. "Jamie, stop. You're going to hurt yourself further."

He whimpers again as if he understands me, though he continues his fool's errand another minute. I watch, hand still hovering near the gun, until he finally gives up and lies down directly below me. I do not know if he is hoping I will fall so he can have a midnight snack or guarding me. Either way, when he begins licking his hurt paw I feel safe enough to lay in my 5X4 enclosure with the cool wind wafting against my skin from the Irish moors. I rest my head on my hands, pulling my legs to my chest with a sigh. What a day. Realized I was in love, shot the man, killed a vampyre, fell off a dirigible, was chased by a werewolf, and now will sleep in a ruined castle with a monster below. I shut my eyes. I absolutely can wait to see what fresh hell tomorrow brings.

CHAPTER ELEVEN

IRISH HOSPITALITY

Bloody, buggery birds. Their melodic happy chirping brings me out of a dead slumber, and I want to roast them alive for it. The sun is just poking its head over the hills when I pry open my eyes. Yesterday's hangover was a mild annoyance compared to the agony occurring now. From head to toe, I ache like nothing I have ever felt before. At first I am afraid to move in fear all my bones are broken, but even if they are I cannot remain here. I groan and whimper as I sit up, my head swimming when I am upright. Biting my lip to stop the whimpers, I spend ten excruciating minutes moving all my appendages to work the stiffness out, tendons and bones cracking like they're breaking. Feels as if they are. When I can move my body without too much effort, I rest for a few minutes before attempting wall climbing. I'd be amazed if I can lift a cat let alone make that distance but have no choice. At least in daylight I can see larger holds. Get this over with. Even with the bigger and more copious wrings this trek is far more painful than last night. Perhaps I need a werewolf pawing at me as incentive. My arms quiver as I stare at the wall. *Do not look down.*

When I reach my stony hill, I collapse in my nook and burst into tears. I sob into the stones of the once great castle now nothing but rubble until I cannot breathe. But deep down I know crumbling is a luxury I cannot afford. I have to find Jamie. Nothing else matters but making sure he is alright. I conjure up his face, his handsome face as he stares at me when his guard is down. The feel of his lips against mine. Within seconds the tears subside, and I can breathe again. Even when he's not present he helps me. My turn. I push myself up, dust myself off, and continue on.

In the light of day, the view is quite lovely. The dark river and hilly, lush green terrain remind me of Somerset. A pang of homesickness grips my soul. The rate things are going I shall never see it again. I'll never ride Barnabas again. Never pet Brutus. I…what is that smell? About halfway to the rendezvous, over the top of the hill, I spot the smoke Jamie smelled lifting from the top of a stone chimney. Probably a farm with warm beds, food, and no need for death defying acts to locate a place to safely sleep. I briefly consider popping there first, but know I shall not get a moment's peace until I set eyes on Jamie. At least I have found civilization.

It takes triple the time back as when I was running for my life, but I know I find the spot of last night's madness from the bloodstained britches, cowboy boots, strips of black shirt, goggles, and bloody stake with a pile of ash beside it. That must be what is left of the vampyre once the sun rose. I hope she felt it, every excruciating second of pain. A little farther down the creek I spot another gruesome sight, a gutted deer lying dead on the ground, grey entrails poking out of its ravaged skin. Dear Lord. As I walk closer, I see smears of blood surrounding it and ragged claw marks on its body and neck. The source of its demise lies close by.

Nude. So very nude.

Splotches of I hope deer blood smeared like war paint everywhere except his derrière, which my eyes immediately appraise. I know I should look away but cannot. I have never seen anyone but myself naked before, never mind a man. A beautiful, virile broad shouldered, tan Adonis of a man I might add. I've viewed paintings and sculptures, but they did not prepare me for this visual bounty. He is so exquisite, taught tight with hard muscles poking out like fleshy peaks, especially his buttocks. Lust overshadows the ever present pain for a few glorious seconds before necessity quashes it. There is no time for ogling. I suppose I have to wake him. Someone might pass and find him like this.

Naked. Gloriously naked. I shake my head. Bloody hell, get control of yourself, Verity. He—

Jamie turns over, and I all but swoon. His chiseled, hairy torso is even bloodier than the back with a musky film all over, even in his hair, but after I assess that my gaze moves southward. The paintings never showed one like *that*. Do they always do that in the morning? I—

Jamie groans, and before his eyes open, I turn my back to him. "Jamie? Jamie, wake up." He doesn't make another sound. "Jamie!" I shout.

Behind me there's another soft groan. I do not dare turn around. "What…" he groans. Seconds later he sighs. "I feel like I fell off a dirigible."

I smile, relief washing over me. "Are you alright?"

"I think so. I'm fucking exhausted."

"Here," I say, holding out his pants behind me. "I found these."

I believe he stands. "I need to clean up first."

"Yes. Right. Of course. I shall just…" I drop the rest of his clothes, jacket and gun belt included, and scurry back the way I came. When I am far enough away, I breathe a sigh of relief. Last thing I need is him catching me letching again. While he is getting the muck off, I should do the same. I am tacky with sweat, blood, and dirt. Oh damn it. My gloves are ripped and ruined beyond repair, as is my dress. Neither are fit for use even as rags. I unbutton my shoes and stockings, hike up what remains of my skirt, and wade into the chilly water. I wash my face and hands, feeling a bit better or at least not as sticky.

At the very least we need to find new clothes, how I know not. We have no money, and the only thing of value on me is my cameo and perhaps the silver bullets, but we'll need the latter. By now the vampyres will have worked out I slipped through their claws again and will move onto the next plot. The guns and Artemis are all we have to defend ourselves against the next assault, which could be at any moment. The gravity of our situation hits me, and I stop washing. We have no clothes, no money, no way of getting any, and no idea where we are, let alone how to get to Galway. For the first time since this nightmare began I haven't a clue how to proceed.

"Your face will stay that way if you keep it like that much longer."

I was so deep in thought I did not notice him approach the creek bed. His wet hair is slicked back and the bloody jacket is buttoned up. He looks as haggard as I am sure I do. I cannot even muster a smile as I spot his eyes apprizing my exposed legs. "How do you feel?" I ask.

"Exhausted. The change always takes it out of me."

Still holding up my skirt, I wade toward him through the calm water."Beyond that, how are you? Your chest, your arm?"

He holds up the arm he broke as a wolf. "Good as new." He half smiles. "I'm, uh, sorry if I scared you last night. If it's any consolation I wasn't trying to hurt you, I don't think."

"Then what…never mind. I'm fine, you're fine, that is all that matters." I lower myself onto the grass to put my stockings and shoes back on. As I roll the dirty fabric up my leg, I notice him out of the corner of my eye watching. At least I am not the only letch around. "I found a house a mile downriver. We should ask for assistance, maybe they'll take pity on us." I glance down at my blood splattered dress. "Or contact the Garda."

"We'll cover the blood with mud, then use the same story we did in Bridgenorth."

"Whatever you say."

"Damn. You must be rundown to nothing too," he says with a chuckle.

"Why is that?"

He walks over to me, holding out his hand to help me stand. "That's the first time you've agreed to *anything* without a fight. Sure you're Verity Hart?"

Even exhausted he's trying to make me feel better. In this instant I want to throw myself into his arms, fall onto the soft grass, and spend the rest of the day with his warmth enveloping me in every conceivable way. I've bloody well earned it. And for a split-second I was worried last night's attack would diminish my love for him. If that did not, I doubt much could. He gazes into my eyes, and as if reading my mind, steps away as if I were about to mawl him. It would certainly make us even. "Let's get to that house," he says.

After smearing mud over the bloodstains, we slowly trudge downstream in silence. We pass the ashes, exchange a look, but continue walking. There is a lot of blood on the grass but the rain will eventually wash it away. I do not think either of us wishes to dwell on what occurred here last night. We pick up the pace until we are safely away from the bad memories.

When we reach the house the smoke still billows. In our beaten states, the small hill may as well be a mountain, but we reach the small grey stone cottage with thatched roof and wooden barn. A pregnant woman close to my age dressed in a worn brown dress and apron, waddles out of the barn with a pail. When she spots us, both her mouth and pail drop. What she must think.

"Dear Lord. Fergus!" she shouts with an Irish accent. The frightened woman maintains her distance until her husband and three small children step out of the house.

He takes one look at us and his long face falls. We must look worse than I thought. "Children go inside. *Now*." The children obey. Fergus moves toward his wife, putting a protective arm around her shoulder. "What do you want?"

"We were on our way to Galway when our coach lost a wheel," Jamie says. "We've been walking for hours, and yours is the first house we've passed. We just need something to eat, a place to lie down, maybe some clothes if you can spare any."

Both sets of eyes narrow. They are not buying the lie. "You lost your luggage as well?" the wife asks.

"You were taking a coach instead of a train?" asks Fergus. "And why are you covered in mud?"

I glance at Jamie, but his mouth hangs open. He looks about ready to fall over he's so bone-weary. "You are right, we are lying," I say. "We were attacked last night. We barely survived, and I would tell you more but it is simply too unbelievable a story. All you need to know is that we are good people in desperate, *desperate* need of aid. I swear to God above no harm shall come to you or yours if you aid us. I am begging you. He—here," I say, taking off my grandmother's cameo, "as payment. I—we don't have anything else of value on us at present. Please."

I shove the cameo in my grubby scabbed hands at the woman, who appears both disgusted and ashamed all at once. "No, that's not necessary. Fergus..."

He meets his wife's eyes and sighs. "Come in," Fergus says reluctantly.

"Thank you, thank you so much," I almost cry.

"Thank you," Jamie says. He takes a step and stumbles. Our trek was too much for him. I throw his arm over my shoulder for him to lean on me. It hurts, but I help him inside.

The inside of the cottage is dark with a roaring fireplace, table and chairs, and three children under age ten playing with their large dog. It whimpers when we enter and runs toward the back of the house. The children chase after him as the woman puts the pail on the table. Fergus shuts the door. "We have some fresh bread and apples, and Maggie can make you eggs."

"I need to sleep," Jamie says.

"There's a bed in the back room," Fergus says.

"Thank you," I say, leading Jamie toward the bedroom. It has a double bed and twin in the corner for one of the children. He doesn't even take off his boots before falling into bed. "I need about three more hours, then I'll be fighting fit, I swear. You should sleep too."

"I'm fine. Besides, one of us has to figure out how we are getting to Galway. We cannot linger here too long."

"Umh." He sighs, and one second later he's asleep. Poor man, I am shocked he made it all this way. He went through far worse than I. Shot, broken, metamorphsized in a single hour. I remove his boots and cover him as best I can with the brown wool blanket before brushing a stray strand of wet hair off his forehead. He looks so peaceful there. I could curl up beside him in that bed, fall asleep in his warm arms, but there is far too much left to do. First on the daunting list, clean myself up. People in the East End would shy away from me as is. I would not blame them one whit.

The family is still on guard when I come out, watching as I move toward them to sit at the table. "He's asleep. Thank you so much for the bed. I'll, um, take that bread now." I take one bite of the fresh bread and realize I am starving. Within seconds the bread is gone, along with an apple. "Thank you. Thank you, you're so kind. I shall not forget it. When I return home, I shall make sure I send you compensation for all you have done, I swear it."

"That's not necessary," Maggie says. "It's our Christian duty."

As it is my Christina duty to send them fifty pounds for their troubles. "Thank you," I say with a smile before taking another apple. "How far away are we from Galway?"

"Thirty miles," Fergus says. "The train station in Ballinasloe is seven."

Which would be excellent save for the fact we have no money and cannot ask these people for any. Perhaps we can walk to town, find a pawn broker, I don't know. Except even if we do the vampyres are most likely waiting at the Galway train and dirigible stations for us. Blast. A coach? Far too expensive even with the cameo. We might have no choice but to walk. It would take a full day, and we would have to sleep outside. Together. Under the stars. Our bodies pressed against one another to keep warm, his arm around me, his breath hot against my—

"Are you feeling unwell, ma'am? You're flushed," Maggie says.

"I'm sorry? Oh…I need to get clean, change my clothes and whatnot."

"I'll see what I can find," Maggie says, retreating into the bedroom.

I enjoy my second apple until she returns with a calico dress and bar of soap. I accept them gratefully and retreat to the river. My beautiful, Saville Row dress is ruined and the blood stains have reached even my corset and chemise. Blast. I undo my hair, which flows down to my waist, and wade into the cold river. It's no hot bath but still feels heavenly as I wash the night's horrors away. I scrub until all the grime, the blood, all is gone. Well, not all. My body is covered in bruises the size of countries and raw cuts I do not recall earning. Disgusting. The calico dress is too large for me so I forgo my corset and let my tangled hair stay loose to dry.

With basic needs covered, it is time to formalize a plan. Walking is the best option, but we get to Barna and then what? They'll probably be watching my trunk, so we have no way to defend ourselves save for two guns and the Artemis. That against a house full of vampyres? No. We need help. Luckily, I knew where we can try.

When I return up to the cottage, hammering in the barn draws me in. I find Fergus attaching a plank of wood to a horse's gate. It's a small barn with only a small chicken coop in the far corner where the eldest boy collects eggs, and a cow next to the horse paddock. What really captures my attention is the metallic monopede covered in spider webs near the coop. I have not seen one of those in years. They fell out of fashion a decade ago when everyone went doolally over bicycles. It is easy to understand why. The monopede is nothing more than a six foot circular track with a rubber tyre around the outside, a precursor to the bicycle yet without the physical fitness benefit. Affixed to the brass rim inside is a cracked glass windscreen with a seat and leavers attached to the base, leading to a small steam powered motor on the back that moves the tyre, propelling the rider forward at ten miles per hour. They never completely caught on as they are incredibly hard to ride with only those with exceptional balance or months of practice able to stay on. I fall into the latter category. I believe God just provided our way to Galway.

"You have a monopede?" I ask.

"Aye," Fergus says. "Won it in a county raffle years ago."

I brush away the cobwebs from it, sneezing from the dust. "Do you use it?"

"I forgot we even had it. The engine broke years ago. We never used it, so there was no point spending money to fix it."

I examine the tyre which is cracked in places but still usable. "Do you have tools?"

"Why?"

"I wish to see if I can repair it."

He does a double take. "You?"

"Yes, me," I say with my best smile. "If I do get it running, may we borrow it? I promise to return it to you later."

"I, um, suppose," he says.

"Marvelous! Thank you. Thank you so much." My smile grows. "One more favor, if I may? Can I use your tools?"

After assisting me in moving the contraption outside so I have room to move, I get to work. First, I examine the rest of the machine to make sure the levers and brake pedals are not the source of the problem, but aside from a moderate rust problem, solved in part by oil and grease, it seems to be in excellent shape. The engine is another story. At first glance there seems to be nothing wrong with it, no bent valves or eroded bolts, which only makes my task harder. I have to take the entire thing apart and rebuild it, which shall take hours. As I do, I'm aware the Reilly family occasionally passes by or sits down to watch me in the case of the young girl. With a proud smile, she even helps me screw in a few bolts before her mother calls her in. I do believe hours pass, but as always when I work they feel like mere minutes. The world all but vanishes except for these pieces of metal, and the puzzle they present.

As I re-couple the outside shell, in my periphery I notice another person behind me remaining motionless for a full minute. I finish screwing in the last bolt and glance back. Jamie stands staring at me and my mess with a small, private smile on his face. I wipe the sweat from my brow. "Oh, hello," I say. "How was your nap?"

"Great," he says, strolling toward me. He appears rested and even dapper in a loose white shirt and brown trousers. His black cowboy boots were salvageable as was the holster and belt he sports. "I was just, uh, admiring your hair ornament there."

"Oh." I pull out the screwdriver I used to hold my hair in place out. My damp hair falls.

"So, um, what's going on here? What did I miss?"

"Just repairing the monopede so we can continue on. I believe I located the problem. One of the pressure valves was sluggish, most likely not firing in time with the others. I repaired it as best I can. I just have to reattach the engine to the levers, fill it with water, and to Galway we go. Should be about half an hour more." I gaze up to see Jamie with awe in his eyes. "What?"

He remembers himself, shaking it away. "Nothing. Uh, can I help?"

"Actually, yes." I hand him the engine which is about the size of a shoebox. "Hold this in place, please."

He bends down beside me, putting it too far up on the monopede. "Here?"

"No, right here." I place my exposed hand on top of his to guide it in place. My hand lingers, flesh on flesh, as our eyes meet. For a moment, only a moment there is nothing else in the world but that touch. But what a moment. After a quick smile, I pull away. *Focus*, Verity. Easier thought than done with him in such close proximity. We catch each other stealing glances once or twice, and each time I blush. I recognise the shift inside him with each glance. His guard is down, either from exhaustion or last night's events. Perhaps it was watching me fall. I can just imagine it now. I am pulled over the edge with the vampyre tumbling after. There's no thought involved, emotion overpowers his rationality. There is no guarantee he'll catch her, but he takes the leap regardless. For me. If that isn't love, or at least the seeds of it, I do not know what is. But this is not the time nor the place to capitalize on this fact. I attach the engine and when I add the water, the engine begins puffing away without a problem. I smile at Jamie, who proudly smiles back. I am *very* good at what I do. Galway ahoy.

I change into trousers, Fergus' white shirt, and twist my hair into a bun so nothing gets caught in the wheel. The Reilly's also provide us with a knapsack with cheese, bread, apples, and directions to a road half a mile away before we say good-bye. I know they refused it, but I leave the cameo in the bedroom anyway. It is the least I can do. The *very* least. With food in our bellies, clean clothes, and a mode of transportation, we take our leave. God bless the Reilly family.

"Irish hospitality, huh?" Jamie says as we walk to the monopede. "Can't be beat." I certainly hope not. I am banking on it. The monopede does not work well on grass, not enough traction, so we push it to the road. When we do reach the gravel road surrounded by rolling fields as emerald green as all have claimed they are, we take a break to allow the engine to heat up, steam billowing higher and higher each second. "You ever ridden on one of these?"

"Yes. Father purchased one years ago at the behest of a friend but David and I used it more than he did. You?"

"Nope. Saw too many people fall off 'em to ever try."

"Then I guess you are at my mercy, Mr. McQueen," I say with an amused grin, which he reciprocates at double radiance. God, I adore that smile. There isn't a hint of insincerity. They only recommend one person ride at a time but two is possible if not tricky. Jamie sits first, then having no choice—not that I mind—I lower myself onto his lap. "Sorry." His body tenses the moment my bum touches his body. "You'll have to hold me."

"Um, okay." Hesitantly, he wraps his arms around my waist, hands meeting at the base of my sternum. I think we are both aware of my loose breasts resting on the tops of his arms as much as the fact I am pressed against the most intimate area of his, the one that held such fascination for me this morning.

"It's like riding a bicycle. I shall start slowly until we find our centre of gravity. When we do, try not to move too much," I instruct.

"Aye, aye captain."

After affixing on my goggles, another present from the Reilly family, I move the brass lever to release the brakes, edging us forward at less than a snail's pace. We wobble but do not fall, even as I increase the speed, the steam engine puffing away as the tire gyrates at an equal pace. Jamie clamps tighter around my chest. I smile to myself. I have the feeling I shall enjoy this rise immensely and plan to savor every second. And away we go. I can only pray he forgives me for what's to come.

*

The road is almost deserted, with only the odd horse drawn carts passing us as we overtake them. More than a few even smile and wave. Ireland is certainly growing on me. It is a beautiful country with lush green grass folding onto rocky crags, blooming purple heather, gentle hills with sheep and thick flowering trees, and more decaying ruins. Churches and castles reclaimed by the land. It's breathtaking. And with the man I love's arms around me, his head resting upon my shoulder when his neck aches, his hot breath against my bare flesh, this is like a beautiful dream. Better. Once or twice I have to adjust myself on his lap to get comfortable, and I can feel that familiar bulge growing. At his behest we stop then. I just smile to myself as he takes a walk to calm himself. When we finally cross the stone bridge, salmon jumping out of the water to greet us, into Galway six hours later, I am so relieved I could cry. We did it. We made it. There but for the grace of God.

Galway, another sea village, is most reminiscent of Treddur with all manner of ship from steam to dirigible in the sapphire blue harbor, tall yet bijou shops, some stone and others whitewashed yet one right next to the other in one in a straight line along the two lane main road. We are not the only people enjoying the summer day. Street performers juggle or play instruments, as inhabitants stroll to their homes and pubs as we drive by what must be the heart of the town, Eyre Square, done in the Georgian style with ash trees, stone wall around the perimeter with cannons on display. With our outdated mode of travel, me in men's clothes, and Jamie's guns visible, we cause quite the stir. People actually point and stare. How rude. "Ideas?" Jamie asks as we roll out of the square.

To avoid lying, I do not answer. Instead I don't utter a word as I drive around until I find the waterfront where a veritable fleet of fishing boats sail in or out of the bay. I park the monopede at the beginning of a long wooden dock with a dozen or so moored ships along the expanse sharing the calm blue water the seagulls and swans lazing about. "What are we doing here?" asks Jamie.

"Trust me." He must because he follows me to the end of the quay past the net and wood lobster cages where an old man in a fishing cap with multiple hooks adorning it winds up rope beside his small blue and white vessel, *The Caledonia* scrawled across the side. "Excuse me, sir?"

"Yes, lass?"

"Could you please help us? We're a bit lost. We're trying to get to the Roarke family island, and—"

Out of nowhere, Jamie's hand wraps around my arm, jerking it to cut short my words. "Sorry. Excuse us." Almost snarling, he pulls me away from the fisherman. "What the hell are you doing? I told you we're not going there."

"Well, circumstances have changed a bit since you made that proclamation. We have no money, we have no clothes, we have a lackluster weapons reserve. We need help. And at this point, we cannot exactly be picky where it comes from."

"We will figure something else out."

I fold my arms across my chest. "I am all ears. But need I not remind you we are in the lion's den now. The vampyres know we escaped, and they know we are coming. We cannot trust anyone else in this village. We are in dire straits. Even if we had sufficient funds, we cannot check into an inn on the chance they alert Michael to our arrival, same with the dirigible station to retrieve our luggage. There is no other option available, Jamie. Not if we desire to see another day let alone save my brother. So suck up your damneable pride, and let's go meet your family."

"I—we—you," he stammers before groaning. Logic reigns supreme once more. "They probably won't even see us. Hell they'll probably kill me then hold you hostage. Or worse."

I cock an eyebrow. "Only one way to find out, Mr. McQueen." He scowls, but when his shoulders slump I know I have him. That was far easier than I'd anticipated. I smile before sidestepping him to return to the fisherman. "Excuse us, I apologize for that."

"You look like him," the man says to Jamie.

"I'm sorry?" Jamie asks.

"James Roarke. You look just like him. Different eyes, though. His were blue."

"You knew him?" I ask.

"Oh, aye. He bought me my first pint over fifty years ago. Hard man, but he'd have to be to rule that lot. You one of them?"

"One of what?" Jamie asks coldly.

"One of *them*. You know. All of us in town do. Vampyres to the left, werewolves to the right, probably some fae folk hiding in the hills, though that's only a rumor. If you're a Roarke you must be one."

"You know of the vampyres? What about the one called Michael in Barna?" I ask.

"Sorry, love. We try to stay away from that lot as much as possible around here. We tolerate the wolves because they keep themselves to themselves and haven't hurt anyone in centuries."

"That ain't exactly accurate," Jamie says with a hard edge.

Squeezing his muscled arm, his tension wanes. "So, is there a way we reach the island? We haven't any money, but we can get you some in a day or so."

He glances at me, then Jamie. "You sure you want to go there?"

I say "yes", and Jamie says "no" in unison.

I narrow my eyes at him before turning back to the fisherman. "We do. Is there a ferry?"

"No ferry, but I can take you. I was heading that way anyway. It's only two miles, won't take long. But I won't stick around. You have to find your own way back."

"That's fine," I say. "We appreciate this so much. You are saving our lives."

"Or ending them a hell of a lot more quickly," Jamie mutters.

We manage to load the monopede onto the boat, a small sixty footer with piles of nets and coils of rope leaving little room for passengers. It reeks of dead fish and other rotting meat with splatters of blood and fish guts all over the wooden deck and roped nets large enough to catch a giant squid. The view makes up for the stench. I take in the blue waves crashing onto the rocky shores, the lone white lighthouses holding vigil on high cliffs, the emerald green hills, even the flocks of gulls gliding into the water for dinner, and people strolling along the shore content in the beautiful day. I seem to be enjoying it far more than Jamie, who hasn't looked at me once since we left port, but judging from how tense his shoulders are, he is not taking in nature's visual bounty. When we reach open water, I join him aft. He's scowling again and so deep in thought, he does not notice me.

"You know, if you keep your face that way too long, it will stick," I chide playfully.

He doesn't smile. "I'm not in the mood."

"Jamie, it will be fine. I know it."

"Based on what? Our great luck so far? You vast experience with werewolves? You can't know, shug."

"Well, we've gotten this far. We've survived vampyres, bullets, Newton's law. Whatever comes next if it isn't, we will conquer it as we have everything else." I entwine my hand in his. "Together."

He glances down at our hands then up at me, brown eyes grim as a reaper before pulling away from my touch. "We'll see," he says as he stomps away from me.

Oh, please let me be right about this. *Please.*

Our destination soon sails into view, a small island with high cliffs where a small lighthouse is perched above, and rocky flatlands with scattered trees and tufts of grass breaking through every so often. Not the most welcoming place I have ever seen. Atop the highest point of the island sits a huge three-storey grey stone medieval castle complete with two turrets that I fear may soon begin expelling arrows from the narrow slits that act as windows. Newgate redux. It has the same friendly feeling of the prison as well. This is a hard, foreboding corner of the world that all but shouts, "You are not welcome. Abandon hope all ye who enter here." My resolve that all shall work out in our favor cracks, at least on the inside. When Jamie glances at me with that same scowl, I smile my brightest. He just turns back around.

The hollow ring of a tolling bell echoes like a death knell from the castle as we pull up to the small wooden dock with two smaller crafts tied up. We disembark with the monopede after saying, well I say our farewells to the good Samaritan. Jamie pushes the monopede down the dock without a word. I follow behind. The dock ends at a stone path that must wind up the steep hill to the castle, though I cannot see our destination as the path is surrounded by thick foliage. We make it a hundred exhausting meters up when Jamie stops dead in his tracks. Oh, this cannot be good. Jamie does not acknowledge my presence as I step beside him. His head cocks to the side, and that expression of serious determination returns. Trouble.

"Should we—"

"Let *them* come to us."

I cock the Artemis and wait. Jamie's hand lingers near his gun. Oh, please let me be right about this. A second later, I hear footsteps running towards us. Jamie remains stone still, not even blinking until two men round the corner. I wouldn't put either of them above age twenty, but are still imposing, easily as large and tall as Jamie. The one on the right looks remarkably like him as well with the same jaw and black hair, while the one on the left's hair is a lighter brown with a pinched nose. Their steely expressions, another family trait, falter a tad when they set eyes upon Jamie, or the guns I suppose. The boys exchange a glimpse but continue walking.

"This is, um, private property," righty says with a thick Irish brogue. "You shouldn't be here."

"My name is James McQueen. My mother was Anne Roarke, daughter of James Roarke, former pack leader. My companion and I want to speak to whoever is in charge now."

"What about?" the one on the left asks, eyes not moving from the gun centimeters from Jamie's hand.

"That's between me and him."

The boys look at each other again, hoping that the other will know how to proceed. Righty turns back to us. "Give us the guns first."

"Or I can just shoot you both and go up anyway," Jamie counters. The boys are taken aback at this prospect, but Jamie smiles. "If I meant harm it would have happened by now. I swear on my mother, your kin's grave I am here without evil intentions. That will have to be enough." He takes a step toward them, and their eyes double in size. "Or you can try for my guns, but I sure hope you ain't that stupid. Your choice."

Every muscle in the boy's faces tense in horror at the mere prospect. "Follow us," righty says. And I thought werewolves would be tougher.

We walk a quarter mile up the path to the castle, the boys glancing back on occasion to see if we are up to something. I smile to reassure them, but it does nothing to assuage their fears. A bird chirps and they jerk from fright. Who knew werewolves could be such 'fraidy cats. There are more surprised people of all ages as we draw closer to the castle, some carrying sacks, other pushing carts or cleaning brush from around the mortar. I doubt they get many visitors on Werewolf Isle, so we are a unique sight. I maintain my Lady Hart smile and receive a few back in return.

The inside of the small castle—well small by castle standards—is dark with actual torches instead of gas lamps hanging between tapestries of knights riding alongside wolves or graphic battle scenes like something out of a nightmare. The passage ends at the great hall. At the centre of the cavernous stone room is a huge coat-of-arms with a wolf carved onto a metal plate, which hangs over a well worn maroon upholstery chair fit for a king. On either side of the arms are portraits of men who, though some have red hair or have different noses, are obviously Jamie's relatives. The second to last portrait might as well be of my McQueen. Must be James Roarke, his grandfather. Our light haired escort tells his companion, "I'll go get Grand-Da," before leaving.

"Who is your grandfather?" I ask.

The boy and Jamie do not take their eyes off one another. "Our pack leader."

"Oh." I am too nervous to remain still, so I saunter around the large space taking a better look at the portraits. The boy takes no notice of me. The first painting appears to be five hundred years old, judging from the hairstyle and clothes. The plaque underneath reads "William Roarke." The first of a dynasty ending with James and finally Albert Roarke. Compared to his predecessors Albert has grey hair, thinner lips, and wrinkles around his eyes and mouth, but still inherited the Roarke good looks. James was much younger when he ascended to the throne, about my age. "Is this your grandfather? Albert?"

For the first time the boy acknowledges me. "Yes."

"How is he related to James?"

"James was my great-grandfather," the boy says.

Which makes the man coming to greet us Jamie's uncle. He grew up with Anne. If Jamie cares, it does not show. He remains expressionless as does our guard. What a merry family. Another minute passes before we hear footsteps on the stone floor from more than one person. I quickly move beside Jamie, whose back straightens to its maximum length. He's had years to perfect his intimidating stance and gaze. It probably worked on the Jesse James gang so why not the Roarke clan?

Albert literally leads the pack of five men with ages ranging from sixty to sixteen. Not a one is happy to see us. Glares all around. Irish hospitality indeed.

"Is this him?" Albert asks as he struts in.

"He wouldn't give up his guns, Grand-Da," our guard says.

"Did you even try, Kieran?" Albert asks.

"They were wise enough not to," Jamie says. "Guess we're about to find out if brains run in the family."

"If you're any indication, they aren't," Albert says as he sits on his throne. The others flank him on either side, all folding their arms across their wide chests. "Not that you've given me any proof that what you claim is true."

"Then you must be blind, *uncle*."

Albert bristles, a familiar scowl crossing his face. "Likeness proves nothing. And even if it did, it has been over sixty years since my sister was stolen from us. You are not pack."

"Nor do I have any desire to be. I want to be here as much as you want me here, believe me, but we have no place else to go."

"All we are asking for is a fresh set of clothes, some food, and a bed for the night," I say.

"We? And who are you? Another long lost relative, or my nephew's whore?"

Judging from the snarl, I know Jamie's about to literally go for the jugular as his uncle desires. Jamie takes a step toward Albert, but I sidestep in front of him to act as a shield. He bumps into my back, and I hold onto his forearms from behind, "I am the Lady Verity Hart, daughter of Lord Edmund Hart, Tenth Earl of Carlisle and a member of the House of the Lords, along with sister to the famed inventor D.V. Hart. And I swear on my family's honor this man is your nephew, son of Anne Roarke, your beloved sister. Now we did not come to cause trouble, we are simply looking for familial or Christian charity. If that is not enough, I can compensate you for your hospitality at a later date. But I ask, no sir I *beg*, please take pity on us, if not for our sakes then for your sister's. This is her only child, your kin, who has never asked for anything before. All he desires now is mercy. As do I. Please, Mr. Roarke. *Please.*"

The wolf studies me with hard blue eyes which I cannot read. "I don't think—"

"Oh, Albert, do shut up," a woman with an English accent says from the other room. All eyes move toward the door as a short, not even topping five feet tall, frail old woman easily in her nineties dressed in all black slowly walks in with the use of a cane. "Of course they can stay."

"Mam, we don't know anything about them," Albert says. "I—"

She whacks his arm with her cane. "What's the matter with you?"

"Mam!" he says, rubbing his arm.

"It is obvious he is kin. Any fool can see that. Even you. You are just looking for a fight because you're bored. Well, you are not picking it with my grandson and his mate. They are staying as long as they need, and that is final." Albert's mouth snaps shut. The other men cow their heads when her gaze passes over them. The real Alpha has arrived. She moves toward us next. "Now you, boy. Come here so I can get a better look at you." I release his arms and step aside so Jamie can comply. "Bend down. Do not make an old woman crane her neck."

"Yes, ma'am," he says as he kneels.

She examines him as if he were a fine painting. "You are James reborn, you truly are. Except for the eyes, those belong to your father." She frowns. "Forgive an old woman lad, but I cannot seem to recall your name."

"James. Jamie McQueen, ma'am."

She nods. "That's right. I am surprised Christopher agreed to the name, but I guess he would have done anything for our Annie. Your father wrote us, you know, after you were born to let us know about you and her. He always was a thoughtful boy. He was a good father? Raised you right?"

"He was the best, ma'am."

"Stop calling me ma'am. We're family. It's Nan." She gazes into his eyes in search of something. "Yes, he did a good job. I can see it. I knew he would, better than we would have. Your grandfather wanted to snatch you back when he heard Annie died, but your place was with your father as Annie would have wanted. Yet here you are. You have returned to the bosom of your family." She glances at me. "And you've bought your beautiful wife with you."

"We are not—"

"Yes, I did," Jamie cuts in. "This is my wife. Verity."

The old woman smiles. "You both look exhausted and filthy. Let's get you taken care of before you explain why you're in such a sorry state, and how we can help. Duncan, show them up to the spare room on the second floor in the east wing at the end of the hall."

"Yes, Nan," the dark haired boy says. "This way."

"Thank you so much," I say as I leave the room. "Everyone."

There are more portraits and tapestries on the hallway walls from eras long past, but I cannot stop to view them as Duncan and Jamie practically run toward the stone staircase to the second floor. There are no people in the halls, though shadows fall in the corners, giving me chills. I hate castles, so gloomy and cold. The ruin from last night was far homier than this tomb. Our destination is behind a large wooden door on the second floor, a dusty, darkened room. "Someone will be up to bring you wood for the fire," Duncan says.

"Thank you," I say.

The boy nods and walks away. I shut the door as Jamie opens the shutters to let the air and light in, though it does little good. Our room is as cheerless as the rest of the house. It has a double bed with carved wooden headboard and animal pelt comforter, bookcase, armoire, wooden window seat, and dark green fainting couch with old dolls on it. The only gaiety in the room originates from numerous small watercolours on the wall of the castle and grounds with "A.R." scrawled in the bottom corners. What really captures my attention is the portrait above the fireplace of a young girl with black hair, green eyes, pale skin, and very familiar sweet smile. The plaque below reads, "Anne Maud Roarke, 1816-1834." My mouth drops open.

"What?" Jamie asks as he moves beside me. He looks at the portrait, all the colour draining from his face.

"She was beautiful," I say.

"Yeah," he says so quietly I barely hear. He just stares at the painting with confusion, which becomes torment like a turning tide.

"What is the matter?"

"This is…the first time I've ever seen her. I mean, Pa described her, but there were no photographs then. He didn't even have a locket or nothing with her likeness. I never knew what she really looked like. Until now. This is…" He cannot finish the sentence. I suppose it's as if a missing puzzle piece finally found, yet the puzzle was destroyed years ago. My hand finds his. Our fingers entwine together. He closes them, then without taking his eyes off the portrait, he pulls me closer to his side. I know precisely what he needs. I put my arms around his waist and rest my head on his chest as his arm encircles my waist. Even tough werewolves require a hug on occasion.

The knock on the door a few seconds later breaks the spell. Shaking his head, Jamie pulls away, no doubt embarrassed by the momentary loss of the strong façade he clings to. "Come in."

A woman in livery enters carrying a jug of water with cousin Kieran behind with a pile of wood, which they set down in the appropriate places. "Someone else is getting you clothes and food," Kieran says. "Do you need help with the fire?"

"I can manage," Jamie says.

"Thank you," I say as the two depart. Alone again.

He is all business again. As Jamie works on the fire, with the occasional glance at the portrait above, I slide onto the window seat. "So, what do you think?"

"About?"

"Here. This. The family. I think your grandmother's a treasure."

"If you say so."

I know by now when he does not wish to talk. Instead, I gaze out the window at the people below. Servants cart wood or coal in wheelbarrows inside the castle while men in casual clothes, more Roarke's by the look of them, walk and talk around the courtyard. As a minute or two pass while Jamie builds the fire, I realize I have not seen another female not in service. I wonder…what on Earth is that? I move my finger over some indentations in the wood. When I glance down, I notice words have been painted over but remain visible despite this. I smile when I realize what it says. "Jamie. Come here."

He finishes lighting the fire before stepping over. "What?"

I stand and guide his hand to the spot. "Feel. Look. A.R. + C.M. with a heart around. Your mother probably carved this. This must have been her room!"

Jamie yanks his hand away as if the wood were on fire. "Maybe," he says, walking to the bookcase in the corner as far from the seat as possible.

"I can just imagine it," I say as I sit on the window seat once more. "There she was, sitting in this very spot waiting for the man she loved to climb through her window in the dead of night. She's nervous, excited, elated, about to jump out of her skin from anticipation until she hears the thump of the ladder outside the window. He leaps inside like a faeiry tale prince, literally whisks her off her feet, and carries her to bed as they both had been dreaming of all day. You were probably conceived in this very room. I—"

"Will you please stop talking?" he snaps, baring his teeth with a sneer. "Shut up. Just shut up, okay? You're driving me crazy."

I am taken aback by his vehemence. "Why? What is the matter now?"

"You're just...too damn excited and happy, alright? You think everything is great and wonderful and perfect, but it ain't. That Albert—"

"Oh, he was just posturing. Your grandmother will not let harm come to us."

"You don't know that, shug. You're too damn trusting." He starts pacing like a caged animal. "I don't like this, not a bit. I have a powerful bad feeling about this whole thing. That old woman has some angle. There is something I ain't seeing. Something...bad. I sure as hell didn't like the way they were eyeing you. They're gonna get me out of the way and try for you, I know it. I do. They're as bad as the damn vampyres. Worse maybe. At least those bastards don't pretend to be anything but what they are. No, we're leaving. It ain't safe here. Especially not for you. They're gonna hurt you. I won't let them. I won't let them get you. Not one damn hair on your head. I'll kill them first, every last one of them. We—"

He's frightening me now. Did he feel this helpless when I was being irrational? I rush over to him, grabbing his arms to stop the pacing. "Stop. Just stop. You are making yourself crazy."

"Crazy was coming here! I can't believe I let you talk me into this. I—"

"Jamie, stop! Just stop!" He stops moving though his nostrils continue to flare. "Look at me. *Look at me*," I order, voice hard. His hard eyes meet mine. "This is a lot to take in, I know. You are exhausted and overwhelmed, and it is making you go a bit mad right now. But there is nothing to fear, I know it to my bones. They have no reason to harm us. Deep down you know that. We will be fine here. We will be safe here, I swear it. We will simply…continue to look out for one another as we have done from the very beginning. You may not trust them, but trust *me*. Do you trust me?"

He remains silent for a few seconds, breathing heavily, before saying, "Yes."

"That means more than words can say. Thank you."

"You're welcome," he says, glancing away.

I would press, but have no desire to take advantage of him. Much. "Good. Come on, you need to lie down." Taking his hand once more, I lead him to the bed, which without further prompting he falls onto face first with a sigh.

I start pulling off his boots, but he sits up, saying, "You don't have to—"

"You have been taking care of me for days, let me return the favor." He mulls my proposition over before begrudgingly lying back down. I tug off his boots and socks. "Better? Pistols next." He allows me to remove the arm straps and drop the holster beside the boots. His shoulders are still as tight as a banker holding purse strings. I bite my lower lip. Dare I? Fortune favors the bold, Verity. "I can…do something else to help. But it would require touching you."

"What do you have in mind, shug?" he chuckles.

"Just a shoulder massage. David does it when I am strained. If you are not comfortable, I do not have to—"

"You just spent all day sitting on my lap, shug. Hands on my shoulders is nothing."

"Okay." Before I lose my courage, I perch on the bed beside him and place my hands on his clenched shoulders, kneading the knots out. I'm not wearing gloves, so when my bare thumbs brush against his exposed neck, I savor it. "Is this alright?"

"More than alright, shug. Go to town." As I work on his shoulders, the rest of him relaxes as well. Thank God. I was growing concerned he might spontaneously combust. "That feels real nice. You sure are good with your hands." I work out a few knots, and he all but melts under my fingers. "I'm sorry I yelled at you. Again. Guess you're used to it by now, huh?"

"No apology necessary. Even the strongest of us lose our way from time to time. Then we just need someone to show us the way back."

He grins. "Wise words."

"I only steal from the best, Mr. McQueen." With his shoulders tended to, I move down his back, kneading out those hard spots as well. "You are more knots than muscle."

"Been a rough week," he says after a weak chuckle.

"The worst is over."

"You know, when you say it, I almost believe it." I massage in silence, my grin growing with each contented groan I inflict. When I make it all the way down to his waist, to his sides, he chuckles and tries to squirm away. "Quit."

"Oh, someone's ticklish I see."

When I tickle again he laughs, while trying to push my hands away. "Stop! Stop!" I titter as he wiggles under my torture, and actually guffaw when he flips over, grabs my wrists, and rolls me onto my back for retribution. Straddling me, I half heartedly try to push him away as I twist and turn against his tricky fingers. "How do you like it? Huh? Huh?"

"Stop," I laugh. "Uncle. Uncle!"

He relents for a moment, pretends to consider a truce, then says, "Hell no." The onslaught begins anew with my laughter ringing out as he tortures me with his fingertips. He stops a few seconds later, smiling down at me as I beam up at him. This man. This marvelous, breathtaking, dazzling, bewitching man. The world vanishes, leaving nothing but him and me and this astonishing, magical thing passing between us. This...*love*. For a moment, it is as if all the secrets of the universe have been presented to him and deep happiness overflowing from his eyes, replaced almost immediately with something akin to panic. I am losing him again. "I can't—"

He attempts to rise, but I lock my legs around his waist, giving him no quarter. "*No*."

He is not running from me, from us this time. His terror transforms to confusion as he meets my determined eyes. Slowly, as if I were about to pet a tiger at the zoo, I reach up to stroke his stubbled cheek. He flinches as if my touch would scald him but does not stop me. I run my fingers lightly over his cheek, his strong jaw, his furrowed brow with a feather light embrace. That confusion fades with the first caress, replaced with a deep craving. He stays perfectly still, not a blink, not a twitch, except for his chest heaving as if he had just run straight from England. I have never seen a man so frightened before, so in conflict, but I will not stop. My thumb traces his lips. His hands tighten around the animal pelt as if he was hanging onto a lifeline. He yearns to touch me, to lose control as much as I ache for him to. I move my hand to his fist, loosening his grip and weaving his fingers with mine again. "Jamie…"

The knock on the door obliterates all my hard won effort. We're both so startled we jerk, breaking the spell. "Let me go," he whispers harshly. "Come in!"

I release him, and he has enough time to roll away and I to sit up before a young servant boy steps in with a tray of food. "Sir, Mrs. Roarke asks that you meet her in the library once you've settled in."

"I'm settled enough," he says as he stands. "Take me to her."

"Jamie, we have not finished—"

"You need to rest," he orders. "It's been a long day. Eat, sleep, read, do whatever. Just stay in the room until I come get ya. Don't go wandering around alone."

"Jamie—" He follows the boy out walks out the door before I can finish.

That…! Ugh! I grab one of the pillows and scream into it. After a few seconds the frustration is bearable enough to stop. I toss the pillow back, flopping onto it. He is insufferable! Anne stares across the room at me. "Was his father this much bloody trouble?" Her frozen smile speaks for her. "Thought so."

With a sigh, I flip on my side, resting my head on my hands. So close yet so far away. But still I cannot help to smile. I saw it, only for an instant, but it *was* there. Love. He's hiding it, possibly even from himself, but it was unmistakable even to a novice like me. Jamie McQueen is in love with me. He *loves* me. Now I simply have to convince him of it. Every inch of him is struggling against it, but if there is a force on earth strong enough to win against his stubbornness, it is love. "Anne, if you can hear me, if your spirit is watching over your son as I hope it is, help me. *Help me.*"

As I utter the last syllable a cool breeze wafts in from the window, carrying with it the scent of the sea. "Thank you." I close my eyes with a grin. I knew coming here was a marvelous idea.

CHAPTER TWELVE

IN A DEN OF WOLVES

Another bloody knock on the door draws me out of peaceful slumber, the first I've had in days. According to the clock only two hours have passed, but the sun has almost set. Despite the sudden wake up, I am instantly alert. "Come in."

The same female servant from before walks in carrying a pile of clothes complete with corset, petticoats, and suit for Jamie with Nan shuffling in behind her, torch in hand. "Get up, Sleeping Beauty," the ancient woman orders, lighting the other torches along the wall. "Time to prepare for your dinner. Should be a good one. Getting the whole pack together, well those still in the area. Sent a few people out to collect them. One of my granddaughters-in-law gave me some clothes that should fit you." She gazes at me and puckers her lips. "To look at you I would never have guessed you were raised a lady, except you talk and carry yourself like one. Bridget, she needs a good scrubbing."

"Yes, ma'am," the servant says.

Nan glares at me. "Well? Need an engraved invitation? Get up!" Her vehemence makes me immediately hop to my feet. "And take those filthy rags off."

I am used to being nude in front of my ladies maid while she helps me dress, but I still balk. "I don't...I can wash myself. I—"

"Stop acting like a convent girl. You don't have anything we don't. Off! Now!" Having no desire to provoke the ire of my savior, I pad over to Bridget and remove my dress. The sea breeze tickles my bare skin as I stare out the window at the orange and blue sky in an attempt to block out the fact I am as naked as the day I was born in front of perfect strangers. As Bridget wipes the sweat and dirt off, Nan appraises me much like Father does a new horse he wishes to purchase. "Good hips and teats. You'll appreciate that when the children come. You're a bit old for a human to just be starting, but you appear to be of good stock. My grandson seems to have chosen well enough."

"Thank you, Mrs. Roarke," I say for lack of a better retort.

"Nan or Maud. You're the mother of my future great-grandchildren, though I am surprised it hasn't happened yet."

My eyes narrow in confusion. "I beg your pardon?"

"Children, girl! Babies! You do share a bed with my grandson, don't you?"

"I...we have not been married that long."

"Three months is plenty of time. I conceived Anne the first night."

"It will happen when God wills it, I suppose," I chuckle nervously.

"Of course it may not be your fault," she says, circling me as a bird does a carcass. "Some believe those born of a human/wolf crossing like your husband are like mules, cursed with the inability to breed, but I think that's a load of hogwash our fathers told us to keep the bloodlines pure. We only stopped marrying brother to sister a generation ago. James and I might as well have been siblings with all the relatives we had in common. I lost five children in the womb, one stillborn so deformed we thought it was a demon, and my poor Peter living every one of his three years in agony. I only have two living children now, Albert and Matthew, and James married them to cousins too. Every generation the same problems repeating. We're a shadow of what we once were. Thank the gods the young ones are leaving in droves into the world to find mates." She glances at Anne's portrait. "New blood, strong blood, that's what we need. I was just thinking that today, and who shows up on my doorstep? The gods have answered my prayers."

I haven't a clue how to respond, so I just smile. Bridget has finished my cleaning and helps me on with the white chemise. I still feel naked under the old woman's gaze. "We're just so happy to be here. You literally saved our lives."

"Yes, it took some prodding, but my grandson told me about your brother." She shakes her head. "Vampyres. The pack has had a truce with Lucian for close to a hundred years, ever since he took over the cabal. They leave us alone, we leave them alone, just as we all like it. This Michael, though. When he moved in he approached us about an alliance against Lucian, but I told Albert to dismiss it. I did not appreciate the way he spoke to us, as if *he* were doing *us* a favor. Then came the veiled threats right in our own home. The next night his vampyres accosted some of the younger wolves in town." She scoffs. "He finally got the message when those same vampyres returned to the manor with wounded bodies and pride. He has not dared to cross us since, but I told Albert it was only a matter of time. This, what happened to your brother, could be retaliation. Did Michael know who your brother was in relation to my grandson when he was abducted?"

For a moment, I consider lying. They would be more inclined to assist if this mess was their fault, but the woman's stare knocks the lie from my lips. I have the feeling she is already suspicious of me, and I have no idea what Jamie told her already. That and Bridget is pulling so tight on my stays I cannot muster a more than a syllable. "No."

Her lips purse. "A pity. I saw the devil in that vampyre's eyes. It would have been the perfect reason to remove them."

"He *is* dangerous," I point out between the winces. "A murderer who has insulted your pack, that should be reason enough. He's a threat to you regardless."

"Not an immediate one, and with any luck both cabals will wipe each other out, which is the most likely outcome."

"Not necessarily," I say desperately. "Michael is building a war machine. If he wins against Lucian, who is to say he shall not turn around and use it against your pack as well? I have limited experience with vampyres, but I do know they are unlikely to forgive a slight. It may not be tomorrow or even a year from now, but he will decide he wants your castle, or simply desires a fight because he is bored, and he will come. If you strike first, if you strike now, you have the greatest weapon in all of warfare: the element of surprise."

Nan mulls this over for a moment, but then shakes her head. "No. We are too few in strength, and as much as I love Albert, he has no head for battle. My boy is hard when he needs to be soft, and emotional when a clear head is required. The pack is falling apart with the young ones leaving as soon as they can, and those who stay do so because they lack disciple or intelligence." She grimaces. "This age of technology and peace has made us soft. The wolf has laid dormant for too long. It's useless. Timid. There is no place for it in this world anymore."

I step toward her, clutching her free hand in mine. "There is now. I need it. My brother needs it. I know about being tame, taking the safe course, denying what is desperately aching to break out inside you. Although it may lie dormant, without a doubt it is there when you truly need it. And if you don't take the opportunity to let it be free when you can, you will never know true happiness. You are no better than a vampyre. You may be living, but damn it you are not alive."

The room is silent as the old woman reads my face with a hint of amusement. "A keen mind as well as beauty. My grandson *has* done well for himself. I hope he appreciates it." She pulls her hand from mine. "Finish dressing. The guests of honor cannot be late." She hobbles to the door, and when she opens it, I am shocked to find Jamie sitting in a chair off to the side. He must have been out there the entire time. Which means he heard about my hips and…oh, bugger. "You too. You can go in now, son. We're done. Supper in about half an hour." Jamie rises from his guard post and nods at Nan before stepping in. "Be ready," she says as she shuts the door.

Even Bridget sighs in relief when she departs. What a woman.

Jamie remains by the door, I suppose in case he feels the need to flee again. I almost wish he would. Neither of us can look at the other. Oh he absolutely heard the entire conversation. "Did you, um, sleep well?"

"Yes, thank you," I say as Bridget fastens my petticoats. "Um, Bridget, we can manage the rest. Thank you."

"Are you sure, ma'am?"

"Yes. You may go."

"Yes, ma'am," the girl says before she walks out.

Jamie still refuses to move from the door. "They brought clothes for you as well," I say, gesturing to the pile.

"Thank you." He takes the clothes over to the basin, giving me a wide berth as he does.

"How long were you sitting out there?"

"Um…" He pulls off his holster then shirt. Once again the sight of his bare, beautiful torso causes flutters inside my stomach. "About an hour and half. The old lady interrogated me for about half an hour. When I came back here, I found one of them skulking around the room. I don't want you alone for even a minute while we're here, okay?"

"I have no qualms with that." He starts wiping his body with the rag, and I know propriety states I should look away, but instead I sit on the bed facing him. "But I do maintain your fears are unwarranted. I am convinced now more than ever we are amongst friends, your grandmother in particular. I believe she shall help us, I really do."

"Don't get your hopes up, shug. There is no real reason for them to help."

"There was no real reason for them to let us stay, either," I point out.

Shaking his head, Jamie pulls off his boots and socks. "Giving us a bed for the night and killing a house full of vampyres are two very, *very* different things. No, we stay here tonight, wake at dawn to check out this manor of his, extract your brother, and go straight to the police and newspapers just like we planned. With any luck they'll pick up your trunk at the airport like I asked, and we'll have enough firepower so we can at least fool ourselves into thinking this ain't a suicide mission."

"Or we spend our evening convincing your grandmother and uncle it is in their best interest to align themselves with this vampyre Lucian to help us wipe out these vermin. Or at the very least convince them to introduce us to Lucian so we can inform him of Michael's plot. If he is not a total imbecile, he will have no choice but to help us."

"Or he'll take a page from Michael's book and keep you hostage until you finish building *him* a war machine. I trust vampyres about as much as werewolves."

"You have to trust someone sometime."

"Apparently, I trust you. Turn around."

"I'm sorry?"

He starts unbuttoning his trousers. "Turn around."

Blast. Yet I do as he asks. "Then you should trust my judgment on this."

Water splashes behind me. "Shug, the hardest lesson I ever learnt was never go into battle with people you can't trust. You'll just end up gut-shot in the middle of Death Valley. I speak from experience."

"And I've learnt sometimes you have no choice but to rely on faith if something is as important to you as David is to me. I took that leap of faith with you, and it was the smartest decision I have ever made. I have not regretted it even for a moment."

When he does not retort, the temptation to turn grows stronger with each passing second, before he finally says, "I've almost gotten you killed three times."

"But you saved me those three times as well," I point out.

"You helped."

I smirk. "True, but I would never have made it this far without you, and it all began with faith. My faith that you were a good, honorable, stalwart man who would not abandon me even when he should have. And I have faith in your grandmother. She will do the right thing."

"You give me too much credit, shug. Her too." I hear clothes rustling, then he says, "You can turn around now."

I have to stop myself from outright leering at his still bare torso. I clear my throat and rise. "I had best finish dressing as well." I keep my back to him as I put on the dress. Brown is not my colour and the muslin and rivets up and down the bodice are tarnished and worn, but at least it fits.

The buttons are on the back, and I manage a few, but I feel him move behind me. "Let me."

"Thank you." The heat from him standing so close prickles my skin that delicious way of his. "What would I do without you?"

I must have said the wrong thing because he hesitates before the next button. "You would call the maid." Those words destroy all the butterflies. He finishes the last two buttons. "There." He moves back to the other side of the room to continue dressing.

I know him well enough to glean when he desires silence, so I grant it to him as I fix my hair. There's a brush on the vanity which I use to tame rat's nest that was once my glorious hair. As I stroke out the tangles, I watch my beloved in the mirror, first dressing then peering out the window. I can hear voices as the guests arrive. Jamie's dour expression, the same one he sports when we are about to enter a dangerous situation and he's weighing the options, never leaves his rugged face. He has already made up his mind that they are the enemy. He will not lift a finger to convince them to assist us. Which leaves the task squarely on my shoulders.

After last night seeing what only two vampyres are capable of, any illusion that the two of us can defeat them alone shattered. I have one goal tonight: convince Albert to aid us any way I can. *Any way* possible. I glance at Jamie again. I pray Albert is more receptive to my charm than his nephew.

Even if he is not, this should make for an interesting dinner.

*

Kieran comes for us promptly at nine, and we are ready for him. Even in a brown dress without make-up, clean up quite well. Natural beauty does come in handy every so often. The only piece of jewelry I wear is the Artemis. I trust the pack but not enough to dine unarmed. Jamie shares my sentiment as he dons his gun belt and holster under his black coat. He looks wild tonight with messy black hair and days worth of stubble, neither of which he sees the point in correcting. I prefer him like this anyway, it suits him far more than the tamed visage he sported when we met at the ball, but our hosts might take offense. When I broach the subject, he scoffs and returns to peering out the window. If Kieran is any indication, my fears are unfounded. The boy wears a simple white shirt and brown pants, but at least he brushed his brown hair.

We follow him back down to the great hall, which we easily could have found alone. The sound of laughter, talking, and even slamming of tables and chairs echoes through the castle. I get the distinct feeling my idea of a formal dinner is far different from theirs. My apprehension must be apparent because right before we enter, Jamie slides his hand around my waist. I know it is mostly for show but makes me feel safer regardless.

In the passing hours the great hall has been transformed. The throne has been replaced by a small table with a longer one in front forming a "T" the length of the room. It's more welcoming as both red table clothed daises are lined both with candelabras between the jugs of mead and wine. There are perhaps twenty people, with men outnumbering women three to one, and those few females seem paired off with the older werewolves with one or two exceptions. Those, even the little girl about ten, command the attention of every male within five feet of her. Male or female, all the attendees resemble one another, with most having black hair, the same strong jaw and lips.

Albert and Nan sit at the head of the table with two empty chairs to the left of them for us. "There they are. Our honored guests," Albert says. All eyes turn to us as Kieran leads us to the table. "Everyone, may I present my nephew James McQueen, son of my dearly departed sister Anne, and his beautiful wife Verity."

"Thank you all for having us," I say with my best Lady Hart smile. All the men eye me as if I were a pork chop and are not shy in their attentions. Jamie's grip on my waist tightens. I position myself behind the empty seat to Albert's left, which garners a scowl from Jamie as he pulls out my chair. Albert doesn't hide his felicity at this turn of events, roving eyes resting at the swell of my breasts. Nan smiles to herself as she pours more wine. "I cannot believe you did all of this for us," I say. "Thank you so much for such a warm welcome."

"You're welcome," Albert says with a grin. "It's not often we get guests, especially ones as stunning as you."

"Oh, thank you for that lovely lie. I know I look a fright," I say, touching my hair. "Traveling and other…occurrences have taken their toll."

"Nonsense. I do not believe this castle has ever given shelter to a more beautiful woman before in all its centuries."

"You are far too kind, sir," I say demurely, forcing a blush to my cheeks. Flirting is just like riding a monopede, once you begin again it is as if you never stopped. I glance at Jamie, whose scowl has grown deeper, before looking away like a good lady. "You have a beautiful home," I say as I sip my wine. "I have never seen such interesting tapestries. How many of you live here?"

"Only about ten now, not including servants. Most have chosen to live in town, except when the full moon rises."

"How large is the pack in total?" I ask.

"Now? About twenty strong."

"It was almost double that in my heyday," Nan says into her wine.

"Mam," Albert snaps before returning to me with a smile. "Some have chosen to live rogue to find mates and work. We're still one of the largest packs in the world."

"And I am sure there is not a person in this room who is not grateful to have such a strong, understanding leader guiding them through their trials and travails. Those who are not here are probably kicking themselves for their ill decision."

Albert positively beams until Jamie says, "Not fucking likely."

Albert's mouth sets straight at this insult. Blast. I glower at my companion before returning my gaze to his uncle. "You will have to forgive my husband. He grew up wild as a gypsy, and though I have tried to smooth them, some rough edges remain."

"It's understandable," Nan says. "Manners have never run in the family. I guarantee you one fistfight will break out tonight. I'm surprised it has not already."

I hope the smile I give her translates to, "Thank you." It must because my savior nods and begins talking to Albert about the stables, giving me a chance to wrap my arm around Jamie's, lean in, and whisper, "Unless you desire to take on twenty livid werewolves singlehandedly, please stop antagonizing him. Trust me. I know what I'm doing." Aware that people are watching, I plant a kiss on his cheek. "Thank you, my love."

The main course is brought out, giant plates of meat, pork judging from the two pigs heads carried in as well, with smaller plates stacked high with potatoes and cabbage. A pig's head is placed right in front of me, and I suppress a shudder. "I hope you're hungry," Albert says.

"Famished." That becomes a lie as I watch the others grab the greasy meat with their hands and chew it without benefit of fork and knife. Even so, I use my utensils to serve myself pork and potatoes. Cabbage makes me belch, not that his crowd would notice. Every few minutes someone belches or passes gas, with some of the younger ones making it a contest. If my mother were here, she would literally swoon. The food is not as disgusting as it appears at least if I do not look at it. "Delicious."

"So how did my nephew manage to marry such an angel as yourself?" Albert asks.

Cue another blush. "Mr. Roarke, you really must stop saying such things. As my good husband can assure you, I am no angel."

"That's for damn sure," Jamie mutters. "Your angel threw herself at me at a ball just minutes after we met, got me all by my lonesome, then tracked me down a few days later. She insisted we run off that same day. Been making my life close to hell ever since."

"I find that quite hard to believe, nephew," Albert says.

"I don't really give a damn what you believe, uncle," Jamie retorts with a cruel smile.

"We have been through our trials, that is certain," I say, taking Jamie's hand, "but what does not kill us only makes us stronger. And without a doubt, those same trails make it abundantly clear what is important in life. Trust. Respect. And above all…love."

"Whatever you say," Jamie says as he yanks his hand away to down his wine, "*dear.*"

I am ready to kill him with my bare bloody hands, I really am. Instead I keep them busy by cutting my meat. "And what about you, Mr. Roarke? Such a handsome man as yourself must be married. It would be a crime against nature otherwise."

He chuckles. "Oh, I'm married alright. Father made me a fine match. Caroline's her name. She has just chosen to return to her pack in Newport for the past forty years or so."

"Oh, you poor dear, I am so sorry," I say, putting down my fork to pat his hand.

"They're welcome to her, but thank you," he says, placing his other hand over mine. "She gave me two healthy sons before she left, so her obligation was done."

"Still, you must get quite lonely."

"Oh, for the love of—" Jamie says before I kick him under the table. "Ow! Why—"

"Verity, hon, I have some catching up to do with my grandson there," Nan interjects. "Change seats with me for a bit?"

"She's fine where—"

I pick up my plate and cup before rising. God bless the old woman. "Of course, Nan. Whatever you desire." We make the switch, and I sit with a grin Albert's way. "There. Now I have you all to myself." I lean into his ear. "I am so sorry for his ill behavior. When uncomfortable my husband has a tendency to lash out. I simply ignore it."

"He should not speak like that to you under any circumstance."

"We have both been under tremendous stress what with recent events." I remove the mirth from my face. "My brother and the vampyres and all. Lately, we have been acting more as employer and employee than husband and wife."

"Yes, Mam told me about your troubles. I am sorry about your brother. What do they want with him?"

I gaze down at my lap, and my gloved hands ringing a napkin in it. "I am—I'm frightened to tell you the real reason. You've been so kind to us, more than kind, so I feel you have a right to know. And I shall understand if you ask us to leave when you hear the terrible truth," I say, meekly glancing up.

His eyes narrow. "What is it?"

I pause for effect and clench my jaw, pretending to gather my strength. "It's me they want," I whisper. "They are hunting for *me*." I grab his hands, clutching desperately, while meeting his eyes. "We had no choice but to seek aid here, I am so sorry. Jamie did not want to. He said it was too dangerous, that it would be unfair to place you in harm's way, but I insisted. Please do not blame him. Please. They shall never know we were here, I swear it. I just…they have attempted to kill Jamie twice and abscond with me. They're holding my brother hostage because of me. I am just so scared and so tired. I am at the end of my tether. But it is just Jamie and I against a horde of vampyres. We—we're going to lose. We do not stand a chance. They are going to kill us, kill my brother, for some silly territory dispute." I do not have to force the tears as I thought I might, they come naturally. "I'm frightened. So frightened. I…excuse me. Forgive me." I cover my mouth before springing up and rushing out of the hall into the dark corridor. I keep my back to the door to wipe the tears. *Please, please, please…*

Seconds later when I hear the footsteps behind me it is an excellent thing Albert cannot see me because I smile. Fish in a bloody barrel. "Mr. Roarke, I—"

For once the sight of Jamie does not bring joy to my heart. Instead, I have the strongest desire to throw a torch at him. "You okay?" he asks.

I stalk over to him, gazing over his shoulder. "Is your uncle coming?"

"No," he snaps. "I told him I'd check on you."

My mouth drops open. "Why would you do that?"

"Because you're my wife, and he upset you."

"Oh my God, can you be that bloody dense? He did not upset me. Do I appear upset? Are you purposely trying to ruin this? Every time I make progress with him you sweep in and blow it to bits!"

"Progress in what? Pissing me off?"

"No, you imbecile! Progress in acquiring twenty powerful supernatural beings to help us retrieve David so we can walk out of the vampyre cabal alive."

"And you acting the whore is gonna accomplish that? How far exactly are you going to go with this charade?"

"If it saves our lives, as far as I have to."

"And I assume the same goes for me, huh?" he snarls. "Do whatever or say whatever to get me to stick around?"

"*What?*" I shout. "You believe that I…I have been toying with you? After all we have been through, all you know of me, you suspect my feelings toward you have all been an act? That I do not lo—" I stop talking to compose myself. "Do you really think so little of me? How could you…? Go to hell. Just go to hell." I brush past him, still reeling as if he had just slapped me. That would actually hurt less.

"Shit, Verity, I'm sorry. Please—"

The pack eyes me as I return, and even Albert stands as I approach. "Are you unwell? You're ashen." he asks, putting his hand on my back.

Jamie rushes into the room, pain and concern brimming from his eyes, but I cannot bear to look at him. "I'm fine," I say none too convincingly as I sit. "Thank you."

Albert glowers at his nephew as he returns to his seat. Jamie picks up a jug of mead, pouring himself a hefty portion. "I am so sorry for my ill-timed display of emotion. I hope I did not ruin the feast for you."

"Nonsense. I just hope you're feeling better."

Not in the least. "I am. Thank you, Mr. Roarke."

He pats my hand as I glance at Jamie, who seems oblivious to all but his mead. "Good. One as beautiful as you should never be sad." He squeezes my hand. "And fear not, I don't let anyone, let alone vampyres, dictate who my guests are. You're welcome to stay as long as you need to."

"Does that go for me as well, uncle?"

We both look at the acrimonious, glaring Jamie. Albert releases my hand. "That goes without saying, nephew."

"Just so we're clear," Jamie says before sipping his mead.

I shake my head and suppress a sigh. I am not going to accomplish much with Jamie around, that much is clear. To Nan as well, because she steers the conversation to my life in London where I make sure to mention David's accomplishments, and the world's need for him all the while batting my eyes at Albert, who seems more than pleased with the attention, often smiling and leaning in while asking conversations. Conversation shifts to Albert's reign as pack leader, which takes us through pie. Part One of my plan appears complete as the dishes are cleared. Judging from the way Albert has taken every opportunity to touch me and the seductive smiles, he is quite besotted by me. Part Two should be that much easier for it.

Even here the sexes separate after the meal, the men enjoying cigars while the women gossip, so the servants can re-stage the hall for the bacchanalia. I'm just about to follow Nan and the other ladies to the parlor when Jamie steps beside me. He appears about as happy to be there as I am to have him. "What are you doing?" I ask.

"Mr. McQueen," Albert calls from the other side of the room, "the cigars are this way. Nothing but clucking that way."

"I'm not leaving my wife alone."

"She won't be alone, boy, she'll be with us," Nan snaps. "I won't allow harm to come to her. Or can you just not live without her for ten minutes?" She pokes him with her cane. "Go. Make nice."

He glances at me, greeted by my scowl. "I will be fine."

"Of course she will," Nan says, yanking me toward the door. When we're through it alone, she says, "I am all for being protective of the one you love, but he is just being ridiculous."

I smile sadly. "I fear love does not factor into it, only honor." Oh, Lord, I cannot believe I said that. Let down my guard for one moment, and I may have ruined the whole charade.

The old woman remains impassive though. "Men. I had five brothers, four sons, seven grandsons, twelve great-grandsons, not to mention a father and husband, and all of them some of the finest werewolves in the world. Great fighters. Wonderful head in the battlefield. But when it comes to women, they are hopeless. We scare them more than any sword ever forged. That's why they force us down, and we're far too busy running a household and raising our husband and children to fight back. But we do love them." She pats my hand. "And though they may not show it the way we want them to, we may got get sonnets and strolls through the moonlight, they love us as well. They would lay down their lives for us in a heartbeat. And that *does* run in the blood."

We walk into the small, dim drawing room where the other women are already conversing on brown sofas and love seats around a wooden table. The two younger teenage girls sit on a bench beside the entrance giggling about how handsome Kieran and Duncan are, but that ceases when I enter. Instantly, seven women are upon me, firing questions about London, the Season, the latest fashions, and if I know this person or that. I would put money on the fact not a one has been to the city, London or otherwise. I answer the questions with ease until Mathilda of the furrowed brow, mate of Cullen, whoever that is, asks, "What about your husband? What does he do on the full moon?"

A lie does not come to the forefront of my mind. "I'm sorry?" I ask to buy time.

"It just seems odd he would remain in town then. It would be incredibly dangerous for you and your family to have him around. Does your family even know about his condition?"

My mouth opens as my mind reels for answers. I never considered these things, these tangible problems. Where *would* we live? He misses America, I know that. Could I bear to leave England? David? He would never be accepted, not by my peers and certainly not my parents, even without them knowing his werewolf lineage. I may not care about his lack of manners or money, but they will never let him forget his lack of station. These considerations have barely crossed my mind. They have crossed his, though. Every time he pulls away, every time he looks at me, they must be there. He has been trying to convince himself he is not good enough for me, that our problems are insurmountable. That's why he…oh, I do love him. But he is an idiot at times.

"My parents hate him, my father especially," I begin. "I was almost disowned, but the scandal would have been too great had we not married. After the initial shock, they have begun to grown accustomed to the idea. They at least pretend to tolerate him just as they always have me. As for my friends…once they saw how happy he made me, how much he loved me, my real friends grew to accept him. The rest, well, no great loss there. And we barely spend any time in London, a month at the most. Really we live at Foxfire Manor in Somerset, which suits us both. There is plenty of room and privacy there. He can even run free on the full moon if he so chooses without worry. My brother lives there as well, and we work on inventions together still. He and Jamie get along so well. They are alike in so many regards. True to themselves, intelligent, caring. I'm so blessed to have them both. And when I am not working, Jamie and I stroll through the fields talking, me about my troubles with my inventions, him regaling me with tales of his wild adventures, or the both of us traveling into town to fleece unsuspecting travelers in cards. Then at night we fall into each other's arms, drifting off to sleep. It is…bliss."

"He doesn't miss America?" Mathilda asks.

"Oh, he does. A great deal. He still has a farm in Oklahoma. We were talking about visiting, and maybe one day we'll build a grand house there, but until then we are happy wherever we are. America, Somerset, here. It is not perfect, but neither are we. And I thank God for that. Perfection is so dreadfully dull. No, when everything is stripped away, and you get down to bare essentials, you realize all you ever really need in this life is someone who loves and respects you for you, warts and all."

"Do you agree, gentlemen?" Nan asks behind me.

I spin around to find Albert, Jamie, and two others standing by the door. I was so deep in my fantasy I failed to hear them enter. Oh bugger. Unsure how much Jamie heard, I study him. He seems impassive, that poker face of his acting as a mask, but by now I can see the cracks in it, the torment leaking through. He heard it all.

"Of course," Albert says, gazing down at me. "Without love, what do we have?" After a wink, he looks up at the girl with red hair across from me. "Heather, I do hope you will grace us with a song or two. There is no finer voice in Ireland."

"Of course, sir" Heather, a pretty thing a few years older than Margot, says.

"We have quite a few accomplished musicians in the family who have agreed to play. I hope you enjoy dancing, Verity."

"I adore it."

"Then I request the first dance," he says with a sly smile.

"Um, my husband might—"

"Nonsense," Albert says. He places one hand on my bare shoulder and I have to stop myself from tensing and recoiling from his touch. "I insist."

I glance at Jamie. Still a rock of apathy. Fine. "Very well then," I say. "I would be honored."

Mercifully, Albert removes his hand from my personage, extending it out. "Excellent. Shall we?"

My hand resting on top of his, Albert and I lead the others to the great hall where preparations are still underway. His throne has returned this time with two wooden high backed chairs beside it, and benches along the wall, giving us ample room to dance. Five of the men, now finished with their cigars and brandy, sit in the corner, one with a mandolin, others with a flute, banjo, violin, and accordion, which makes horrid noises as he tunes it. Albert steers me to the centre of the room, smirking like the cat that killed the canary or whatever the werewolf equivalent is, as his subordinates watch. Jamie, scowl affixed, sits in the corner as far from the others as he can get. I glance at him but he looks away, folding his arms across his chest for good measure. Why is he acting like such a—oh, my.

Albert's arm snakes around my waist as he tugs me against his body so there is no space between us. I gasp in surprise, which is nothing compared to Jamie's reaction. Like lighting he goes from slumped to back straight as a rod. Ready to pounce. Albert smiles down at me as he lifts my arm into waltz position. "You'll find we do things a little different here."

"I gathered," I say, smiling nervously. My eyes shoot to Jamie to warn him away, and though I did not think it possible, his scowl deepens down to his craggy soul. It might as well be carved in stone. A large part of me wants him to rush over to claw me from Albert's arms, but my rational side is glad when he relaxes a tad at least in the shoulders. I have a mission to complete.

The music begins, the violin and other instruments playing furiously right away, and it is certainly not like a waltz I have ever encountered. It is far faster and jauntier, which is reflected in how we dance to it. Instead of elegant, fluid movements I find myself swept about, bouncing like a ball all around the room. At first it discombobulates me, but then I find myself in the spirit of the event, laughing like mad as I bounce and twirl in time to the mirthful melody. This is far more fun than I thought it possible. Albert even throws in a few new movements, swings and double steps that throw me for a loop, but do keep me literally on my toes. When the song ends far too soon, I am almost out of breath from the dance and laughter. We all applaud, even Jamie.

"You dance beautifully," Albert says as he applauds.

"As do you," I chuckle.

Duncan steps over to us. "May I have the next dance, Mrs. McQueen?"

Albert winds his arm around my waist. "I'm not done with her yet, son." He sweeps me away as what sounds like a reel begins. The pace is slower this time, but we do not follow traditional reel steps, so I have no choice but to stare down at his feet.

"I am sorry, I do not know this one," I say, narrowly missing stepping on his foot.

"That's because I'm making it up as I go." I glance around and find that the others are doing the same, some just rocking to and fro in each other's arms without even moving their feet. The women rest their heads on their mate's shoulder with their eyes closed. Oh my. This would be considered lewd anywhere else but with the sweet music, the candlelight, and their contented smiles pressed against the ones they love. I may never wish to dance any other way again. "How many dances do you think I can have before my nephew objects?"

"Quite a few I imagine. He abhors dancing."

"He is quite serious. Reminds me so much of my father, it's damn unnerving."

"Do not tell him that. He is convinced your father was Nero reborn."

"Christopher's fault, no doubt. Bastard. Broke my parent's hearts when he stole Anne from us. What my sister saw in him I have no idea. He was a damn weakling. The one time Martin and I tried to play with him, he went crying to his Daddy. We were just practicing our stalking. We weren't even in wolf form. He couldn't take a punch either, even when we were just toying with him. Thin blood. Hope your husband hasn't inherited that."

Inside I am aghast at his nonchalance about terrorizing a young boy for years, Jamie's father or no, but do not let it show. "I do not believe he has. He is the strongest, most honorable man I have ever known. Bar none." I must have said the wrong thing again because his smile falters. "That is until I met the rest of you. Those traits must run in the blood as well. You obviously have them in enormous quantities. Albert Roarke."

"Depends on who you ask," he says, ruining whatever mirth remained.

"What do you mean? Everyone here seems to hold you in such high regard."

"But I am no James Roarke, as my mother keeps reminding me."

"Well, from the little I know of him, that might not be such a terrible thing. He sounded like a tyrant."

"Maybe that's what the pack needs. *He* didn't lose twelve wolves to the world in ten years. He didn't lose that many in his seventy year reign. Last full moon Duncan almost bested me in a fight. I know what they think. I'm weak. I bowed to Lucian on the dock purchases, I let the Newport pack down in their struggle with the Rennes pack, I ignored Michael's threats."

"I am sure you are doing the best you can." Three, two...one. "But there must be something you can do to assure them of your strength. Just picture it. You leading the charge, all your wolves at your back, fighting the good fight. Nothing unites people like a common enemy." His eyes have narrowed, and I know I have overstepped. I stare down demurely. "At least that's what my father always says."

"Maybe."

The song ends, and we applaud again. That's enough for now. The seed is planted, best give it time to sprout. "Oh, I'm parched. Do you mind if I rest?"

"Of course not. Heather! Give us a song." As I step toward Jamie, Albert blocks me. "Come. Sit," he says, gesturing to his throne. He places his arm around my waist again, leading me away from a glowering Jamie. "Bring us wine. Now!"

I sit to Albert's left, with Nan on his right, sipping my wine as Heather moves to the centre of the room. Gone is the giggly girl only a few older than Margot enthralled by my talk of fashion and plays. Instead she is self conscious and playing with her skirt. She begins softly, singing in Gaelic, but her mournful voice sweeps us all away. The tune, along with her haunting voice, is soul piercing. Even Jamie seems moved as he does not take his eyes off the girl or sip his wine. After a few seconds he notices me staring and meets my eyes. For an instant the room, the others, all but us and the music vanish. The corners of his mouth move in unison with mine until we are both smiling.

"Beautiful, no?" Albert whispers, breaking the spell. My smile drops, but is quickly replaced with a strained one as I nod yes. When I glance back at Jamie his eyes are downcast again. Blast.

Albert has Heather perform four more songs, each more resplendent than the last. I would enjoy myself if Jamie did not appear so miserable alone in his corner nursing a drink. Our eyes catch a few times, but he looks away with a scowl. Applause breaks our gaze this time. "Thank you, Heather," Albert says as we clap. "Now, let's lighten the mood. Gentlemen?"

A song style I have never heard before, with the violinist sawing like a demon, begins. Everyone hoots with joy and leaps to the floor, even men without partners. At one of his soirees last year Orrlock invited gypsy dancers to perform. They danced in the same fashion, letting the music sway them however they wished. A few men start a complex dance that involves kick steps in rapid succession as if stepping on hot coals with spins. I believe it is called a jig. I love it.

Not waiting for Albert, I spring up to join in on the fun. It takes me a few seconds to learn how they are doing what they are, but then take to it like a fish to water, step kicking with my skirt pulled up. Some people start clapping in time to the music as others hop up. Kieran locks elbows with me, spinning me like a gear. I lose my concentration, almost tripping on my own feet. Even my fumble brings large guffaws from us all. I appear to have left my grace in London. As I take a few seconds to catch my breath, I spy Jamie in the corner smiling and tapping his feet to the music. I knew it. My grin grows. He notices me approaching, and the smile drops as if I was a cat and he the mouse about to be devoured. He is not far off.

"Jamie McQueen, may I have this dance?"

"I don't dance."

"You do tonight. Dance with me."

He is almost aghast at the prospect. "I don't know the steps. I—"

"Jamie…" I extend my hand to him, "*dance with me. Please.*"

Indecision wracks his face as if I asked him to jump into a volcano, but when he meets my smiling eyes, it vanishes. He takes my hand, and I lead him into the fray. As everyone else spins and twirls around him, he tenses as if they were all about to attack him with clubs. He really is a terrible dancer, stiff and awkward, just moving side to side. Holding his hands in mine we do a sidestep until he is at least in time to the music, then I release him and add shoulder and hip motions along with a side kick. He smiles as he attempts to imitate me, but steps on his own feet, almost tripping himself, we both double over with laughter.

"You really are terrible at this!"

"Told ya." We return to basics until the song ends, and with the widest grins on our faces we applaud. Jamie even whistles. I knew he'd enjoy himself. Our smiles remain as they begin a more somber song. As we meet each other's eyes the smiles fade. "I had better—"

I grab his hand, moving it to my waist. "Dance with me."

Seconds pass as the hesitation returns. *Please, God…* His grip on me tightens as he raises my hand in position. "I may step on your feet."

I wrap my arm around his waist too. "I can handle it."

This receives another smile from us both. He moves right first, stepping on my foot. We chuckle. "I warned ya."

"We will figure it out."

Like some of the others we rock side-to-side in each other's arms. I close my eyes, resting my head on his chest right above his heart. He smells of smoke and lavender and is as warm as wildfire.

For a moment he ceases moving, only to pull me in tighter to him. Where I belong. "See? Isn't this perfect?" I ask.

"Pretty damn close," he whispers into my hair.

"Mind if I cut in?"

My eyes fly open to find Albert smirking at me as if Jamie doesn't exist. "Um…" The proper thing to do is say yes, but the word will not leave my mouth. Not now. Please not now. I will not let a dominance game ruin this moment for us. Jamie begs to differ. He releases me with a matching smirk. "She's all yours," he says as he steps aside.

"If you were mine," Albert says as he wraps me in his clutches, "I would never let another man look at you, let alone touch you."

"Good thing I'm not yours then," I say without thinking. Albert's expression turns sour, bordering on a scowl fixed only with my Lady Hart smile. "For the other men, I mean."

I endure seven more dances with our host who gives me a reprieve only to return a minute later to inform me there were two of Michael's vampyres hanging near my trunk at the dirigible airport. "We'll try again tomorrow," he says with the vocal equivalent of a pat on the head as if I were a child. I "accidently" stomp my heel into his foot soon after. I am getting exhausted, bored, not to mention sweaty when the eighth song begins. Enough is enough. Time to go in for the kill.

Fanning myself with my hand, I shake my head and when I take a step I fall against Albert, putting my free hand on his chest to steady myself. "Oh, my."

"Are you unwell?" Albert asks.

"Just a bit dizzy."

"Let's get you some air." I allow him to slip his arm around my waist proprietarily as he walks me out of the hall. Jamie, who was joined by Nan in his corner around dance five, glances at me as we pass. I momentarily meet his eyes, shame gripping me enough I must look away. He knows. He knows what I am about to do. Whatever is necessary. For David. I *will* do this. Oh Jamie, please do not hate me. *Please.*

It's a warm night not much better than in the hall than out here on the stone terrace. The stars twinkle above, Perseus and Andromeda together in the heavens until the end of time. They were so much closer last night, more brilliant and glorious as I viewed them with him last night. A rock falls into my stomach. He'll forgive me…oh please let him forgive me for this.

"Lovely night, no?" Albert asks.

"It really is," I say after a deep breath. I force my face down to give myself an air of melancholy.

He takes the bait. "What is it?"

"I was just thinking of my brother." I hug myself. "Does he get to enjoy the night, or do they have him locked in some dungeon? Are they torturing him? Is he calling out for me? I just realized he's so close, only a few miles away, and I'm…I've failed him. Oh, I miss him so much. If I do not get him back…I don't think I could continue on. I really do not. I'm sorry," I choke out, covering my mouth to hide my whispers.

As I anticipated he wraps his arms around me in a hug. "It's okay. Don't cry. It will work itself out."

"How? We have no weapons without my trunk, and even if we did, Jamie and I are just two people. You know how dangerous vampyres are. We barely escaped with our lives last night. And that Michael is the devil himself. I heard he even threatened *you*. If only I could go to the police or military or find someone brave enough who could help us. Could you, I do not know, introduce me to Lucian, so I could tell him about Michael?"

"Maybe," Albert says, holding me tighter. "Let me think about it."

"There's no time Albert! The longer they have David the likelier it becomes they shall kill him. Something must be done now."

"I'm not on the best of terms with Lucian. He probably won't even agree to meet."

"You can try. His life is in danger as well."

"Good. Maybe they'll kill each other off."

I pull from the embrace to meet his eyes. "With my brother and I as collateral damage. And if they do not? Michael will have the advantage, and who is to say he will not set his sights on ridding himself of the wolves who insulted him next? Your mother told me what transpired when you met. From any angle you view it, he is a threat to you anyway you."

"If he comes, he comes. I'll rip his fangs out with my bare hands."

"Or you can neutralize him now. Join with Lucian and rid yourself of the pest while he does not anticipate it."

Albert remains quiet for a few seconds, I hope mulling over my logic. "I don't know...maybe if I had a little incentive."

"What kind—" My words are stopped as his dry lips assault mine. I am so shocked and revolted, I jerk my head away. "What are you doing?"

His arms coil me even tighter against his body, my own tensing. "Stop playing coy. This is what you've been after all night." He leans in again, and I move back as far as possible while still wrapped in his clutches. I knew this might happen, but now it has nausea grips me. Every inch of me screams to flee, to claw his face.

"I'm married."

Any kindness and gentility is wiped away. "And I am pack Alpha, and you are both in my territory. Not to mention it seems as if you need my help with your vampyre problem. This is not the way to receive favors from me. Understand?"

I swore I would do whatever it took to save him. Even this. I have destroyed my reputation, almost died, killed. I can do this. Nothing else matters but David. It takes a lot, but I swallow my revulsion, shut my eyes, and kiss him. Just pretend its Jamie. These are Jamie's lips, Jamie's tongue, Jamie's bulge...oh, God. This is wrong, every fiber of my being knows this is wrong. I feel disgusting. Dirty. Especially when his hand moves to my bottom, kneading it roughly as his swell grinds against me. Bile rises into my throat. This is madness. I cannot allow this to happen. I will lose Jamie forever. David would not want this, selling my body and soul not even for him. I pull away, this time from his entire grasp. "I cannot do this. I cannot do this to Jamie. I love him, I can't. Not even for your help. I'm sorry."

I run to the door, coming face to face with the man I love as I step inside. He must have been out here the entire time, watching me make a slattern of myself. "I'm sorry," I cry, "I am so sorry."

Without a word, he grabs my hand and yanks me through the hall, into the corridor, and up to our room so fast I have to run to keep up. He flings me into our bedroom, slamming the door shut. "Please don't hate me, I could not bear it. I'm sorry. I—"

He spins around, stalks over, pulls me into him, and mashes his lips against mine in a savage, hard, miraculous kiss. The kiss is like the rest of him, the perfect mixture of soft and hard. No hesitation. I kiss him back, devouring him with ferocity and passion I never knew I possessed. For him. No one else but him until the end of eternity. When he backs me into the bed, there is not a part of me that protests. We were made for this, for each other. No matter what anyone says, nothing that comes from this, from us, from love can be a sin. I fall against the soft mattress and he on top of me so there is no space between us. Neither of us could suffer that. Even as I remove my gloves, our lips do not unseal, our tongues never stop exploring its mate. Tobacco and wine. I shall become an addict for their taste as well.

My bare hand moves through his silky hair as the other yanks at his shirt to grip the hot flesh of his back. Even with his trousers and my undergarments, as he rubs his bulge against me, a sensational tingling and almost burning begins deep inside me, literally aching to be quenched. I wrap my legs around him, drawing him even closer. His lips move down my neck with petal soft kisses until he reaches where neck meets shoulder. Once again soft becomes hard as his teeth bite down on my tender flesh, marking me as his.

"Oh, Jamie…" I moan, grinding into him like a cat in heat, the burning pleasure building to maddening proportions.

His lips leave my body as he gazes down at me. I meet his eyes as a million emotions run through those dark orbs. Elation, confusion, fury, regret, and love. Pure love. Pure miraculous, eternal, brilliant love shining brighter than a million suns. Until he allows the darkness to creep in. That love is followed by an equally deep look of sheer terror and revulsion. He is so horrified he tosses me out of his arms and backs away as if I were about to suck out his soul. "Shit, fuck, shit, fuck, *fuck*!" he shouts. And once again he runs out of the room, away from me and away from himself.

I am too shocked to even blink. He…I burst into tears, hard wracking sobs that overtake my body. But not from despair. From absolute, utter *pure* joy like nothing I have ever felt before. He loves me. Truly, madly, deeply *he* loves *me*. Any doubt in my mind has vanished. Something shifts inside me. Something glorious. All my fear burns away, and for the first time in my life I feel...happy. Strong. Powerful. Free. *Alive*. I'm alive. I will rise like the break of dawn every time you try to put me down and I shall burn you to ashes. I conquered love, what are a few vampyres?

So hang the werewolves. Hang the vampyres. Hang my bastard father, my weak mother, a society afraid of its own shadow. You cannot touch me now. The Lady is dead.

Long live Verity Hart.

CHAPTER THIRTEEN

TO THE MANOR BORN,
THEN DEAD,
THEN UNDEAD

Jamie does not return after that. At least to the room. About ten minutes after he storms out, I hear the chair outside the door creak. Even now his honor will not allow him to abandon me to the wolves. Of course I want to throw open that door and kiss and stroke his worry away, but I know what he is going through. Realizing you are in love is terrifying at first, especially in our unique circumstances, so he needs to go through the motions and acclimate to his new state of being as I did. I do not envy him. I fall asleep listening to his steady breathing out in the hall. My centurion.

A shutting door brings me out of a dream where I run with wolves across the moors, keeping pace even, though I have two legs to their four. "Jamie?"

"No, ma'am," Bridget, the maid, says. She stands at the door with a tray of food. "Mrs. Roarke told me to bring you breakfast."

"What time is it?" I ask, sitting up.

"A little past eight, ma'am." She places the tray on my lap. Eggs, bacon, ham, and toast. Delicious. "I'll just fetch your clothes, ma'am."

"Thank you, Bridget," I say as she walks to the door. "And see if you can find my husband fresh clothes a well. He's being stubborn out there."

Confusion fills her face. "Mr. McQueen has left, ma'am."

"I beg pardon?"

"He went into town at dawn."

"What?" I shout. I move the tray and fly out of bed. He wouldn't... When I toss open the door, I find Duncan whittling in the guard post chair. He did. "Where is Jamie?"

"I don't...I cannot tell ya, ma'am. He said not to. He just said he'd give me two pounds if I watched out for you today. Made sure you did not leave the island."

Indignant rage flares within me. That bastard. He has lost his bloody mind. "Do you know the location of the vampyre Michael's manor?"

"I don't, I can't—"

"Ten pounds. I shall give you ten pounds if you take me there."

He exchanges a look with Bridget, who is as horrified at this turn of events as he is. "It's dangerous, ma'am, far too dangerous for...you." He smartly does not add "for a woman" but may as well have.

"That is my concern, not yours. All you need concern yourself with is which fine necklace you shall purchase Heather with your ten pounds to aid in your wooing. Do we have a bargain?"

Duncan mulls it over for half a second. Me or Heather, no question there. "I can show you where the manor is, but cannot go in with you. Grand-Da has forbidden it."

"I never expected you to. But I need you both to fetch me a few items. A maid's uniform, a cross or crucifix, and any silver blades the pack possesses. *Now.*" I go back into the room, kick myself, then poke my head out again. "Please." Even at times like these, manners should never be forgotten.

Half an hour later, I am ready for battle. In keeping with our original plan, I am dressed in one of Bridget's black and white livered dresses to blend in with the staff at the manor. Stuffed in my cleavage is a cross, in each of my stockings a small silver blade, along with the Artemis. Not ideal but better than nothing. Duncan leads me through the near empty castle, and those who do pass do not acknowledge us. The disguise works thus far. May my luck continue. Oh please let my luck continue. We have almost made it out of the servant's exit when a familiar voice asks, "And where are you two sneaking off to?"

Blast. I spin around to find Nan at the kitchen door. "Just for a walk. I wanted to see the island."

Her eyes narrow. "You are a fine liar, you know. I might have believed that, if not for the silly get-up." She takes a step. "What you are thinking of doing is suicide. It's pure madness."

"So I have been told. I am still going."

"I'm just showing her where it is, Nan," Duncan says. "I'm not helping, I promise."

"Stop sniveling, Duncan," she snaps, before turning back to me. "My grandson left you behind for a reason, consider that. He could not bear it if something happened to you."

"And I couldn't bear it if something happened to him!" I shout. "Either of them. It is the lives of my brother and the man I love at stake. I shall not sit by and knit whilst they remain in mortal danger. If I die, I die. I am prepared for that. What I am not prepared for is to bury them because I was too afraid to fight for them as they would for me. So I am sorry but I am leaving now. Thank you for your hospitality. It was very nice meeting you. Good-bye." I spin around and take a step out.

"Mrs. McQueen?" Nan calls. I turn around with my hands on my hips. A sly smile fills her face. "If you survive this foolishness, please come back and visit anytime. I told my grandson the same this morning before he left. Perhaps next visit will prove more rewarding. You are family after all. Be safe." With that, she turns and hobbles away. What an odd woman.

Duncan and I hurry down to the dock to avoid further delays. Jamie took the monopede so the best way to the manor, according to Duncan, is to follow the shore in a skiff, land in

Barna, and walk the two remaining miles. So that is what I do, foot tapping nervously the whole way. When we finally dock over an hour later my escort refuses to leave the boat, so I continue the rest of the way alone, walking uphill through a heavily wooded area with flourishing trees and bramble like something out of a faeiry story. Apprehension creeps in with each step. Bloody hell, this is it. All I have been through, all I have survived has led to today. I could very well die this day, or worse find it was all for naught. David could be dead. He could have been dead since that first night. Jamie as well. He could have gone in already, already been discovered, and as punishment they killed them both. Unthinkable. I shall burn down the entire manor if they have harmed one hair on their heads.

I know I am getting closer to the manor when the acrid stench of death begins filling the woods every so often. Probably the corpses of their victims in shallow graves. This new development makes the crackling branches I have heard since entering the forest far more alarming. I cock the Artemis.

The forest recedes less than a quarter mile later onto the clearing with the manor at the centre. It reminds me of Foxfire with the same Elizabethan architecture with Dutch gables, large mullion bay windows, pinnacles on the roofs adorned with gargoyles, and made with the same grey stone, though Foxfire does not have a turret tower in its centre poking out like a finger pointing to the heavens. I spot three people in the surrounding field slowly shambling back and forth as if on an automatic track like automatons. Guards? They are too far away to make out clear details, but there are two men and a woman judging from the clothes. There is something not right about them, but I cannot pinpoint exactly what. No matter. Jamie would have seen them too and repositioned to the servant's entrance in back to avoid detection.

Using the trees as cover, I dash along the edge of the forest as quietly as possible until I locate the perfect vantage of that door.

It's closer than the front entrance as well, only about a fifty meters through the clearing. There are no signs of life here, no people going in or out, which is most odd. There should be groomsmen, maids, kitchen staff, grounds men milling about. Perhaps there are no servants. No, the door opens and a woman my age in a similar outfit to mine, a simple black dress with white apron, walks out with a pail. She is as skittish and tense as a cat, glancing every which way as if a lion could leap out of the jungle and eat her. What is she nervous about? It's daylight, the vampyres are asleep.

Branches snap behind me and the woman gasps, even dropping the pail. What on earth? She retrieves the bucket and disappears around the side of the house, running as fast as she can. How odd. I glance back, finding nothing but a squirrel. I keep watch as the woman returns with a full pail and rushes back inside. I suppose if I worked for a vampyre I would be…what on earth is that stench?

This time when I look back, my heart catches in my throat, strangling my scream. A familiar man stands a few feet away with the yellow sagging skin, blood and dirt stained suit, cloudy eyes, and several ravaged pulpy bites on his neck. Even in his horrific state, I recognise him. Dr. Charles Rathbone, the no longer missing inventor. And he's dead, yet still moves with lips pulled over rotting black teeth, snarling at me. He is dead, I know it as I know anything. A ghoul. Oh, Charles, what have they done to you? There is no time to mourn. The monstrosity takes one step toward me, and I dash to the right with him hot on my trail. Who knew the dead could run so fast? I have no plan, no idea if there are more ghouls this way, I just know to run. He—

"Verity! Stop!"

Even now I trust him implicitly. I cease running and spin around. Rathbone continues his charge, but that is not where my eyes land. Just as the ghoul is a few feet away and closing, I see movement in one of the trees. Jamie pushes the branches aside and launches himself off his perch, landing right on Rathbone. Both men fall face first onto the ground near my feet. Jamie recovers faster, thumping the grunting ghoul's head against a rock several times before rolling off him. Rathbone turns over, black congealed blood all over his forehead. That is the spot Jamie aims for with the large branch he now wields, clubbing and clubbing the ghoul as more gore and pulp spills from his caved-in head and face. My breakfast rises into my throat.

When the ghoul finally ceases moving and moaning ten agonizing seconds later, a breathless Jamie tosses his weapon away. His menacing gaze whips over to me. "What the *fuck* are you doing here?" he hisses.

I am taken aback by his anger enough to flinch. "Well, what the…fuck are you doing leaving me behind?"

His eyes grow even wider as he rises. "I left you behind because you'll be a liability in there."

"Oh, as I was a liability when I saved you on the train? Or when that vampyre was gnawing on you? Or when I secured us transportation and a place to sleep? Twice? There are most likely two dozen rooms in that manor, it will take forever to search them and I know the layout. And I think by now we have established you and I are better together than alone." I put my hands on my hips and take a step toward him. "Or is that the true problem?"

"What?" he spits out.

I did not anticipate having this conversation beside a corpse but strangely it is fitting. "You're in love with me."

His mouth twitches, and the scowl grows. "The hell I am."

I grab the stubborn mule by the jacket, pulling his lips to mine. At first he resists, his mouth stiff, but only for an instant. He kisses me back with equal intensity, clutching onto me as if I were attempting to flee, tongue matching mine stroke for stroke. I pull away first, licking my lips then grinning from my victory. "The hell you aren't." Disgusted at giving in so easily, his mouth twists into a grimace. He turns on his heel and walks the way I came. I roll my eyes before giving chase. "That's it, do what you always do. Flee from me when you might, just *might*, have to face what we both know to be true. Be a coward."

"Lady, call me yellow again and I will give you a split lip. I mean it," he says as he continues running away from me.

"Then stop acting like one, you silly man. You know what I am saying is true. You admitted it to yourself last night. I know, I saw it. I felt it. So admit it to me. Look, it's easy. Jamie McQueen, I love you. I am completely, passionately in love with you, and I shall be until the day I die."

He moves even faster. "Shut up, lady."

"No. I love you. I am in love with you."

Out of nowhere he spins around, stalking toward me angrier than I have ever seen him. "Just shut up. Shut your damn mouth, Lady. You do not love me. You want me, and love and lust are two very different things."

"You think I do not know that? Without question, it began as lust, no question, and I assume it was the same for you. But as I got to know you, I saw your gentility, your misplaced honor, your strength, your intelligence, your…accepting nature. How could I not fall in love with such a man? So I shall say it again. I love you, Jamie McQueen. And you love me. I know this because you grow petrified every time you look at me, you who leapt off a dirigible. Love is the most frightening force on this planet, especially for people such as us. Oddities. Freaks. We know how rare this force is; just as we know it can be taken in a moment with one misstep. And I am not blind to our challenges, I am altogether aware of them, perhaps even more than you. But we have survived gunfights, mercenaries, vampyres, dirigibles, your animal instincts, and an evening with your family. What is geography, one night a month apart, and the opinions of idiots against that? We will figure it all out as we have everything else. Together." I shrug. "We have no other choice. We found one another now. There is no going back, and even if there was a chance to, would you really be able to take it? To turn your back on all that this could be? To consign us both to the purgatory we called our lives? Because the man I love would never contemplate it for a moment, not even out of fear. Not even a vampyre would be that cruel."

We stand staring at each other, me with my shoulders back and he almost seething with emotion, though none shows on his face. He is working so hard not to let my words penetrate that thick skull of his, but they will. Without question. Jamie McQueen would never let me down. "This ain't the time or place to discuss this. Let's go get your brother."

We have a lifetime ahead of us, so I nod. "To be continued then."

Without another word, I follow him to the edge of the clearing to survey the manor. He keeps his eyes straight ahead, refusing to look at me the entire time. "I was watching the house for awhile when another of those corpses found me. There are three more out front, two in back, and God knows how many in the woods and house. This Michael must have brought them back as ghouls after he drained them."

"That was Dr. Rathbone back there, the inventor they kidnapped before David. He must have attempted to escape, and judging from his wounds, the human bite marks, a ghoul killed him. Poor Charles."

"We learn from his mistakes. We enter through the servant's door, we come out the same way. The monopede is straight back about two hundred feet. We go in, grab props to make it seem like we work there, but keep our heads down and avoid gazes while we search. Blend in."

"It will go faster if we split up."

"I am not leaving you…" He catches himself possibly even literally biting his tongue judging from the sneer. "You're right. If he's not in a dungeon or that tower, look for rooms away from others. They'd want him isolated."

"I understand." I take a deep breath to calm my nerves.

It's time.

I take a step into the clearing, but Jamie grabs my hand. "Wait." I turn to him, greeted by a grave expression more frightening than a ghoul. "If something goes wrong, if something happens to me or you get caught, don't hesitate. If they're a threat, take them out and you run. You don't worry about me or your brother, you just run. You go back to the Roarke's. My grandmother will make sure they protect you. But you run and you don't look back. Do you understand me?"

"I will not leave you to them, Jamie. I will not abandon—"

"You may have no other choice. It may be the only way to save us all. *You. Run.* Promise me." He squeezes my hand hard. "Promise me, or we're not going in there."

The words stick in my throat, but I say, "I promise."

He half nods and releases my hand. "Good. Then let's go rescue your brother."

*

Like at Foxfire the servant's entrance opens onto a small, dark foyer with muddy coats and shoes lined up on the floor leads to a hall that branches out to various rooms such as the kitchen, pantry, servant's dining room, washing room, and a half dozen others needed to maintain the routine of the house. I grab a feather duster, and Jamie a long brown coat to conceal his gun belt. Though we look the part of stable hand and still-maid, we walk the empty corridor with our heads bowed. There is one staircase to the women's quarters, another to the men's, and the winding one leading up to the manor. The house should have at least a dozen servants, not counting those responsible for the stables and grounds, but we only pass one maid too busy ironing to bother with us. So far so good.

The stairs end at another dim hallway, though this one is far grander with red carpet over hardwood floor, antique vases with wilting or dead flowers and oil paintings of previous landowners of decades past or hunts lining the walls. It is as quiet as a crypt with the air of one as well. There is no life in this house. No mirth. Just a void. "You go left, I'll go right. We'll meet at the main staircase in ten minutes," Jamie whispers.

"Be careful," I whisper back.

"Remember your promise," he says before rushing left down the hall.

How could I forget?

I check the billiard, drawing, and morning rooms along with the parlor, study, library and not a soul. Nothing. Perhaps we're in the wrong location. Perhaps the vampyres have come and gone. Oh God, that would be worse than facing an entire squadron of ghouls. I find Jamie skulking in the corner of the staircase. "Have you seen anyone?"

"There was a man in the parlor, but no one else," Jamie says as we walk upstairs.

"Did he see you?"

"No, his back was to me."

When we reach the second floor, he goes right and I left when the stairs branch off in opposite directions. The second floor is even gloomier than the first with dark wood panels along the walls, matching high back wooden chairs, and heavy velvet curtains keeping out all the light from the bay windows in the hall. At least they have gas lamps or I might bump into the tables and shatter the vases on them. I try the first door on the right beside a grandfather clock, but the handle will not turn. Locked. *David.* I lightly knock but there is no answer, only snores. I peer in through the keyhole, and though there is minimal light, I can make out the outline of what could be a coffin beside the bed with a slumbering woman snoring away. Blast. The next room yields the same result. There are vampyres on the other side of these doors, all seven of them. If one of those coffins is David's, all is lost. When I return to the stairs, it seems Jamie has beaten me again.

"I found eight vampyres," Jamie says as we hurry to the next staircase around the corner.

"Seven," I say. "At least they are asleep."

"For now. Let's just be gone when they wake."

When we reach the third floor, we stop dead. Down the dark hallway, a valet dressed in livery steps into one of the bedrooms as a few feet away a maid dusts a vase. She glances over at us, half smiles, then moves around the corner to continue her tasks.

"We must hurry," I whisper.

"Yep."

He veers right, and I left. Keeping my head down, I try the knobs, but if a door is locked and keyhole dark I move on. I cannot take the chance of being caught snooping. On door four, the maid returns to this hallway. I begin dusting a vase. "I already did this hall," she says. I nod and move on, but do not dare look back as I am sure she is apprising me. I round the corner she came from and take a deep breath, slowly letting it out. At least this passage is empty. I find two more locked rooms before reaching the double doors with light rimming its edges from the other side. Three locks as well. Curiouser and curiouser. When I bend to peer through the keyhole, I see stairs. It must lead to the tower. How—

"What are you doing?" a man asks behind me.

My entire body stiffens upon hearing his voice. Keep calm, Verity. "I, um, dropped my duster, sir," I say with a wretched Irish accent as I rise. "I'm sorry, sir."

"Turn around." Though keep my head bowed I obey. It's the valet from the hallway. He is barely in his twenties, and handsome with brown hair. "I don't know you."

"I started today, sir. I arrived late last night with my husband. He is working in the stables."

The valet stares as he weighs my story. "Mrs. O'Bannon did not inform you that room was forbidden?"

"No sir. She just told me not to enter the rooms if the door was locked. I haven't, sir."

He appraises me with a scowl. *Oh, please...* "Finish dusting this passage then see if they need help with the ironing."

"Yes, sir," I say with a curtsey.

"And remove that bracelet. You should know better."

"Yes, sir, Thank you, sir." I unlatch the Artemis, putting it in my open pocket, and begin dusting the suit of armor beside the door. After what feels like forever, the valet walks back down the hall.

I continue working for a minute in case this is a trick. Good thing too because after only thirty seconds he pokes his head around the corner again. I wait another minute before putting down the duster. That was close. We have to hurry. He'll most likely check with Mrs. O'Bannon now. I examine the double doors again. Oak. Hard to break, and I haven't a clue how to pick a lock let alone three. David *has* to be in there. After putting the Artemis back on, I run down the hall in search of Jamie. He—

When I round the corner, I physically run into the valet. My mouth drops open with a gasp. Blast.

"You!" he says, grabbing my arm. "I knew it. You're her, Lady Hart, aren't you?"

"Unhand me, sir," I say.

"We've been waiting for—"

Bugger this. With all my might, I thrust my knee into his bollocks, making the man double over, before I grab a marble bust from a nearby table and brain him in the back of the head. He falls unconscious to the floor. "Sorry," I whisper, replacing the bust on the table. I take him by the arms and drag him around the corner out of sight, checking his pockets for keys after. None. It is never that easy, is it? I sigh. We need to get into the tower. Quickly.

I locate my partner leaving a bedroom in the end of the east wing. I nod backwards, and he knows what I mean. He follows me back the way I came, slowing only when we pass the stairs where the maid descends. She glances back at us, greeted by smiles. The valet remains dead to the world when we return. Jamie takes one look at him, picks him up, and puts him in an empty room without a word of recrimination.

"Can you pick a lock?" I ask.

"I don't have my set, and…" He kicks the doors, and they splinter open. "This takes less time."

His smile falters as his head cocks to the side like a dog's. With one fluid movement he pushes aside his coat, whips out a knife from his belt and tosses it as a man with a gun dashes down the steps into view. It enters right below the guard's Adam's apple, sliding in like a peg into a hole. Blood spurts from the man's mouth before he collapses on the stairs. Emotionless, Jamie walks up to him, pulls the knife out, garnering another spurt, and takes the man's gun and keys as well. "Come on. We don't got much time."

As I step over the dying man, I close my eyes. I shall say a prayer for him later. At the top of the stairs we find an iron door with a now empty chair beside it. Jamie hands me the keys before he stands guard with the gun pointed down the stairs. I knock. "David?" No answer. I knock furiously. "David?" He has to be here. He has to. He—

"Verity?"

Upon hearing my brother's voice, fresh tears spring from my eyes. There was a large part of me that was sure I would never hear it again. He's alive. Thank you, God. "Yes it's me. We're going to get you out of here right now," I say, voice quaking.

"Hurry," Jamie orders.

It takes a few attempts, but I find the keys for the three locks. When I throw the door open my brother stands on the other side, pale and drawn, but alive. He's truly alive. I leap into his arms. "I feared I would never see you again," I say, clutching onto his almost skeletal body.

His grip tightens. "I feared the same. What—"

"Run now, reunion later," Jamie barks.

I pull away. "He's right. We have to go." I take David's hand and lead him out the door. We rush down the steps close behind Jamie.

"Who is that?" David asks.

"Long story."

David gasps as we pass the dead guard, but I barely notice him. My tolerance for the horrid has increased tenfold this week. I yank my brother away from the corpse just as Jamie moves though the double doors into the hall with us a second behind. Everything happens at once. There is little time to react.

The moment David and I move through the doors, I realize Jamie has stopped dead in the middle of the hall. He levels his gun toward the way of our escape. At the same time I look in that direction, finding three men cocking their pistols at us. David gasps again, but my breath cannot escape. I'm paralyzed mentally and physically. No. *No*. We were so close. So close. This cannot be happening. Not now.

"Drop your gun," one of the men orders with an Irish brogue.

"You drop yours," Jamie says.

"It's three to one, mate. We will fire."

"Do that and you might hit the lady. I hear your boss is a real asshole. Imagine what he would do if you killed the woman he's been so damn desperate to get hold of. Want to take that chance?"

For a moment, I think they will stand down as their faces contort with trepidation. Beautiful, wonderful logic. This may—

A horrible pain rips through the back of my head as something heavy smashes into it. I lose all control. My limbs, my thoughts, all give way to agony. As the world turns black, the last thing I hear is my name screamed in terror by my brother.

We were so close. Blast.

*

Something cool and wet against my forehead draws me out of the darkness. Why couldn't I stay there? Pain soon follows so intense I almost vomit.

"Very, don't move," David instructs.

I open my eyes, though even the dim light from the windows and flickering gas lamps ratchets up the torment. I blink to clear my cloudy vision. In the past week I have awoken in some strange locals, but this one at least resembles home. It is a workshop much like mine with a large drafting table in the centre of the room covered with scraps of metal, tools, a rounded silver helmet with faceplate like an old knight's, and the rest of the man-sized suit of armor held together with tubes, rivets, and hydraulics standing in the corner of the large room. There are also bookcases, wooden chairs, and another door off to the side of the grey stonemason room. What an interesting prison cell.

I am vaguely aware I am in David's lap on a couch as he tends to the back of my head with a wet cloth partially stained red. "What happened?"

"A valet snuck up behind us and hit you on the head with a marble bust. Your friend surrendered after that."

"Jamie?" I call, which sends shards of glass further into my cranium. I hope that valet is experiencing similar agony right now. Bastard.

"They took him someplace else. I do not know where."

"Good. He can come rescue us then." I shut my eyes, which helps with the pain a fraction. "We just have to wait." I feel my pilfered blades from the Roarke castle still in my stockings, and cross in my cleavage, but not the Artemis. "They took the Artemis?"

"Yes. I believe they recognised it from the article in the paper last week."

"That was only a week ago? Seems like a lifetime."

"I know. I feel as if I have been locked up here a month."

I grimace. "I'm sorry."

"What for?"

"Not arriving sooner. Failing." He does not speak for several seconds. I open my eyes again and gaze up. Oh my, he is on the verge of tears. "What?"

"I…I am the one who should apologize," he says, voice cracking. "I—I tried to work on the machine, I did, but I wrecked the engine. He…was going to drain me. I was half dead, and it just flowed out. I am so sorry, Very. *So sorry*. You would not be here, imprisoned, in mortal danger if I were stronger. I—"

"David, stop," I say, caressing his hollow cheek. "There is nothing to forgive. You had no other option, I know that. You're alive, that is all I care about. Whatever you did to remain that way you will find no recrimination by me. Just as I pray all I did to get here, to get to you, shall be extended the same courtesy."

His eyes narrow. "What did you do, Very?" he asks, almost fearful.

As I slowly recover from my second concussion this week, we share our tales of terror. After they flew off that night in London, the vampyres took him directly to a steamer ship waiting in the harbor, and as I thought, made him write that letter. They left him handcuffed, gagged, and frightened out of his mind the entire twenty-four hour voyage from ship to manor where this Michael demanded he finish the suit Rathbone almost completed before his ill-fated escape attempt. When they finally discovered their mistake after the steam engine exploded and set the curtains on fire, Michael was about to drain him of every last drop of blood. Only then did my brave brother reveal the truth. I meant what I said. I do not blame him one whit for the disclosure. I would have broken sooner. Since that night he has been locked in this room waiting to die.

My adventure takes longer to recount. When I finish, David's expression is priceless with his brown eyes popping out of his head, mouth agape.

"*Him?*"

"Him."

"The man, no sorry, *werewolf* responsible for the dead man on the steps? A murderer? You are in love with a killer?"

"I'm a killer as well now, David," I point out. "We did what was necessary to save us all. I would do it all again in a heartbeat."

"It is bad enough he's an American. A crude, vulgar, violent, penniless American I might add, but…he transforms into a wolf? An animal? Very, you absolutely cannot be in love with this man. You cannot."

"But I am."

For the first time in over an hour, I sit up. The world tilts but only for a second. "David, he has risked his life countless times for me. For you. He could have abandoned me, given up, but no matter what, he stood by my side."

"But Very, you are paying him. A great sum on money."

"You do not know him as I do," I say with a scowl. Even that hurts. "You have not seen what I have, felt what I have whilst we are together. He is…my equal, and he treats me as such. He has seen me at my worst and never wavered. He is the love of my life. I know it. Just as I knew you were alive when everyone told me it was impossible."

"I do not doubt your love for him, Very. You have always known your own heart. But it is impossible to gaze into someone else's. I simply do not wish to see you hurt again."

"He is not Jolyon. You shall see, brother dear. He loves me as I love him."

David wraps his arm around my shoulders, pulling me close so I can rest my head on his bony shoulder. He kisses my forehead. "How could he not?"

We sit in silence for a moment as I stare at the metal man in the corner. The source of all this trouble.

"So what exactly is that thing? An automaton?"

"Best I can glean, it is a mechanical suit of armor. A person, I presume Michael, is meant to be inside controlling it. There is something called a Gatling gun he wants added along with a flamethrower, both of which he can regulate from inside the suit. It also has to be sun tight, whatever that means."

"It means he plans to attack his rival Lucian during the day, wiping out the whole cabal whilst they slumber. He assumes command of the survivors if any, and all of Lucian's business ventures. He becomes the Lord of Galway all for the price of a few inventors' lives. Clever. What is he like?"

"Frightening. Evil incarnate."

"In that case…" I gaze at the metal monster in the corner. The things I could do with that. I grin. "I cannot wait to meet him."

*

As the sun begins to set, and Jamie still does not storm the tower, my anxiety grows. David swore up and down he was taken alive, but all manner of foul things could have happened between then and now. One lesson I've learnt this week is to have a back-up plan. Or three. When I can stand without assistance, I take stock of what we have at our disposal. Our captor has provided an ample bounty of tools and materials we can use to build weapons. How kind of him. A few possibilities spring to mind, and with the aid of headache powder, I begin formulating a plan. After the sun sets, as I'm drafting a blueprint, one of the henchmen from earlier in the hall, gun still in hand, steps inside our cell. "Michael wishes to see you. Both."

Time to face mine enemy. About bloody time.

The manor is bustling with activity now the sun has set. All the vampyres have risen from those coffins of theirs and now stalk the halls, one paler than the last. They eye us as if we are dinner, some even hissing and baring their fangs. I simply keep my head up and eyes straight as if they were not there. We are escorted to the large drawing room where a man in his early twenties, dressed in a black velvet smoking jacket with a ruby encrusted gear on his white cravat, lounges on the white silk divan reading the newspaper and sipping a goblet of what I assume is blood. As with the rest of the manor's inhabitants, our host is most pale with curly auburn hair, emaciated frame, and almost coal black eyes complete with clipped moustache. A familiar face, Francis Smith from London minus his better half Megan, stands beside Michael still as a coat rack with a pitcher of blood ready to serve his master once more. The vampyre folds up the paper and smiles at me, exposing those fangs, I suppose to intimidate me. After this week it shall take more than that. "Lady Hart. Finally," he says with an Irish accent.

"You must be Michael."

"My reputation precedes me." He sips the blood. "As does yours. You are a difficult woman to get a hold of. When Megan and Joseph failed to return, I was about to give up hope and drain your brother. Yet here you are. *You* came to *me*. Tell me, what did happen to those I sent after you?"

"Which ones? The men on the train or vampyres on the dirigible? I suppose it does not matter, the answer is the same. They are dead."

The corner of his thin mouth twitches upon the news. "I assumed as much. Such a waste. Now, was it you or your werewolf friend responsible for their fates?"

"Half and half. We try to keep our relationship fair and equal."

He twitches again. "It seems I underestimated you."

"Most do," I say with a grin. "Just like now. I do not know if you have been informed, but my companion is Albert Roarke's nephew. You remember Albert. The leader of twenty plus werewolves you threatened a few years past? He is no admirer of yours, I can tell you that. What do you think the pack shall do when they discover you intend to harm us? They are quite fond of us both. They even threw a fete in our honor last night."

The way every muscle in his face falls, I glean he was not privy to this information. "You lie."

"Ask Mr. McQueen if you do not believe me. The family resemblance is astounding. Or better yet send a message to the island. I am sure Albert is waiting with bated breath by the door to hear from us. That was the plan at least." Even I am close to believing this lie.

The vampyre's eyes narrow. "Then why only the two of you? Why didn't the whole pack invade my house?"

"We insisted they not get involved unless absolutely necessary. I believe we have reached that point, yes? The sun has set. I expect them shortly."

Michael studies my self-assured face but must see behind the façade as a small smile creeps along his face. "Liar." He turns to Francis. "Bring the werewolf." The vampyre hops to, scurrying out of the room. "Please sit down."

With a gracious smile, I sit on the loveseat with David beside me across from the divan. "Thank you." I finger the dagger taped to my forearm for reassurance. David has one as well. I am confident Jamie has whipped up a plan by now, and we Harts are prepared to implement it.

A few minutes later I hear chains rattling. As the sound grows closer, I look to the door. Oh thank God. I smile brightly as Jamie enters, held at gunpoint by Francis, but he gives me such an enraged glare it wipes the smile away. How odd. Though it could just be due to his current predicament. Both hands and feet are shackled, and judging from the burns on his wrists, they are made of silver.

"Our other unexpected guest. Welcome. Mr. Roarke, is it?"

"McQueen. Jamie McQueen."

"But your mate here said your last name was Roarke."

"She's not my mate," he snaps. "She's my boss."

"Your boss?" he asks with amusement.

"She hired me to bring her here. Get the brother. A thousand pounds."

"My, my that is quite a bounty. I am honored." He examines Jamie up and down. "You look like a Roarke though."

"Half of one. James was my grandfather, and Albert is my uncle. We ain't exactly close, but I know they wouldn't take kindly to one of their kin being killed by one of yours just for doing his job. I am still blood after all, and I know you two have had your troubles. You strike me as a smart man. You don't want to piss off the local pack unless you have to."

"So I should just allow you and the Harts to just waltz out after all the trouble I've been through to get them here?" The vampyre scoffs. "I think not."

"Well, you can keep them," he says, nodding at us. My stomach drops. He did not just suggest...? "Just let me go. They're nothing to the pack, and you don't need me for your stupid war with whatever his name is."

"Really?" Michael asks with amusement. "You would leave them here to our mercy?"

"For safe passage to the first steamer out of this fucking hellhole of a country, and the balance of what's owed me? Yeah."

"You blackguard!" David shouts.

"Jamie..." I say, stunned.

The man I love looks at me, expressionless. "Sorry, shug. You're a hell of a woman, and a damn fine kisser to boot, and it has been fun, but...I ain't dying for you. Certainly not like this," he says so nonchalantly it stops my breath. He turns back to Michael. "So you give me five hundred pounds, the rest of her balance, undo these shackles, and not only will I telegraph the Roarkes I'm safe, but one of your buddies can ride all the way to America with me if you're not the trusting sort."

"And if I do not release you?"

"Then after my grandmother doesn't hear from me by midnight she convinces my uncle, the hothead with twenty wolves at his disposal, to spin a tale to your friend Lucian and both arrive to kick your bony ass. I don't know what you want her to build, but unless it's a device to raise the full force of hell to your side, we both know you wouldn't stand a chance. I am absolutely not worth that risk."

As Michael considers his options, I just stare at Jamie in shock. He spoke with such conviction even *I* am inclined to believe he truly desires to desert us. He must have a plan. At any moment he shall spring into action. Any moment.

"You killed several of my people," Michael says.

"Only the ones trying to kill me. Wasn't personal."

"I will not pay you a farthing. Consider it a fine for those I lost. And you draft a handwritten letter on the ship denouncing any further action against us which we shall deliver to the pack."

"Not a problem," Jamie says, not missing a beat.

"And someone accompanies you onto the first ship to America leaving tonight. But know that if he does not return by dawn, or I see one werewolf from here on, I throw Lord Hart to my ghouls for supper and turn Lady Hart."

Jamie doesn't even flinch. "Want that in the letter too?" he asks as if it was nothing.

"Yes. And the shackles remain on until you reach the ship."

"Well, since I ain't in any position to negotiate further, guess we got ourselves a deal. I would like my suitcase though."

"We'll bring it out to you." He nods at a willowy vampyre wearing my Artemis, who rushes out.

"Thank you," Jamie says.

Michael nods to Francis, who nods back. "Come on," Francis says.

Jamie turns around without even a glance my way. Okay, anytime now. He shuffles to the door. Anytime. But when he reaches the threshold, I cannot contain myself a moment longer. I leap up. "Jamie!" He ceases walking, and turns as I run over to him. "What…?"

"I'm sorry, shug," he says blithely. "I'm sure you'll be fine. You're tough. Just do what he asks, it'll go better for ya."

"You're not...I do not understand," I say, voice cracking.

He lets out a sad sigh as his shoulders slump. "You gotta know when to hang up the fiddle, shug. We lost. I'm sorry, but I know when to get out while the getting's good. I can't save you this time. Sorry." He plants a chaste kiss on my quivering lips. "Sorry. Bye."

I clutch onto his hands to stop him. "Jamie, you cannot do this. You cannot leave us here," I cry, the tears falling down my cheeks.

"I got no choice," he says through gritted teeth, eyes wild. "I ain't being tortured in some cell or drained alive by them, I ain't. Not for you, not for anyone. Besides, I told you to stay behind at the castle, didn't I? The only thing I ever asked of you was to listen, and you didn't. This is your own fault. I ain't paying for it, I'm just not."

"Wh—What about honor? Where is the honor in leaving us with them?"

"What good is honor if you're dead?" he says harshly. He yanks his hands from mine. "Sometimes it ain't us versus them, it's you or me. *I choose me.* You get the chance, you do the same Lady Hart. I'm sorry. Bye."

He shuffles away again, and I stand too shocked and heartbroken to move for a few seconds. David comes behind me, putting his hands on my shoulders. "Verity—"

I shrug them off and stomp into the foyer after him. "I love you!" He continues toward the door as if he cannot hear me. "Did you hear me? I love you." Jamie slowly turns, and I wipe my tears. "And I thought you loved me."

"Oh, shug," he says sadly, meeting my eyes. "*No.* I don't love you. I'm sorry."

"But you... I—I saw..."

"I lost myself a few times in the moment, that's all," he says nonchalantly. "We went through hell together. What happened between us happens all the time. Hell, I've lost count of how many times I've fallen into bed with a gal after a crazy situation. I didn't mean to lead you on or hurt you, I mean it. Really, I'm sorry. For all of this."

I violently shake my head. "No. I—I don't believe you."

He shrugs. "Believe what you want. I don't care."

"No," I whimper.

"Bye, Lady Hart. We had a hell of a ride together. I won't soon forget it. You're a hell of a gal." He looks down at the floor, properly cowed for someone leaving us to die. "Bye, shug."

The man I love turns again and strolls to the entrance without a glance back. The moment the door shuts the moment he abandons us, I gasp as my legs give out. I collapse onto the red carpet unable to breathe. I gasp and gasp, but no air will enter.

"Verity!" David shouts, rushing to my side. He kneels down, takes me in his arms, and rocks me back and forth as I wheeze against this shoulder. He's gone. He is really gone. He's left us to the mercy of monsters.

"You will finish my machine, Lady Hart," Michael says behind me, "or lose the other man you love." He moves in front of me, gazing down without emotion. "At least this one seems to deserve said love." Michael glances at the guard before sauntering to the drawing room. "Take them back to the tower. I do so loathe hysterical women."

"Come on, Very," David whispers as he helps me rise.

I sob on my brother's shoulder the entire way back to the tower. He pets my hair and whispers that all will be well. When we reach our prison, I pull away, throwing myself onto the couch, crying hysterically against the arm. "I'd get working if I were you," the guard says. "Don't make him angrier than he already is." The door shuts.

David hurries over to me. "Oh, Very. I'm so sorry. Very—" I look up at my concerned brother and as if I flick a switch, I immediately stop sobbing. He is visibly taken aback by my reversal. I would be too. "What?"

I wipe my eyes. "You believed that malarkey?" I smile my brightest. "I was quite good, wasn't I? Almost had myself fooled there for a moment." I rise and straighten my shirt. "Think Mr. Stoker would put me on the stage? That'd shock Father, no?"

"Verity, I don't think he—"

"His eyes kept moving left," I say as I walk to the window. "Saw it clear as day. That's his tell. He was lying."

"What? Very, I know you love that man, but he left us. He abandoned us to them," he says through gritted teeth.

I scoff. "He did not abandon us. He may not be here in body, but he is in spirit. He's free to put his plan into motion. He'll be back, I know it."

"Because he moved his eyes left?" David asks incredulously.

I pull aside the curtain and watch as below the man I love leaves in an automaton horse drawn carriage. "Because I trust him. Because I have faith in him. Because he is the most honorable man I have ever met. And he loves me. Of that I have no doubt." I rest my head against the wall and watch as the carriage disappears into the dark night. "And what are a few dozen vampyres against true love?" Turning to my brother, I smile again. "Now brother dear, I believe we have a war machine to build. I feel one approaching. We must be ready. Chop chop."

See you soon, my love. I shall be waiting.

CHAPTER FOURTEEN

THE GLOVES COME OFF

So we wait. And wait. And wait. My faith never wavers.

Not the next morning when we are informed not only did Jamie board a ship for Boston, but the vampyre with him sailed with him all the way past the Airen Islands. Not the following day when I am read a letter from the Roarke pack promising no retaliation for my capture per Jamie's request. Not even six days into my captivity when we receive a telegram from Boston stating he arrived. Each time we receive word David grows concerned for me, as if I have lost contact with reality.

"The man jumped off a train and dirigible for me. What's a ship?"

"He has not spoken to the pack yet. I am sure he has a plan involving them."

"Jamie has friends all over America. No doubt he telegrammed one of them in Boston asking them to send one from there in his name. It's what I would do. Stop fretting, he's coming."

My brother simply shakes his head sadly and continues working. He is finally learning there is no convincing me Jamie has forsaken us, so why try? We must be ready when he arrives. I ordered our captors to acquire a chemistry set for David as the war machine needs compounds, special oil and such, to run. Which is a load of bunkum of course. As I assemble the metal man, which should really have taken only two days but they do not know that, David creates our ammunition. Flammable liquid for the Incinerators I assemble from spare parts, and crystals that explode on impact. Feels like old times. Except unlike at Somerset or in London an enraged vampyre visits nightly to rant about our lack of progress and threatens to kill us. I could do without that, thank you very much.

And every night, when I cannot keep my eyes open a moment longer, I sleep and dream of him. Some nights we lie in a field of gold just holding one another as the breeze tickles my skin. Others we are riding horses wildly cackling like banshees through the streets of London firing at the outlaws chasing us. I cannot wait to drift off most nights.

On the sixth night, a few hours after I was informed of the telegram, I am instructed to join Michael in the drawing room. I am not given the chance to change out of my work clothes I insisted they provided. Black leather bloomers, white shirt with buckled leather vest over it, black gloves, and goggles. I believe I am wearing dead Megan's flying outfit. They look better on my anyway. It is my first time out of the room, and though I loathe the company, it is lovely to leave my cell. The tower only has two rooms, the workshop and bedroom David and I share, and I am sick of them both. Once again when I enter Michael lounges on the divan, reading and enjoying his bloody nightcap with the bastard valet who knocked me out at his side. "Have you seen the London papers lately, Lady Hart?" the vampyre asks, folding the paper and sitting up. "You might find them interesting. Page six." He hands it to the valet who passes it to me, glaring the entire time. What? I hit him, he hit me. We are even now.

I open to the society page on six. Oh, Lord. If the vampyres don't kill me Father will finish me off.

"*The most whispered about mystery of the Season has been solved. Which fashionable, beautiful daughter of a high ranking Member of Parliament, known as a breaker of at least three harts,*" Well that was very clever. The first ten times they ever used it, "*has thrown away that reputation for one as a fallen woman? This hartbreaker, who has been noted multiple times as missing from the end of the Season, has been reported as far as Ireland in the company of a certain American bounty hunter remembered for the assault of Lord Richard Hopper. It seems that the hartbreaker not only arranged for his release, but the same day ran off to Wales with him. Unaccompanied.*

"However, it appears what goes around does come around. Word has reached this reporter that said American has abandoned her for his native land, leaving the hartbreaker hartbroken. Her exact whereabouts at present are unknown, but rumor has it that she is recovering in Ireland with her brother, who is hard at work on a secret project. More on this story as it develops."

"I, of course, contacted the papers with the story," Michael informs me with pride. "My sources told me people, including your family, were beginning to worry. We could not have them come looking for you, could we?"

"You…" I crumple up the paper. "Bastard."

"I know your father is a powerful man with many friends in the government and military, so we have been sending him telegrams in both you and your brother's names for some time. Your father is not coming for you, and neither is your werewolf. And I am running out of patience, Lady Hart. I have treated you and your brother with the utmost hospitality. Until now."

"If you call keeping us locked up against our will hospitality."

"No harm has come to you, has it? We have not starved or beaten you? But that will change. You have three nights from now to complete my machine. If it is not ready by then, I turn you, then lock you and your brother alone in a room. A newborn vampyre is a vicious creature, with no humanity whatsoever. You will kill him without hesitation. Then we will make it appear you murdered him then took your own life due to your disgrace."

"Why should I do what you ask? When I finish you, will kill us anyway."

"Not necessarily. I *could* let you both go as no one would ever believe the truth. Perhaps even plant false memories in both your minds. I am capable," He sips his blood. "Or I could turn you both. You are resourceful and smart, both of which are in short supply in my cabal. Or I can just give you to my underlings for a light snack. We shall see how effective our project is before I decide."

I want to spew out the epitaphs I learnt from Jamie but hold my tongue. "Then I had best get back upstairs, hadn't I? Am I dismissed?"

He nods. After a cruel grin and curtsey I turn and walk out. "Three nights, Lady Hart," Michael calls. "Three nights."

Bloody bastard.

When I return to the tower, and hear the three locks click in place, I let out the breath I held. I need air. The front window opens only two inches so we cannot climb out onto the slanted roof, but those inches are better than nothing. As I take in the warm breeze, the ghouls below continue their perpetual saunter to and fro under the full moon. The full moon. How glorious it is up there amid the stars. Right now Jamie is running underneath it, wild and free, possibly chasing down a stag or leaping over creeks in search of prey. Is he with the pack? Watching me in those woods? Has the moon even risen in Amer—*no.* No such thoughts are allowed to pass through my mind. I want to answer truthfully that my faith in him did not waver for even a second.

"What did Michael want?" David asks, still perched over his three Bunsen burners with the round goggles hiding his eyes.

"To tell me we are dead in three nights." I step away from the window. "And the whole of Britannia knows of my unladylike adventures and are appalled. No doubt Father is cursing the day I was born, and praying I never return. In three nights, he may be granted that wish."

"Are you alright?"

"Well, my exploits were bound to come out, especially when I bring Jamie home. At least now they can warm to the idea, get all their sniggers and self-righteousness under control before we return."

"I meant about the fact in three nights Michael intends to kill us."

"Oh. That," I say, picking up my blow torch. "Yes, it is a pickle," I say, putting on my dark tinted goggles. "What if Jamie needs more time? We should have—"

"Stop!" David shouts with a ferocity I have only heard from him once before. He rips off his goggles so I see the full force of his glare. "You *have* to stop this. I have tried to hold my tongue as long as I could, I really have, because we all need hope in this life, especially in our current situation. But not when it becomes detrimental. Like now. We cannot simply wait anymore for rescue when none is coming. *And none is coming.* We are on our own, as always. Accept it or we die. Do you understand me?"

He is so frightened, my big brother. I take him in my arms, hugging tight. "I know you think I've gone around the bend. If the roles were reversed, I would believe the same. And I am as scared as you are, I truly am." I release him. "But I am not mad nor a fool. We know now we have three nights left. So we wait the three nights, and if Jamie does not arrive, we go it alone."

"Okay," David says.

I meet my brother's eyes. "But we give Jamie the three nights. Even if we flee during daylight, there are at least ten servants and who knows how many ghouls between us and freedom. Then even if we do get away, where can we go that is safe? We know too much. They will continue coming after us. Perhaps not right away, but they will. I see that now. And I refuse to spend the remainder of my life glancing over my shoulder. I would rather go out fighting now than living half a life scared of a single misstep. I have done it for too long. Even if it costs you everything, if the cause is just, you *fight*. You fight until you cannot get up. Until you lose every ounce of blood. You fight. *He* made me see that. At least if we strike back, Michael may think twice about coming after us. Jamie knows this too. He *will* come."

I pick up the oil pencil I use on metal, walk over to the window, and draw, "4, 3, 2, 1" on the window panes so anyone outside can read them. "And when he does…" I cross out the four. "We shall be ready."

*

Michael's visits grow in number, with him often staying to watch our progress, so our side projects are hidden away and only worked on in daylight hours such as David practicing the operation of the suit. At first he insisted I be the one inside, protected against the wages of war, but since it was built for a man I am too small. David will clear the path, taking the brunt of the assault while I will follow behind, armed with all our new goodies. We are so busy and exhausted the days go by in a flash. The "3" is soon crossed out, then the "2" an hour after sunset. As I mark that last one, I glance at David, who looks away, fear all over his wan face. I feel the same, but attempt not to show my terror. Damn it, Jamie. Where are you?

"Tomorrow. At first light then," I say as I set the pencil down.

David grips the edge of the cluttered table, hanging his head. "We give it to him."

"I beg your pardon?"

His gaze whips up. "We give Michael the machine. It's what he wants. He — he'll let us go. He will. He has no reason to keep us after we give him what he wants," David says wildly.

"David, he is not releasing us! He can't. We have been over this. We fight or we die, there are no other options. We can do this, I know we can."

"Like you knew the American was coming back?" he spits out. "Very, get your bloody head out of the clouds! We—"

The unfamiliar sound of chugging steam engines beckons us to the window. There are very little comings and goings here. Only three times has anyone left this manor, and tonight was not one of them. With only the moon for illumination it is difficult to make out any details of the carriage beyond the two steaming automaton horses. The slanting roof below blocks me viewing the carriage reach the door, let alone who climbs out of it. "Who could it be?" David asks.

"I do not know." I open the window and start shouting, "Help! We're up here! Help us!"

The iron door swings opens, and the guard enters, pointing his pistol at us. "Shut up or I'll cut out your tongues! Get away from that window."

We step away. "Who has arrived?" I ask.

"None of your damn business. Get back to work!"

I believe I shall enjoy killing you tomorrow.

I am tightening the bolts on the machine's arm and glancing at the guard, who remains in the room for ten minutes, when there is a knock on the door. "Gregory, it's Colin," a man says on the other side. With his gun still on us, the guard opens the door. The bastard valet steps in. "Michael wants her ladyship."

So it begins.

The bastard valet escorts me to the usual drawing room, though this time it is filled with at least ten vampyres and one little old lady werewolf. I do not hide my joy this time. "Nan!" I try to move toward her, but Colin grips my arm whilst keeping his pistol on me with this other hand.

"Lady Hart," Nan says with a nod as I am shoved onto the divan beside our host. Michael wraps his arm around my shoulders, and begins twining a stray strand of my hair for show. Even through the leather, I can feel his cold dead skin.

"As you can see, she has been left unharmed." He kisses my cheek. "Thus far. Though why you care is beyond me."

"I am an old woman with a soft heart. Even if she did lie to me."

"She did? Pray tell," Michael says.

"She claimed to be kin. That she was the wife of my grandson. Even tried to get my son to fight you in her name and all. Still. Hate to see her or anyone else mistreated."

"Obviously not, because here *you* are. Did your grandson not inform you before he fled like a coward that if one wolf set foot on this property, I would eat her alive? Literally."

"What? Are you afraid of an old woman, son?"

The vampyre snarls, and faster than I can register, I am yanked onto his lap, with his hand in my hair pulling my head to the side and those fangs mere inches from my artery. He'll eat me faster because my blood is pumping furiously now. Nan doesn't balk. "What do you want, Mrs. Roarke?"

She straightens her twisted back as far as she is capable of. "Against my advice, my son has decided he wishes to discuss a possible alliance."

"Why now?"

"You have what? Twenty, twenty-two vampyres here?"

"Four and twenty."

"Lucian has but twenty, though his castle is far more fortified. But now you have Lady Hart and the automaton. With your superior numbers and now the machine, even a dunce can glean who has the upper hand. So my son has sent me to ask for a meeting tomorrow night in town. A public setting of course, one of your choosing."

"And why would I agree to that? You mongrels have treated me with nothing but disrespect since I arrived."

"You can discuss that with my son tomorrow. I am simply here to deliver his message, nothing more. Though the offer expires when I leave this house."

"And I suppose you will inform Lucian of my plans should I not agree?"

"We haven't told him yet, have we? We just want to be left alone, and we will promise you the same." Nan meets my eye for a moment. "And a Roarke *always* keeps their word."

Michael is silent for a few seconds as he contemplates this. I stare at Nan, but she keeps her eyes on the vampyre. "I suppose a meeting in public cannot be too detrimental. Ten o'clock, Campbell's Pub. Albert and I alone."

"I will tell him. Thank you for your time." Nan glances at me again and nods. "Lady Hart, I do hope things work out for you. And I am sorry about my grandson. Consider yourself lucky. Weak blood, that one, not like the rest of us. Saw it straight away. No honor, none whatsoever." She shakes her head with regret. "I hope he allows you to live, I really do. Even if deep down you ain't no lady." She turns on her cane and walks out. "And thank God for that."

My mouth twitches in a smile but only for a moment.

No one says a word until they hear the front door shut. "Do we believe her?" the willowy vampyre wearing the Artemis asks her leader.

"She is a mongrel, do you even need ask? Sweep the woods and see if any wolves are around." He shoves me off his lap onto the floor as three vampyres run out. "Is my machine done?"

"Al—almost. I just ha—have to solve the circulation problem. By tomorrow—"

"By dawn."

"I don't not think I can—"

"Dawn," he snaps. He rises and the others cower. "Everyone stays in tonight and keeps their senses about them." He turns to Colin the valet. "Take her back upstairs and stay in the room. Now!" he roars.

Everyone flinches and rushes away to their tasks. Once again, I am yanked and manhandled by hand and gun alike to the tower. "You're hurting me," I say as the valet pokes me with the pistol on the tower stairs.

"Shut up," Colin says, shoving me through the iron door, "you bit—"

The instant we enter the room, he and I recognise something is amiss. A sheet-white David stands trembling in the corner with the window flung open with a broken glass pane. I notice that first, though why this and not the dead guard on the carpet with blood all over him I know not. Blood. Blood everywhere. The valet is as shocked by the gore as I am. "What—"

A blur streaks down from the ceiling, silencing the valet. Forever. In a blink, Colin lies prostrate on the floor with another man on top of him. Before the valet can scream, the blur covers his mouth and bites into the terrified man's neck. Blood spurts everywhere, even on my leather trousers. I watch in silent horror as the attacker literally sucks the life out of the valet. A vampyre. What is going on? David sinks to the floor, small moans escaping him. I do not know how much time passes, probably seconds, before the valet stops struggling. Until his limbs cease flailing. Dead. He's dead.

The vampyre, a man my age with long brown hair, olive skin, and black eyes stares up at me, face and clothes saturated with the valet's blood. He grins, flashing his dripping fangs. "Lady Hart, pleasure to finally make your acquaintance. I have heard much about you." He rises, standing over the corpse to bow at me as if we were about to dance. "I am Lucian Magnus, leader of the Galway Cabal. I am here to aid in your rescue."

I am far too shocked to do anything but mutter a quiet, "Hello."

"Hello." He nods and steps over the valet to go to the worktable. "May I trouble you for a clean shirt? Quickly, please. Time is of the essence." Eager to leave the room, I rush into the bedroom and retrieve one of David's clean shirts. When I return, the wash basin is red, and Lucian has removed his top. His lean torso is still smeared with gore. "Will your brother be up to our task?"

In the chaos, I forgot David. He is still in the corner rocking back and forth, staring at nothing. He is in shock. I would be in the same state if this were a fortnight ago. Having no choice and no time, I give him a hard slap. His eyes focus on me. "David you need to get up. It is time to leave."

"Leave?" he asks, still far away.

"Jamie's here. We are going home. Get up, love." I help him find his feet. "You recall the plan? Get everything together." On shaking legs, he walks into the other room still in a daze. I return to Lucian as he buttons the shirt. "Jamie did send you, correct?"

"Of course. Your lover can be quite persuasive. Frightening as well. He is a fierce one. Arrived at my castle over a week ago with quite the story." I follow the vampyre to the intact war machine, which he inspects. "Impressive."

It is. Dr. Rathbone should be proud. All the panels on the six foot tall machine are completely open now so the person wearing it simply has to step back into it as you would an iron maiden before the front armor is pulled down and fastened to the back fully enclosing the operator. "I was inclined to believe Mr. McQueen, but since Michael has superior numbers and made no overt threats, I could not risk my people. It was not until he brought the wolves into the bargain that I could agree. Is it complete?"

"I just need to install one more part. It shall take two minutes."

"Hurry, please." I dash to the cabinet and remove the coupler for the steam engine the size of a bread box with two small steam stacks on either side attached to its back as David begins assembling our arsenal. "Are the weapons systems functional?"

"Not the Gatling gun on the left shoulder, no. They would not provide bullets. Everything else, yes. David, please load them." As I ratchet in the coupler, David adds the explosive crystals each the size of a fist to the launcher on the left arm and flammable liquid to the flamethrower on the right. "Why did the pack finally agree to the alliance?" I ask.

"Mr. McQueen defeated his uncle and three others in a dominance match. I hear he almost ripped Albert's front paw off. It has not fully healed even now. The pack would follow him to Hades if ordered after such an impressive display." Lucian knocks on the steel panel. "This truly is a remarkable device, Lady Hart. Without question, Michael could have strolled in, knocked down our doors, and murdered us all while slumbering. I underestimated his cunning."

I tighten the last bolt. "There. Done." After switching on the boiler to heat up the engine, I move to help David with the other preparations. "So what exactly is the plan? Why was Nan here?"

"Distraction. To gain knowledge of their numbers. To have Michael send some of those numbers outside where we are awaiting them. To let you know we were coming. Your lover is quite the strategist."

"What's going to happen?" David asks, fear cracking in his voice.

"War," I say.

"I need to know how to operate this machine," Lucian says.

"Wait. No. David should—"

"The machine is mine now, Lady Hart. *I* will be operating it, no one else. Yet you need not worry. You shall be protected, I assure you. Two of my best men are assigned to be your guards. We fought in Gaul together."

David and I exchange a look. Yes, neither of us wishes to enrage the ancient vampyre who slaughtered two men with pistols in front of us. "David will show you how to use it."

"I will?" I glare at my brother. He smiles nervously at Lucian. "I will."

While David instructs our rescuer which leaver performs what function, and how to move the limbs, I finish loading the ammunition and move onto our personal arsenal, which is now up two guns thanks to the dead guards. Colin finally proved useful.

Shame the pistols do not contain silver bullets. We still have the small silver blades from the botched rescue, and I re-made the Incinerator, one for each of us, and fill it with one of David's concoctions that burns like Greek fire. As for the highly volatile crystals, I developed something of an enclosed crossbow bucked to my arm. After cocking the lever back, the crystals inside the cooper tube buckled to my arm propel forward with great speed like an exploding arrow. I call her the Crossfire. I feel like Queen Boadicea reborn.

"All that is unnecessary," Lucian say, practicing moving his leg, the hydraulics at the joints whirring as he does. Only his face is visible inside the shining suit. "You shall immediately be flown to safety."

"If this fortnight has taught me anything, Mr. Magnus it is that I would rather have a weapon than not should I need it," I say, latching the Incinerator over my black leather glove. David is having difficulty with his Incinerator as his hands will not stop quaking. I move over to him, fastening it on. "It is almost over. We are going home."

"I am sorry I doubted you, I—"

I pull him into a tight hug in case I never get the chance again. "I love you, David."

He hugs me back. "I love you too, Very. *So* much. Thank you."

"For what?"

"Coming to my rescue."

"Well, we promised to be on each other's side come hell or high water, right? And a Hart always keeps their word." I release him from my embrace. "Besides, I still owe you about twenty rescues. This one erases ten."

"Deal," my brother, my best friend, my champion says with a genuine smile.

I step away, cocking the Incinerator to ignite the flame on the tip of the reservoir before pulling back the lever on the

Crossfire. The satchel with the crystals and Colin's gun go around my shoulder. "I believe we are ready, Mr. Magnus."

"Then open the door, turn off all the lights, and wait by the window. My men shall fly you safely to the rendezvous."

"I am not letting Jamie fight alon—"

"Those are Mr. McQueen's orders, Lady Hart. I believe his exact words were, 'Tell her to stop being so damn ornery, or he will have a powerful mind to tan your hide next time he sees you.' Americans," Lucian says with disdain. "Please latch the faceplate, hold open the door, and wait until I am at the end of the stairs to turn off the lights. That is the signal to charge. Be ready."

And away we go.

I do as he asks. The steam from the exhaust pipes shoots out like geysers as Lucian begins moving. One would think that the machine would move slowly what with it weighing half a ton, but Lucian does not lumber. His gait is slower than typical walking speed but not by much. It really is little more than a mechanical suit of armor, an updated version of those downstairs worn centuries ago by brave knights of the realm. I wonder if they had the Incinerator on their arm and mini-cannon attached to their shoulders the Hundred Years War would have ended after one battle. Dr. Rathbone truly was a genius, may he rest in peace.

I wait by the window, peering out into the night, but see nothing but the ghouls on their endless tromp. They are out there, though. *He* is out there. Probably has been a dozen instances before, simply watching me through the window as he is now. He never left and never will. I blow the man I love a kiss.

David rushes back into the room. "Lucian is in place."

"Then douse the lights." He switches off the gas lamps, and we are in darkness save for the moonlight. David joins me by the window, breath ragged already from nerves. He is a hair's breadth from panic. "It will be fine, David. Have faith."

A few seconds pass. Nothing happens. The ghouls continue on, the forest remains still. For a brief moment, I consider we have been duped. That Lucian simply took the machine and fled. He is a vampyre after all. I cannot—

Someone steps into the clearing. A lone man wearing a cowboy hat presses his hand to his mouth and waves it toward me, kissing me back. Not a moment of doubt.

A second later, a large wolf creeps out from the trees, then another, then more men standing tall and wolves. The final tally is ten wolves, and twenty men or I suppose vampyres, as some hover above the ground. An army. The love of my life brought me an army.

The ghouls start running toward the men, as right below us, vampyres filter out of the manor to figure out the cause of the undead charge. A mistake. Three wolves sprint forward, reaching the ghouls in a heartbeat. In another heartbeat the ghouls are pinned by the animals before heads literally roll.

"Sic 'em," Jamie bellows, voice booming.

The entire line flies, some literally, toward the manor. Below, a woman shrieks and the rest flee inside. Smart but useless. Two of the gliders reach the manor first, coming straight up to our window. David and I leap back as they move through the window.

The men formally bow when their feet touch the floor. "I am Marius, and this is Octavian. We are to escort you out of the manor."

Below us I hear glass breaking, people shouting, gunshots, and screams of pain. "What an excellent idea. Thank you."

Octavian is the first out the window carrying David. Marius takes me in his arms as if I were a bride, and we lift off before my fear of heights cripples me. My stomach lurches from the change. I hold onto his neck as we sail out the window.

We do not make it far.

Like a jack-in-the-box from hell, a vampyre pops up just as we are about to clear the landing, slamming against Marius. He drops me onto the slanted roof. I skid down for a second, but I have enough forethought to latch my hand onto a loose shingle.

The two vampyres smash through the tower window into the dark room, out of sight. I am definitely not meant to be airborne. Ever.

As I try to pull myself up toward the window, there is a commotion above me with breaking glass and wood splitting inside the tower. I barely make it a few inches before the tower grows silent. I cease movement. If the other vampyre won, I am better off out here. But seconds later a bleeding Marius pokes his head and hand out, pulling me up. Just as I reach the window's landing, our attacker apparates behind Marius with one of my hammers raised high.

"Look out!"

The claw end smashes into Marius' head with a squish I still hear over my shriek. My rescuer releases me again, but I hold onto the landing for dear life. Marius howls in pain while disappearing back into the darkness inside. He needs me. As I propel myself into the room, arms aching from the strain, the vampyre continues his assault on my protector. I lose count of the hammer's blows. Marius finally collapses just as I vault through the window. The vampyre tosses the beside the body and looks up at me, fangs bared. Excellent target. I lift my left arm and lower my ring finger with the trigger chain on it. A thin jet of fire shoots out of the reservoir into his mouth then clothes as I angle the destruction down. The man shrieks in agony as he burns, limbs flailing, setting the table and curtains alight as he knocks against them. I sprint for the iron door before my cell becomes naught but ashes.

Compared to the rest of the house the third floor is relatively quiet in that there are only distant explosions around the corner and no screams as there are above and below. Quiet yet stomach churning horrific with smoldering or exploded bodies and walls rippling with fire. Onwards. *Fast.* As I dash down the hall, black smoke billowing everywhere, a portly vampyre walks out of a bedroom, takes one look at me, and charges. I trigger the Crossfire on my right arm, the two crystals speeding his way. They reach him first, hitting him square in his huge chest. I have enough time to cover my ears as the burst of light and smoke sends the man reeling back, his chest blooming open with blood and pulp from the explosion. Disgusting but effective.

Covering my mouth from the stench of burnt flesh and smoke, I sprint down hall past the smoldering vampyre and around the corner. I stop dead in my tracks. Far down the hall, past the staircase, the war machine dispatches two vampyres with a jet of orange fire. The walls, chairs, even the carpet becomes engulfed as the vampyres wail in pain, one even floating to the ceiling, setting it ablaze as well. I give it ten minutes before fire brings the whole manor down. I have no desire to be here for that. Swiftly but cautiously, I hurry down the hall toward the stairs, loading the Crossfire with two more crystals from my satchel, and pulling the lever back. When I reach the staircase, two wolves on the next level sprint in and out of view, followed by their General. My breath catches at the sight of him, clothes speckled with blood and guns literally blazing. "Jamie!"

His gaze whips up at me. Surprise becomes delight becomes alarm. "Down!"

I drop to the floor as his guns rise toward the ceiling. He fires twice from each pistol. The eviscerated, portly vampyre crashes from the air beside me with four smoking holes in his forehead. I gasp. Suppose I should have checked to see if he was still alive after I disemboweled him. Must not make that mistake again. I glance from the corpse then to Jamie as I slowly find my feet. We simply stare at one another amid the screams and explosions as if blinking would break the spell and make us each vanish for all eternity. Then a small groan of relief escapes him, and we run into each other's arms. He dips me before kissing me with a ferocity only near death and separation can bring forth from my soul. I return his ardor, savoring the feverish feel and taste of him. Cigar and peppermint. More intoxicating than absinthe. I am an addict. He pulls away first, gazing down at me as if we had been parted for a millennia. "Oh, I do love you," he says, breathless.

Out of the corner of my eye, I spy a vampyre charging up the stairs toward us. Not breaking our gaze, I extend my arm out and pull the trigger on the Crossfire, literally blowing the vampyre's head off. "I know."

Hand-in-hand, we dash down the steps before he maneuvers me into a bedroom, kicking shut the door. He runs his hands up and down my body, examining me. "Are you okay? Are you hurt?"

"No, I'm fine."

"Your brother?"

"He made it out."

He nods as he cups my jaw with his hands, running his rough, calloused hands over my cheeks. "I'm sorry, shug. I am *so* sorry for leaving you like that. For everything I said. I didn't—"

I plant a small kiss on his lips to cease his words. "I know." I kiss him again. "I knew what you were doing all along. You would never abandon me. *Never*."

He kisses me again, a hot engulfing kiss. For a few seconds amid the hell we've wrought, we lose ourselves in each other, in bliss, where nothing else matters but one another. Never again. No matter what occurs from now on, no matter what this life attempts to throw in our paths, I shall never let this man go. He is for me, and I him. The wild man I adore. The love of my life.

The explosion that rattles the door draws us back to reality. We break apart, staring where the noise was. "We need to get you out of this house." Jamie empties this six shooter and begins reloading it with silver bullets from his belt as I load the Crossfire. There are more screams of agony and howling wolves outside. "I'm sorry I didn't come sooner," Jamie says.

I cock the Crossfire. "You sounded busy. Lucian told me all you accomplished."

"Nan helped. She told me where Lucian lived, how to get Albert cowed, put me in touch with her gunsmith for the silver bullets. You made quite an impression on her." Jamie snaps the barrel back into the gun and takes my hand. "Her only price was I marry ya."

"*What*?" I ask as he yanks me out of the room.

The second we step into the hall two wolves, one brown and the other black both covered in blood with chunks of skin in their teeth, gallop over to us. Jamie nods down the hall. "Duncan, Kieran clear the path for us. Go!"

The wolves obey, and we follow behind hand in hand. "Yeah, she saw the newspaper about us," he continues. "Michael must have sent it to us. That woman was as mad as a peeled rattler. Said I brought shame to the family and to you."

A vampyre, Francis from London, rounds the far corner and is immediately set upon by the wolves. They both leap on him as a hound does a fox, his screams are ceased by powerful jaws ripping out his throat. We don't stop walking. "Said the honorable thing to do was marry ya. I agree with her."

"The honorable thing? Just what a girl always wants to hear during a proposal. 'I have to marry you, honor and my grandmother demand it'. How utterly romantic."

We reach the main staircase where three vampyres encircle a dead body lying in a pool of blood. The men nod with reverence at Jamie, who returns the gesture. On the floor below are more decimated bodies missing heads or with holes in their chests with blood streaking the walls and oil paintings. The vampyres fall behind us as we stroll down the staircase as our two wolves run past toward the main entrance. We follow slowly behind them. Back the way we came, the ceiling creaks. Several seconds later Lucian lumbers to the top of the stairs as the walls crumble behind him, flames spilling out and all around. "Six months in England, six in America."

My gaze whips back to Jamie. "I'm sorry?" I ask, my senses over stimulated by all the carnage.

"We'll spend six months in England and six in Oklahoma. That's fair, I reckon. Right?"

"I suppose." We reach the ground floor, maneuvering through the corpses toward the main entrance. "At least until the children arrive, then we shall have to reassess."

"Naturally."

The majority of our army have already assembled on the lawn, with wolves chasing the few stragglers and Lucian's vampyres savoring the sight of the burning manor. Michael's human servants stand off to the side, quaking in terror as vampyres with pistols guard them.

"Lucian?" one of the vampyres asks Jamie.

"Coming. Michael?"

"Over there," he says, nodding to the left.

"Thank you." We stroll toward our captive as if we were enjoying the day in Hyde Park. I must take him there when we return to London. We can have a picnic. "Your friends and family will never accept me," Jamie says. "Never."

I shrug. "Bugger them all. They do not even accept *me.*"

"And I won't be a kept man. I need to make my own money, so I'll take bounties from time to time just like always."

"Perhaps we can track them together. I seem to have quite an aptitude for this line of work, would you not say?"

"You're a natural, shug," he says with a proud smile.

Two of Lucian's vampyres and Albert stand guard over Michael, who lies on the ground, his right arm and legs contorted at sickening angles, broken so he cannot flee. Albert points a rifle at him regardless. "Lady Hart," Albert says sheepishly.

"Mr. Roarke, always a pleasure," I say with a gracious smile. "I am glad to see your arm has healed." The man looks away in embarrassment.

"You will all pay for this," Michael hisses through the pain. "I will kill you all. You—"

I kick him in the side. "Oh, do shut up." I gaze over at the smiling Jamie. "May we please kill him already? I have lost enough of my precious life because of this monster. I do not wish to give him a moment more."

"As the lady wishes." Jamie switches guns with Albert, then hands me the rifle. "Lady Hart, care to do the honors? You've earned it."

I take the rifle. "Why, yes, Mr. McQueen, I believe I would. How kind of you to think of me." I train the barrel against Michael's heart, who is too gripped by fear to do anything but tremble. "Thank you for the hospitality, Michael. It was an experience I will not soon forget." With one last smile, I squeeze the trigger three times over his heart, then once in the head for good measure before handing the rifle back to a slack jawed Albert. "I warned him not to underestimate me," I say with a wink.

And that's that. Victory has never smelled so much like a burning manor.

As I remove my cuffs and gloves, Jamie says, "Throw him in the fire with the rest. Don't want to take any chances." The men, Albert included, hop to.

"It is so good to see you getting on with your family," I say, dropping the last glove with a raised eyebrow. "It is most important, do you not think?"

"You have made me a believer, shug."

"Verity!"

"Speaking of…" Jamie says with a grin. Oh, I do so hope our children inherit their father's smile.

I spin around and find Octavian swooping down from the sky with my brother still in his arms. "David!" The moment they land, David rushes toward me as I do him. We hug each other so tight neither of us can draw breath.

"Are you alright?" he asks after we break apart. "You vanished. I made him bring me back. I was—"

"I'm fine." I kiss his cheek. "I'm bloody marvelous. It is over. It's all over. We won."

"Lucian!" Octavian calls. We watch as all the vampyres congregate around the metal man sauntering out of the burning manor as the roof collapses. He earned that machine without question.

"That really is a fine piece of machinery, shug," Jamie says as he walks over to David and me. "Can't wait to see what you cook up next." When he reaches us, Jamie nods and extends his hand to my brother. "It's nice to formally meet you, Lord Hart. Heard nothing but great things. I'm Jamie McQueen," he says shaking hands, "I'm marrying your sister."

My eyes narrow. "Are you now? I believe you have forgotten a crucial step, Mr. McQueen."

It takes a second before it comes to him. Jamie shakes his head. "Oh, sorry shug. Forgot how important rules and propriety are to you. I haven't asked you yet, have I?"

"You had other things on your mind," I say casually. "I forgive you."

"Most kind of you." He takes a step away to face me. "Right, well…" He clears his throat and pulls something out of his jacket pocket, holding it up to me. My mouth opens from surprise. The Artemis. He meets my eyes. "Don't have a ring yet, shug. Hope this will do." He falls to one knee, holding her up to me. "Lady Verity Hart, will you marry this coarse, rude, prejudiced, penniless werewolf before ya who loves you more than anything?"

Though my eyes are filling with tears, I pretend to mull it over for a second then frown for effect. "It is the honorable thing to do, I suppose."

Our knowing smiles grow in unison until they are stretched across our faces as he rises. When they cannot go any further, I laugh and launch myself into his open arms. He gazes down at me, caressing my blood stained cheek. "I love you so damn much, lady."

I beam up at him, meeting those ardent brown eyes of his and smile mischievously. "Darling…" I say, snaking my hand into his hair. I push his lips millimeters from mine. "I ain't no lady."

And I kiss my American werewolf as the blood soaked vampyres fly off into the night, as the wolves howl, as the corpses burn, and the manor falls to ashes.

Lady indeed.

THE END

ACKNOWLEDGEMENTS

First, to all of you who write, Tweet, review, even send me presents. I have the best fans ever. Thank you.

Thanks to all who gave me shit about this book: Susan Dowis, Jill Kardell, Ginny Dowis, Kim Weaver, and Sandy Lu. You were right. I took your suggestions but YOU made this book better.

To all the people at KBOARDS who share their experiences and insights into indie and e-book publishing. You've saved me so much time and money. Anything I can do to pay it forward, let me know.

To Trevor and especially Mom for the Photoshop help. See that cover? I DID THAT. With their help.

Finally, to my Grandma for introducing me to all things British.

ABOUT THE AUTHOR

Jennifer Harlow spent her restless childhood fighting with her three brothers and scaring the heck out of herself with horror movies and books. She grew up to earn a degree at the University of Virginia which she put to use as a radio DJ, crisis hotline volunteer, bookseller, lab assistant, wedding coordinator, and government investigator. Currently she calls Atlanta home but that restless itch is ever present. In her free time, she continues to scare the beejepers out of herself watching scary movies and opening her credit card bills. She is the author of the Amazon best-selling F.R.E.A.K.S. Squad, Midnight Magic Mystery series and The Galilee Falls Trilogy. For the soundtrack to her books and other goodies visit her at www.jenniferharlowbooks.com

www.ingramcontent.com/pod-product-compliance
Lightning Source LLC
Chambersburg PA
CBHW070838250626

47159CB00003B/826